More praise for Jonathan Kellerman and *Dr. Death*

"[Kellerman] has shaped the psychological mystery novel into an art form."
—*Los Angeles Times Book Review*

"More than satisfying . . . Kellerman delves deep into the psyche of his characters, peeling back the layers of secrets to uncover a stunning truth."
—*The Orlando Sentinel*

"Kellerman uses bloody killings, psychological intrigue and a straight-ahead writing style to keep readers turning pages well into the night."
—*The Denver Post*

"Often, mystery writers can either plot like devils or create believable characters. Kellerman stands out because he can do both. Masterfully."
—*USA Today*

"[An] intriguing thriller . . . A heady blend of criminal profiling and police procedural and another surefire hit for the bestselling Kellerman."
—*Booklist*

Books by Jonathan Kellerman

Fiction
TWISTED (2004)
THERAPY (2004)
THE CONSPIRACY CLUB (2003)
A COLD HEART (2003)
THE MURDER BOOK (2002)
FLESH AND BLOOD (2001)
DR. DEATH (2000)
MONSTER (1999)
BILLY STRAIGHT (1998)
SURVIVAL OF THE FITTEST (1997)
THE CLINIC (1997)
THE WEB (1996)
SELF-DEFENSE (1995)
BAD LOVE (1994)
DEVIL'S WALTZ (1993)
PRIVATE EYES (1992)
TIME BOMB (1990)
SILENT PARTNER (1989)
THE BUTCHER'S THEATER (1988)
OVER THE EDGE (1987)
BLOOD TEST (1986)
WHEN THE BOUGH BREAKS (1985)

Nonfiction
SAVAGE SPAWN:
REFLECTIONS ON VIOLENT CHILDREN (1999)
HELPING THE FEARFUL CHILD (1981)
PSYCHOLOGICAL ASPECTS OF CHILDHOOD CANCER (1980)

For Children, Written and Illustrated
JONATHAN KELLERMAN'S
ABC OF WEIRD CREATURES (1995)
DADDY, DADDY, CAN YOU TOUCH THE SKY? (1994)

With Faye Kellerman
DOUBLE HOMICIDE (2004)

DR. DEATH

A NOVEL

Jonathan Kellerman

BALLANTINE BOOKS • NEW YORK

This book contains an excerpt from *Flesh and Blood* by Jonathan Kellerman. This excerpt has been set for this edition only and may not reflect the final content of the edition.

A Ballantine Book
Published by The Random House Publishing Group
Copyright © 2000 by Jonathan Kellerman

Excerpt from *Flesh and Blood* copyright © 2001 by Jonathan Kellerman

All rights reserved under International and Pan-American Copyright Conventions. Published in the United States by Ballantine Books, an imprint of The Random House Publishing Group, a division of Random House, Inc., New York, and simultaneously in Canada by Random House of Canada Limited, Toronto.

Ballantine and colophon are trademarks of Random House, Inc.

www.ballantinebooks.com

ISBN 0-345-41388-1

This edition published by arrangement with Random House, Inc.

Manufactured in the United States of America

First Mass Market Edition: September 2001

OPM 10 9 8 7 6 5

THIS ONE'S FOR
DR. JERRY DASH

CHAPTER

1

IRONY CAN BE a rich dessert, so when the contents of the van were publicized, some people gorged. The ones who'd believed Eldon H. Mate to be the Angel of Death.

Those who'd considered him Mercy Personified grieved.

I viewed it through a different lens, had my own worries.

Mate was murdered in the very early hours of a sour-smelling, fog-laden Monday in September. No earth-quakes or wars interceded by sundown, so the death merited a lead story on the evening news. Newspaper headlines in the *Times* and the *Daily News* followed on Tuesday. TV dropped the story within twenty-four hours, but recaps ran in the Wednesday papers. In total, four days of coverage, the maximum in short-attention-span L.A. unless the corpse is that of a princess or the killer can afford lawyers who yearn for Oscars.

No easy solve on this one; no breaks of any kind. Milo had been doing his job long enough not to expect otherwise.

He'd had an easy summer, catching a quartet of lov-ingly stupid homicides during July and August—one domestic violence taken to the horrible extreme and three brain-dead drunks shooting other inebriates in squalid Westside bars. Four murderers hanging around long enough to be caught. It kept his solve rate high, made it a bit—but not much—easier to be the only openly gay detective in LAPD.

"Knew I was due," he said. It was the Sunday after the murder when he phoned me at the house. Mate's corpse had been cold for six days and the press had moved on.

That suited Milo just fine. Like any artist, he craved solitude. He'd played his part by not giving the press anything to work with. Orders from the brass. One thing he and the brass could agree on: reporters were almost always the enemy.

What the papers *had* printed was squeezed out of clip-file biographies, the inevitable ethical debates, old photos, old quotes. Beyond the fact that Mate had been hooked up to his own killing machine, only the sketchiest details had been released:

Van parked on a remote section of Mulholland Drive, discovery by hikers just after dawn.

DR. DEATH MURDERED.

I knew more because Milo told me.

The call came in at eight P.M. just as Robin and I had finished dinner. I was out the door, holding on to the straining leash of Spike, our little French bulldog. Pooch and I both looking forward to a night walk up the glen. Spike loved the dark because pointing at scurrying sounds let him pretend he was a noble hunter. I enjoyed getting out because I worked with people all day and solitude was always welcome.

Robin answered the phone, caught me in time, ended up doing dog-duty as I returned to my study.

"Mate's yours?" I said, surprised because he hadn't told me sooner. Suddenly edgy because that added a whole new layer of complexity to my week.

"Who else merits such blessing?"

I laughed softly, feeling my shoulders humping, rings of tension around my neck. The moment I'd heard about Mate I'd worried. Deliberated for a long time, finally made a call that hadn't been returned. I'd dropped the issue because there'd been no good reason not to. It really *wasn't* any of my business. Now, with Milo involved, all that had changed.

I kept the worries to myself. His call had nothing to do with my problem. Coincidence—one of those nasty little overlaps. Or maybe there really are only a hundred people in the world.

His reason for getting in touch was simple: the dreaded W word: whodunit. A case with enough psychopathology to make me potentially useful.

Also, I was his friend, one of the few people left in whom he could confide.

The psychopathology part was fine with me. What bothered me was the friendship component. Things I knew but didn't tell him. *Couldn't* tell him.

CHAPTER

2

I AGREED TO meet him at the crime scene the following Monday at 7:45 A.M. When he's at the West L.A. station, we usually travel together, but he was already scheduled for a 6:15 meeting downtown at Parker Center, so I drove myself.

"Sunrise prayer session?" I said. "Milking the cows with guys in suits?"

"Cleaning the stable while guys in suits rate my performance. Gonna have to find a clean tie."

"Is the topic Mate?"

"What else. They'll demand to know why I haven't accomplished squat, I'll nod a lot, say 'Yassuh, yassuh,' shuffle off."

Mate had been butchered fairly close to my home, and I set out at seven-thirty. The first leg of the trip was ten minutes north on Beverly Glen, the Seville fairly sailing because I was going against traffic, ignoring the angry faces of commuters incarcerated by the southbound crush.

Economic recovery and the customary graft had spurred unremitting roadwork in L.A., and hellish traffic was the result. This month it was the bottom of the glen: smug men in orange CalTrans vests installing new storm drains just in time for the next drought, the usual munici-

4

pal division of labor: one guy working for every five standing around. Feeling like a pre-Bastille Royalist, I sped past the queue of Porsches and Jaguars forced to idle with clunkers and pickups. Democracy by oppression, everyone coerced into bumper-nudging intimacy.

At Mulholland, I turned left and drove four miles west, past seismically strained dream houses and empty lots that said optimism wasn't for everyone. The road coiled, scything through weeds, brush, saplings, other kindling, twisted upward sharply and changed to packed, ocher soil as the asphalt continued east and was renamed Encino Hills Drive.

Up here, at the top of the city, Mulholland had become a dirt road. I'd hiked here as a grad student, thrilling at the sight of antlered bucks, foxes, falcons, catching my breath at the furtive shifting of high grass that could be cougars. But that had been years ago, and the suddenness of the transformation from highway to impasse caught me by surprise. I hit the brakes hard, steered onto the rise, parked below the table of sallow dirt.

Milo was already there, his copper-colored unmarked pulled up in front of a warning sign posted by the county: seven miles of unfinished road followed, no vehicles permitted. A locked gate said that L.A. motorists couldn't be trusted.

He hitched his pants, loped forward, took my hand in both of his giant mitts.

"Alex."

"Big guy."

He had on a fuzzy-looking green tweed jacket, brown twill pants, white shirt with a twisted collar, string tie with a big, misshapen turquoise clasp. The tie looked like tourist junk. A new fashion statement; I knew he'd put it on to needle the brass at this morning's meeting.

"Going cowboy?"

"My Georgia O'Keeffe period."

"Natty."

He gave a low, rumbling laugh, pushed a lick of dry black hair off his brow, squinted off to the right. Focusing on a spot that told me exactly where the van had been found.

Not up the dirt road, where untrimmed live oaks would have provided cover. Right here, on the turnoff, out in the open.

I said, "No attempt to conceal."

He shrugged and jammed his hands in his pockets. He looked tired, washed-out, worn down by violence and small print.

Or maybe it was just the time of year. September can be a rotten month in L.A., throat-constrictingly hot or clammy cold, shadowed by a grimy marine layer that turns the city into a pile of soiled laundry. When September mornings start out dreary they ooze into sooty afternoons and sickly nights. Sometimes blue peeks through the clouds for a nanosecond. Sometimes the sky sweats and a leaky-roof drizzle glazes windshields. For the past few years resident experts have been blaming it on El Niño, but I don't recall it ever being any different.

September light is bad for the complexion. Milo's didn't need any further erosion. The gray morning light fed his pallor and deepened the pockmarks that peppered his cheeks and ran down his neck. White sideburns below still-thick black hair turned his temples into a zebra-striped stunt. He'd gone back to drinking moderately and his weight had stabilized—240 was my guess—much of it settling around his middle. His legs remained skinny stilts, comprising a good share of his seventy-five inches. His jowls, always monumental, had given way around the edges. We were about the same age—he was nine months older—so I supposed my jawline had surrendered a bit, too. I didn't spend much time looking in the mirror.

He walked to the kill-spot and I followed. Faint chevrons of tire tracks corrugated the yellow soil. Nearby lay a scrap of yellow cordon tape, dusty, utterly still. A week of dead air, nothing had moved.

"We took casts of the tracks," he said, flicking a hand at them. "Not that it matters. We knew where the van came from. Rental sticker. Avis, Tarzana branch. Brown Ford Econoline with a nice big cargo area. Mate rented it last Friday, got the weekend rate."

"Preparing for another mercy mission?" I said.

"That's what he uses vans for. But so far no beneficiary's come forth claiming Mate stood him up."

"I'm surprised the companies still rent to him."

"They probably don't. The paperwork was made out to someone else. Woman named Alice Zoghbie, president of the Socrates Club—right-to-die outfit headquartered in Glendale. She's out of the country, attending some sort of humanist convention in Amsterdam—left Saturday."

"She rented the van and split the next day?" I said.

"Apparently. Called her home, which also doubles as the Socrates office, got voice mail. Had Glendale PD drive by. No one home. Zoghbie's message says she's due back in a week. She's on my to-do list." He tapped the pocket where his notepad nestled.

"I wonder why Mate never bought a van," I said.

"From what I've seen so far, he was cheap. I tossed his apartment the day after the murder, not much in the way of creature comforts. His personal car's an old Chevy that has seen better days. Before he went automotive he used budget motels."

I nodded. "Bodies left on the bed for the cleaning crew to find next morning. Too many traumatized maids turned into bad publicity. I saw him on TV once, getting defensive about it. Saying Christ had been born in a barn full of goat dung, so setting doesn't matter. But it does, doesn't it?"

He looked at me. "You've been following Mate's career?"

"Didn't have to," I said, keeping my voice even. "He wasn't exactly media-shy. Any tracks of other cars nearby?"

He shook his head.

"So," I said, "you're wondering if the killer drove up with Mate."

"Or parked farther down the road than we checked. Or left no tracks—that happens plenty, you know how seldom forensic stuff actually helps. No one's reported seeing any other vehicles. Then again, no one noticed the damn *van*, and it sat here for hours."

"What about shoe prints?"

"Just the people who found the van."

"What's the time-of-death estimate?" I said.

"Early morning, one to four A.M." He shot his cuff and looked at his Timex. The watch crystal was scarred and filmed. "Mate was discovered just after sunrise—six-fifteen or so."

"The papers said the people who found him were hikers," I said. "Must've been early risers."

"Coupla yuppies walking with their dog, came up from the Valley for a constitutional before hitting the office. They were headed up the dirt road and noticed the van."

"Any other passersby?" I pointed down the road, toward Encino Hills Drive. "I used to come up here, remember a housing development being built. By now it's probably well-populated. That hour, you'd think a car or two would drive by."

"Yeah, it's populated," he said. "High-priced development. Guess the affluent get to sleep in."

"Some of the affluent got that way by working. What about a broker up early to catch the market, a surgeon ready to operate?"

"It's conceivable someone drove past and saw something, but if they did they're not admitting it. Our initial canvass produced zip by way of neighborly help. How many cars have you seen while we stood here?"

The road had been silent.

"I got here ten minutes before you," he said. "One truck. Period. A gardener. And even if someone did drive by, there'd be no reason to notice the van. No streetlights, so before sunrise it would've been pure black. And if someone did happen to spot it, no reason to give it a thought, let alone stop. There was county construction going on up here till a few months ago, some kind of drain line. CalTrans crews left trucks overnight all the time. Another parked vehicle wouldn't stand out."

"It stood out to the yuppies," I said.

"Stood out to their *dog*. One of those attentive retrievers. They were ready to walk right past the van but the dog kept nosing around, barking, wouldn't leave it alone. Finally, they had a look inside. So much for walking for health, huh? That kind of thing could put you off exercise for a long time."

"Bad?"

"Not what *I'd* want as an aerobic stimulant. Dr. Mate was trussed up to his own machine."

"The Humanitron," I said. Mate's label for his death apparatus. Silent passage for Happy Travelers.

Milo's smile was crooked, hard to read. "You hear about that thing, all the people he used it on, you expect it to be some high-tech gizmo. It's a piece of junk, Alex. Looks like a loser in a junior-high science fair. Mismatched screws, all wobbly. Like Mate cobbled it from spare parts."

"It worked," I said.

"Oh yeah. It worked fine. Fifty times. Which is a good place to start, right? Fifty families. Maybe someone didn't approve of Mate's brand of travel agency. Potentially, we're talking hundreds of suspects. Problem one is we've been having a hard time reaching them. Seems lots of Mate's chosen were from out-of-state—good luck locating the survivors. The department's lent me two brand-new Detective-I's to do phone work and other scut. So far people don't want to talk to them about old Eldon, and the few who do think the guy was a saint—'Grandma's doctors watched her writhe in agony and wouldn't do a damn thing. Dr. Mate was the only one willing to help.' Alibi-talk or true belief? I'd need face-to-faces with all of them, maybe you there to psychoanalyze, and so far it's been telephonic. We're making our way through the list."

"Trussed to the machine," I said. "What makes you think homicide? Maybe it was voluntary. Mate decided it was his own time to skid off the mortal coil, and practiced what he preached."

"Wait, there's more. He was hooked up, all right—I.V. in each arm, one bottle full of the tranquilizer he uses—thiopental—the other with the potassium chloride for the heart attack. And his thumb was touching this little trip-wire doohickey that gets the flow going. Coroner said the potassium had kicked in for at least a few minutes, so Mate would've been dead from that, if he wasn't dead already. But he was. The gizmo was all for *show*, Alex. What *dispatched* him was no mercy killing: he got slammed on the head hard enough to crack his skull and cause a subdural hematoma, then someone cut him up, none too neatly. 'Ensanguination due to extensive genital mutilation.' "

"He was castrated?" I said.

"And more. Bled out. Coroner says the head wound was serious, nice columnar indentation, meaning a length of pipe or something like that. It would've caused big-time damage if Mate had lived—maybe even killed him. But it wasn't immediately fatal. The rear of the van was soaked with blood, and the spatter says arterial spurts, meaning Mate's heart was pumping away when the killer worked on him."

He rubbed his face. "He was vivisected, Alex."

"Lord," I said.

"Some other wounds, too. Deliberate cuts, eight of them, deep. Abdomen, groin and thighs. Squares, like the killer was playing around."

"Proud of himself," I said.

He pulled out his notepad but didn't write.

"Any other wounds?" I said.

"Just some superficial cuts the coroner says were probably accidental—the blade slipping. All that blood had to make it a slippery job. Weapon was very sharp and single-edged—scalpel or a straight razor, probably with scissors for backup."

"Anesthesia, scalpel, scissors," I said. "Surgery. The killer must have been drenched. No blood outside the van?"

"Not one speck. It looked like the ground had been swept. This guy took *extreme* care. We're talking wet work in a confined space in the dead of night. He had to use some kind of portable light. The front seat was full of blood, too, especially the passenger seat. I'm thinking this bad boy did his thing, got out of the van, reentered on the passenger side—easier than the driver's seat because no steering wheel to get in the way. That's where he cleaned most of the mess off. Then he got out again, stripped naked, wiped off the rest of the blood, bundled the soiled stuff up, probably in plastic bags. Maybe the same plastic he'd used to store a change of clean clothes. He got into his new duds, checked to cover any prints or tracks, swept around the van and was gone."

"Naked in full view of the road," I said. "That would be risky even in the dark, because he'd have to use a flashlight to check himself and the dirt. On top of operating in the van using light. *Someone* could've driven by, seen it shining through the van windows, gone to check, or reported it."

"The light in the van might not have been that big of a problem. There were sheets of thick cardboard cut to the right size for blocking the windows on the driver's seat. Also streaked with arterial blood, so they'd been used during the cutting. Cardboard's just the kind of homemade thing Mate would've used in lieu of curtains, so my bet is Dr. Death brought them himself. Thinking he was gonna be the trusser, not the trussee. Same for the mattress he was lying on. I think Mate came ready to play Angel of Death for the fifty-first time and someone said, Tag, you're it."

"The killer used the cardboard, then removed it from the windows," I said. "*Wanting* the body to be discovered. Display, just like the geometrical wounds—like leaving the van in full sight. Look what *I* did. Look who I *did* it to."

He stared down at the soil, grim, exhausted. I pictured the slaughter. Vicious blitz assault, then deliberate surgery on the side of an ink black road. The killer silent, intent, constructing an impromptu operatory within the confines of the van's rear compartment. Picking his spot, knowing few cars drove by. Working quickly, efficiently, taking the time to do what he'd come to do—what he'd fantasized about.

Taking the time to insert two I.V. lines. Positioning Mate's finger on the trigger.

Swimming in blood, yet managing to escape without leaving behind a dot of scarlet. Sweeping the dirt . . . I'd never encountered anything more premeditated.

"What was the body position?"

"Lying on his back, head near the front seat."

"On the mattress he provided," I said. "Mate prepares the van, the killer uses it. Talk about a power trip. Co-optation."

He thought about that for a long time. "There's something that needs to be kept quiet: The killer left a note. Plain white paper, eight by eleven, tacked to Mate's chest. Nailed into the sternum, actually, with a stainless-steel brad. Computer-typed: *Happy Traveling, You Sick Bastard.*"

Vehicle noise caused us both to turn. A car appeared from the west, on the swell that led down Encino Hills. Big white Mercedes sedan. The middle-aged woman at the wheel kept to forty miles per while touching up her makeup, sped past without glancing at us.

"Happy Traveling," I said. "Mate's euphemism. The

whole thing stinks of mockery, Milo. Which could also be why the killer coldcocked Mate before cutting him up. He set up a two-act play in order to parody Mate's technique. Sedate first, then kill. Piece of pipe instead of thiopental. Brutal travesty of Mate's ritual."

He blinked. The morning gloom dulled his leaf-green eyes, turned them into a pair of cocktail olives. "You're saying this guy is playing doctor? Or he *hates* doctors? Wants to make some sort of *philosophical* statement?"

"The note may have been left to get you to *think* he's taking on Mate philosophically. He might even be telling *himself* that's the reason he did it. But it ain't so. Sure, there are plenty of people who don't approve of what Mate did. I can even see some zealot taking a potshot at him, or trying to blow him up. But what you just described goes way beyond a difference of opinion. This guy enjoyed the *process*. Staging, playing around, enacting the *theater* of death. And at this level of brutality and calculation, it wouldn't surprise me if he's done it before."

"If he has, it's the first time he's gone public. I called VICAP, nothing in their files matches. The agent I spoke to said it had elements of both organized and disorganized serials, thank you very much."

"You said the amputation was clumsy," I said.

"That's the coroner's opinion."

"So maybe our boy's got some medical aspirations. Someone with a grudge, like a med-school reject, wanting to show the world how clever he is."

"Maybe," he said. "Then again, Mate *was* a legit doc and *he* was no master craftsman. Last year he removed a liver from one of his travelers, dropped it off at County Hospital. Packed with ice, in a picnic cooler. Not that anyone would've accepted it, given the source, but the liver was garbage. Mate took it out all wrong, hacked-up blood vessels, made a mess."

"Doctors who don't do surgery often forget the little they learned in med school," I said. "Mate spent most of his professional life as a bureaucrat, bouncing from public health department to public health department. When did this liver thing happen? Never heard about it."

"Last December. You never heard about it because it was never made public. 'Cause who'd want it to get out? Not Mate, because he looked like a clown, but not the D.A.'s office, either. They'd given up on prosecuting Mate, were sick of giving him free publicity. I found out because the coroner doing the post on Mate had seen the paperwork on the disposal of the liver, had heard people talking about it at the morgue."

"Maybe I wasn't giving the killer enough credit," I said. "Given the tight space, darkness, the time pressure, it couldn't have been easy. Perhaps those error wounds weren't the only time he slipped. If he nicked himself he could've left behind some of his own biochemistry."

"From your mouth to God's ears. The lab rats have been going over every square inch of that van, but so far the only blood they've been able to pull up is Mate's. O positive."

"The only common thing about him." I was thinking of the one time I'd seen Eldon Mate on TV. Because I had followed his career, had watched a press conference after a "voyage." The death doctor had left the stiffening corpse of a woman—almost all of them were women—in a motel near downtown, then showed up at the D.A.'s office to "inform the authorities." My take: to brag. The man had looked jubilant. That's when a reporter had brought up the use of budget lodgings. Mate had turned livid and spat back the line about Jesus.

Despite the public taunt, the D.A. had done nothing about the death, because five acquittals had shown that bringing Mate up on charges was a certain loser. Mate's triumphalism had grated. He'd gloated like a spoiled child.

A small, round, bald man in his sixties with the constipated face and the high, strident voice of a petty functionary, mocking the justice system that couldn't touch him, lashing out against those "enslaved to the hypocritic oath." Proclaiming his victory with rambling sentences armored with obscure words ("My partnership with my travelers has been an exemplar of mutual fructification"). Pausing only to purse slit lips that, when they weren't moving, seemed on the verge of spitting. Microphones shoved in his face made him smile. He had hot eyes, a tendency to screech. A hit-and-run patter had made me think *vaudeville*.

"Yeah, he was a piece of work, wasn't he?" said Milo. "I always thought when you peeled away all the medicolegal crap, he was just a homicidal nut with a medical degree. Now he's the victim of a psycho."

"And that made you think of me," I said.

"Well," he said, "who else? Also, there's the fact that one week later I'm no closer to anything. Any profound, behavioral-science insights would be welcome, Doctor."

"Just the mockery angle, so far," I said. "A killer going for glory, an ego out of control."

"Sounds like Mate himself."

"All the more reason to get rid of Mate. Think about it: If you were a frustrated loser who saw yourself as a genius, wanted to play God publicly, what better than dispatching the Angel of Death? You're very likely right about it being a travel gone wrong. If the killer did make a date with Mate, maybe Mate logged it."

"No log in his apartment," Milo said. "No work records of any kind. I'm figuring Mate kept the paperwork with that lawyer of his, Roy Haiselden. Mouthy fellow, you'd think he'd be blabbing nonstop, but nada. He's gone, too."

Haiselden had been at the conference with Mate. Big man in his fifties, florid complexion, too-bushy auburn toupee. "Amsterdam, also?" I said. "Another humanist?"

"Don't know where yet, just that he doesn't answer calls. . . . Yeah, everyone's a humanist. Our *bad* boy probably thinks he's a humanist."

"No, I don't think so," I said. "I think he likes being bad."

Another car drove by. Gray Toyota Cressida. Another female driver, this one a teenage girl. Once again, no sideward glance.

"See what you mean," I said. "Perfect place for a nighttime killing. Also for a travel jaunt, so maybe Mate chose it. And after all the flack about tacky settings, perhaps he decided to go for scenic—final passage in a serene spot. If so, he made the killer's job easier. Or the killer picked the spot and Mate approved. A killer familiar with the area—maybe even someone living within walking distance—could explain the lack of tire tracks. It would also be a kick—murder so close to home and he gets away with it. Either way, the confluence between his goals and Mate's would've been fun."

"Yeah," Milo said, without enthusiasm. "Gonna have my D-I's canvass the locals, see if any psychos with records turn up." Another glance at his watch. "Alex, if the killer set up an appointment with Mate by faking terminal illness, that implies theater on another level: acting skills good enough to convince Mate he was dying."

"Not necessarily," I said. "Mate had relaxed his standards. When he started out, he insisted on terminal illness. But recently he'd been talking about a dignified death being anyone's right."

No formal diagnosis necessary. I kept my face blank.

Maybe not blank enough. Milo was staring at me. "Something the matter?"

"Beyond a tide of gore in the morning?"

"Oh," he said. "Sometimes I forget you're a civilian. Guess you don't wanna see the crime-scene photos."

"Do they add anything?"

"Not to me, but . . ."

"Sure."

He retrieved a manila packet from the unmarked. "These are copies—the originals are in the murder book."

Loose photos, full-color, too much color, the van's interior shot from every angle. Eldon Mate's body was pathetic and small in death. His round white face bore *the look*—dull, flat, the assault of stupid surprise. Every murdered face I'd seen wore it. The democracy of extinction.

The flashbulb had turned the blood splatter greenish around the edges. The arterial spurts were a bad abstract painting. All of Mate's smugness was gone. The Humanitron behind him. The photo reduced his machine to a few bowed slats of metal, sickeningly delicate, like a baby cobra. From the top frame dangled the pair of glass I.V. bottles, also blood-washed.

Just another obscenity, human flesh turned to trash. I

never got used to it. Each time I encountered it, I craved faith in the immortality of the soul.

Included with the death photos were some shots of the brown Econoline, up close and from a distance. The rental sticker was conspicuous on the rear window. No attempt had been made to obscure the front plates. The van's front end so ordinary . . . the front.

"Interesting."

"What is?" said Milo.

"The van was backed in, not headed in the easy way." I handed him a picture. He studied it, said nothing.

"Turning around took some effort," I said. "Only reason I can think of is, it would've made escape easier. It probably wasn't the killer's decision. He knew the van wouldn't be leaving. Although I suppose he might have considered the possibility of being interrupted and having to take off quickly. . . . No, when they arrived, Mate was in charge. Or thought he was. In the driver's seat literally and psychologically. Maybe he sensed something was off."

"It didn't stop him from going through with it."

"Could be he put his reservations aside because he also enjoyed a bit of danger. Vans, motels, sneaking around at night say to me he got off on the whole cloak-and-dagger thing."

I handed him the rest of the photos and he slipped them in the packet.

"All that blood," I said. "Hard to imagine not a single print was left anywhere."

"Lots of smooth surfaces in the van. The coroner did find smears, like finger-painting whirls, says it might mean rubber gloves. We found an open box in the front. Mate was a dream victim, brought all the fixings for the final feast." He checked his watch again.

"If the killer had access to a surgical kit, he could've also brought sponges—nice and absorbent, perfect for cleanup. Any traces of sponge material in the van?"

He shook his head.

I said, "What else did you find, in terms of medical supplies?"

"Empty hypodermic syringe, the thiopental and the potassium chloride, alcohol swabs—that's a kicker, ain't it? You're about to kill someone, you bother to swab them with alcohol to prevent infection?"

"They do it up in San Quentin when they execute someone. Maybe it makes them feel like health-care professionals. The killer would've liked feeling legitimate. What about a bag to carry all that equipment?"

"No, nothing like that."

"No carrying case of any kind?"

"No."

"There had to be some kind of case," I said. "Even if the equipment was Mate's, he wouldn't have left it rolling around loose in the van. Also, Mate had lost his license but he still fancied himself a doctor, and doctors carry black bags. Even if he was too cheap to invest in leather, and used something like a paper sack, you'd expect to find it. Why would the killer leave the Humani-tron and everything else behind and take the case?"

"Snuff the doctor, steal his bag?"

"Taking over the doctor's practice."

"*He* wants to be Dr. Death?"

"Makes sense, doesn't it? He's murdered Mate, can't exactly come out into the open and start soliciting terminally ill people. But he could have something in mind."

Milo rubbed his face furiously, as if scrubbing without water. "More wet work?"

"It's just theory," I said.

Milo gazed up at the dismal sky, slapped the packet of death photos against his leg again, chewed his cheek. "A sequel. Oh that would be peachy. Extremely *pleasant*. And this theory occurs to you because *maybe* there was a bag and *maybe* someone took it."

"If you don't think it has merit, disregard it."

"How the hell should *I* know if it has merit?" He stuffed the photos in his jacket pocket, yanked out his pad, opened it and stabbed at the paper with a chewed-down pencil. Then he slammed the pad shut. The cover was filled with scrawl. "The bag coulda been left behind and ended up in the morgue without being logged."

"Sure," I said. "Absolutely."

"Great," he said. "That would be great."

"Well, folks," I said, in a W. C. Fields voice, "in terms of theory, I think that's about it for today."

His laughter was sudden. I thought of a mastiff's warning bark. He fanned himself with the notepad. The air was cool, stale, still inert. He was sweating. "Forgive the peckishness. I need sleep." Yet another glance at the Timex.

"Expecting company?" I said.

"The yuppie hikers. Mr. Paul Ulrich and Ms. Tanya Stratton. Interviewed them the day of the murder, but they didn't give me much. Too upset—especially the girl. The boyfriend spent his time trying to calm her down. Given what she saw, can't blame her, but she seemed . . . delicate. Like if I pressed too hard she'd disintegrate. I've been trying all week to arrange the re-interview. Phone tag, excuses. Finally reached them last night, figured I'd go to their house, but they said they'd rather meet up here, which I thought was gutsy. But maybe they're thinking some kind of self-therapy—

whatchamacallit—working it *through*." He grinned.
"See, it *does* rub off, all those years with you."

"A few more and you'll be ready to see patients."

"People tell *me* their troubles, they get locked up."

"When are they due to show up?"

"Fifteen minutes ago. Stopping by on their way to
work—both have jobs in Century City." He kicked dust.
"Maybe they chickened out. Even if they do show, I'm
not sure what I'm hoping to get out of them. But got to
be thorough, right? So what's your take on Mate? Do-
gooder or serial killer?"

"Maybe both," I said. "He came across arrogant, with
a low view of humanity, so it's hard to believe his altruism was pure. Nothing else in his life points to excep-
tional compassion. Just the opposite: instead of taking
care of patients, he spent his medical career as a paper
pusher. And he never amounted to much as a doctor until
he started helping people die. If I had to bet on a primary
motive, I'd say he craved attention. On the other hand,
there's a reason the families you've talked to support
him. He alleviated a lot of suffering. Most of the people
who pulled the trigger of that machine were in torment."

"So you condone what he did even if his reasons for
doing it were less than pure."

"I haven't decided how I feel about what he did,"
I said.

"Ah." He fiddled with the turquoise clasp.

There was plenty more I could've said and I felt low,
evasive. Another burst of engine hum rescued me from
self-examination. This time, the car approached from
the east and Milo turned.

Dark-blue BMW sedan, 300 model, a few years old.
Two people inside. The car stopped, the driver's window
lowered and a man with a huge, spreading mustache

looked out at us. Next to him sat a young woman, gazing straight ahead.

"The yuppies show up," said Milo. "Finally, someone respects the rule of law."

CHAPTER

3

MILO WAVED THE BMW up, the mustachioed man turned the wheel and parked behind the Seville. "Here okay, Detective?"

"Sure—anywhere," said Milo.

The man smiled uncomfortably. "Didn't want to mess something up."

"No problem, Mr. Ulrich. Thanks for coming."

Paul Ulrich turned off the engine and he and the woman got out. He was medium-size, late thirties to forty, solidly built, with a well-cured beach tan and a nubby, sunburned nose. His crew cut was dun-colored, soft-looking to the point of fuzziness, with lots of pinkish scalp glowing through. As if all his hair-growing energy had been focused on the mustache, an extravagance as wide as his face, parted into two flaring red-brown wings, stiff with wax, luxuriant as an old-time grenadier's. His sole burst of flamboyance, and it clashed with haberdashery that seemed chosen for inconspicuousness on Century Park East: charcoal suit, white button-down shirt, navy and silver rep tie, black wing-tips.

He held the woman's elbow as they made their way toward us. She was younger, late twenties, as tall as he, thin and narrow-shouldered, with a stiff, tentative walk that belied any hiking experience. Her skin tone said indoors, too. More than that: indoor pallor. Chalky-white edged with translucent blue, so pale she made Milo look ruddy. Her hair was dark brown, almost black, boy-short, wispy. She wore big, black-framed sunglasses, a mocha silk blazer over a long brown print dress, flat-soled, basket-weave sandals.

Milo said, "Ms. Stratton," and she took his hand reluctantly. Up close, I saw rouge on her cheeks, clear gloss on chapped lips. She turned to me.

"This is Dr. Delaware, Ms. Stratton. Our psychological consultant."

"Uh-huh," she said. Unimpressed.

"Doctor, these are our witnesses—Ms. Tanya Stratton and Mr. Paul Ulrich. Thanks again for showing up, folks. I really appreciate it."

"Sure, no prob," said Ulrich, glancing at his girlfriend. "I don't know what else we can tell you."

The shades blocked Stratton's eyes and her expression. Ulrich had started to smile, but he stopped midway. The mustache straightened.

He, trying to fake calm after what they'd been through. She, not bothering. The typical male-female mambo. I tried to imagine what it had been like, peering into that van.

She touched a sidepiece of her sunglasses. "Can we get this over quickly?"

"Sure, ma'am," Milo said. "The first time we talked, you didn't notice anything out of the ordinary, but sometimes people remember things afterward—"

"Unfortunately, we don't," said Tanya Stratton. Her voice was soft, nasal, inflected with that syllable-stretching California female twang. "We went over it last night because we were coming here to meet you. But there's nothing."

She hugged herself and looked to the right. Over at the spot. Ulrich put his arm around her. She didn't resist him, but she didn't give herself over to the embrace.

Ulrich said, "So far our names haven't been in the paper. We're going to be able to keep it that way, aren't we, Detective Sturgis?"

"Most likely," said Milo.

"Likely but not definitely?"

"I can't say for sure, sir. Frankly, with a case like this, you never know. And if we ever catch who did it, your testimony might be required. I certainly won't give your names out, if that's what you mean. As far as the department's concerned, the less we reveal the better."

Ulrich touched the slit of flesh between his mustaches. "Why's that?"

"Control of the data, sir."

"I see . . . sure, makes sense." He looked at Tanya Stratton again. She licked her lips, said, "At least you're honest about not being able to protect us. Have you learned anything about who did it?"

"Not yet, ma'am."

"Not that you'd tell us, right?"

Milo smiled.

Paul Ulrich said, "Fifteen minutes of fame. Andy Warhol coined that phrase and look what happened to him."

"What happened?" said Milo.

"Checked into a hospital for routine surgery, went out in a bag."

Stratton's black glasses flashed as she turned her head sharply.

"All I meant, honey, is celebrity stinks. The sooner we're through with this the better. Look at Princess Di— look at Dr. Mate, for that matter."

"We're not celebrities, Paul."

"And that's good, hon."

Milo said, "So you think Dr. Mate's notoriety had something to do with his death, Mr. Ulrich?"

"I don't know—I mean, I'm no expert. But wouldn't you say so? It does seem logical, given who he was. Not that *we* recognized him when we saw him—not in the condition he was in." He shook his head. "Whatever. You didn't even tell us who he was when you were questioning us last week. We found out by watching the news—"

Tanya Stratton's hand took hold of his biceps.

He said, "That's about it. We need to get to work."

"Speaking of which, do you always hike before work?" said Milo.

"We walk four, five times a week," said Stratton.

"Keeping healthy," said Ulrich.

She dropped her hand and turned away from him.

"We're both early risers," he said, as if pressed to explain. "We both have long workdays, so if we don't get our exercise in the morning, forget it." He flexed his fingers.

Milo pointed up the dirt road. "Come here often?"

"Not really," said Stratton. "It's just one of the places we go. In fact, we rarely come up here, except on Sundays. Because it's far and we need to drive back, shower off, change. Mostly we stick closer to home."

"Encino," said Milo.

"Right over the hill," said Ulrich. "That morning we were up early. I suggested Mulholland because it's so pretty." He edged closer to Stratton, put his hand back on her shoulder.

Milo said, "You were here, when—six, six-fifteen?"

"We usually start out by six," said Stratton. "I'd say

we were here by six-twenty, maybe later by the time we parked. The sun was up already. You could see it over that peak." Pointing east, toward foothills beyond the gate.

Ulrich said, "We like to catch at least part of the sunrise. Once you get past there"—hooking a thumb at the gate—"it's like being in another world. Birds, deer, chipmunks. Duchess goes crazy 'cause she gets to run around without a leash. Tanya's had her for ten years and she still runs like a puppy. Great nose, thinks she's a drug dog."

"Too good," said Stratton, grimacing.

"If Duchess hadn't run to the van," said Milo, "would you have approached it?"

"What do you mean?" she said.

"Was there anything different about it? Was it conspicuous in any way?"

"No," she said. "Not really."

"Duchess must've sensed something off," said Ulrich. "Her instincts are terrific."

Stratton said, "She's always bringing me *presents.* Dead squirrels, birds. Now *this.* Every time I think about it I get sick to my stomach. I really need to go, have a pile of work to go through."

"What kind of work do you do?" said Milo.

"Executive secretary to a vice president at Unity Bank. Mr. Gerald Van Armstren."

Milo checked his notes. "And you're a financial planner, Mr. Ulrich?"

"Financial consultant. Mostly real-estate work."

Stratton turned abruptly and walked back to the BMW.

Ulrich called out "Honey?" but he didn't go after her. "Sorry, guys. She's been really traumatized, says she'll never get the image out of her head. I thought coming up here might actually help—not a good idea at all." He shook his head, gazed at Stratton. Her back was to him. "Really *bad* idea."

Milo strode over to the car. Tanya Stratton stood with her hand on the handle of the passenger door, facing west. He said something to her. She shook her head, turned away, revealing a tight white profile.

Ulrich rocked on his heels and exhaled. A strand of mustache hair that had eluded wax vibrated.

I said, "Have you two been together long?"

"A while. She's sensitive . . ."

Over by the car, Stratton's face was a white mask as Milo talked. The two of them looked like Kabuki players.

"How long have you been into hiking?" I said.

"Years. I've always exercised. It took a while to get Tanya into it. She's not—let's just say this'll probably be the conclusion of that." He looked over at the BMW. "She's a great gal, just needs . . . special handling. Actually, there *was* one thing I remembered. Came to me last night, isn't that bizarre? Can I tell you or do I have to wait for him?"

"It's fine to tell me."

Ulrich smoothed his left mustache. "I didn't want to say this in front of Tanya. Not because it's anything significant, but she thinks anything we say will get us more deeply involved. But I don't see how this could. It was just another car. Parked on the side of the road. The south side. We passed it as we drove up. Not particularly close, maybe a quarter mile down that way." Indicating east. "Couldn't be relevant, right? Because by the time we arrived Mate had been dead for a while, right? So why would anyone stick around?"

"What kind of car?" I said.

"BMW. Like ours. That's why I noticed it. Darker than ours. Maybe black. Or dark gray."

"Same model?"

"Can't say, all I remember is the grille. No big deal, there've got to be lots of Beemers up here, right? I just thought I should mention it."

"You didn't happen to notice the license plate?"

He laughed. "Yeah, right. And the facial features of some psychotic killer drooling at the wheel. No, that's all I can tell you—a dark Beemer. The only reason I even remembered it was that when Detective Sturgis called last night, he asked us to search our minds for any other details, and I really gave it a go. I can't even swear it was that dark. Maybe it was medium-gray. Brown, whatever. Amazing I remembered it at all. After seeing what was inside that van, it's hard to think about anything else. Whoever did that to Mate must have really hated him."

I said, "Rough. Which window did you look through?"

"First the front windshield. Saw blood on the seats and I said, 'Oh shit.' Then Duchess ran around the back so we followed her. That's where we caught a full view."

Milo backed away and Stratton got in the car.

Ulrich said, "Better hustle. Nice to meet you, Dr. Delaware."

He jogged toward the blue car, saluted Milo as he entered. Starting up, he shifted into gear, hooked a U-turn and sped down the rise.

I told Milo about the dark BMW.

"Well, it's something," he said. Then he laughed coldly. "No, it's not. He's right. Why would the killer stick around for three, four hours?" He stashed the notepad back in his pocket. "Okay, one reinterview heard from."

"She's a tense one," I said.

"Blame her? Why? She set off some buzzers?"

"No. But I see what you meant about delicacy. What did she tell you when you spoke to her alone?"

"It was *Paul's* idea to come up here. *Paul's* idea to hike. *Paul's* a superjock, would live in a tree if he could. They probably weren't in the throes of love when they found Mate. Guess it didn't spice up their relationship."

"Murder as aphrodisiac."

"For some folks it is. . . . Now that I know about the second BMW I'm gonna have to log and do *some* kind of follow-up . . . hopefully a basic DMV will sync with some neighbor's vehicle and that'll be it." He rubbed his ear, as if dreading phone work. "First things first. Follow up with my junior D's to see how the family list is going. If you're so inclined, you could do some research on Mate."

"Any particular *theories* you want checked out?"

"Just the basic one: someone hated him bad enough to slaughter him. Not necessarily a news item. Maybe someone popping off about Mate in cyberspace."

"Our killer's a careful fellow. Why would he go public?"

"It's beyond long shot, but you never know. Last year we had a case, father who molested and murdered his five-year-old daughter. We suspected him, couldn't get a damn bit of evidence. Then a half year later, the asshole goes and brags about it to another pedophile in a chat room. Even then it was only a lucky accident that we heard about it. One of our vice guys was monitoring the kiddie-rapers, thought the details sounded familiar."

"You never told me about that one."

"I'm not out to introduce *pollution* into your life, Alex. Unless I need help."

"Sure," I said. "I'll do what I can."

He slapped a hand on my shoulder. "Thank you, sir. The suits are right miffed about a high-profile case popping up right now, just when the crime rate was allegedly dropping. Just when they thought they'd get some *good* publicity before funding time. So if you produce, I might even be able to get you some money fairly soon."

I panted like a dog. "Oh, Master, how wonderful."

"Hey," he said, "hasn't the department always treated you well?"

"Like royalty."

"Royalty . . . you and old Duchess . . . Maybe it's *her* I should be interviewing. Maybe it'll come to that."

CHAPTER

4

I DROVE DOWN Mulholland and eased into the traffic at Beverly Glen. The jazz station had gotten talky of late so the radio was tuned to KUSC. Something easy on the ears was playing. Debussy was my guess. Too pretty for this morning. I switched it off and used the time to think about the way Eldon Mate had died.

The phone call I'd made when I'd first heard about it.

No answer, and trying again was a much worse idea than it had been last week. But how long could I work with Milo without clearing things up?

As I tossed it back and forth, the ethical ramifications spiraled. Some of the answers were covered in the rule books, but others weren't. Real life always transcends the rule books.

I arrived home hyped by indecision.

The house was quiet, cooled by the surrounding pines, oak floors gleaming, white walls bleached metallic by eastern light. Robin had left toast and coffee out. No sign of her, no panting canine welcome. The morning paper remained folded on the kitchen counter.

She and Spike were out back in the studio. She had several big jobs backordered. With obligation on both our minds, we hadn't talked much since rising.

I filled a cup and drank. The silence was annoying.

Once, the house had been smaller, darker, far less comfortable, considerably less practical. A psychopath had burned it down a few years ago and we'd rebuilt. Everyone agreed it was an improvement. Sometimes, when I was alone, there seemed to be too much space.

It's been a long time since I've pretended to be emotionally independent. When you love someone for a long time, when that love is cemented in routine as well as thrill, her very presence fills too much space to be ignored. I knew Robin would interrupt her work if I dropped in, but I was in no mood to be sociable, so instead of continuing out the back door, I reached for the kitchen phone and checked with my service. And the problem of the unanswered call solved itself.

"Morning, Dr. Delaware," said the operator. "Only one message, just a few minutes ago. A Mr. Richard Doss, here's the number."

An 805 exchange, not Doss's Santa Monica office. Ventura or Santa Barbara County. I punched it in and a woman answered, "RTD Properties."

"Dr. Delaware returning Mr. Doss's call."

"This is his phone-routing service, one moment."

Several clicks cricketed in my ear, followed by a rub of static and then a familiar voice. "Dr. Delaware. Long time."

Reedy tone, staccato delivery, that hint of sarcasm. Richard Doss always sounded as if he was mocking someone or something. I'd never decided if it was intentional or just a vocal quirk.

"Morning, Richard."

More static. Fade-out on his reply. Several seconds passed before he returned. "We may get cut off again, I'm out in the boonies, Carpinteria. Looking at some land. Avocado orchard that'll do just fine as a minimall if my cold-blooded capitalist claws get hold of it. If we lose each other again, don't phone me, I'll phone you. The usual number?"

Taking charge, as always. "Same one, Richard." Not *Mr. Doss*, because he'd always insisted I use his first name. One of the many rules he'd laid down. The illusion of informality, just a regular guy. From what I'd seen, Richard T. Doss never really let down his guard.

"I know why you called," he said. "And why you think I called back."

"Mate's death."

"Festive times. The sonofabitch finally got what he deserved."

I didn't reply.

He laughed. "Come on, Doctor, be a sport. I'm dealing with life's challenges with humor. Wouldn't a psychologist recommend that? Isn't humor a good coping skill?"

"Is Dr. Mate's death something you need to cope with?"

"Well . . ." He laughed again. "Even positive change is a challenge, right?"

"Right."

"You're thinking how vindictive I'm being—by the way, when it happened I was out of town. San Francisco. Looking over a hotel. Trailed by ten clinically depressed Tokyo bankers. They paid thirty million five years ago, are itching to unload for considerably less."

"Great," I said.

"It certainly is. Do you recall all that yellow-peril nonsense a while back: death rays from the Rising Sun, soon our kids will be eating sushi for school lunch? About as realistic as Godzilla. Everything cycles, the key to feeling smart is to live long enough." Another laugh. "Guess the *sonofabitch* won't feel smart anymore. So . . . that's my alibi."

"Do you feel you need an alibi?" The first thing I'd wondered when I'd heard about Mate.

Silence. Not a phone problem this time; I could hear him breathing. When he spoke again, his tone was subdued and tight.

"I wasn't being literal, Doctor. Though the police *have* tried to talk to me, probably have some kind of list they're running down. If they're proceeding sequentially, I'd be at the bottom or close to it. The sonofabitch murdered another two women after Joanne. Anyway, enough of that. *My* call wasn't about him, it's about Stacy."

"How's Stacy doing?"

"Essentially fine. If you're asking did the sonofabitch's death flash her back to her mother, I haven't noticed any untoward reactions. Not that we've talked about it. Joanne hasn't been a topic since Stacy stopped seeing you. And Mate's never been of interest to her, which is good. Dirt like that doesn't deserve her time. Essentially, we've all been fine. Eric's back at Stanford, finished up the year with terrific grades, working with an econ professor on his honors paper. I'm flying up to see him this weekend, may take Stacy with me, give her another look at the campus."

"She's decided on Stanford?"

"Not yet, that's why I want her to see it again. She's in good shape application-wise. Her grades really picked up after she saw you. This semester she's going the whole nine yards. Full load, A.P. courses, honors track. We're still trying to decide whether she should apply for early admission or play the field. Stanford and the Ivys are taking most of their students early. Her being a legacy won't hurt, but it's always competitive. That's why I'm calling. She still has problems with decision-making, and the early-admit deadlines are in November, so there's some time pressure. I assume you'll be able to find time for her this week."

"I can do that," I said. "But—"

"Payment will be the same, correct? Unless you've raised your fee."

"Payment's the same—"

"No surprise," he said. "With the HMOs closing in, you'd be hard-pressed to raise. We've still got you on computer, just bill through the office."

I took a single deep breath. "Richard, I'd be happy to see Stacy, but before I do you need to know that the police have consulted me on Mate's murder."

"I see . . . Actually, I don't. Why would they do that?"

"I've consulted to the department in the past and the primary detective is someone I've worked with. He hasn't made a specific request, just wants open-ended psychological consultation."

"Because the sonofabitch was crazy?"

"Because the detective thinks I might be helpful—"

"Dr. Delaware, that's ambiguous to the point of meaninglessness."

"But true," I said, inhaling again. "I've said nothing about having seen your family, but there may be conflict. Because they *are* running down the list of Mate's—"

"Victims," he broke in. "Please don't give me that 'travelers' bullshit."

"The point I'm trying to make, Richard, is that the police *will* try to reach you. Before I go any further, I wanted to discuss it with you. I don't want you to feel there's a conflict of interest, so I called—"

"So you've found yourself in a conflictual situation and now you're trying to establish your position."

"It's not a matter of position. It's—"

"Your sincere attempt to do the right thing. Fine, I accept that. In my business we call it due diligence. What's your plan?"

"Now that you've called and asked me to see Stacy again, I'll bow off Mate."

"Why?"

"She's an ongoing patient, continuing as consultant is not an option."

"What reason will you give the police?"

"There'll be no need to explain, Richard. One thing, though: the police may learn about our relationship anyway. These things have a way of getting out."

"Well, that's fine," he said. "Don't keep any secrets on my account. In fact, when they do get hold of me, I'll inform them myself that Stacy's seen you. What's to hide? Caring father obtains help for suffering children? Even better, go ahead and tell them yourself."

He chuckled. "Guess it's fortunate that I do have an alibi—you know what, Doctor? Bring the police on. I'll be happy to tell them how I feel about the sonofabitch. Tell them there's nothing I'd like better than to dance on the sonofabitch's grave. And don't even think about giving up your consultant money, Dr. Delaware. Far be it for me to reduce your income in the HMO age. Keep right on working with the cops. In fact, I'd *prefer* that."

"Why?"

"Who knows, maybe you'll be able to dig around in the sonofabitch's life, uncover some dirt that tells the world what he really was."

"Richard—"

"I know. You'll be discreet about anything you find, discretion's your middle name and all that. But everything goes into the police file and the police have big mouths. So it'll come out . . . I like it, Dr. Delaware. By working for them you'll be doing double duty for *me*. Now, when can I bring Stacy by?"

I made an appointment for the next morning and hung up feeling as if I'd stood on the bow of a small boat during a typhoon.

Half a year had passed since I'd spoken to Richard Doss, but nothing had changed about the way we interacted. No reason for it to be any different. Richard hadn't changed, that had never been his goal.

One of the first things he'd let me know was that he despised Mate. When Mate's murder had flashed on the tube, my initial thought had been: *Richard went after him.*

After hearing the details of the murder, I felt better. The butchery didn't seem like Richard's style. Though how sure of that could I be? Richard hadn't disclosed any more about himself than he'd wanted to.

In control, always in control. One of those people who crowds every room he enters. Maybe that had been part of what led his wife to seek out Eldon Mate.

The referral had come from a family-court judge I'd worked with named Judy Manitow. The message her clerk left was brief: a neighbor had died, leaving behind a seventeen-year-old daughter who could use some counseling.

I called back, hesitant. I take very few therapy cases, stay away from long-termers, and this didn't sound like a quickie. But I'd worked well with Judy Manitow. She was smart, if authoritarian, seemed to care about kids. I phoned her chambers and she picked up herself.

"Can't promise you it'll be brief," she admitted.

"Though Stacy's always impressed me as a solid kid, no obvious problems. At least until now."

"How did her mother die?"

"Horribly. Lingering illness—severe deterioration. She was only forty-three."

"What kind of illness?"

"She was never really diagnosed, Alex. The actual cause of death was suicide. Her name was Joanne Doss. Maybe you read about her? It happened three months ago. She was one of Dr. Mate's . . . I guess you couldn't call her a patient. Whatever he calls them."

"Travelers," I said. "No, I didn't read about it."

"It wasn't much of a story," she said. "Back of the Westside supplement. Now that they don't prosecute Mate, guess he doesn't get prime coverage. I knew Joanne for a long time. Since we had our first babies. We did Mommy and Me together, preschool, the works. Went through it twice, had kids the same years. My Allison and her Eric, then Becky and Stacy. Becky and Stacy used to hang out. Sweet kid, she always seemed . . . grounded. So maybe she won't need long-term therapy, just a few sessions of grief work. You used to do that, right? Working on the cancer wards at Western Pediatrics?"

"Years ago," I said. "What I did there was mostly the reverse. Trying to help parents who'd lost kids. But sure, I've worked with all kinds of bereavement."

"Good," she said. "I just felt it was my duty because I know the family and Stacy seems to be a little depressed—how *couldn't* she be? I know you'll like her. And I do think you'll find the family interesting."

"Interesting," I said. "Scariest word in the English language."

She laughed. "Like someone trying to fix you up with an ugly blind date. 'Is he cute?' 'Well, he's *interesting*.'

That's not what I meant, Alex. The Dosses are smart, just about the brightest bunch I've ever met. *Individuals,* each of them—one thing I promise you, you won't be bored. Joanne earned two PhDs. First in English from Stanford, she'd already gotten an appointment as a lecturer at the U. when they moved to L.A. She switched gears suddenly, enrolled as a *student,* took science courses when she was pregnant with Eric. She ended up getting a doctorate in microbiology, was hired by the U. to do research. Before she got sick, she ran her own lab. Richard's a self-made millionaire. Stanford undergrad and MBA. He and Bob were in the same fraternity. He buys distressed properties, fixes them up, develops. Bob says he's amassed a fortune. Eric's one of those extreme geniuses, won awards in everything—academics, sports, you name it, a fireball. Stacy never seemed to have his confidence. More . . . internal. So it makes sense she'd be the one hit hardest by Joanne's death. Being a daughter, too. Mothers and daughters have something special."

She paused. "I've gone on a bit, haven't I? I guess it's because I really like the family. Also, to be honest, I've put myself in a spot. Because Richard was resistant to the idea of therapy. I had to work on him a bit to get him to agree. It was Bob who finally got through. He and Richard play tennis at the Cliffside; last week Richard mentioned to Bob that Stacy's grades had slipped, she seemed more tired than usual, did he have a recommendation for vitamins. Bob told him he was being a damn fool, Stacy didn't need vitamins, she needed counseling, he'd better get his own act in gear."

"Tough love," I said. "Must have been some tennis game."

"I'm sure it was testosterone at its finest. I love my guy, but he's not a master of subtlety. Anyway, it worked.

Richard agreed. So, if you *could* see Stacy, it would help me not look like a complete idiot."

"Sure, Judy."

"Thank you, Alex. There'll certainly be no problem paying the bills. Richard's doing great financially."

"What about emotionally?"

"To tell the truth, he seems fine there, too. Not that he'd ever show it. He did have time to adjust, because Joanne was sick for over a year. . . . Alex, I've never seen such a negative transformation. She gave up her career, withdrew, stopped taking care of herself. Gained weight—I'm talking a tremendous amount, really huge, maybe seventy, a hundred pounds. She became this . . . inert lump. Stayed in bed, eating and sleeping, complaining of pain. Her skin broke out in rashes—it was a horror."

"And there was never any diagnosis?"

"None. Several doctors saw her, including Bob. He wasn't her internist—Bob likes to stay away from people he knows socially, but he worked up Joanne as a favor to Richard. Found nothing, referred her to an immunologist who did his thing and sent her to someone else. And so on and so on."

"Whose decision was it to go to Mate?"

"Definitely Joanne's—not Richard's, Joanne never told him, just disappeared one night and was found the next morning out in Lancaster. Maybe that's why Richard *hates* Mate so much. Being left out. He found out when the police called him. Tried to get in touch with Mate but Mate never returned his calls. Enough, I'm digressing."

"On the contrary," I said. "Anything you know could be helpful."

"That's all I know, Alex. A woman destroyed herself

and now her kids are left behind. I can only imagine what poor Stacy's going through."

"Does she look depressed to you?"

"She's not the kind of kid to bleed all over, but I'd say yes. She *has* gained some weight. Nothing like Joanne, maybe ten pounds. But she's not a tall girl. I know how my girls watch themselves, at that age they all do. That and she seems quieter, preoccupied."

"Are she and Becky friends?"

"They used to be really close," she said. "But Becky doesn't know anything, you know kids. We're all very fond of Stacy, Alex. Please help her."

The morning after that conversation, a secretary from RTD Properties called and asked me to hold for Mr. Doss. Pop music played for several minutes and then Richard came on sounding alert, almost cheerful, not at all like a man whose wife had killed herself three months before. Then again, as Judy had said, he'd had time to prepare.

No hint of the resistance Judy had described. He sounded eager, as if readying himself for a new challenge.

Then he began laying out the rules.

No more of that "Mr. Doss," Doctor. Call me Richard.

Services to be billed monthly through my corporate office, here's the number.

Stacy can't afford to miss school, so late-afternoon appointments are essential.

I expect some definition of the process you foresee, specifically what kind of treatment is called for and how long it will take.

Once you've completed your preliminary findings,

please submit them to me in writing and we'll take it from there.

"How old is Stacy?" I said.

"She turned seventeen last month."

"There's something you should know, then. Legally, she has no rights to confidentiality. But I can't work with a teen unless the parent agrees to respect confidentiality."

"Meaning I'm shut out of the process."

"Not necessarily . . ."

"Fine. When can I bring her in?"

"One more thing," I said. "I'll need to see you first."

"Why?"

"Before I see a patient, I take a complete history from the parent."

"I don't know about that. I'm extraordinarily busy, right in the middle of some complex deals. What would be the point, Doctor? We're focusing on a rather discrete topic: Stacy's grief. Not her infancy. I could see her development being relevant if it was a learning disability or some kind of immaturity, but any school problems she's experiencing have got to be a reaction to her mother's death. Don't get me wrong, I understand all about family therapy, but that's not what's called for here.

"I consulted a family therapist when my wife's illness intensified. Some quack referred by a doctor I no longer employ, because he felt someone should inquire about Stacy and Eric. I was reluctant, but I complied. The quack kept pressuring me to get the entire family involved, including Joanne. One of those New Agey types, miniature fountain in the waiting room, patronizing voice. I thought it was absolute nonsense. Judy Manitow claims you're quite good."

His tone implied Judy was well-meaning but far from infallible.

I said, "Whatever form treatment takes, Mr. Doss—"

"Richard."

"I'll need to see you first."

"Can't we do history-taking over the phone? Isn't that what we're doing right now? Look, if payment's the issue, just bill me for telephonic services. God knows my lawyers do."

"It's not that," I said. "I need to meet you face-to-face."

"Why?"

"It's the way I work, Richard."

"Well," he said. "That sounds rather dogmatic. The quack insisted on family therapy and you insist upon face-to-face."

"I've found it to be the best way."

"And if I don't agree?"

"Then I'm sorry, but I won't be able to see your daughter."

His chuckle was flat, percussive. I thought of a mechanical noisemaker. "You must be busy to afford to be that cavalier, Doctor. Congratulations."

Neither of us talked for several seconds and I wondered if I'd erred. The man had been through hell, why not be flexible? But something in his manner had gotten to me—the truth was, he'd pushed, so I'd pushed back. Amateur hour, Delaware. I should've known better.

I was about to back off when he said, "All right, I admire a man with spine. I'll see you once. But not this week, I'm out of town. . . . Let me check my calendar . . . hold on."

Click. On hold again. More pop music, belch-tone synthesizer syrup in waltz-time. "Tuesday at six is my only window this week, Doctor."

"Fine."

"Not *that* busy, eh? Give me your address."

I did.

"That's residential," he said.

"I work out of my house."

"Makes sense, keep the overhead down. Okay, see you Tuesday. In the meantime, you can begin with Stacy on Monday. She'll be available anytime after school—"

"I'll see her after we've spoken, Richard."

"What a *tough* sonofabitch you are, Doctor. Should've gone into *my* business. The money's a helluva lot better and you could still work out of your house."

CHAPTER

5

AN ALIBI.

Richard's call made me want to get out of the house. I filled a cup for Robin and carried it, along with mine, out through the house and into the garden. Passing the perennial bed Robin had laid down last winter, crossing the footbridge to the pond, the rock waterfall. Placing the coffee on a stone bench, I paused to toss pellets to the koi. The fish darted toward me before the food hit the water, coalescing in a frothy swirl at the rim. Iron skies bore down, dyeing the water charcoal, playing on metallic scales. The air was cool, odorless, just as stagnant as up at the murder site, but greenery and water burble blunted the sense of lifelessness.

Up in the hills, September haze can be romanticized as fog. Our property's not large, but it's secluded because of an unbuildable western border, and surrounded by old-growth pines and lemon gums that create the illusion of solitude. This morning the treetops were capped with gray.

I crouched, allowing one of the larger carp to nibble my fingers. Reminding myself, as I sometimes did, that life was transitory and I was lucky to be living amid beauty and relative quiet. My father destroyed himself with alcohol and my mother was heroic but habitually sad. No whining, the past isn't a straitjacket. But for people breast-fed on misery, it can be an awfully tight sweater.

No sounds from the studio, then the chip-chip of Robin's chisel. The building's a single-story miniature of the house, with high windows and an old, burnished pine door rescued by Robin from a downtown demolition. I pushed the door open, heard music playing softly—Ry Cooder on slide. Robin was at her workbench, hair tied up in a red silk scarf, wearing gray denim overalls over a black T-shirt. Hunched in a way that would cause her shoulders to ache by nightfall. She didn't hear me enter. Smooth, slender arms worked the chisel on a guitar-shaped piece of Alaskan spruce. Wood shavings curled at her feet, creating a cozy bed for Spike. His bulldog bulk had sunk into the scrap, and he snored away, flews flapping.

I watched for a while as Robin continued to tune the soundboard, tapping, chiseling, tapping again, running her fingers along the inner edges, pausing to reflect before resuming. Her wrists were child-size, seemed too fragile to manipulate steel, but she handled the tool as if it were a chopstick.

Biting her lower lip, then licking it, as her back humped more acutely. A stray bit of auburn curl sprang loose from the kerchief and she tucked it back impatiently. Oblivious to my presence though I stood ten, fifteen feet away. As with most creative people, time and space have no meaning for her when her mind's engaged.

I came closer, stopped at the far end of the bench. Mahogany eyes widened, she placed the chisel on the workbench and the ivory flash of those two oversize incisors appeared between full, soft lips. I smiled back and held out a cup, enjoying the contours of her face, heart-shaped, olive-tinted, decorated by a few more lines than ages ago when we'd met, but still smooth. Usually, she wore earrings. Not this morning. No watch, no jewelry or makeup. She'd rushed out too quickly to bother.

I felt a nudge at my ankle, heard a wheeze and a snort. Spike grumbled and butted my shin. We'd both adopted him, but he'd adopted her.

"Call off your beast," I said.

Robin laughed and took the coffee. "Thanks, baby." She touched my face. Spike growled louder. She told him, "Don't worry, you're still my handsome."

Setting the cup down, she wrapped both her arms around my neck. Spike produced a poor excuse for a bark, raspy and attenuated by his stubby bulldog larynx.

"Oh, Spikey," she told him, snaring her fingers in my hair.

"If you stop to pet him," I said, "*I'll* start snorting."

"Stop what?"

"This." I kissed her, ran my hands over her back, down to her rear, then up again, grazing her shoulder blades. Starting at the top and kneading the knobs of her spine.

"Oh that's good. I'm a little sore."

"Bad posture," I said. "Not that I'd ever preach."

"No, nothing like that."

We kissed again, more deeply. She relaxed, allowing her body—all 110 pounds of it—to depend upon mine. I felt the warmth of her breath at my ear as I undid the straps of her overalls. The denim fell to her waist but no farther, blocked by the rim of the workbench. I stroked her left arm, luxuriating in the feel of firm muscle under soft skin. Slipping my fingers under her T-shirt, I aimed for the spot that tended to pain her—two spots, really, a pair of knots just above her gluteal cleft. Robin's by no means skeletal; she's a curvy woman, blessed with hips and thighs and breasts and that sheath of body fat that is so wonderfully female. But a small frame meant a back narrow enough for one of my hands to cover both tendernesses simultaneously.

She arched toward me. "Oh . . . you're bad."

"Thought it felt good."

"That's why you're bad. I should be working."

"I should be, too." I took her chin in one hand. Reached down with my other hand and cupped her bottom. No jewelry or makeup, but she had taken the time for perfume, and the fragrance radiated at the juncture of jawline and jugular.

Back to the sore spots.

"Fine, go ahead," she whispered. "Now that you've corrupted me and I'm completely distracted." Her fingers fumbled at my zipper.

"Corruption?" I said. "This is nothing."

I touched her. She moaned. Spike went nuts.

She said, "I feel like an abusive parent." Then she put him outside.

When we finished, the coffee was long cold but we drank it anyway. The red scarf was on the floor and the wood shavings were no longer in a neat pile. I was sitting in an old leather chair, naked, with Robin on my lap. Still breathing hard, still wanting to kiss her. Finally, she pulled away, stood, got dressed, returned to the guitar top. A private-joke smile graced her lips.

"What?"

"We moved around a bit. Just want to make sure we didn't get anything on my masterpiece."

"Like what?"

"Like sweat."

"Maybe that would be a good thing," I said. "Truly organic luthiery."

"Orgasmic luthiery."

"That, too." I got up and stood behind her, smelling her hair. "I love you."

"Love you, too." She laughed. "You are such a *guy.*"

"Is that a compliment?"

"Depends on my mood. At this moment, it's a whimsical observation. Every time we make love you tell me you love me."

"That's good, right? A guy who expresses his feelings."

"It's great," she said quickly. "And you're very consistent."

"I tell you other times, don't I?"

"Of course you do, but this is . . ."

"Predictable."

"One hundred percent."

"So," I said, "Professor Castagna has been keeping a record?"

"Don't have to. Not that I'm complaining, sweetie. You can always tell me you love me. I just think it's cute."

"My predictability."

"Better that than instability."

"Well," I said, "I can vary it—say it in another language—how about Hungarian? Should I call Berlitz?"

She pecked my cheek, picked up her chisel.

"Pure guy," she said.

Spike began scratching at the door. I let him in and he raced past me, came to a short stop at Robin's feet, rolled over and presented his abdomen. She kneeled and rubbed him, and his short legs flailed ecstatically.

I said, "Oh you Jezebel. Okay, back to the sawmill."

"No saw today. Just this." Indicating the chisel.

"I meant me."

She looked at me over her shoulder. "Tough day ahead?"

"The usual," I said. "Other people's problems. Which is what I get paid for, right?"

"How'd your meeting with Milo go? Has he learned anything about Dr. Mate?"

"Not so far. He asked me to do some research on Mate, thought I'd try the computer first."

"Shouldn't be hard to produce hits on Mate."

"No doubt," I said. "But finding something valuable in the slag heap's another story. If I dead-end, I'll try the research library, maybe Bio-Med."

"I'll be here all day," she said. "If you don't interrupt me, I'll push my hands too far. How about an early dinner?"

"Sure."

"I mean, baby, don't stay away. I want to hear you say you love me."

Pure guy.

Often, especially after a day when I'd seen more patients than usual, we spent evenings where I did very little talking. Despite all my training, sometimes getting the words out got lost on the highway between Head and Mouth. Sometimes I thought about the nice things I'd tell her, but never followed through.

But when we made love . . . for me, the physical released the emotional and I supposed that put me in some sort of Y-chromosome file box.

There's a common belief that men use love to get sex and women do just the opposite. Like most alleged wisdom about human beings, it's anything but absolute; I've known women who turned thoughtless promiscuity into a fine art and men so bound by affection that the idea of stranger-sex repulsed them to the point of impotence.

I'd never been sure where Richard Doss fell along that continuum. By the time I met him, he hadn't made love to his wife for over three years.

He told me so within minutes of entering the office. As if it was important for me to know of his deprivation. He'd resisted any notion of anyone but his daughter being my patient, yet began by talking about himself. If he was trying to clarify something, I never figured out what it was.

He'd met Joanne Heckler in college, termed the match "ideal," offered the fact that he'd stayed married to her over twenty years as proof. When I met him, she'd been dead for ninety-three days, but he spoke of her as having existed in a very distant past. When he professed to have loved her deeply, I had no reason to doubt him, other than the absence of feeling in his voice, eyes, body posture.

Not that he was incapable of emotion. When I opened the side door that leads to my office, he burst into the house talking on a tiny silver cell phone, continuing to talk in an animated tone after we'd entered the office and I'd sat behind my desk. Wagging an index finger to let me know it would be a minute.

Finally, he said, "Okay, gotta go, Scott. Work the spread, at this point that's the key. If they give us the rate they promised, we're in like Flynn. Otherwise it's a deal-killer. Get them to commit now, not later, Scott. You know the drill."

Eyes flashing, free hand waving.

Enjoying it.

He said, "We'll chat later," clicked off the phone, sat, crossed his legs.

"Negotiations?" I said.

"The usual. Okay, first Joanne." At his mention of his wife's name, his voice went dead.

Physically, he wasn't what I'd expected. My training is supposed to endow me with an open mind, but everyone develops preconceptions, and my mental picture of Richard Doss had been based upon what Judy Manitow had told me and five minutes of phone-sparring.

Aggressive, articulate, dominant. Ex–frat boy, tennis-playing country-club member. Tennis partner of Bob Manitow, who was a physician but about as corporate-looking as you could get. For no good reason, I'd guessed someone who looked like Bob: tall, imposing, a bit beefy, the basic CEO hairstyle: short and side-parted, silver at the temples. A well-cut suit in a somber shade, white or blue shirt, power tie, shiny wing-tips.

Richard Doss was five-five, tops, with a weathered leprechaun face—wide at the brow tapering to an almost womanish point at the chin. A dancer's build, very lean, with square shoulders, a narrow waist. Oversize hands sporting manicured nails coated with clear polish. Palm Springs tan, the kind you rarely saw anymore because of the melanoma scare. The fibrous complexion of one who ignores melanoma warnings.

His hair was black, kinky, and he wore it long enough to evoke another decade. White man's afro. Thin gold chain around his neck. His black silk shirt had flap pockets and buccaneer sleeves and he'd left the top two buttons undone, advertising a hairless chest and extension of the tan. Baggy, tailored gray tweed slacks were held in place by a lizard-skin belt with a silver buckle.

Matching loafers, no socks. He carried a smallish black purselike thing in one hand, the silver phone in the other.

I would've pegged him as Joe Hollywood. One of those producer wanna-bes you see hanging out at Sunset Plaza cafés. The type with cheap apartments on month-to-month, poorly maintained leased Corniches, too much leisure time, schemes masquerading as ideas.

Richard Doss had made his way south from Palo Alto and embraced the L.A. image almost to the point of parody.

He said, "My wife was a testament to the failure of modern medicine." The silver phone rang. He jammed it to his ear. "Hi. What? Okay. Good . . . No, not now. Bye." Click. "Where was I—modern medicine. We saw dozens of doctors. They put her through every test in the book. CAT scans, MRIs, serologic, toxicologic. She had two lumbar punctures. No real reason, I found out later. The neurologist was just 'fishing around.' "

"What were her symptoms?" I said.

"Joint pain, headaches, skin sensitivity, fatigue. It started out as fatigue. She'd always been a ball of energy. Five-two, a hundred and ten pounds. She used to dance, play tennis, powerwalk. The change was gradual—at first I figured a flu, or one of those crazy viruses that's going around. I figured the best thing was stay out of her face, give her time to rest. By the time I realized something serious was going on, she was hard to reach. On another planet." He hooked a finger under the gold chain. "Joanne's parents didn't live long, maybe her constitution . . . She'd always been into the mom thing, that went, too. I suppose *that* was her main symptom. Disengagement. From me, the kids, everything."

"Judy told me she was a microbiologist. What kinds of things did she work on?"

He shook his head. "You're hypothesizing the obvious: she was infected by some pathogen from her lab. Logical but wrong. That was looked into right away, from every angle—some sort of rogue microbe, allergies, hypersensitivity to a chemical. She worked with germs, all right, but they were *plant* germs—vegetable pathogens—molds and funguses that affect food crops. Broccoli, specifically. She had a USDA grant to study broccoli. Do you like broccoli?"

"Sure."

"I don't. As it turns out, there *are* cross-sensitivities between plants and animals, but nothing Joanne worked with fit that category—her equipment, her reagents. She went through every blood test known to medicine." He thumbed his black silk cuff. His watch was black-faced with a gold band, so skinny it looked like a tattoo.

"Let's not get distracted," he said. "The precise reason for what happened to Joanne will never be known. Back to the core issue: her disengagement. The first thing to go was entertaining and socializing. She refused to go out with anyone. No more business dinners—too tired, not hungry. Even though all she did in bed was eat. We're members of the Cliffside Country Club and she'd played tennis and a little golf, used the gym. No more. Soon, she was going to bed earlier and rising later. Eventually, she started spending all her time in bed, saying the pain had gotten worse. I told her she might be aching because of inactivity—her muscles were contracting, stiffening up. She didn't answer me. That's when I started taking her to doctors."

He recrossed his legs. "Then there was the weight gain. The only thing she *didn't* withdraw from was food. Cookies, cake, potato chips, anything sweet or greasy." His lips curled, as if he'd tasted something bad. "By the end she weighed two hundred ten pounds. Had more than doubled her weight in less than a year. A hundred and ten extra pounds of pure fat—isn't that incredible, Doctor? It was hard to keep seeing her as the girl I married. She used to be lithe. Athletic. All of a sudden I was married to a stranger—some asexual alien. You're with someone for twenty-five years you just don't stop liking them, but I won't deny it, my feelings for her changed— for all practical purposes she was no longer my wife. I tried to help her with the food. Suggesting maybe she'd be just as satisfied with fruit as with Oreos. But she wouldn't hear of it and she arranged the grocery deliveries when I was at work. I suppose I could've taken drastic measures—gotten her on fen-phen, bolted the refrigerator, but food seemed to be the only thing that kept her going. I felt it was cruel to withdraw it from her."

"I assume every metabolic link was checked out."

"Thyroid, pituitary, adrenal, you name it. I know enough to be an endocrinologist. The weight gain was simply Joanne drowning herself in food. When I made suggestions about cutting back, she responded the same way she did to any opinion I offered. By turning off completely—here, look."

Out of the purse came a pair of plastic-encased snapshots. He made no effort to hand them to me, merely stretched out his arm so I had to get up from my chair to retrieve them.

"Before and after," he said.

The left photo was a color shot of a young couple. Green lawn, big trees, imposing beige buildings. I'd collaborated with a Stanford professor on a research project years ago, recognized the campus.

"I was a senior, she was a sophomore," said Doss. "That was taken right after we got engaged."

For many students, the seventies had meant long coifs, facial hair, torn jeans and sandals. Counterculture giving way to Brooks Brothers only when the realities of making a living sank in.

It was as if Richard Doss had reversed the process. His college 'do had been a dense black crew cut. In the picture he wore a white shirt, pressed gray slacks, horn-rimmed glasses. And here were the shiny black wing-tips. Study-pallor on the elfin face, no tan.

Youthful progenitor of the corporate type I'd expected him to be.

Distracted expression. No celebration of the engagement that I could detect.

The girl under his arm was smiling. Joanne Heckler, petite as described, had been pretty in a well-scrubbed way. Fair-skinned and narrow-faced, she wore her brown hair long and straight, topped by a white band. Glasses for her, too. Smaller than Richard's, and gold-framed. A diamond glinted on her ring finger. Her sleeveless dress was bright blue, modest for that era.

Another elf. Marriage of the leprechauns.

They say couples who live together long enough start to look like each other. Richard and Joanne had begun that way but diverged.

I turned to the second photo, a washed-out Polaroid. A subject who resembled no one.

Long-view of a king-size bed, shot from the foot. Rumpled gold comforter strewn across a tapestry-covered bed bench. High mound of beige pillows propped against the headboard. In their midst, a head floated.

White face. Round. So porcine and bloated the features were compressed to a smear. Bladder-cheeks. Eyes buried in folds. Just a hint of brown hair tied back tight from a pasty forehead. Pucker-mouth devoid of expression.

Below the head, beige sheets rose like a bell-curved, tented bulk. To the right was an elegant carved night-stand in some kind of dark, glossy wood, with gold pulls. Behind the headboard was peach wallpaper printed with teal flowers. A length of gilded frame and linen mat hinted at artwork cropped out of the photo.

For one shocking moment, I wondered if Richard Doss had a postmortem shot. But no, the eyes were open . . . something in them . . . despair? No, worse. A living death.

"Eric took it," said Doss. "My son. He wanted a record."

"Of his mom?" I said. Hoarse, I cleared my throat.

"Of what had happened to his mom. Frankly put, it pissed him off."

"He was angry at her?"

"No," he said, as if I were an idiot. "At the situation. That's how my son deals with his anger."

"By documenting?"

"By organizing. Putting things in their place. Person-ally, I think it's a great way to handle stress. Lets you wade through the emotional garbage, analyze the factual content of events, get in touch with how you feel, then move on. Because what choice is there? Wallow in other people's misery? Allow yourself to be destroyed?"

He pointed a finger at me, as if I'd accused him of something.

"If that sounds callous," he said, "so be it, Doctor. You haven't lived in my house, never went through what I did. Joanne took over a year to leave us. We had time to figure things out. Eric's a brilliant boy—the smartest person I've ever met. Even so, it affected him. He was in his second semester at Stanford, came home to be with Joanne. He devoted himself to her, so if taking that picture seems callous, bear that in mind. And it's not as if his mother minded. She just lay there—that picture captures exactly what she was like at the end. How she ever mobilized the energy to contact the sonofabitch who killed her I'll never know."

"Dr. Mate."

He ignored me, fingered the silver phone. Finally our eyes met. I smiled, trying to let him know I wasn't judging. His lids were slightly lowered. Beneath them, dark eyes shone like nuggets of coal.

"I'll take those back." He leaned forward, holding out his hand for the pictures. Again, I had to stand to return them.

"How did Stacy cope?" I said.

He took his time zipping open the purse and placing the snapshots within. Crossing his legs yet again. Massaging the phone, as if hoping a call would rescue him from having to answer.

"Stacy," he said, "is another story."

CHAPTER

6

I BOOTED UP the computer. Eldon Mate's name pulled up over a hundred sites.

Most of the references were reprints of newspaper columns covering Mate's career as a one-way travel agent. Pros, cons, no shortage of strong opinions from experts on both sides. Everyone responding on an intellectual level. Nothing psychopathic, none of the cold cruelty that had flavored the murder.

A "Dr. Death Home Page" featured a flattering photo of Mate, recaps of his acquittals and a brief biography. Mate had been born in San Diego sixty-three years ago, received a degree in chemistry from San Diego State and worked as a chemist for an oil company before entering medical school in Guadalajara, Mexico, at the age of forty. He'd served an internship at a hospital in Oakland, gotten licensed as a general practitioner at forty-six.

No specialty training. The only jobs the news pieces had mentioned were civil service positions at health departments all over the Southwest, where Mate had overseen immunization programs and pushed paper. No indication he'd ever treated a patient.

Beginning a new career as a doctor in middle age but avoiding contact with the living. Had he been drawn to medicine in order to get closer to death?

The name and phone number at the bottom of the page was Attorney Roy Haiselden's. He'd listed no e-mail address.

Next came several euthanasia stories:

The first few covered the case of Roger Damon Sharveneau, a respiratory therapist at a hospital in Rochester, New York, who'd confessed eighteen months earlier to snuffing out three dozen intensive-care patients by injecting potassium chloride into their I.V. lines—wanting to "ease their journey." Sharveneau's lawyer claimed his client was insane, had him examined by a psychiatrist who diagnosed borderline personality and prescribed the antidepressant imipramine. A few days later, Sharveneau recanted. Without his confession, the only evidence against him was proximity to the ICU every night a questionable death had occurred. The same applied to three other techs, so the police released Sharveneau, terming the case "still under investigation." Sharveneau filed for disability benefits, granted an interview to a local newspaper and claimed he'd been under the influence of a shadowy figure named Dr. Burke, whom no one had ever seen. Soon after, he overdosed fatally on imipramine.

The case prompted an investigation of other respiratory techs living in the Rochester area. Several with criminal backgrounds were found working at hospitals and convalescent homes around the state. The health commissioner vowed to institute tighter controls.

I plugged Sharveneau's name into the system, found only one follow-up article that cited lack of progress on the original investigation and doubts as to whether the thirty-six deaths had been unnatural.

The next link was a decade-old case: four nurses in Vienna had killed as many as three hundred people using overdoses of morphine and insulin. Arrest, conviction, sentences ranging from fifteen years to life. Eldon Mate was quoted as suggesting the killers might have been acting out of compassion.

A similar case from Chicago: two years later, a pair of nurses' aides who'd smothered elderly terminal patients to death as part of a lesbian romance. Plea bargain for the one who talked, life without parole for the other. Once again, Mate had offered a contrarian opinion.

Onward. A Cleveland piece dated only two months earlier. Kevin Arthur Haupt, an emergency medical tech working the night shift on a city ambulance, had decided to shortcut the treatment of twelve drunks he'd picked up on heart-attack calls by clamping his hand over their noses and mouths during transport to the hospital. Discovery came when one of the intended victims turned out to be healthier than expected, awoke to find himself being smothered and fought back. Arrest, multiple murder charge, guilty plea, thirty-year sentence. Mate wondered in print if spending money to resuscitate habitual alcoholics was a wise use of tax dollars.

An old wire-service piece about the Netherlands, where assisted suicide was no longer prosecuted, claimed that doctor-initiated killings had grown to 2 percent of all recorded Dutch deaths, with 25 percent of physicians admitting they'd euthanized patients deemed unfit to live, without the patients' consent.

Years ago, while working Western Pediatrics Medical Center, I'd served on something called the Ad Hoc Life Support Committee—six physicians and myself, drafted by the hospital board to come up with guidelines for ending the treatment of children in final-stage illness. We'd been a fractious group, producing debate and very little else. But each of us knew that scarcely a month went by when a slightly-larger-than-usual dose of morphine didn't find its way into the mesh of tubes attached to a tiny arm. Kids suffering from bone or brain cancer, atrophied livers, ravaged lungs, who just happened to "stop breathing," once their parents had said good-bye.

Some caring soul ending the pain of a child who would've died anyway, sparing the family the agony of a protracted deathwatch.

The same motivation claimed by Eldon H. Mate.

Why did it feel different to me from Mate's gloating use of the Humanitron?

Because I believed the doctors and nurses on cancer wards had been acting out of compassion, but I suspected Mate's motivations?

Because Mate came across obnoxious and publicity-seeking?

Was that the worst type of hypocrisy on my part, accepting covert god-play from those I greeted in the hall while allowing myself to be repelled by Mate's in-your-face approach to death? So what if the screeching little man with the homemade killing machine wouldn't have won any charm contests. Did the *psyche* of the travel agent matter when the final *destination* was always the same?

My father had died quietly, fading away from cirrhosis and kidney failure and general breakdown of his body after a lifetime of bad habits. Muscles reabsorbing, skin bagging as he devolved into a wizened, yellowed gnome I hardly recognized.

As the poisons in his system accumulated, it took only a few weeks for Harry Delaware to sink from lethargy to torpor to coma. If he'd gone out screaming in agony, would I now harbor any reservations about the Humanitron?

And what about people like Joanne Doss, suffering but undiagnosed?

If you accepted death as a civil rights issue, did a medical label matter? Whose life *was* it, anyway?

Religion supplied answers, but when you took God out of the equation, things got complicated. That was as good a reason as any for God, I supposed. I wished I'd been blessed with a greater capacity for faith and obedience. What would happen if one day I found myself being devoured by cancer, or deadened by paralysis?

Sitting there, hand poised to strike the ENTER key, I found that my thoughts kept flying back to my father's last days. Strange—he rarely came to mind.

Then I pictured Dad as a healthy man. Big bald head, creased bull neck, sandpaper hands from all those years turning wood on the lathe. Alcohol breath and tobacco laughter. One-handed push-ups, the too-hard slap on the back. He'd been well into his fifties by the time I could hold my own against him in the arm wrestles he demanded as a greeting ritual during my increasingly rare trips back to Missouri.

I found myself edging forward on the chair. Positioning myself for combat, just as I'd done as Dad's forearm and mine pressed against each other, hot and sticky. Elbows slipping on the Formica of the kitchen table as we purpled and strained, muscles quivering with tetany. Mom leaving the room, looking pained.

By the time Dad hit fifty-five, the pattern was set: mostly I'd win, occasionally we'd tie. He'd laugh at first. *Alexander-er, when I was young I could climb walls!* Then he'd light up a Chesterfield, frown and mutter, leave the room. My visits thinned to once a year. The ten days I spent sitting silently holding my mother's hand as he died was my longest stay since leaving home for college.

I shuttered the memories, tried to relax, punched a key. The computer—perfect, silent companion that it was—obliged by flashing a new image.

A site posted by a Washington, D.C.–based handicapped-rights group named Still Alive. A position statement: all human life was precious, no one should judge anyone else's quality of life. Then a section on Mate—to this group, Hitler incarnate. Archival photo of Still Alive members picketing a motel where Mate had left a traveler. Men and women in wheelchairs, lofting banners. Mate's reaction to the protest: "You're a bunch of whiners who should examine your own selfish motivations."

Quotes from Mate and Roy Haiselden followed:

"The storm troopers came for me, but I wouldn't play passive Jew" (Mate, 1991).

"Darwin would have loved to meet [District Attorney] Clarkson. The idiot's living proof of the missing link between pond slime and mammalian organisms" (Haiselden, 1993).

"A needle in a vein is a hell of a lot more humane than a nuclear bomb, but you don't hear much outrage from the morality mongoloids about atomic testing, do you?" (Mate, 1995).

"Any pioneer, anyone with a vision, inevitably suffers. Jesus, Buddha, Copernicus, the Wright brothers. Hell, the guy who invented stickum on envelopes probably got abused by the idiots who manufactured sealing wax" (Mate, 1995).

"Sure, I'd go on *The Tonight Show*, but it ain't gonna happen, folks! Too many stupid rules imposed by the network. Hell, I'd help someone *travel* on *The Tonight Show* if the fools who made the rules would let me.

I'd do it live—so to speak. It would be their highest-rated show, I can promise you that. They could play it during sweeps week. I'd play some music in the background—something classical. Use some poor soul with a totally compromised nervous system—maybe an advanced muscular dystrophy case—limbs out of control, tongue flapping, copious salivation, no bladder or bowel control—let them leak all over the soundstage, show the world how pretty decay and disease are. If I could do that, you'd see all that sanctimonious drivel about the nobility of life fade away pronto. I could pull off the whole thing in minutes, safe, clean, silent. Let the camera focus on the traveler's face, show how peaceful they were once the thiopental kicked in. Teach the world that the true nature of compassion isn't some priest or rabbi claiming to be God's holy messenger or some government mongoloid lackey who couldn't pass a basic biology course trying to tell me what's life and what isn't. 'Cause it's not that complex, amigos: when the brain ain't workin', you ain't livin'. *The Tonight Show* . . . yeah, that would be educational. If they let me set it up the right way, sure, I'd do it" (Mate, 1997, in response to a press question about why he liked publicity).

"Dr. Mate should get the Nobel Prize. Double payment. For medicine *and* peace. I wouldn't mind a piece of that, myself. Being his lawyer, I deserve it" (Haiselden, 1998).

Other assorted oddities, ranked lower for relevance:

A three-year-old Denver news item about a Colorado "outsider" artist with the improbable name of Zero Tollrance who'd created a series of paintings inspired by Mate and his machine. Using an abandoned building in a run-down section of Denver, Tollrance, previously unknown, had exhibited thirty canvases. A freelance writer had covered the show for *The Denver Post*, citing "several portraits of the controversial 'death doctor' in a wide range of familiar poses: Gilbert Stuart's George Washington, Thomas Gainsborough's Blue Boy, Vincent van Gogh's bandaged-ear self-portrait, Andy Warhol's Marilyn Monroe. Non-Mate works included collages of coffins, cadavers, skulls and maggot-infested meat. But perhaps the most ambitious of Tollrance's productions is a faithfully rendered re-creation of Rembrandt's *Anatomy Lesson*, a graphic portrayal of human dissection, with Dr. Mate serving a dual role, as scalpel-wielding lecturer as well as flayed cadaver."

When asked how many paintings had sold, Tollrance "walked away without comment."

Mate as cutter and victim. Be interesting to talk to Mr. Tollrance. Save. Print.

Two citations from a health-issues academic bulletin board posted by Harvard University: a geriatric study found that while 59.3 percent of the relatives of elderly patients favored legalizing physician-assisted suicide, only 39.9 percent of the old people agreed. And a study done at a cancer treatment center found that two-thirds of the American public endorsed assisted death but 88 percent of cancer patients suffering from constant pain had no interest in exploring the topic and felt that a doctor's bringing it up would erode their trust.

In a feminist resource site I found an article in a journal called *S(Hero)* entitled "Mercy or Misogyny: Does Dr. Mate Have a Problem with Women?" The author wondered why 80 percent of Mate's "travelers" had been female. Mate, she claimed, had never been known to have a relationship with a woman and had refused to answer questions about his personal life. Freudian speculation followed.

Milo hadn't mentioned any family. I made a note to follow up on that.

The final item: four years ago, in San Francisco, a group calling itself the Secular Humanist Infantry had granted Mate its highest award, the Heretic. Prior to the ceremony, a syringe Mate had used on a recent "travel venture" had been auctioned off for two hundred dollars, only to be confiscated immediately by an undercover police officer citing violation of state health regulations. Commotion and protest as the cop dropped the needle into an evidence bag and exited. During his acceptance speech, Mate donated his windbreaker as a consolation prize and termed the officer a "mental gnat with all the morals of a rotavirus."

The name of the winning bidder caught my eye.

Alice Zoghbie. Treasurer of the Secular Humanist Infantry, now president of the Socrates Club. The same woman who'd leased the death van and left that day for Amsterdam.

I ran a search on the club, found the home page, topped by a logo of the Greek philosopher's sculpted head surrounded by a wreath that I assumed was hemlock. As Milo'd said, headquarters on Glenmont Circle in Glendale, California.

The Socrates mission statement emphasized the "personal ownership of life, unfettered by the outmoded and barbaric conventions foisted upon society by organized religion." Signed, Alice Zoghbie, MPA. A hundred-dollar fee entitled the fortunate to notification of events and all other benefits of membership. AMEX, VISA, MC, and DISC accepted.

Zoghbie's master's in public administration didn't tell me much about her professional background. Searching her name produced a long article in *The San Jose Mercury News* that filled in the blanks.

Entitled "Right-to-Die Group's Leader's Comments Cause Controversy," the piece described Zoghbie as

fiftyish, pencil-thin and tall. The former hospital personnel director is now engaged full-time running the Socrates Club, an organization devoted to legalizing assisted suicide. Until recently, members have maintained a low profile, concentrating upon filing friend-of-court briefs in right-to-die cases. However, recent remarks by Zoghbie at last Sunday's brunch at the Western Sun Inn here in San Jose have cast the club into the limelight and raised questions about its true goals.

During the meeting, attended by an estimated fifty people, Zoghbie delivered a speech calling for the "humane dispatch of patients with Alzheimer's disease and other types of 'thought impairment,' " as well as disabled children and others who are legally incapable of making "the decision they'd clearly form if they were in their right minds."

"I worked at a hospital for twenty years," the tan, white-haired woman said, "and I witnessed firsthand the abuses that took place in the name of treatment. Real compassion isn't creating vegetables. Real compassion is scientists putting their heads together to create a measurement scale that would quantify suffering. Those who score above a predetermined criterion could then be helped in a timely manner even if they lacked the capacity to liberate themselves."

Reaction to Zoghbie's proposal by local religious leaders was swift and negative. Catholic Bishop Armand Rodriguez termed the plan "a call to genocide," and Dr. Archie Van Sandt of the Mount Zion Baptist Church accused Zoghbie of being "an instrument of cancerous secularism." Rabbi Eugene Brandner of Temple Emanu-El said that Zoghbie's ideas were "certainly not in line with Jewish thought at any point along the spectrum."

An unattributed statement by the Socrates Club issued two days later attempted to qualify Zoghbie's remarks, terming them "an impetus to discussion rather than a policy statement."

Dr. J. Randolph Smith, director of the Western Medical Association's Committee on Medical Ethics, viewed the disavowal with some skepticism. "A simple reading of the transcript shows this was a perfectly clear expression of philosophy and intent. The slippery slope yawns before us, and groups such as the Socrates Club seem intent on shoving us down into the abyss of amorality. Given further acceptance of views such as Ms. Zoghbie's, it's only a matter of time before the legalization of murder of those who say they want to die gives way to the murder of those who have never asked to die, as is now the case in the Netherlands."

I logged off, called Milo at the station. A young man answered his phone, asked me who I was with some suspicion and put me on hold.

A few seconds later, Milo said, "Hi."

"New secretary?"

"Detective Stephen Korn. One of my little helpers. What's up?"

"Got some stuff for you, but nothing profound." Got a resolved ethical issue, too, but I'll save that for later.

"What kind of stuff?" he said.

"Mostly biography and the expected controversy, but Alice Zoghbie's name came up—"

"Alice Zoghbie just called me," he said. "Back in L.A. and willing to talk."

"Thought she wasn't due for two days."

"She cut her trip short. Distraught about Mate."

"Delayed grief reaction?" I said. "Mate's been dead for a week."

"She claims she didn't hear about it till yesterday. Was up in Nepal somewhere—climbing mountains, the Amsterdam thing was the tail end of her trip, big confab of death freaks from all over the world. Not the place to choke on your chicken salad, huh? Anyway, Zoghbie says she had no access to news in Nepal, got to Amsterdam three days ago, her hosts met her at the airport and gave her the news. She slept over one day, booked a return flight."

"So she arrived two days ago," I said. "Still a bit of delay before she called you. Giving herself time to think?"

"Composing herself. Her quote."

"When are you meeting her?"

"Three hours at her place." He recited the Glenmont address.

"Socrates Club headquarters," I said. "Found their website. Hundred bucks to join, credit-card friendly. Wonder how many of her bills that pays."

"You don't trust this lady's intentions?"

"Her views don't inspire trust. She thinks senile old folks and handicapped kids should be put out of their misery, whether they want to be or not. Got the quotes for you—part of today's work product. Along with assorted other goodies, including some other death-freak stuff and more weirdness."

I told him about Roger Sharveneau and the other hospital ghouls, finished with Zero Tollrance's exhibition.

"Cute," he said. "The art world's always been a warm and fuzzy place."

"One thing about Tollrance I found particularly interesting: he posed Mate in *The Anatomy Lesson* as wielding the scalpel *and* getting flayed."

"So?"

"It implies a certain ambivalence—wanting to play doctor *on* the doctor."

"You're saying I should take this guy seriously?"

"Might be interesting to talk to him."

"Tollrance, like that's a real name . . . Denver . . . I'll see what I can find."

"How far down the family list have your little helpers gotten?" I said.

"All the way down in terms of locating phone numbers and first attempts at contact," he said. "They've talked to about half the sample. Everyone loves Mate."

Not everyone. "Want me to come along to meet Alice in Deathland?"

"Sure," he said. "Look how cruel life can be. Climbing mountains in Nepal one day, enduring the police the next . . . She's probably one of those fit types, body image *über alles*."

"Depends on whose body you're talking about."

CHAPTER

7

WE AGREED TO meet at the station in two hours and I hung up. I'd intended to bring up the Doss family but hadn't. My excuse: some topics didn't lend themselves to phone chat.

I wanted to know more about Eldon Mate the physician, so I drove over to the Bio-Med library at the U., found myself a terminal. The periodicals index gave me a few more magazine articles but nothing new. I scanned scientific databases for any technical articles Mate might have published, not expecting anything in view of his lackluster career, but I found two citations: a Chemical Abstracts reference that led me to a thirty-year-old letter to the editor Mate had written in response to an article about polymerization—something about small molecules combining to create large molecules and the potential for better gasoline. Mate disagreed crankily. The author of the article, a professor at MIT, had dismissed Mate's comments as irrelevant. Mate's title, back then, had been assistant research chemist, ITEG Petroleum.

The second reference appeared in MEDLINE, sixteen years old, also a letter, this time in a Swedish pathology journal. Mate had his MD by then, cited his affiliation at Oxford Hill Hospital in Oakland, California. No title. No mention that he was a lowly intern.

The second letter didn't argue with anyone. Titled "Precise Measurement of Time of Death: A Social Boon," it began with a quote by Sir Thomas Browne:

"We all labour against our own cure, for death is the cure of all diseases."

Mate went on to bemoan the

stigma associated with cellular cessation, and subsequent moral cowardice exhibited by physicians when dealing with parathanatological phenomena. As the ultimate caretakers of body and that fiction known as "soul," we must do everything in our power to demystify the process of life termination, utilizing the scientific tools at our disposal to avoid needless prolongation of "life" that is the fruit of theology-based myths.

In this regard, quantification of precise time of death will be useful in robbing the myth mongers of their fictions and save costs that accrue from the needless employment of so-called heroic measures that create nothing more than respirating corpses.

Along these lines, I have attempted to discern which outward physical manifestations advertise the precise shutoff of vital systems. The central nervous system often continues to fire synaptically well after the heart stops beating and vice versa. Even a high-school biology student can keep a pithed frog's heart beating for a substantial "postmortem" period through the use of stimulant drugs. Furthermore, brain death is not a discrete event, and this fact leads to confusion and uncertainty.

I have thus looked for other changes, specifically ocular and muscular alterations, that correlate with our best judgment of thanatological progress. I have sat at the bedside of numerous premortem patients, gazing into their eyes and studying minute movements of their faces. Though this research is in the formative stage, I am encouraged by what appears to be a dual manifestation of cardiac and neurological shutoff typified by simultaneous twitchlike movement of the eyes combined with a measurable slackening of the lips. In some patients, I have also discerned an audible noise that appears to manifest sublaryngitically— perhaps the "death rattle" commonly cited in popular fiction. However, this does not occur in all patients and is best dispensed with in favor of the aforementioned ocular-muscular phenomenon I label the "lights-out" syndrome. I suggest that this event be studied in great detail for its potential in serving as a simple yet precise indicator of cellular surrender.

Interns back then worked hundred-hour weeks. This intern had found the time to indulge his extracurricular interest.

Sitting and staring into the eyes of the dying, trying to capture the precise moment.

My hunch about his intentions, confirmed. Early in the game, Mate's obsession had been with the minutiae of death, not the quality of life.

No comments from the Swedish journal editor. I wondered how Mate's side activities had been received at Oxford Hill Hospital.

Leaving the reading room, I found a pay phone in the hallway, got Oakland Information and asked for the number. No listing.

Returning to the computers, I looked up the call

number of the Joint Commission on Accreditation of Healthcare Organizations rosters, found the bound volumes in the stacks, and beginning with the year of Mate's internship looked up Oxford Hill. In business and accredited fully. Same for the following five years, then nothing.

The place had been legitimate, but it had closed down. Good luck finding someone who remembered the middle-aged intern with the ghoulish hobby.

What use was there excavating Mate's past, anyway? He'd become the victim, and it was the butcher I needed to understand, not the slab of meat in the back of the rented van.

I left the library and drove to the West L.A. station.

When I pulled up, Milo was standing in front with two men in their late twenties. Both wore gray sport coats and dark slacks and held notepads against their thighs. Both were tall as Milo, each was forty pounds lighter. Neither looked happy.

The man to the left had a puffy face, squashed features and wheat-colored blow-dried hair. The other D-I was dark, balding, bespectacled.

Milo said something to them and they returned inside.

"Your little elves?" I said, when he came over.

"Korn and Demetri. They don't like working for me, and my opinion of them ain't too grand. I put them back on the phones, recontacting families. They whined about scut work—oh this younger generation. Ready for Zoghbie? Let's take my Ferrari, in case we need a police presence."

He crossed the street to the police lot and I followed in the Seville, waiting till he backed out, then sliding into his parking space. Signs all over said POLICE PERSONNEL ONLY, ALL OTHERS WILL BE TOWED.

I got in the unmarked and handed him the material I'd printed from the Internet. He put it on the backseat, wedged between two of the file boxes that filled the space. The car smelled of old breakfast. The police radio was stuttering and Milo snapped it off.

"What if?" I said, pointing to the warning signs.

"I'll go your bail." Stretching his neck to one side, he winced, cleared his throat, pressed down on the gas and sped to Santa Monica Boulevard, then over to the 405 North, toward the Valley. I knew what I had to do and my body responded by tightening up. When we passed the mammoth white boxes that the Getty Museum comprised, I told him about Joanne Doss.

He didn't say anything for a while. Opened his window, spit, rolled it up.

Another minute passed. "You were waiting for the right moment to inform me?"

"As a matter of fact, I was. Till a few hours ago, I couldn't tell you anything, because even the fact that I'd seen them was confidential. Then Mr. Doss called and asked me to see his daughter and I figured I'd have to bow off Mate. But he wants me to continue."

"First things first, huh?" His jaw worked.

I kept quiet.

"And if he'd said *not* to mention it?"

"I'd have bowed off, told you I couldn't explain why."

Half mile of silence. He stretched his neck again. "Doss . . . yeah, local family—the Palisades. Toward the end of the list—the missus was in her early forties."

"Traveler number forty-eight," I said.

"You knew her?"

"No, she was already dead when I saw Stacy—the daughter."

"Mr. Doss is one of those who has not returned our repeated calls."

"He travels a lot."

"That so . . . Anything about him I should worry about?"

"Such as?"

He shrugged. "You tell me. He said you could blab, right?"

He kept his eyes on the freeway, but I felt surveilled.

"Sorry if this is rubbing you the wrong way," I said. "Maybe I should've begged off the case right from the beginning."

Pause. Long pause, as if he was considering that. Finally, he said, "Nah, I'm just being a hard-ass. We've all got our rule books. . . . So what was the matter with Mrs. Doss that led her to consult Dr. Mate?"

"She was one of the undiagnosed ones I mentioned. Had been deteriorating for a while. Fatigue, chronic pain, she withdrew socially, took to bed. Gained a hundred pounds."

He whistled, touched his own gut. "And no clue as to why all this happened?"

"She saw a lot of doctors, but no formal diagnosis," I said.

"Maybe a head case?"

"Like I said, I never knew her, Milo."

He smiled. "Meaning you're also thinking she might've been a head case . . . and Mate killed her anyway—'scuse me, assisted her *passage*. That could irritate a family member, if they didn't think she was really sick."

He waited.

I said nothing.

"How long after she died did you see the daughter?"

"Three months."

"Why're you seeing her again? Something to do with Mate's murder?"

"That I can't get into," I said. "Let's just say it's nothing you have to worry about."

"Something that just happens to come up now, after Mate's killed?"

"College," I said. "Now's when kids get serious about applying to college."

He didn't answer. The freeway was uncommonly clear and we sped toward the 101 interchange. Milo pumped the unmarked up the eastbound ramp and we merged into slightly heavier traffic. Orange signs on the turnoff announced impending construction for one and a half years. Everyone was going fifteen miles over the limit, as if getting in some last speed licks.

He said, "So you're telling me Mr. Doss is like all the others—big fan of Mate?"

"I'll leave it to him to express his opinion on that."

He smiled again. Not a nice smile at all. "The guy didn't like Mate."

"I didn't say that."

"No, you didn't." He eased up on the gas pedal. We cruised past the Van Nuys exits, Sherman Oaks, North Hollywood. The freeway turned into the 134.

I said, "I found a feminist journal that claimed Mate hated women. Because eighty percent of his travelers were female and he'd never been seen with a woman. Know anything about his personal life?"

Graceless change of subject. He knew what I was

doing but let it ride. "Not so far. He lived alone and his landlady said she'd never seen him go out with anyone. I haven't checked marriage licenses yet, but no one's turned up claiming insurance benefits."

"Wonder if a guy like that would carry life insurance," I said.

"Why not?"

"I don't think he valued life."

"Well, maybe you're right, 'cause I didn't find any policies at his apartment. Then again, all his papers might be with that goddamn attorney, Haiselden, who is still incommunicado. Maybe Ms. Zoghbie can direct us to him."

"Find out anything else about her?"

"No criminal record, not even parking tickets. Guess she just gets off on people dying. There seems to be a lot of that going around, doesn't there? Or maybe it's just my unique perspective."

Any attraction Alice Zoghbie had to the culture of death wasn't reflected by her landscaping.

She lived in a vanilla stucco English country house centered on a modest lot in the northern hills of Glendale. Cute house. The spotless shake roof over the entry turret was topped by a copper rooster weather vane. White pullback drapes framed immaculate mullion windows. A flagstone path twisted its way toward an iron canopy over a carved oak door. Banks of flowers rimmed the house, arranged by descending height: the crinkled foliage and purple bloom of statice, then billowing clouds of multicolored impatiens fringed by a low border of some sort of creeping white blossom.

A white Audi sat in the cobblestoned driveway, shaded

by a young, carefully shaped podocarpus tree, still staked. On the other side of the flagstone stood an equally tonsured, much larger sycamore. Where the sun hit, the sloping lawn was so green it appeared spray-painted. The big tree had started to release its leaves, and the sprinkle of rusty brown on grass and stone was the sole suggestion that not everything could be controlled.

Milo and I parked on the street and climbed the pathway. The door knocker was a large brass goat's head, and he lifted the front part of the animal's face, causing it to leer, allowed the jaw piece to fall, setting off oak vibrations. The door opened before the sound died.

"Detectives?" said the woman in the doorway. Thrust of hand, firm dry handshake for both of us. "Please! Come on in!"

Alice Zoghbie was indeed fiftyish—early fifties was my guess. But despite sun-worn skin and a cap of white-hot hair, she seemed more youthful than middle-aged.

Tall, slim, full-busted, strong square shoulders, long limbs, rosy overlay on the outdoorsy dermis, wide sapphire eyes. As she led us through the round entry hall created by the turret into a small, elegant living room, her stride took on a dancer's bounce—speedy, well-lubricated, arms swinging, hips swaying.

The room was set up as carefully as the flower beds. Yellow walls, white moldings, a red damask sofa, various floral-print chairs. Little tables placed strategically by someone with an eye. California oil paintings hung on the walls, all in period gilt frames. Nothing that looked expensive, but each picture was right for its place.

Alice Zoghbie stood in front of a blue brocade chair and cocked a hip, indicating the red couch for us. After we sat, she folded herself on the chair, tucked one leg under the other and smoothed back a feather of white bangs. Down cushions on the sofa made us sink low. Milo's weight plunged him below me and I noticed him shifting uncomfortably.

Alice Zoghbie laced her fingers in her lap. Her face was round, taut around the mandible, seamed at the eyes. She wore a bulky baby-blue cashmere turtleneck, pressed blue jeans, white socks, white suede loafers. Big silver pearls covered her earlobes, and a gold chain interspersed with multicolored cabochons followed the swell of her chest. Bare fingers. Between us was a tile-inlaid coffee table set with a Japanese Imari bowl full of hard candy. Gold and green nuggets; butterscotch and mint.

"Please," she said, pointing to the candy. Managing to sound lighthearted while wearing a grave expression.

"No, thanks," Milo said. "Appreciate your seeing us, ma'am."

"This is all so hideous. Do you have any idea who sacrificed Eldon?"

"Sacrificed?"

"That's what it was," she said. "Some fanatic asshole making a point." One hand clenched. She stared down at her fist, opened the fingers.

"Eldon and I talked about the risk—some lunatic deciding to make headlines. He said it wouldn't happen and I believed him, but it did, didn't it?"

"So Dr. Mate wasn't afraid."

"Eldon didn't function from fear. He was his own man. Knew the only way to dictate your own passage was to dictate the terms. And Eldon was committed— vital. He intended to be around for a long, long time."

Milo moved his bulk again, as if trying to remain

afloat in a sea of red silk. The movement served only to plunge him lower and he edged forward on the couch. "But you and he did discuss danger."

"I brought it up. In general terms, so no, there's no specific asshole I can direct you toward. Maybe it was one of those pathetic cripples who used to carp at him."

"Still Alive," I said.

"Them, their ilk."

Milo said, "You spoke in general terms, but did something happen to make you worry, ma'am?"

"No, I simply wanted Eldon to be more careful. He didn't want to hear it. He just didn't believe anyone would hurt him."

"What kind of cautions did you want him to take?"

"Simple security. Have you seen his apartment?"

"Yes, ma'am."

"Then you know. It's a joke, anyone could just walk in. It wasn't that Eldon was reckless. He simply wasn't attuned to his surroundings. Most brilliant people aren't. Look at Einstein. Some foundation sent him a ten-thousand-dollar check and he never cashed it."

"Dr. Mate was brilliant," said Milo.

Alice Zoghbie stared at him. "Dr. Mate was one of the great minds of our generation."

That didn't jibe with med school in Mexico, internship at an obscure hospital, the bureaucratic jobs. Alice Zoghbie might have known what I was thinking, because now she turned to me and said, "Einstein worked as a clerk until the world discovered him. The world wasn't smart enough to understand him. Eldon had a mind that just never stopped working. Thinking all the time. Science, history, you name it. And unlike most people, he wasn't blinded by personal circumstance."

"Because he lived alone?" I said.

"No, no, that's not what I *mean*. He didn't get distracted by irrelevancies. I'll bet you assume his own parents died in pain and that's why he decided to dedicate his life to relieving pain." Her hand drew an invisible X. "*Wrong*. Both his mother and his father lived to ripe old ages and passed on peacefully."

"Maybe *that* impressed him," said Milo. "Seeing the way it should be."

Alice Zoghbie uncrossed a long leg. "What I'm trying to get across to you people is that Eldon had a worldview perspective."

"Seeing the big picture."

Zoghbie shot him a disgusted look. "Talking about him is making me very *sad*."

Stating it calmly, almost boastfully. Milo remained expressionless and I did the same.

She gazed back at both of us, as if waiting for further response. Suddenly, the lower lids of the sapphire eyes pooled and twin rivulets flowed down her cheeks.

Tears flowing perfectly parallel to her slender nose. She sat there, immobile, allowing the tracks to reach the corners of her mouth before reaching up and dabbing with spidery fingers. Pink glossy nail polish. From somewhere in the house, a clock chimed.

She said, "I sure as hell hope you find the vicious fuck who did this. They just can't get away with this. That would be the worst thing."

"They?"

"They, he, whoever."

"What would be the worst thing, ma'am?"

"No consequences. Everything should have consequences."

"Well," said Milo, "my job is catching vicious fucks."

Zoghbie's expression went flat.

"Ma'am, is there anything you can tell us that might help the process along?"

"Enough with the ma'am, *okay*?" she said. "It's coming across patronizing. Is there anything I can tell you? Sure, look for a fanatic—probably a religious extremist. My bet would be a Catholic, they seem to be the worst. Though I was married to a Muslim, and they're no great shakes." Her head bobbed forward as she studied Milo's face. "What's your background?"

"Actually, I was raised Catholic, ma'am."

"So was I," said Zoghbie. "Down on my knees confessing my sins. What rubbish. The pity for both of us. Candles and guilt and bullshit spewed by impotent old men in funny hats—yes, I'd definitely look for a Catholic. Or a born-again Christian. Anyone fundamentalist for that matter. Orthodox Jews are just as bad, but they don't seem as predisposed to violence as the Catholics, probably because there's not enough of them to get cocky. Fanatics are all cut out of the same mold: God's on my side, I can do whatever the fuck I please. As if the Pope or Imam Whatever is going to be around when your loved one is writhing in agony and choking on their own vomit. The whole right-to-life thing is obscene. Life's sacred but it's okay to set off bombs at abortion clinics, pick off doctors. Eldon was made an example of. Look for a religious fanatic."

She smiled. It didn't fit the diatribe. Her eyes were dry again.

"Talk about sin," she said. "Hypocrisy's the worst sin. Why the hell can't we get past the bullshit they feed us in childhood and learn to think independently?"

"Conditioning," I said.

"That's for lower animals. We're supposed to be better."

Milo pulled out his pad. "Do you know of any actual threats against Dr. Mate?"

The specificity of the question—the police routine—seemed to bore her. "If there were, Eldon never told me."

"What about his attorney, Roy Haiselden. Do you know him, as well?"

"Roy and I have met."

"Any idea where he is, ma'am? Can't seem to locate him."

"Roy's all over the place," she said. "He owns laundromats up and down the state."

"Laundromats?"

"Coin-ops in strip malls. That's how he makes his money. What he does for Eldon doesn't pay the bills. It basically killed the rest of his law practice."

"Have you known him and Dr. Mate for a long time?"

"I've known Eldon for five years, Roy a little less."

"Any reason Mr. Haiselden wouldn't return our calls?"

"You'd have to ask him that."

Milo smiled. "Five years. How'd you get to know Dr. Mate?"

"I'd been following his career for a while." Her turn to smile. "Hearing about him was like a giant lightbulb going on: someone was finally shaking things up, doing what needed to be done. I wrote him a letter. I guess you could call it a fan letter, though that sounds so adolescent. I told him how much I admired his courage. I'd been working with a humanist group, had retired from my job—got retired, actually. I decided to find some meaning in all of it."

"You were fired because of your views?" I said.

Her shoulders shifted toward me. "Big surprise?" she snapped. "I was working in a hospital and had the nerve to talk about things that needed talking about. That chafed the hides of the assholes in charge."

"Which hospital?"

"Pasadena Mercy."

Catholic hospital.

She said, "Leaving that dump was the best thing that ever happened to me. I founded the Socrates Club, kept up with the SHI—my first group. We were having a convention in San Francisco and Eldon had just won another victory in court, so I thought, Who better to deliver the keynote? He answered my invitation with a charming note, accepting." Blink. "After that, Eldon and I began to see each other—socially but not sexually, since you're obviously going to ask. Life of the mind; I'd have him over for dinner, we'd discuss things, I'd cook for him. Probably the only decent meals he had."

"Dr. Mate didn't care about food?" said Milo.

"Like most geniuses, Eldon tended to ignore his personal needs. I'm a great cook, felt it was the least I could do for a mentor."

"A mentor," said Milo. "He was training you?"

"A philosophical guide!" She jabbed a finger at us. "Stop wasting your time with me and catch this fuckhead."

Milo sat back, sank in, surrendered to gravity. "So the two of you became friends. You seem to be the only female friend he had—"

"He wasn't *gay,* if that's what you're getting at. Just *choosy.* He was married and divorced a long time ago. Not an edifying experience."

"Why not?"

"Eldon didn't say. I could see he didn't want to talk

about it and I respected his wishes. Now, is there anything else?"

"Let's talk about the weekend Dr. Mate was murdered. You—"

"Rented the van? Yes, I did. I'd done it before because when Eldon showed up at the rental company, sometimes there were troubles."

"They didn't want to rent to him."

Zoghbie nodded.

"So," said Milo, "the night he was murdered, Dr. Mate was planning to help another traveler."

"I assume."

"He didn't tell you who?"

"Of course not. Eldon never discussed his clinical activities. He called and said, 'Alice, I'll be needing a van tomorrow.' "

"Why didn't he discuss his work?" said Milo.

"Ethics, Detective," Zoghbie said with exaggerated patience. "Patient confidentiality. He was a doctor."

The phone rang, distant as the clock chime.

"Better get that," she said, standing. "Could be the press."

"They've been in touch?"

"No, but they might be, once they find out I'm back."

"How would they know that, ma'am?"

"Please," she said. "Don't be naïve. They have their ways." She dance-walked through the dining room and out of sight.

Milo rubbed his face and turned to me. "Think Mate was boffing her?"

"She did take the time to mention that their relationship was social but not sexual. Because we were obviously going to ask. So maybe."

Alice Zoghbie returned, looking grim.

"The press?" said Milo.

"A nuisance call—my accountant. The IRS wants to audit me—big surprise, huh? I've got to go gather my tax records, so if there's nothing else . . ." She pointed to the door.

We stood.

"You climb mountains for fun?" said Milo.

"I hike, Detective. Long-distance walks on the lower slopes, no pitons or any of that stuff." She gave Milo's gut a long appraisal. "Stop moving and you might as well die."

That reminded me of something Richard Doss had told me six months ago:

I'll rest when I'm dead.

Milo said, "Did Dr. Mate stay active?"

"Mentally, only. Never could get him to exercise. But what does that have to do with—"

"So you have no idea who Dr. Mate was going to help the weekend he died?"

"No. I told you, we never discussed patient issues."

"The reason I'm asking is—"

"You think a traveler killed him? That's absurd."

"Why, ma'am?"

"These are sick people we're talking about, Detective. Weak people, quadriplegics, Lou Gehrig's disease, terminal cancer. How could they have the strength? And why would they? Now, please."

Her foot tapped. She looked jumpy. I supposed an audit could do that to you.

"Just a few more details," said Milo. "Why'd you choose the Avis in Tarzana? Far from here and from Dr. Mate's place."

"That was the *point*, Detective."

"What was?"

"Covering our tracks. Just in case someone got suspicious and refused to rent to us. That's also why I chose Avis. We alternated. Last time was Hertz; before that, Budget."

She hurried to the door, opened it, stood tapping her foot. "Forget about it being a traveler. None of Eldon's people would hurt him. Most of the time they required help just to get over to the travel site—"

"Help from who?"

Long silence. She smiled, folded her arms. "No. We're not going there."

"Other people have been involved?" said Milo. "Dr. Mate had assistants?"

"Unh-unh, no way. Couldn't tell you even if I wanted to, because I don't know. Didn't want to know."

"Because Dr. Mate never discussed clinical details with you."

"Now please leave."

"Let's say Dr. Mate did have confederates—"

"Say whatever you please."

"What makes you so sure one of them couldn't have turned on him?"

"Because why *would* they?" She laughed. Harshly. Too loudly. "I can't get you to see: Eldon was brilliant. He wouldn't have trusted just anyone." She put a foot out onto her front porch, jabbed a manicured fingernail. "Look. For. A. Fanatic."

"What about a fanatic passing himself off as a confederate?"

"Oh please." Another loud laugh. Zoghbie's hands flew upward, fingers fluttering. She dropped them quickly. A series of clumsy movements, at odds with the dancer's grace. "I can't answer any more stupid questions! This is a very hard *time* for me!"

The tears returned. No more symmetrical trickle.
A gush.

This time she wiped them hastily.

She slammed the door behind us.

CHAPTER

8

BACK IN THE unmarked, Milo looked up at the vanilla cottage. "What a harpy."

"Her attitude changed after that phone call," I said. "Maybe it was the IRS. Or she was let down that it wasn't the press. But maybe it was someone who'd worked with Mate, telling her to be discreet."

"Dr. Death had his own little elves, huh?"

"She did everything but confirm their existence. Which leads me to an interesting question: this morning we talked about the killer luring Mate to Mulholland by posing as a traveler. What if he was someone Mate already knew and trusted?"

"Elf goes bad?"

"Elf gets next to Mate because he likes killing people. Then he decides he's finished his apprenticeship. Time to co-opt. It would fit with playing doctor, taking Mate's black bag."

"So I shouldn't start rounding up Catholics and Orthodox Jews, huh? Old Alice would have been an asset to the Third Reich. Too bad her alibi checks out—flights confirmed by the airlines." He punched the dashboard lightly. "A confederate gone bad . . . I've gotta get hold of Haiselden, see what kind of paper he's been stashing."

"What about storage lockers in Mate's name?" I said.

"Nothing, so far. No POBs either. It's like he was covering his tracks all the time—the same kind of crap you get with a vic who's a criminal."

"All part of the intrigue. Plus, he did have enemies."

"Then why *wasn't* he more careful? She's right about the way he lived. No security at all."

"Monumental ego," I said. "Play God long enough, you can start to believe your own publicity. Mate was out for notoriety right from the beginning. Fooled around on the edge of medical ethics long before he built the machine." I told him about the letter to the pathology journal, Mate's death-side vigils, staring into the faces of dying people.

He said, "Cellular cessation, huh? Goddamn ghoul. Can you imagine being one of those poor patients? Here you are, stuck in the ICU, fading in and out of consciousness, you wake up, see some schmuck in a white coat just sitting there, *staring* at you. Not doing a damn thing to help, just trying to figure out exactly when you're gonna croak? And how could he look in their eyes if they were that sick?"

"Maybe he lifted the lids and peeked," I said.

"Or used toothpicks to prop them up." He slapped the dash again. "Some childhood *he* must've had." Another glance at the vanilla house. "An ex-wife. First I've heard of it. Don't want her popping up in the press and making me look like the fool I feel." Smile. "And some of my best sources have been exes. They *love* to talk."

He got on the cell phone: "Steve, it's me. . . . No, nothing earthshaking. Listen, call County Records and see if you can find any marriage certificate or divorce papers on old Eldon. If not, try other counties . . . Orange, Ventura, Berdoo, try 'em all."

"Before med school, he worked in San Diego," I said.

"Try San Diego first, Steve. Just found out he was based there before he became a doc. . . . Why? Because it might be important . . . What? Hold on." He turned to me: "Where'd Mate go to med school?"

"Guadalajara."

That made him frown. "Mexico, Steve. Forget trying to pry anything out of there."

I said, "He interned in Oakland. Oxford Hills Hospital, seventeen years ago. It's out of business, but there might be some kind of record."

"That's Dr. Delaware," said Milo. "He's been doing some independent research. . . . Yeah, he does that. . . . What? I'll ask him. If none of what I told you pans out, try our buds at Social Security. No one's filed for insurance benefits, but maybe there're some kind of federal payments going out to dependents. . . . I know it's an hour of voice mail and brain death, Steve, but that's the job. If you get nothing with SS, go back to the counties, Kern, Riverside, whatever, just keep working your way through the state. . . . Yeah, yeah, yeah . . . Any callback from Haiselden? Okay, stay on him, too. . . . Leave *fifty* goddamn messages at his house and his office if you have to. Zoghbie said he runs laundromats . . . yeah, as in clean clothes. Check that out. If that doesn't lead anywhere, bug his neighbors, be a pest— What's that? Which one?" Tiny smile. "Interesting . . . yeah, I know the name. I definitely know the name."

He hung up. "Poor baby is getting bored . . . he wanted me to ask you if working with me will turn him psychotic."

"There's always that chance. What made you smile?"

"Your man, Doss, finally called back. Korn and Demetri are gonna talk to him tomorrow."

"Progress," I said.

"Mrs. Doss," he said. "Was she able to move around on her own?"

"As far as I know. She may have driven herself to meet Mate."

"May have?"

"No one knows."

"She just walked out on hubbie?"

I shrugged. But she had. Middle of the night, no note, no warning.

No good-bye.

The deepest wound she'd inflicted on Stacy . . .

"Not very considerate," he said.

"Pain will do that to you."

"Time to call in Dr. Mate . . . Take two aspirins, hook yourself up to the machine and *don't* call me in the morning."

He started up the car, then swiveled toward me again, wedging his bulk against the steering wheel. "Seeing as we'll be face-to-face with Mr. Doss soon, are there any blanks you want to fill in?"

"He didn't like Mate," I said. "Wanted me to tell you."

"Bragging?"

"More like nothing to hide."

"What was his beef with Mate?"

"Don't know."

"Maybe the fact that Mate killed his wife and he never knew it was going to happen?"

"Could be."

He leaned across the seat, moved his big face inches from mine. I smelled aftershave and tobacco. The wheel dug into his sport coat, bunching the tweed around his neck, highlighting love handles. "What's going on here,

Alex? The guy said you could talk. Why're you parceling info out to me?"

"I guess I'm still not comfortable talking about patients. Because sometimes patients feel really communicative, then they change their minds. And what's the big deal, Milo? Doss's feelings about Mate aren't relevant. He has an alibi as tight as Zoghbie's. Out of town, just like Zoghbie. The day Mate was killed he was in San Francisco looking at a hotel."

"To buy?"

I nodded. "He was in the company of a group of Japanese businessmen. Has the receipts to prove it."

"He told you all that?"

"Yes."

"Well, ain't that fascinating." He knuckled his right eye with his left hand. "In my experience, it's mostly criminals who come prepared with an alibi."

"He wasn't prepared," I said. "It came up in the course of the conversation."

"What, like 'How's it going, Richard?' 'Peachy, Doc—and by the way I have an alibi'?"

I didn't answer.

He said, "Buying a hotel. Guy like that, rich honcho, gotta be used to delegating. Why would he do his own dirty work? So what the hell's an *alibi* worth?"

"The job done on Mate, all that anger. All that personal viciousness. Did it smell like hired help to you?"

"Depends upon what the help was hired to do. And who got hired." He reached out, placed a heavy hand on my shoulder. I felt like a suspect and I didn't like it. "Do you see Doss as capable of setting it up?"

"I've never seen any signs of that," I said in a tight voice.

He released his hand. "That sounds like a maybe."

"This is exactly why I didn't want to get into it. There's absolutely nothing I know about Richard Doss that tells me he's capable of contracting that level of brutality. Okay?"

"That," he said, "sounds like expert-witness talk."

"Then count yourself lucky. 'Cause when I go to court I get paid well."

We stared at each other. He shifted away, looked past me, up at Zoghbie's house. Two California jays danced among the branches of the sycamore.

"This is something," he said.

"What is?"

"You and me, all the cases we've been through, and now we're having a wee bit of *tension*."

Veneering the last few words in an Irish brogue. I wanted to laugh, tried to, more to fill time and space than out of any glee. The movement started at my diaphragm but died, a soundless ripple, as my mouth refused to obey.

"Hey," I said, "can this friendship be saved?"

"Okay, then," he said, as if he hadn't heard. "Here's a direct question for you: Is there anything else you know that I should know? About Doss or anything else?"

"Here's a direct answer: no."

"You want to drop the case?"

"Want me to?"

"Not unless you want to."

"I don't want to, but—"

"Why would you want to stay on it?" he said.

"Curious."

"About what?"

"Whodunit, whydunit. And riding around with the po-lice makes me feel oh-so-safe. You want me off, though, just say so."

"Oh Christ," he said. "Nyah-nyah-nyah-nyah-*nyah*-nyah."

Now we both laughed. He was sweating again and my head hurt.

"So," he said. "Onward? You do your job, I do mine—"

"And I'll get to Scotland afore ye."

"It ain't Scotland I care about," he said. "It's Mulholland Drive—gonna be interesting hearing what Mr. Doss has to say. Maybe I'll interview him myself. When are you seeing the daughter—what's her name?"

"Stacy. Tomorrow."

He wrote it down. "How many other kids in the family?"

"A brother two years older. Eric. He's up at Stanford."

"Tomorrow," he said. "College stuff."

"You got it."

"I may be talking to her, too, Alex."

"She didn't carve up Mate."

"Long as you've got a good rapport with her, why don't you ask her if her daddy had it done."

"Oh sure."

He shifted into drive.

I said, "I wouldn't mind getting a look at Mate's apartment."

"Why?"

"To see how the genius lived. Where is it?"

"Hollywood, where else? Ain't no bidness like *shooow* bidness. C'mon, I'll *shooow* you—fasten your seat belt."

CHAPTER

9

MATE'S BUILDING WAS on North Vista, between Sunset and Hollywood, the upper level of a seventy-year-old duplex. The landlady lived below, a tiny ancient named Mrs. Ednalynn Krohnfeld, who walked stiffly and wore twin hearing aids. A sixty-inch Mitsubishi TV ruled her front room, and after she let us in she returned to her chair, folded a crocheted brown throw over her knees and fastened her attention upon a talk show. The skin tones on the screen were off, flesh dyed the carotene orange of a nuclear sunburn. Trash talk show, a pair of poorly kept women cursing at each other, setting off a storm of bleeps. The host, a feloniously coiffed blonde with lizard eyes behind oversize eyeglasses, pretended to represent the voice of reason.

Milo said, "We're here to take another look at Dr. Mate's apartment, Mrs. Krohnfeld."

No answer. The image of a hollow-eyed man flashed in the right-hand corner of the screen. Gap-toothed fellow leering smugly. A written legend said, *Duane. Denesha's husband but Jeanine's lover.*

"Mrs. Krohnfeld?"

The old woman quarter-turned but kept watching.

"Have you thought of anything since last week that you want to tell me, Mrs. Krohnfeld?"

The landlady squinted. The room was curtained to gloom and barricaded with old but cheap mahogany pieces.

Milo repeated the question.

"Tell you about what?" she said.

"Anything about Dr. Mate?"

Head shake. "He's dead."

"Has anyone been by recently, Mrs. Krohnfeld?"

"What?"

Another repeat.

"By for what?"

"Asking about Dr. Mate? Snooping around the apartment?"

No reply. She continued to squint. Her hands tightened and gathered the comforter.

Duane swaggering onstage. Taking a seat between the harridans. Giving a so-what shrug and spreading his legs wide, wide, wide.

Mrs. Krohnfeld muttered something.

Milo kneeled down next to her recliner. "What's that, ma'am?"

"Just a bum." Fixed on the screen.

"That guy up there?" said Milo.

"No, no, no. Here. Out there. Climbing up the stairs." She jabbed an impatient finger at the front window, slapped both hands to her cheeks and plucked. "A bum—lotsa hair—dirty, you know, street trash."

"Climbing the stairs to Dr. Mate's apartment? When?"

"No, no—just tried to get up there, I shooed him away." Glued to the orange melodrama.

"When was this?"

"Few days ago—maybe Thursday."

"What did he want?" said Milo.

"How would I know? You think I let him in?" One of

the feuding women had jumped to her feet, pointing and cursing at her rival. Duane was positioned between them, relishing every strutting-rooster moment of it.

Bleep bleep bleep. Mrs. Krohnfeld read lips and her own mouth slackened. "Such talk!"

Milo said, "The bum, what else can you tell me about him?"

No answer. He asked the same question, louder. Mrs. Krohnfeld jerked toward us. "Yeah, a bum. He went . . ." Jabbing over her shoulder. "Tried to go up. I saw him, yelled out the window to get the hell outa there, and he skedaddled."

"On foot?"

Grunt. "That type don't drive no Mercedes. What a louse." This time, directing the epithet at Duane. "Stupid idjits, wasting their time on a louse like *that*."

"Thursday."

"Yup—or Friday . . . look at that." The women had raced toward each other and collided, alloying into a clawing, hair-pulling cyclone. "Idjits."

Milo sighed and rose. "We're going upstairs now, Mrs. Krohnfeld."

"When can I put the place up for rent?"

"Soon."

"Sooner the better—*idjits*."

The steps to Mate's unit were on the right side of the duplex, and before I climbed I had a look at the rear yard. Not much more than a strip of concrete, barely space for the double carport. An old Chevy that Milo identified as Mate's was parked next to an even older Chrysler New Yorker. Unused laundry lines sketched crosshatch shadows across the cement. Low block fencing revealed neighbors on all sides, mostly multiple-unit apartment buildings, higher than the duplex. Throw a barbecue down here and lots of people would know the menu.

Mate had chased headlines, desired no privacy in his off-hours.

An exhibitionist, or had Alice Zoghbie been right? Not cued into his surroundings.

Either way, easy victim.

I mentioned that to Milo. He sucked his teeth and took me back to the entrance.

Mate's front door was capped by a small overhang. Ads from fast-food joints littered the floor. Milo picked them up, glanced at a few, dropped them. Yellow tape banded the plain wood door. Milo yanked it loose. One key twist and we were in. A single lock, not a dead bolt. Anyone could've kicked it in.

Mold, must, rot, the nose-tweaking snap of decaying paper. Air so heavy with dust it felt granular.

Milo opened the ancient venetian blinds. Where light penetrated the apartment it highlighted the particulate storms that we set off as we moved through tight, shadowed spaces.

Tight because virtually the entire front of the flat was filled with bookshelves. Plywood cases, separated by narrow aisles. Unfinished wood, warped shelves suffering under the weight of scholarship.

Life of the mind. Eldon Mate had turned his entire domicile into a library.

Even the kitchen counters were piled high with books. Inside the fridge were bottles of water, a moldering slab of hoop cheese, a few softening vegetables.

I walked around reading titles as dust settled on my shoulders. Chemistry, physics, mathematics, biology, toxicology. Two entire cases of pathology, forensics, another wall of law—civil liability, jurisprudence, the criminal codes of what appeared to be every state of the union.

Mostly crumbling paperbacks and cold shabby texts with torn spines and flaking pages, the kind of treasures that can be found at any thrift shop.

No fiction.

I moved to the tiny back room where Mate had slept. Ten feet square, low-ceilinged, lit by a bare bulb screwed to a white porcelain ceiling fixture. Bare gray walls jaundiced by western light seeping through parchment-colored window shades. The cheap cot and nightstand took up most of the space, leaving barely enough room for a raw-looking three-drawer pine dresser. Ten-inch Zenith TV atop the dresser—as if Mate had had to make up for Mrs. Krohnfeld's video excess.

A door led to the adjoining bathroom, and I went in there because bathrooms can sometimes tell you more about a person than any other space. This one didn't. Razor, shaving cream, laxatives, antigas tablets, and aspirin in the medicine cabinet. Amber ring around the tub. Bar of green soap bottomed by slime, sitting like a dead frog in a brown plastic dish.

The closet was skinny and crammed full, sharp with the reek of camphor. A dozen wash-and-wear white shirts, half that many pairs of gray twill slacks, all Sears label; one heavy charcoal suit from Zachary All, wide lapels testifying to a long-ago fashion cycle; three pairs of black cap-toe oxfords stretched by cedar shoe trees; two beige windbreakers, also Sears; a pair of narrow black ties hanging from a hook—polyester, made in Korea.

"What was his financial situation?" I said. "Doesn't look like he spent much on clothes."

"He spent on food, gas, car repairs, books, phone and

utilities. I haven't gotten his tax forms yet, but there were some bankbooks in there." Indicating the dresser. "His basic income seems to have been his U.S. Public Health Service pension. Two and a half grand a month deposited directly into the savings account, plus occasional cash payments, two hundred to a thou each, irregularly spaced. Those I figure were donations. They add up to another fifteen a year."

"Donations from who?"

"My guess would be satisfied travelers—or those who survived them. None of the families we've talked to admit paying Mate a dime, but they'd want to avoid looking like they hired someone to kill Grandma, wouldn't they? So he was pulling in around fifty grand a year, and in terms of assets he was no pauper. The three other passbooks were for jumbo CDs of a hundred grand each. Dinky interest, doesn't look as if he cared about investing. I figure three hundred would be about a decade of income minus expenses and taxes. Looks like he's just about held on to every penny he's earned since going into the death business."

"Three hundred thousand," I said. "An MD in practice could put away a lot more than that over ten years. So he wasn't in the travel business to get rich. Notoriety was the prize, or he really was operating idealistically. Or both."

"You could say the same for Mengele." Flipping the skimpy mattress, he peered underneath. "Not that I haven't done this already." His back must have twinged, because he sucked in breath as he straightened.

"Okay?" he said.

Suddenly the room felt oppressive. Some of the book aroma had made its way in here, along with a riper smell, more human—male. That and the mothballs added up to the sad, sedate aroma of old man. As if nothing here was expected to ever change. That same sense of staleness and stasis that I'd experienced up on Mulholland. I was probably getting overimaginative.

"Anything interesting on his phone bills?" I said.

"Nope. Despite his publicity-seeking, once he got home, he wasn't Mr. Chatty. There were days at a time when he never phoned anyone. The few calls we did find were to Haiselden, Zoghbie, and boring stuff: local market, Thrifty Drugs, couple of used-book stores, shoemaker, Sears, hardware store."

"No cell phone account?"

He laughed. "The TV's black-and-white. Guy didn't own a computer or a stereo. We're talking manual typewriter—I found blank sheets of *carbon* paper in the dresser."

"No sheets with any impressions for a hot clue? Like in the movies?"

"Yeah, right. And I'm Dirty Harry."

"Old-fashioned guy," I said, "but he pushed the envelope ethically."

I opened the top drawer of the dresser on mounds of folded underwear, white and rounded like giant marshmallows. Stuffed on each side were cylinders of rolled black socks. The middle drawer contained stacks of cardigans, all brown and gray. I ran my hand below them, came up empty. The next drawer was full of medical books.

He said, "Same with the bottom. Guess next to killing people, reading was his favorite thing."

I crouched and opened the lowest drawer. Four hardbacks, the first three with warped bindings and foxed edges. I inspected one. *Principles of Surgery.*

"Copyright 1934," I said.

"Maybe if he'd kept up, that liver would've fared better."

The fourth book caught my eye. Smaller than the others. Ruby-red leather binding. Shiny new . . . gold-tooled decorations on the ribbed spine. Ornate gilt lettering, but a crude, orange-peel texture to the leather—leatherette.

Collector's edition of *Beowulf* published by some outfit called the Literary Gem Society.

I picked it up. It rattled. Too light to be a book. I lifted the cover. No pages within, just hollow, Masonite space. MADE IN TAIWAN label affixed to the underside of the lid.

A box. Novelty-shop gag. Inside, the source of the rattle:

Miniature stethoscope. Child-size. Pink plastic tubing, silvered plastic earpieces and disc. Broken earpieces—snapped off cleanly. Silvery grit in the box.

Milo's eyes slitted. "Why don't you put that down."

I complied. "What's wrong?"

"I checked that damn drawer the first time I tossed the place and that wasn't in there. The other books were, but not that. I remember reading each of the copyrights, thinking Mate was relying on antiques."

He stared into the red box.

"A visitor?" I said. "Our van-boy commemorating what he'd done? Broken stethoscope delivering a message? 'Mate's out of business, *I'm* the doctor now'?"

He bent, wincing again. "Looks like someone clipped the plastic clean. From the dust, maybe he did it right here . . . very clean."

"No problem if you had bone shears. One very nasty little elf."

He rubbed his face. "He came back to celebrate?"

"And to leave his mark."

He walked to the door, looked out at the bookcases in the front room, scowled. "I've been here twice since the murder and nothing else looks messed with. . . ."

Talking to himself more than to me. Knowing full well that with thousands of volumes, there was no way to be sure. Knowing the yellow tape across the door was meaningless, anyone could've pried the lock.

I said, "The bum Mrs. Krohnfeld saw—"

"The bum walked up the stairs in plain sight and ran away when Mrs. Krohnfeld screamed at him. She said he was a mess. Wouldn't you expect our boy to be a little better organized?"

"Like you said, some people delegate."

"What, the killer hires a schizo to break in and stick a box in a drawer?"

"Why not?"

"If it was an attempt to piss on Mate's grave, wouldn't delegating lessen the thrill?"

"Probably, but at this point he's being careful," I said. "And delegating could offer its own thrill: being the boss, wielding power. It could've happened this way: the killer knows the neighborhood because he stalked Mate for a while. He cruises Hollywood, finds a street guy, gives him cash to deliver a package. Half up front, the rest upon completion. He could've even positioned himself up the street. To watch and get off and to make sure the street guy followed through. He picked someone disorganized *specifically*, because it added another layer of safety: If the bum gets caught there's very little he can tell you. The killer used some sort of disguise for extra insurance."

His cheeks bubbled as he filled them with air, bounced it around, blew it out silently. Out of his pocket came a sealed package of surgical gloves and an evidence bag.

"Dr. Milo's in the house," he said, working his hands into the latex. "You touched it, but I'll vouch for you." Fully gloved, he lifted the box, examined it on all sides.

"Someone who knows the neighborhood," he said. "Hollywood Boulevard's full of novelty shops, maybe I can find someone who remembers selling this recently."

I said, "Maybe the choice of titles wasn't a coincidence."

"Beowulf?"

"Valiant hero slays the monster."

We spent another hour in the apartment, going over the kitchen and the front rooms, searching cupboards, scanning the bookcases for other false volumes, coming up with nothing. In some of the books, I found bills of sale going back decades. Thrift shops in San Diego, Oakland, a few in L.A.

Outside on the landing, Milo retaped the door, locked up and brushed dust from his lapels. He looked shrunken. Across the street, a middle-aged Hispanic woman stood in the paltry shade of a wretched-looking magnolia, purse in hand, newspaper folded under her arm. No one else around, and like any midday pedestrian in L.A. she stood out. No bus stop; probably waiting for a ride. She saw me looking at her, stared back for a second, shifted the purse to the other shoulder, removed the paper and began to read.

"If the box is a 'gift,'" I said, "it's another point in favor of the confederate angle. Someone wanting to put himself in Mate's place. Literally. Choosing the bedroom's consistent with that: the most personal space in the apartment. Think of it as a rape of sorts. Which is consistent with the violation of Mate's genitalia. Someone into power, domination. Playing God—a psychopathic monotheist, there can only be one deity, so he needs to eliminate any competition. On the competition's home base. I can see him walking around, exhilarated by triumph. Enjoying the extra bit of thrill of sneaking into an official crime scene. Maybe he came at night to minimize the chance of discovery, but still he couldn't be sure. If you or anyone else from the department had shown up, he'd have been trapped. The bedroom's at the back of the apartment and there's no rear exit. No place to hide except that bedroom closet, so to escape he'd have had to cross the front room, hide in that maze of bookshelves. I think he's jazzed by the danger element. It's the same first impression I had of the murder itself. Choosing an open road to perform surgery on Mate. Removing the cardboard so Mate's body would be discovered. Cleaning up carefully but leaving the scene naked. The note. Extreme meticulousness combined with recklessness. A psychopath with an above-average IQ. He's bright enough to plan precisely in the short term, but vulnerable in the long run because he gets off on danger."

"Is that supposed to comfort me?"

"He ain't Superman, Milo."

"Good. 'Cause I ain't got no kryptonite."

He stood there thinking and swinging the bag. The woman across the street looked up. Our eyes met. She returned to her paper.

"If the guy walked around," said Milo, "maybe he

touched stuff. After the apartment was printed. Now you and I just mauled it. . . . Asking for new prints is gonna be fun."

"I doubt he left any. That careful, he is."

"I'll ask anyway." He began trudging down the stairs. Stopped midway. "If this is a message, who's it aimed at? Not the public. Unlike the body and the note, there was no way he could be sure it would be found."

"At this point," I said, "he's talking to himself. Doing anything he can to enhance the kick, evoke memories of the kill. He may very well want to return to the scene of the murder but views that as too dangerous, so breaking into Mate's home, directly or by surrogate, would be the next-best thing."

I thought of something Richard Doss had told me . . . *dancing on Mate's grave.*

"Broken stethoscope," I said. "If I'm right about his taking the black bag, the message is clear: '*I* get the real tools, *you* get broken garbage.'"

We resumed our descent. At the bottom of the stairs, Milo said, "The idea of a confederate gets me thinking. About Attorney Haiselden, who should be in town but isn't. Because who spent more time with Mate? Who'd be more familiar with the apartment, maybe even have a key? The guy's behavior is *wrong*, Alex. Here we are, Mate's cold for a week, Haiselden should be throwing *press* conferences. But not a peep out of him. Just the opposite—he rabbits. Collecting coins from laundromats? Gimme a break, this asshole's *hiding* from something. Zoghbie said representing Mate was the only thing Haiselden did as a lawyer. That says overinvolvement. Mate was *Haiselden's* ticket to celebrity. Maybe Haiselden got hooked on it, wanted more, no more second fiddle. He watches Mate I.V. enough travelers, figures it qualifies him as a death doc. Hell, maybe Haiselden's one of those guys who went to law school because he couldn't get into *med* school."

"Interesting," I said. "Something else I pulled off the computer fits that. Newspaper account of a press conference Haiselden *did* call after one of the trials. He said Mate deserved the Nobel Prize, then he added that as Mate's lawyer, *he* deserved part of the money."

His free hand balled. "I've been delegating finding him to Korn and Demetri, but now I'm handling it personally. Going over to his house, right now. South Westwood. I can drop you at the station or you can come along."

I looked at my watch. Nearly five. It had been a long day. "I'll call Robin and come along."

We crossed the street to the unmarked. Milo locked the evidence bag in the trunk, circled to the driver's side, stopped. Glancing to his left.

The Hispanic woman hadn't moved. Milo turned. Her head flipped away, quick as a shuffled card, and I knew she'd been watching us.

Eyes back on the newspaper. Concentrating. The paper waved. No breeze, her hands had tightened. Her bag was a macramé sack that she'd placed on the grass.

Milo studied her. She ignored him. Licked her lips. Buried her nose deeper in newsprint.

He began to turn away from her, and her eyes flicked—just for a second—toward Mate's apartment.

He said, "Hold on."

I followed him as he strode toward her. Her hands were clenching the paper, causing it to shimmy. She folded her lips inward and drew the newsprint closer to her face. I got near enough to read the date. Yesterday's paper. The classifieds. Employment opportunities . . .

Milo said, "Ma'am?"

The woman looked up. Her lips unfolded. Thin purplish lips, chapped and puckered, bleached white around the edges. The rest of her complexion was nutmeg brown. Bags under the eyes.

She was somewhere between fifty and sixty, short and heavy with a plump face and big, gorgeous black eyes. She wore a navy polyester bomber jacket over a blue-and-white flowered dress that reached to midcalf. The dress material looked flimsy, riding up her stocky frame, adhering to bulges. Thick ankles swelled over the top seams of old but clean Nike running shoes. White socks rolled low exposed chafed shins. Her nails were square-cut. Her black hair was threaded with gray and braided past her waist. Her skin was slack around neck, jaw and chipmunk cheeks, but stretched tight over a wide brow. No makeup, no jewelry. A rural look.

While working at Western Peds, I'd known several Latin women who'd chosen that same unadorned appearance. Long hair, always a braid, dresses, never pants. Devout women, Pentecostal Christians.

"Something I can do for you, ma'am?"

"Are you . . . you're police, right?" The old mouth emitted a young voice, breathy and tentative. No accent; the merest softening at the end of each syllable. She could've found employment giving phone sex.

"Yes, ma'am." Milo flashed the badge. "And you are . . ."

She reached into the macramé bag and brought out a red plastic alligator-print wallet. Producing her own I.D., as if it had been demanded of her many times.

Social Security card. She thrust it at Milo.

He read, "Guillerma Salcido."

"Guillerma Salcido *Mate*," said the woman defiantly. "I don't use his name anymore, but that doesn't change a thing. I'm still Dr. Mate's wife—his widow."

10

GUILLERMA MATE STOOD straighter, as if fortified by the claim. Took the Social Security card from Milo's fingers and slipped it back into her purse.

"You're married to Dr. Mate?" He sounded doubtful.

Another dip into the bag, another thrust of paper.

Marriage license, fold marks grubby, photocopied lettering faded to the color of raw plywood. Date of issue, twenty-seven years ago, City of San Diego, County of San Diego. Guillerma Salcido de Vega and Eldon Howard Mate wagering on nuptial bliss.

"There," she said.

"Yes, ma'am. Do you live here in L.A.?"

"Oakland. When I heard—it's been a long time, I didn't know if I should come. I'm busy, got a job taking care of the elderly at a convalescent home. But I figured I should come. Eldon was sending me money, this pension he had. Now that he's gone, I should know what's going on. I took the Greyhound. When I got here I couldn't believe it. What a mess this place is, all the streets dug up. I got lost on the city bus. I've never been here."

"To L.A.?"

"I been to L.A. Never been *here*." Jabbing a stubby finger at the duplex. "Maybe the whole thing was a sign."

"A sign?"

"What happened to Eldon. I don't mean I'm some prophet. But when things happen that aren't natural, sometimes it means you have to take a big step. I thought I should find out. Like who's burying him? He had no faith, but everyone should be buried—he didn't want to be cremated, did he?"

"Not that I know."

"Okay. Then maybe I should do it. My church would help."

"How long exactly has it been since you saw Dr. Mate?"

She touched her finger to her upper lip. "Twenty-five years and . . . four months. Since right after my son was born—his son. Eldon Junior, he goes by Donny. Eldon didn't like Donny—didn't like kids. He was honest about that, told me right at the beginning, but I figured he was just talking, once he had his own he'd change his mind. So I got pregnant anyway. And what do you think? Eldon left me."

"But he supported you financially."

"Not really," she said. "You can't call five hundred a month support—I always worked. But he did send it every month, money order, right on the dot, I'll give him that. Only, this month I didn't get it. It was due five days ago, I have to figure out who to talk to at the army. It was an army reserve pension, they need to send it directly to me now. You have any idea how to contact them?"

"I might be able to get you a number," said Milo. "During the twenty-five years, how often did you and Dr. Mate communicate?"

"We didn't. He just sent the money. I used to think it was because he felt guilty. About walking out. But now I know he probably didn't. For guilt you got to have faith, and Eldon didn't believe in nothing. So maybe he did it out of habit, I don't know. When his mother was alive he used to send *her* money. Instead of visiting. He was always one for habits—doing things the same exact way, every single time. One color shirt, one color pants. He said it left time for important things."

"Like what?"

She shrugged. Her eyes fluttered and she began to sway. Began to fall. Both Milo and I took hold of her shoulders.

"I'm okay," she said, shrugging us off angrily. Smoothing her dress, as if we'd messed it. "Got a little low blood sugar, that's all, no big deal, I just got to eat. I brought food from home, but in the bus station someone stole my Tupperware." The black eyes lifted to Milo. "I want to eat something."

We drove her to a coffee shop on Santa Monica near La Brea. Dulled gold booths, streaked windows, fried-bacon air, the clash and clatter of silverware scooped into gray plastic tubs by sleepy busboys who looked underage. Milo chose the usual cop's vantage point at the back of the restaurant. The nearest patrons were a pair of CalTrans workers inhaling the daily steak-and-eggs special heralded by a front-door banner. Loss leader; the price belonged to the fifties. Unlikely to cover the cost of slaughter.

Guillerma Mate ordered a double cheeseburger, fries and a Diet Dr Pepper. Milo told the waitress, "Ham on rye, potato salad, coffee."

The ambience was doing nothing for my appetite, but I'd put nothing in my stomach since the morning coffee and I asked for a roast-beef dip on French roll, wondering if the meat had been carved from the budget cows.

The food came quickly. My beef dip was lukewarm and rubbery, and from the way Milo picked, his order was no better. Guillerma Mate ate lustily while trying to maintain dignity, cutting her burger up into small pieces and forking morsels into her mouth with an assembly-line pace. Finishing the sandwich, she forked french fries one at a time, consuming every greasy stick.

She wiped her mouth. Sipped Dr Pepper through two straws. "I feel better. Thanks."

"Pleasure, ma'am."

"So who killed Eldon?" she said.

"I wish I knew. This pension—"

"He had two, but I only get one—the five hundred from the reserves. The big one for a couple thousand from the Public Health Service he kept for himself. I don't think I coulda gotten more out of him. We weren't even divorced and he was giving me money." She edged closer across the table. "Did he *make* more?"

"Ma'am?"

"You know, from all the killing he did?"

"What do you think of all the killing he did?"

"What do I think? Disgusting. Mortal sin—that's why I don't go by his name. Had everything changed back to Salcido—he wasn't even a *doctor* when we were married. Went to medical school *after* he walked out. Went down in Mexico, because he was too old for anyplace else. I have friends up in Oakland who know we were married. At my church. But I keep it quiet. It's embarrassing. Some of them used to tell me to go get a lawyer, Eldon's rich now, I could get more out of him. I told them it would be sin money. They said I should take it anyway, give it to the church. I don't know about that—did he leave a will?"

"We haven't found one yet."

"So that means I have to go through that thing—probate."

Milo didn't answer.

"Actually," she said, "we did talk in the beginning, Eldon and me. Right after he walked out. But just a few times. Donny and me were in San Diego, and Eldon wasn't that far, down in Mexico. Then, after he became a doctor, he went up to Oakland to work in a hospital and I did a real stupid thing: I took Donny and we went there, too. I don't know what I coulda been thinking, maybe now that he was a doctor—it was stupid, but there I was with a boy who didn't even know his father."

"Oakland didn't work out?" I said.

"Oakland worked out, I'm still there. But Eldon didn't work out. He wouldn't talk to Donny, wouldn't even pick him up, look at him. I remember it like yesterday, Eldon in his white coat—that scared Donny and he started screaming, Eldon got mad and yelled at me to get the brat out of there—the whole thing just fell apart."

She picked at a scrap of lettuce. "I called him a couple more times after that. He wasn't interested. Refused to visit. Donny's being born just turned him off like a faucet. So I moved across the bridge to San Francisco, got a job. Funny thing is, a few years later I was back to Oakland 'cause the rent was cheaper, but by that time Eldon was gone and the checks were coming from Arizona, he had some kind of government job doing I don't know what. Back *then's* when I thought of getting a lawyer."

"Any reason you didn't file for divorce?" I said.

"Why bother?" she said. "There was no other man I wanted to know, and Eldon was sending me his army pension. You know how it is."

"How is it?" said Milo.

"You don't make a move in the beginning, nothing happens. He sent the check every month, that was enough for me. Then when he started in on that killing business, I knew I was lucky he'd left. Who'd want to live with *that*? I mean, when I heard about that I got sick, really *sick*. I remember the first time. I saw it on TV. Eldon standing there—I hadn't seen him in years and now he was on the TV. Looking older, balder but the same face, the same voice. *Bragging* about what he did. I thought, He's finally gone a hundred percent crazy. The next day I was on the phone, changing my name on the Social Security and everything else I could find."

"So you never talked to him about his new career?"

"Didn't talk to him about anything," she said. "Didn't I just say that?" She shoved her plate away. Pulled more soda through the straws, let the brown liquid drop like the bubble in a carpenter's level before it reached her lips.

"Even if it *was* making him real rich, how would it look if suddenly I showed up wanting more?" She touched the handle of her butter knife. "That was filthy money. I been working my whole life, doing just fine— tell me, *did* he get rich from the killing?"

"Doesn't look like it," said Milo.

"So what was the point?"

"He claimed he was helping people."

"The devil claims he's an *angel*. Back when I knew Eldon, he wasn't interested in helping anyone but himself."

"Selfish?" I said.

"You bet. Always in his own world, doing what he wanted. Which was reading, always reading."

"Why'd you come down here, ma'am?" said Milo.

She held her hands out, as if expecting a gift. Her palms were scrubbed pale, crisscrossed by brown hatch marks. "I told you. I just thought I should—I guess I was curious."

"About what?"

She moved back in the booth. "About Eldon. Where he lived—what had happened to him. I never *could* figure him out."

"How'd the two of you meet?" I said.

She smiled. Smoothed her dress. Sucked soda up the straw. "What? Because he was a doctor and I'm some brown lady?"

"No—"

"It's okay, I'm used to it. When we were married and I used to walk Donny in the stroller, people thought I was the maid. 'Cause Donny's light like Eldon—spitting *image* of Eldon, in fact, and Eldon *still* didn't like him. Go figure. But stuff like that don't bother me anymore, the only thing that matters is doing right for Jesus— that's the real reason I'd never put a claim on Eldon's killing money. Jesus would weep. And I know you're gonna think I'm some kind of religious nut for saying this, but my faith is strong, and when you live for Jesus your soul is full of riches."

She laughed. "Of course, a nice meal once in a while don't hurt, right?"

"How about dessert?" said Milo.

She pretended to contemplate the offer. "If you're having."

He waved for the waitress, "Apple pie. Hot, à la mode. And for the lady . . ."

Guillerma Mate said, "As long as we're talking pie, honey, you got any chocolate cream?"

The waitress said, "Sure," copied down the order, turned to me. I shook my head and she left.

"Eldon didn't believe in Jesus, that was the problem,"

said Guillerma, dabbing at her lips again. "Didn't believe in nothing. You wanna know how we met? It was just one of those *things*. Eldon was living at this apartment complex where my mother did the cleaning—she wasn't legal so she couldn't get a decent job. My dad was a hundred percent legal, had a work permit, did landscaping for Luckett Construction, they were the biggest back then. My dad got citizenship, brought my mom over from El Salvador, but she never bothered to get papers. I was born here, pure American. My friends call me Willy. Anyway, Eldon was living in the complex and I used to run into him when I was washing down the walkways or trimming the flowers. We'd talk."

"This was in San Diego?"

"That's right. I was out of high school only a few years, helping my mom out, taking classes part time at the JC, planning to be a nurse. Eldon was a lot older—thirty-six and he looked in his forties, had lost most of his hair already. I wasn't attracted to him at first, but then I started to like him. 'Cause he was polite. Not just for show, all the time. Quiet, too. That was good, I'd had enough of noisy men. Also, back then I thought he was a genius. He had a job as a chemist, kept science books and all kinds of other books everywhere, reading all the time. Back then, that impressed me. Back then I thought education was the way to get saved."

"No more, huh?"

"Wise man, fool—we're all weak mortals. The only genius is the one up there." Pointing to the ceiling. "Proof is, would a genius go around killing other people? Even those who asked for it? Does that sound like a smart thing to do when we're all gonna answer for our deeds in the next world?"

She shook her head and spoke to the ceiling tiles. "Eldon, I wouldn't want to be in your shoes right now."

The dessert came. She waited until Milo'd taken a forkful before attacking her pie.

I said, "But at the beginning you were impressed with his education."

"I used to think education was everything. I was gonna be a registered nurse—when I moved up to Oakland, I had these . . . fantasies, I guess you'd call 'em. Eldon would open up a doctor's office, I'd work with him. But then he wouldn't have nothing to do with Donny and me, so I had to keep working and never got to finish school." She licked her lips. "I'm not complaining. I take care of the elderly, do what nurses do, anyway. And now I know there's no shortcut to happiness, doesn't matter what your job is in this world. The main world is the one *afterward*, and the only way to get *there* is Jesus. It's exactly what my mother taught me, only back then I wasn't listening to her. No one listened to her, that was the burden she carried around. My father was *godless*. She never turned him around till he was dying, and even then, not till the pain came on real bad, so what else could he do but pray?"

The back of her spoon skated over the chocolate cream pie, picking up a coating of whipped cream. She licked it, said, "My dad smoked all his life, got lung cancer, it spread to his bones, all over his spine. He died in bad pain, choking and screaming. It was horrible. Made a big impression on Eldon."

"Eldon saw your father die?" I said.

"You bet. Dad died right after we were married. We'd go visit Dad in the hospital and he'd be coughing up blood and screaming from the pain and Eldon would turn white as a ghost and have to leave. Who'da figured

he'd be a doctor? You know what *I* think? Seeing Dad
die could be part of what started out Eldon on this killing
business. 'Cause it really *was* horrible, Mom and me got
through it by praying. But Eldon didn't pray. Refused to,
even when Mom begged him. Said he wouldn't be a
hypocrite. If you don't have no faith, seeing something
like that is gonna scare you."

She finished her pie.

Milo said, "Is there anything you can tell us that might
help us learn who killed your husband?"

"I'd say someone didn't like what Eldon was doing."

"Anyone in particular?"

"No," she said. "I'm just talking . . . logical. There's
got to be lots of people who didn't approve of Eldon.
Not God-fearing people, God-fearing don't go running
around killing. But maybe someone . . ." Smile. "You
know, it could be someone *like* Eldon. Got no faith and a
big hate grew inside him *about* Eldon. 'Cause Eldon had
a difficult personality—didn't care what he said or how
he said it. Least, that's the way he was back when we
were married. Always getting into it with people—bring
him into a place like this and he'd be complaining about
the food, marching up to the manager and starting an argument. Maybe he got the wrong person mad and this
person said, Look what he does and gets away with it,
sure, it's okay to kill, it's no different from tying my
shoes. 'Cause let's face it, if you don't believe in the
world hereafter, what's to stop you from killing or raping
or robbing or doing whatever it is your lust tells you
to do?"

Milo sat there, probing the rim of his piecrust with his
fork. I wondered if he was thinking what I was: a lot of
insight in one little speech.

"So," she said, "who do I talk to about that pension? And the will?"

Back in the car, Milo made a series of calls and got her the number of the army pension office.

"As far as the will is concerned," he told her, "we're still trying to contact Dr. Mate's lawyer. A man named Roy Haiselden. Has he ever called you?"

"That big fat guy always with Eldon on TV? Nope— you think *he* has the will?"

"If there is one, he might. Nothing's been filed with County Records. If I learn anything, I'll let you know."

"Thanks. I guess I'll be staying in town for a few days, see what I can find out. Know of any clean, cheap places?"

"Hollywood's a tough area, ma'am. And nothing decent's gonna be that cheap."

"Well," she said, "I'm not saying I don't have any money. I work, I brought two hundred dollars with me. I just don't want to spend more than I have to."

We drove her to a West Coast Inn on Fairfax near Beverly and checked her in. She paid with a hundred-dollar bill, and as we walked her to her first-floor room, Milo warned her about flashing cash on the street and she said, "I'm not stupid."

The room was small, clean, noisy, with a view across Fairfax: cars whizzing by, the sleek, modern lines of the CBS studios a black-and-white subpanel to the horizon.

"Maybe I'll see a game show," she said, parting the drapes. She removed another floral dress from the macramé bag and headed for the closet. "Okay, thanks for everything."

Milo handed her his card. "Call me if you think of anything, ma'am—by the way, where's your son?"

Her back was to us. She opened the closet door. Took a long time to hang the dress. On the top shelf was an extra pillow that she removed. Fluffing, compressing, fluffing.

"Ma'am?"

"Don't know where Donny is," she said.

Punching the pillow. All at once, she looked tiny and bowed. "Donny's real smart, just like Eldon. Did a year at San Francisco State. I used to think he'd be a doctor, too. He got good grades, he liked science."

She stood there, hugging the pillow.

"What happened?" I said.

Her shoulders heaved.

I went over and stood next to her. She edged away, placed the pillow atop a dresser. "They said it was drugs—my friends at church said it had to be that. But I never saw him take any drugs."

"He changed," I said.

She bent, cupped a hand over her eyes. I risked taking her by the elbow. Her skin was soft, gelatinous. I guided her onto a chair, handed her a tissue that she grabbed, crushed, finally used to wipe her face.

"Donny changed totally," she said. "Stopped taking care of himself. Grew long hair, a beard, got filthy. Like one of those homeless people. Only he's *got* a home, if he'd ever come back there."

"How long has it been since you've seen him?"

"Two years."

She sprang up, marched into the bathroom, closed the door. Water ran for a while, then she emerged announcing she was tired. "When I'm ready to eat, where can I get some dinner around here?"

"Do you like Chinese, ma'am?" said Milo.

"Sure, anything."

He phoned up a takeout place and asked them to deliver in two hours. When we left, she was consulting the cable TV channel guide.

Out in the car, Milo sat back in his seat and frowned. "One happy family. And Junior's a homeless guy with mental problems, maybe a druggie. Someone with a reason to kill Mate—who might still want to *be* Mate. Maybe I was wrong to dismiss the street bum so quickly."

"If Donny was intelligent to begin with, even with some sort of mental breakdown, he might've held on to enough smarts to be able to plan. Mate abandoned and rejected him in the worst kind of way. Exactly the kind of primal anger that leads to violence. Mate's getting famous wouldn't have helped things. Maybe Donny smoldered, seethed, decided to come back, take over the family business . . . Oedipus wrecks. Maybe Mate finally agreed to see him, arranged a talk up in Mulholland because he didn't want Donny in his apartment. He could've even had concerns about his safety, that's why he backed the van in. But he went through with it—guilt, or he enjoyed the danger."

He made no comment, got on the phone, hooked up with NCIC, asked for a felony search on Eldon S. Mate. Nothing. But plugging in Eldon *Salcido* pulled up three convictions. All in California, and the vital statistics fit.

Driving under the influence six years ago, larceny two years after that, assault eighteen months ago. Jail time in Marin County. Release six months ago.

"A year and a half in jail and he doesn't call his mother," I said. "Socially isolated. And he progressed from DUI to assault. Getting more aggressive."

"Family values," he said. "Be interesting to see what the grieving widow does when she finds out Mate left over three hundred grand in the bank. Wonder if Alice or anyone else will press a claim—that's really why old Willy came down here. It always boils down to anger and money—okay, I'll look into Donny, but in the meantime let's try to ferret out that goddamn lawyer."

CHAPTER

11

ROY HAISELDEN WAS living better than his prime client, but he was no sultan.

His house was a peach-colored, one-story plain-wrap on Camden Avenue, west of Westwood, south of Wilshire. Mown lawn but no shrubs, empty driveway. Alarm-company sign staked in the grass. Milo rang the bell, knocked on the door—dead-bolted with a sturdy Quikset—pushed open the mail slot and sighted down.

"Just some throwaway flyers," he said. "No mail. So he left recently."

He rang and knocked again. Tried to peer through the white drapes that sheathed the front windows, muttered that it just looked like a goddamn house. A check in back of the house revealed more grass and a small oval swimming pool set in a brick deck, the water starting to green, the gunite spotted with algae.

"If he had a pool man," I said, "looks like he canceled a while back. Maybe he's been gone for a while and put on a mail stop."

"Korn and Demetri checked for that. And the gardener's been here."

The garage was a double, locked. Milo managed to pry the door upward several inches and he peered in. "No car, old bicycle, hoses, the usual junk."

He inspected every side of the house. Most of the windows were barred and bolted and the back door was secured by an identical dead bolt. The kitchen window was undraped but narrow and high, and he boosted me up for a look.

"Dishes in the sink, but they look clean . . . no food . . . another alarm sticker high on the window, but I don't see any alarm leads."

"Probably a fake-out job," he said. "One of those clever boys who thinks appearance is everything."

"Overconfident," I said. "Just like Mate."

He let me down. "Okay, let's see what the neighbors have to offer."

Both of the adjacent houses were empty. Milo scrawled requests to call on the back of his business cards and left them in the mailboxes. In the second house to the south, a young black man answered. Clean-shaven, full-faced, barefoot, wearing a gray athletic shirt with the U. logo and red cotton shorts. Under his arm was a book. A yellow underlining pen was clenched between his teeth. He removed it, shifted the book so I could see the title: *Organizational Structure: An Advanced Text.* The room behind him was set up with two bright-blue beanbag chairs and not much else. Soda cans, potato chip bags, an extra-large pizza box mottled with grease on the thin khaki rug.

He greeted Milo pleasantly, but the sight of the badge caused his face to tighten.

"Yes?" The unspoken overtone: *What now?* I wondered how many times he'd been stopped for driving in Westwood.

Milo stepped back, bent his knee in a relaxed pose. "I was wondering, sir, if you've seen your neighbor Mr. Haiselden recently."

"Who—oh him. No, not for a few days."

"Could you say how many days, Mr. . . ."

"Chambers," said the young man. "Curtis Chambers. I think I saw him drive away five, six days ago. Whether he's been back since, I can't say, 'cause I've been holed up here studying. Why?"

"Do you recall what time of day it was when you saw him, Mr. Chambers?"

"Morning. Before nine. I was going to meet with a prof and he needed to do it by nine. I think it was Tuesday. What's going on?"

Milo smiled and held up a delaying finger. "What kind of car was Mr. Haiselden driving?"

"Some kind of van. Silver, with a blue stripe down the side."

"That his only vehicle?"

"Only one I've seen him in."

"Anyone else live there with him?"

"Not that I know," said Curtis Chambers. "Could you please tell me what's up?"

"We're trying to contact Mr. Haiselden about a case—"

"Dr. Death's murder?"

"You've seen him with Dr. Mate?"

"No, but everyone knew he was Dr. Death's lawyer. People in the neighborhood talk about it. He's a jerk, Haiselden. Last year, we had a party—there are four of us living here, grad students. Nothing wild, we're all grinds, all we had was that single party the entire year to celebrate semester-end. We tried to be considerate, even sent notes around to the neighbors. One woman—Mrs. Kaplan next door—sent us a bottle of wine. No one had a problem with it except Haiselden. *He* called the cops on us. Twenty after eleven and believe me, it was nothing wild, just some music, maybe it got a little loud. What an uptight hypocrite. After all the disruption he brought to the neighborhood."

"What kind of disruption?"

"Reporters, media, all that garbage."

"Recently?"

"No, a few years ago," said Chambers. "I never saw it, wasn't living here back then, but one of my roommates was—he said the whole street was a zoo. This was back when Mate was still getting arrested. He and Haiselden threw press conferences right here. TV crews would show up—lights, cameras, the works. Blocked driveways, cigarettes and garbage left on the lawns. Some of the neighbors finally complained to Haiselden, but he ignored them. So after all that, he goes and calls the cops on *us*. A jerk, always had this irritated look on his face. So why do you want him? Did he kill his buddy?"

"Why would you say that, Mr. Chambers?"

Chambers grinned. "Because I don't like the man . . . and the fact that he split. You'd think, his being Mate's mouthpiece, that he'd stick around, grab some more PR. 'Cause that's what it was all about, right? That's the only problem I have with what Mate did."

"What do you mean?" said Milo.

"The tackiness, making a spectacle out of other people's pain. You want to put a sick person out of their misery, fine. But shouldn't it be private? From what my roommate told me about the way Haiselden used to behave, he loved playing for the cameras. So you'd think he'd be doing the same thing now. Though I guess there's nothing for him to comment on anymore, with Mate gone."

"Guess not," said Milo. "Is there anything else you want to tell me about him?"

"Nope—listen, if you leave me your number and I see him, I'll call you. Siccing the cops on our party. What a jerk."

Driving back to the station, Milo said, "First Mrs. Mate, now him. Insights from the man on the street. Everyone seems to have figured things out except me."

"A lawyer who drives a van."

"Yeah, yeah, psycho killer's transport of choice. Wouldn't that be something? One serial killer representing another in court. And winning."

"Only thing he did win," I said. "He couldn't make a living practicing law, so he turned to coin-ops. Zoghbie said it was because of Mate, but maybe he was struggling before and Mate was his salvation. He latches on to the whole travel thing, rides the coattails, enjoys the glory. Then he and Mate have some kind of rift. Or, as you said, Haiselden starts yearning for more."

"Up the suspect ladder he goes. Time for a pass by his office."

"Where's that?"

"Miracle Mile, the old part, east of Museum Row. He leases some space over a Persian restaurant. Him and some other low-rent outfits. The place has a moldy feel to it, like out of an old movie."

"No secretary?"

"I've been there twice, Korn and Demetri another two times. The door's always locked and no one answers. Time to find the landlord. No sense wasting *your* time. Go home to Robin and Fido."

I didn't argue. I was tired. And Stacy Doss was coming in tomorrow; I needed to review her file.

"So who're you concentrating on?" I said. "Haiselden or Donny Mate?"

"Do I have to choose between Door Number One and Door Number Two, Monty? Can I take Number Three? Better yet, I'll concentrate on both of them. If Donny's our street wacko, it may take a while to find him. I wanna find out if he was released clean or placed on parole. Maybe he's got a P.O. I can talk to. If he was the bum Mrs. Krohnfeld saw, maybe he's still hanging in Hollywood. That would also fit with your idea about stalking Mate."

"Stalking Daddy."

"Who's off in his own world and thinks he's immortal . . . I think I'll touch base with Petra, she's as clued in to the streets as anyone."

Petra Connor was a Hollywood Division homicide detective, young, bright, intense, recently promoted to D-II because of some help she'd given Milo on a series of killings of handicapped people. Just after that, she and her partner had solved the Lisa Ramsey case—ex-wife of a TV actor, found hacked up in Griffith Park. She'd referred me a case, a twelve-year-old boy who'd witnessed the crime while living in the park, a brilliant, complex child, one of the most fascinating patients I'd ever encountered. Rumors were that her partner, Stu Bishop, was in line for a major administrative job and that she'd be a D-III by year's end, then groomed by the new chief for something conspicuous.

"Give her my best," I said.

"Sure," he said, but his tone was detached and his eyes were somewhere off in the distance.

Staring into *his* own world. At that moment, I was happy not to be sharing.

CHAPTER

12

MONDAY, NINE-THIRTY P.M., nearing the end of a very long day.

Robin was soaking in the bath and I was in bed, reviewing Stacy Doss's chart.

Tomorrow morning, Stacy and I would be talking, ostensibly about college.

She'd used college as a cover the first time.

March, a warm Friday afternoon. I'd seen two other kids before her, sad children caught up in the poison of a custody dispute. The next hour was spent writing reports. Then waiting for Stacy. Curious about Stacy.

Despite my preconceptions about Richard Doss—*because* of them—I'd labored to keep an open mind about his daughter. Still, I wondered. What kind of girl would result from the union of Richard and Joanne? I really had no clue.

The red light signaling someone at the side door lit up precisely on time and I went to fetch her. A small girl—five-two in brown loafers. Perfect genetic logic; no reason for the Dosses to produce a basketball player. A bright-green oversize book was sandwiched between her right arm and her chest, the title obscured by her sleeve. She wore a white cotton mock turtle, snug blue jeans, white socks with the loafers.

Normal teenage curves, a bit of flesh on her face, but certainly not overweight. If she'd gained ten pounds, as Judy Manitow had claimed, she'd have been extremely thin before. That made me wonder about Judy—her own tendency toward sharp angles, snapshots of her daughters in her chambers. A pair of bright-eyed blondes in very short, very tight party dresses . . . also skinny. The younger one—Becky—veering too close to skeletal?

No matter, Stacy was the patient. She had full cheeks but a long face that evoked her mother's college picture. Richard's high, broad brow, stippled by a few tiny pimples. Pixie features; another endowment from both parents.

She smiled nervously. I introduced myself and held out my hand. She took it readily, maintained eye contact, flashed a half-second smile that burned lots of calories.

Making an effort.

Prettier than Joanne, with dark, almond eyes and the kind of small-boned good looks that would attract the boys. During my high-school days, she'd have been labeled a Gidget. In any generation, she'd be termed cute.

Another paternal donation: her hair—thick, black, very curly. She wore it long and loose, glossed with some kind of product that relaxed the helixes to dancing corkscrews. Lighter complexion than Richard's—skin the color of clotted cream. Thin skin; traces of blue surfaced at jawline and temple. A cuticle picked raw on her left middle finger had turned red and swollen to a silky sheen.

She hugged the book tighter and followed me in. "That's a pretty pond I passed. Koi, right?"

"Right."

"The Manitows have a koi pond, a big one."

"Really." I'd been in Judy Manitow's chambers several dozen times, never visited her home.

"Dr. Manitow put in an incredible waterfall. You could swim in there. Yours is actually more . . . accessible. You have a beautiful garden."

"Thanks."

We entered the office and she sat down with the green book across her lap. Yellow lettering shouted: *Choosing the Right College for You!*

"No problem finding the place?" I said, settling opposite her.

"Not at all. Thanks for seeing me, Dr. Delaware."

I wasn't used to being thanked by adolescents. "My pleasure, Stacy."

She blushed and turned away.

"Recreational reading?" I said.

Another strained smile. "Not exactly."

She began to look around the office.

"So," I said, "do you have any questions?"

"No, thanks." As if I'd offered her something.

I smiled. Waited.

She said, "I guess I should talk about my mother."

"If you want to."

"I don't know if I want to." Her right index finger curled and moved toward her left hand, located the inflamed cuticle. Stroking. Picking. A dot of blood stretched to a scarlet comma. She covered it with her right hand.

"Dad says he's worried about my future, but I suppose I should talk about Mom." She angled her face so that it was shielded by black curls. "I mean, it's probably the right thing for me. That's what my friend says—she wants to be a psychologist. Becky Manitow, Judge Manitow's daughter."

"Becky's been doing some amateur therapy?"

She shook her head as if thinking about that made her tired. Her eyes were the same dark brown as her father's, yet a whole different flavor. "Becky's been in counseling herself, thinks it's the cure for everything. She lost a lot of weight, even more than her mother wanted her to, so they shipped her off to some therapist and now she wants to be one."

"You two friends?"

"We used to be. Actually, Becky's not . . . I don't want to be cruel, let's just say she's not into school."

"Not an intellectual."

She let out a small, soft laugh. "Not exactly. My mom used to tutor her in math."

Judy had never mentioned her daughter's problem. No reason to. Still, I wondered why Judy hadn't referred Stacy to Becky's therapist. Maybe too close to home, keeping everything in neat little boxes.

"Well," I said, "no matter what Becky or anyone says, you know what's best for you."

"Think so?"

"I do."

"You don't even know me."

"Competent till proven otherwise, Stacy."

"Okay." Another weak smile. So much effort to smile. I wrote a mental note: *poss. depress. as noted by J. Manitow.*

Her hand lifted. The blood on her finger had dried and she rubbed the sore spot. "I don't think I really do. Want to talk about my mother, that is. I mean, what can I say? When I think about it I get down for days, and I've already had enough of those. And it's not as if it was a shock—her . . . what happened. I mean it *was*, when it actually happened, but she'd been sick for so long."

Same thing her father had said. Her own little speech, or his?

"This," she said, smiling again, "is starting to sound like one of those gross movies of the week. Lindsay Wagner as everyone's mom . . . What I'm saying is that what happened to my mother took so long . . . It wasn't like another friend of mine, *her* mother died in a skiing accident. Crashed into a tree and she was gone, just like that." Snap of the inflamed finger. "The whole family watching it happen. *That's* traumatic. My mother . . . I knew it was going to happen. I spent a long time wondering *when*, but . . ." Her bosom rose and fell. One foot tapped. The right index finger sought the sore spot again, curled to strike, scratched, retracted.

"Maybe we *should* talk about my so-called future," she said, lifting the green book. "First could I use the bathroom, please?"

She was gone ten minutes. After seven I started to wonder, was ready to get up to check if she'd left the house, but she returned, hair tied back in a bushy ponytail, mouth shiny with freshly applied lip gloss.

"Okay," she said. "College. The process. My lack of direction."

"That sounds like something someone told you."

"Dad, my school counselor, my brother, everyone. I'm almost eighteen, nearly a senior, so I'm supposed to be into it—career aspirations, compiling lists of extra-curricular activities, composing brag sheets. Ready to sell myself. It feels so . . . phony. I go to Pali Prep, freak-city when it comes to college. Everyone in my class is freaking out daily. I'm not, so I'm the space alien." Her free hand flipped the edges of the green book's pages.

"Can't get into it?" I said.

"Don't *want* to get into it. I honestly don't care, Dr. Delaware. I mean, I know I'm going to end up somewhere. Does it really make a difference *where*?"

"Does it?"

"Not to me."

"But everyone's telling you you should care."

"Either explicitly or, you know—it's in the air. The atmosphere. At school everything's been split down the middle—sociologically. Either you're a goof and you know you'll end up at a party school, or you're a grind and expected to obsess on Stanford or the Ivy League. I *should* be a grind, because my grades are okay. I should have my nose glued to the SAT prep book, be filling out practice applications."

"When do you take the SAT?"

"I already took it. In December. We all did, just for practice. But I did okay enough, don't see why I should go through it again."

"What'd you get?"

She blushed again. "Fifteen-twenty."

"That's a fantastic score," I said.

"You'd be surprised. At PP, kids who get fifteen-eighty take it again. One kid had his parents write that he was American Indian so he'd get some kind of minority edge. I don't see the point."

"Neither do I."

"I honestly think that if you offered most of the senior class a deal to murder someone in order to be guaranteed admission to Harvard, Stanford or Yale, they'd take it."

"Pretty brutal," I said, fascinated by her choice of example.

"It's a brutal world out there," she said. "At least that's what my father keeps telling me."

"Does he want you to take the SAT again?"

"He pretends he's not pressuring me, but he lets me know he'll pay for it if I want to."

"Which is a kind of pressure."

"I suppose. You met him . . . What was that like?"

"What do you mean?"

"Did you get along? He told me you were smart, but there was something in his voice—like he wasn't sure about you." She cracked up. "I've got a big mouth. . . . Dad's super-active, always needs to keep moving, thinking, doing something. Mom's illness drove him crazy. Before she got sick, they were totally active together—jogging, dancing, tennis, traveling. When she stopped living, he was left on his own. It's made him cranky."

That sounded detached, a clinical assessment. The family observer? Sometimes kids assume that role because it's easier than participating.

"Tough adjustment for him," I said.

"Yes, but he finally caught on."

"About what?"

"About having to do things for himself. He always finds a way to adjust."

That sounded accusatory. My raised eyebrow was my next question.

She said, "His main way of handling stress is by staying on the go. Business trips. You know what he does, right?"

"Real-estate development."

She shook her head as if I'd gotten it wrong, but said, "Yes. Distressed properties. He makes money off other people's failures."

"I can see why he'd view the world as brutal."

"Oh yes. The brutal world of distressed *properties*." She laughed and sighed and her hands loosened. Placing the big green book on an end table, she pushed it away.

Her hands returned to her lap. Loose. Defenseless. Suddenly she was slumping like a teenager. Suddenly she seemed truly happy to be here.

"He calls himself a heartless capitalist," she said. "Probably because he knows that's what everyone else says. Actually, he's quite proud of himself."

Undertone of contempt, low and steady as a monk's drone. Deriding her father to a virtual stranger but doing it charmingly. That kind of easy seepage often means the lid's rising on a long-boiling pot.

I sat there, waiting for more. She crossed her legs, slumped lower, fluffed her hair, as if aiming for nonchalance.

Her shrug said, Your turn.

I said, "I get the feeling real estate isn't a strong interest of yours."

"Who knows? I'm thinking of becoming an architect, so I can't hate it that much. Actually, I don't hate business at all, not like some other kids do. It's just that I'd rather build something than be a . . . I'd rather be productive."

"Rather than be a what?"

"I was going to say scavenger. But that's not fair to my father. He doesn't cause anyone else to fail. He's just there to seek opportunities. Nothing wrong with that, it's just not what *I'd* like to do—actually, I have no *idea* what I'd like to do." She rang an imaginary bell. "Dah-*dah*, big insight. I have no *goals*."

"What about architecture?"

"I probably just say that to tell people something when they ask me. For all I know, I might end up despising architecture."

"Do any subjects in school interest you?" I said.

"I used to like science. For a while, I thought medicine

might be a good choice. I took all the A.P. science courses, got fives on the exams. Now I don't know."

"What changed your mind?" *The death of your scientist mother?*

"It just seems . . . well, for one, medicine's not what it used to be, is it? Becky told me her father can't stand his job anymore. All the HMOs telling him what he can and can't do. Dr. Manitow calls it *mis*managed care. After all that school, it would be nice to have some occupational freedom. Do you like *your* job?"

"Very much."

"Psychology," she said, as if the word were new. "I was more interested in real science—oh, sorry, that was rude! What I meant was hard science . . ."

"No offense taken." I smiled.

"I mean, I do respect psychology. I was just thinking more in terms of chemistry and biology. For myself. I'm good with organic things."

"Psychology *is* a soft science," I said. "That's part of what I like about it."

"What do you mean?" she said.

"The unpredictability of human nature," I said. "Keeps life interesting. Keeps me on my toes."

She thought about that. "I had one psych course, in my junior year. Non–honor track, actually a Mickey Mouse. But it ended up being interesting. . . . Becky went nuts with it, picking out every symptom we learned about and pinning it on someone. Then she got real cold to me—don't ask me why, I don't know. Don't care, either, we haven't shared common interests since the Barbies got stored in the closet. . . . No, I don't think any kind of medicine's for me. Frankly, none of it seems too scientific. My mother saw every species of doctor known to mankind and no one could do a thing for her. If I ever decide to do anything with my life, I think I'd like it to be more productive."

"Something with quick results?"

"Not necessarily quick," she said. "Just valid." She pulled the ponytail forward, played with the crimped edges. "So what if I'm unfocused. I'm the second child, isn't that normal? My brother has enough focus for both of us, knows exactly what he wants: to win the Nobel Prize in economics, then make billions. One day you'll read about him in *Fortune*."

"That is pretty specific."

"Eric's always known what he wants. He's a genius— picked up *The Wall Street Journal* when he was five, read an article on supply and demand in the soybean market and gave his kindergarten class a lecture the next day."

"Is that a family tale?" I said.

"What do you mean?"

"It sounds like something you might've heard from your parents. Unless you remember it yourself. But you were only three."

"Right," she said. Confused. "I think I heard it from my father. Could've been my mother. Either of them. My father still tells the story. It probably *was* him."

Mental note: *What stories does Dad tell about Stacy?*

"Does that mean something?" she said.

"No," I said. "I'm just interested in family tales. So Eric's focused."

"Focused and a genius. I mean that literally. He's the smartest person I've ever met. Not a nerd, either. Aggressive, tenacious. Once he sets his mind on something, he won't let go."

"Does he like Stanford?"

"He likes it, it likes him."

"Your parents went there?"

"Family tradition."

"Does that put pressure on you to go there, as well?"

"I'm sure Dad would be thrilled. Assuming I'd get in."

"You don't think you would?"

"I don't know—don't really care."

I'd put some space between our chairs, careful not to crowd her. But now her body arched forward, as if yearning for touch. "I'm not putting myself down, Dr. Delaware. I know I'm smart enough. Not like Eric, but smart enough. Yes, I probably could get in, if for no other reason than I'm a multiple legacy. But the truth is, all that is wasted on me—*smarts* are wasted on me. I really couldn't care less about intellectual goals or tackling challenges or changing the world or making big bucks. Maybe that sounds airheady, but that's the way it is."

She sat back. "How much time do we have left, please? I forgot my watch at home."

"Twenty minutes."

"Ah. Well . . ." She began studying the office walls.

"Busy day?" I said.

"No, easy day, as a matter of fact. It's just that I told my friends I'd meet them at the Beverly Center. Lots of good sales on, perfect time to do some airhead shopping."

I said, "Sounds like fun."

"Sounds mindless."

"Nothing wrong with leisure."

"I should just enjoy my life?"

"Exactly."

"Exactly," she repeated. "Just have fun." Tears welled in her eyes. I handed her a tissue. She took it, crushed the paper, enveloping it with a fine-boned, ivory fist.

"Let's," she said, "talk about my mother."

* * *

I saw her thirteen times. Twice a week for four weeks, then five weekly sessions. She was punctual, cooperative, filled the first half of each session with edgy fast-talk about movies she'd seen, books she'd read, school, friends. Keeping the inevitable at bay, then finally relenting. Her decision, no prodding from me.

The final twenty minutes of each session reserved for her mother.

No more tears, just soft-spoken monologues, heavy with obligation. She'd been sixteen when Joanne Doss began falling apart, remembered the decline, as had her father, as gradual, insidious, ending in grotesquerie.

"I'd look at her and she'd be lying there. Passive—even before, she was always kind of passive. Letting my father make all the decisions—she'd cook dinner but *he'd* determine the menu. She was a pretty good cook, as a matter of fact, but what she made never seemed to matter to her. Like it was her job and she was going to do it and do it well, but she wouldn't pretend to be . . . inspired. Once, years ago, I found this little menu box and she'd put in all these dinner plans, stuff she cut out of magazines. So once upon a time, I guess she cared. But not when I was around."

"So your dad had all the opinions in the family," I said.

"Dad and Eric."

"Not you?"

Smile. "Oh, I have a few, too, but I tend to keep them to myself."

"Why's that?"

"I've found that a good strategy."

"For what?"

"A pleasant life."

"Do Eric and your father exclude you?"

"No, not at all—not consciously, anyway. It's just that the two of them have this . . . let's just call it a big male thing. Two major brains speeding along. Jumping in would be like hopping on a moving train—good metaphor, huh? Maybe I should use it in English class. My teacher's a real pretentious snot, loves metaphors."

"So joining in's dangerous," I said.

She pressed a finger to her lower lip. "It's not that they put me down. . . . I guess I don't want them to think I'm stupid. . . . They're just . . . they're a *pair*, Dr. Delaware. When Eric's home, sometimes it's like having Dad in duplicate."

"And when Eric's not home?"

"What do you mean?"

"Do you and your father interact?"

"We get along, it's just that he travels and we have different interests. He's into collecting, I couldn't care less about accumulating stuff."

"Collecting what?"

"First it was paintings—California art. Then he sold those for a giant profit and got into Chinese porcelain. The house is filled with walls and walls of the stuff. Han dynasty, Sung dynasty, Ming dynasty, whatever. I appreciate it. It's beautiful. I just can't get into accumulating. I guess he's an optimist, buying porcelain in earthquake country. He putties it down with this wax the museums use, but still. If the Big One comes, our house will be one big crockery disaster zone."

"How did it fare during the last quake?"

"He didn't have it back then. He got into it when Mom started to get sick."

"Do you think there's a connection?" I said.

"Between what?"

"Getting into porcelain and your mother becoming ill."

"Why should there be—oh I see. She couldn't do things with him anymore, so he learned to amuse himself. Yes, maybe. Like I said, he knows how to adapt."

"What did your mom think about the porcelain?"

"She didn't think anything, that I saw. She didn't think much about anything—Eric likes the porcelain. He can inherit it, I couldn't care less." Sudden smile. "I'm the Queen of Apathy."

At the end of the sixth session, she said, "Sometimes I wonder what kind of guy I'll marry. I mean, will it be someone dominant like Dad or Eric, because that's what I'm used to, or will I go in a totally opposite direction—not that I'm thinking about that. It's just that Eric was down for the weekend and the two of them went off to some Asian art auction and I watched them leave the house—like twins. That's basically what I know of men."

She shook her head. "Dad keeps buying stuff. Sometimes I think that's what he's all about—expansion. As if one world's not big enough for him—Eric was thinking of coming with me today to meet you."

"Why?"

"He doesn't have classes till tomorrow, asked me if I wanted to hang out before he flies up tonight. Kind of sweet, don't you think? He really is a good brother. I told him I had to see you first. He didn't know about you, Dad makes a big thing about confidentiality. Gave me this whole big speech about even though I was under eighteen, as far as he was concerned I had full rights. Like he was giving me a big gift, but I think he's kind of embarrassed about it. Once, when I brought up Becky's therapy, he changed the subject really fast. . . . Anyway, Eric hadn't known about you and it surprised him. He started asking me all these questions, wanting to know if you were smart, where you got your degree. I realized I didn't know."

I pointed to my diplomas.

She said, "The good old U. Not Stanford or the Ivys, but it'll probably satisfy him."

"Do you feel you need to satisfy Eric?"

"Sure, he's the smart one. . . . No, he's entitled to his opinions, but they don't influence mine. He decided not to come, took a bike ride instead. Maybe one day you'll get to meet him."

"If I behave myself?"

She laughed. "Yes, absolutely. Meeting Eric is a reward of the highest order."

I'd thought a lot about Eric. About the hellish Polaroids he'd shot of his mother. Standing at the foot of the bed, highlighting her misery in cold, unforgiving light. His father considered them trophies, carried them around in that little purse.

How badly had Richard Doss hated his wife?

I said, "How did Eric react to your mother's death?"

"Silence. Silent anger. He'd already dropped out of school to be with her, maybe that did it for him. Because right after, he returned to Stanford." Sudden chill in her voice. She picked at her cuticles, stared down into her lap.

Bad move, bringing up her brother. Keep the focus on her, always on her.

But I wondered if she'd ever seen the snapshots.

"So," I said.

"So." She looked at her watch.

Ten minutes to go. She frowned. I tried to reel her back

in: "A couple of weeks ago, we were discussing how expressing opinions can be tricky in your family. How did your mother—"

"By having none. By turning herself into a nothing."

"A nothing," I said.

"Exactly. That's why I wasn't surprised when I found out what she did—with Mate. I mean I was, when I heard about it on the news. But after the shock wore off, I realized it made sense: the ultimate passivity."

"So you had no warning—"

"None. She never said a word to me. Never said goodbye. That morning she had called me in to say hi before I went to school. Told me I looked pretty. She did that sometimes, there was nothing different. She looked the way she always did. Erased—the truth is she'd already rubbed herself out by the time Mate got involved. The media always make it out like he's doing something but he isn't. Not if the other people were like my mom. He didn't do a damn thing. There was nothing left for him to do. She didn't want to *be*."

I readied my hand for a dive toward the tissue box. Stacy straightened, placed her feet on the floor, sat up straight.

"The whole thing's an incredible pity, Dr. Delaware."

Back to the clinical detachment of the first session.

"Yes, it is."

"She was brilliant, *two* PhDs, she could've won the Nobel Prize if she'd wanted to. *That's* where Eric got his smarts. My father's a bright man, but she was a *genius*. Her parents were brilliant, too. Librarians, they never made much money, but they were brilliant. Both died young. Cancer. Maybe my mother was afraid of dying young. Of cancer, I don't know. She brought Becky Manitow from a D to a B in algebra. When Becky stopped seeing her, she dropped down to a D again."

"Becky stopped because your mother was ill?"

"I suppose."

Long silence. A minute to go.

She said, "Our time's up, isn't it."

"In a moment," I said.

"No. Rules are rules. Thanks for all your help, I'm dealing with stuff pretty well. All things considered." She picked up her books.

"All things considered?"

"One never knows," she said. Then she laughed. "Oh, don't worry about me. I'm fine. What's the choice?"

During the last few sessions, she entered ready to talk about her grief. Dry-eyed, solemn, no changes of subject or digressions to trivia or laughing dance-aways.

Trying.

Yearning to understand why her mother had left her without saying good-bye. Knowing some questions could never be answered.

Asking them anyway. Why her family? Why *her?*

Had her mother even been sick? Had it all been psychosomatic, the way Dr. Manitow said it was—she'd heard him say so to Judge Manitow when the two of them didn't know she was in earshot. Judge Manitow saying, *Oh, I don't know, Bob.* He replying, *Trust me, Judy, there's nothing physically wrong with her—it's slow suicide.*

Stacy, listening from the bathroom next to the kitchen, had been angry at him, really furious, what a bastard, how could he say something like that.

But then she started wondering herself. Because the doctors never did find anything. Her father kept saying doctors don't know everything, they're not as smart as they think. Then he stopped taking her for tests, so didn't that prove that even *he* thought it might be in Mom's head? You'd think *something* would show up on *some* test. . . .

During the eleventh session, she talked about Mate.

Not angry at him, the way Dad was. The way Eric was. That's all the two of them could do when faced with something they couldn't control. Get angry at it. Big male thing, get pissed off, want to crush it.

I said, "Your father wants to crush Mate?"

"Rhetorically. He says that about anything he doesn't like—some guy trying to cheat him in a business deal, he jokes about pulverizing him, wiping him off the planet, that kind of macho BS."

"What do you think of Mate?"

"Pathetic. A loser. With or without him, Mom would have stopped being."

At the beginning of the twelfth session she announced that there was nothing left to say about her mother, she'd better start paying attention to her future. Because she'd finally decided she just might want one.

"Maybe architecture, still." Smile. "I've eliminated everything else. I'm forging straight ahead, Dr. Delaware. Setting my sights on architecture at Stanford. Everyone will be happy."

"Including you?"

"Definitely including me. No point doing anything if it doesn't bring me satisfaction. Thanks for getting me to see that."

She was ready to terminate, but I encouraged her to make another appointment. She came in the next week with brochures and the course catalog from Stanford.

Going over the architecture curriculum with me. Telling me she was pretty sure she'd made the right choice.

"If you don't mind," she said, "I'd like to come in when I apply next year. Maybe you can give me some pointers—if you do that kind of thing."

"Sure. My pleasure. And call any time something's on your mind."

"You're very nice," she said. "It was instructive to meet you."

I didn't have to ask what she meant. I was a male who wasn't her father, wasn't her brother.

CHAPTER

13

It was nearly ten P.M. when I closed the file.

Stacy had left therapy claiming she'd found direction. This morning her father had implied the transformation had been temporary. She'd promised to call but never followed through. Normal teenage flakiness? Not wanting me to view her as a failure?

Despite her declaration of independence, I'd never considered her a therapeutic triumph. You couldn't deal with what she'd been through in thirteen sessions. I suppose I'd known all along that she'd held back.

Would we really talk about college tomorrow morning?

I paged through the file again, found something in my notes of the eleventh session. My deliberately sketchy shorthand, born of too many subpoenas.

Pt. disc. fath. hostility to Mate.

That's all the two of them could do when faced with something they couldn't control. Get angry at it. Big male thing, get pissed off, want to crush it.

The phone rang.

"Dr. Delaware, this came in an hour ago," said the operator. "A Mr. Fusco, he said you can call him back anytime."

The name wasn't familiar. I asked her to spell it.

"Leimert Fusco. I thought it was Leonard but it's

Leimert." She recited a Westwood exchange. "Guess what, Doctor—he says he's with the FBI."

The Federal Building, where the FBI was head-quartered, was in Westwood, on Wilshire and Veteran. Only blocks, as a matter of fact, from Roy Haiselden's house. Something to do with that? Then why call me, not Milo?

Better to check with Milo. I figured the frustrations of the day would push him to keep going, so I tried his desk at the station. No answer there or at his home, and his cell phone didn't connect.

Unsure I was doing the right thing, I punched in Fusco's number. A deep, harsh voice—heavy shoes being dragged over rough cement—recited the usual speech: "This is Special Agent Leimert Fusco. Leave a message."

"This is Dr. Alex Delaware returning your—"

"Doctor," the same voice broke in. "Thanks for getting back so quickly."

"What can I do for you?"

"I've been assigned to look into a police case you're currently working on."

"Which case is that?"

Laughter. "How many police cases are you working on? Don't worry, Doctor, I'm aware of your allegiance to Detective Sturgis, have cleared it with him. He and I will be meeting soon, he wasn't sure whether or not you'd be able to make it. So I thought I'd touch base with you personally, just to see if you've got any information you'd like to share with the Bureau. Psychological insights. By the way, I'm trained as a psychologist."

"I see." I didn't. "The little I know I've told Detective Sturgis."

"Yes," said Fusco. "He as much as said so."

Silence.

He said, "Well, thanks anyway. It's a tough one, isn't it?"

"Looks to be."

"Guess we've all got our work cut out for us. Thanks for calling back."

"Sure," I said.

"You know, Doctor, we do have some expertise in this area. The Bureau."

"What area, specifically?"

"Psychopathic killings. Homicides with psychosexual overtones. Our data banks are pretty impressive."

"Great," I said. "Hope you come up with something."

"Hope so, too. Bye now."

Click.

I sat there feeling like an unwitting character in a candid video.

Something about him . . . I called information and asked for the FBI number. Same prefix Fusco had given, so his number was probably an extension. A female recorded voice said no one was in this late. Rust never sleeps, but the government does.

I tried Milo, again, no success.

Fusco's call bothered me. Too brief. Pointless. As if he'd been checking me out.

Knowing I was being paranoid, I got up, checked all the doors and windows, set the alarm. When I got to the bedroom, Robin was in bed reading, and I slid in beside her. She had on one of my T-shirts and nothing else and I stroked her flank.

"You've been industrious," she said.

"Midwestern work ethic." I reached up under the T-shirt, felt the orange peel of goose bumps between her shoulder blades.

She yawned. "Ready to sleep?"

"I don't know."

She mussed my hair. "Another rough night in store?"

"Hope not."

"You're sure you don't want to try to sleep?"

"In a while," I said. "I promise."

"Well, I've got to nighty-night."

She turned off the light, we kissed, and she rolled away. I got up, closed the bedroom door after me, padded to the kitchen and made some green tea. From his bed in the service porch, Spike played a prolonged snore solo.

I sipped the tea and tried to forget everything. Normally, I like the stuff. Tonight it reminded me of sushi bars minus the food, which is kind of like a concert hall without the music. I reminded myself that it was the only herbal substance proven to the satisfaction of whizbang white-coats to be good for you, crammed as it is with antioxidants. And with all life throws at you, why oxidize needlessly?

When I finished the cup, I gave Milo one last try, reversing the order: cell phone first, then home, then the station. Superstition paid off; he picked up in the detective's room.

"Where've you been?" I said, realizing I sounded like a peeved parent.

"Right here. Why? What's wrong?"

"I just called a few minutes ago and they said you were gone."

"Gone upstairs. The lieutenant's office. Not Mate, bureaucratic BS, seems my poor little baby detectives are unhappy. Insufficiently challenged by their assignment to Homicide. Like I'm running a kindergarten."

"No success finding Haiselden?"

"Rub it in," he said. "Some therapist you are. Locked

office, the landlord's some Chinese guy, barely speaks English, Haiselden's rent isn't due for another two weeks, so what does he care? I guess I should go back to his house, try to find out who does his gardening. . . . Normally, I'd send Korn and Demetri to do it, but all their bitching means I have to be careful."

"You're on the defensive? Thought LAPD was paramilitary."

"More like day care, nowadays. Did you know you can get into the Academy now with prior drug arrests as long as they're not *too* serious. Cokehead cops. Reassuring, huh? Anyway, what's up?"

I told him about Fusco's call.

"Yeah, the grand voice of the federal government. He's got a PhD, I figured he might call you."

"I didn't want to talk to him without clearing it with you. Not that I have anything to tell him."

"Oh," he said. "Yeah, of course. Sorry I didn't tell you it was okay. He's originally from Virginia, big-time pooh-bah from their Behavioral Science Unit. Looks like my call to VICAP triggered something."

"What's he offering?"

"A powwow. I figure what he really wants is to pick my brain—little does he know what a waste that'll be. If the case is hopeless, he bugs out. If I'm onto something, he jumps aboard, sees if he can claim some credit. . . . He faxed a charming note: *Anything I can do, blah blah blah . . . Lem. Assistant Deputy Director, Behavioral Science,* hoo-ha."

"He said you'd be meeting with him soon."

"He wanted tomorrow, I put him off, said I'd be in touch. Gonna keep putting him off, unless the bosses order me to waste time. Or do you think I should be open-minded?"

"Not so open your brain falls out."

"That's already happened. . . . If we do meet, it's gonna be at his expense. Two-pound steaks, hyperthyroid potatoes at the Dining Car or The Palm—I'm making myself hungry. I work three months out of the year to pay the IRS. Let the Bureau pick up the tab for my cholesterol. Anything else?"

"Still planning on seeing Mr. Doss tomorrow?"

"Eleven A.M., his office. Why?"

"How 'bout that," I said. "Eleven's when I'm due to see Stacy."

"There you go," he said. "Synchronicity—something you want to tell me about Daddy?"

"Nope."

"Okay, then, happy therapy, I'm heading home. If I fall asleep at the wheel, you can have my pencil box."

"Take care of yourself," I said.

"Sure, I always do. Sweet dreams, Professor."

"Same to you."

"I don't dream, Alex. Against department regulations."

CHAPTER

14

ELEVEN A.M. TUESDAY. Sun and heat and clarity, an unseasonably beautiful morning. The weather didn't matter much. I'd been waiting in my office for half an hour, no sign of Stacy.

I cleared some paperwork, phoned Pali Prep. The secretary knew my name because I'd treated other students. Yes, Stacy had been excused from class. Two hours ago. I tried the Doss home, no answer. No cancellation message left at my service. I wanted to call Richard's office, but with teenagers you had to be careful not to breach trust, especially when dealing with a parent like Richard.

Also, Milo was with Richard, and that complicated matters.

Ten more minutes and now the session time was gone. Your basic no-show. Happened all the time. It had never happened with Stacy. But I hadn't seen Stacy in half a year, and six months was a long stretch of adolescence. Maybe seeing me had been her father's idea and she'd finally stood up to him.

Or perhaps Mate's death had something to do with it, churning up memories that reminded her what could happen to a woman who allowed herself not to *be*.

I filed the chart, expecting a phone call from one Doss or the other by day's end.

But it was Milo who cleared things up.

He showed up at my house just after one P.M.

"Had a quiet morning, huh?" He walked past me and entered the kitchen. My fridge is an old friend of his, and he greeted it with a small smile, removing a half-gallon of milk and a ripe peach. Looking inside the carton, he muttered, "Not much left, why bother with a glass."

He brought the milk to the table, upended the carton, gulped, wiped his mouth, assaulted the peach as if exacting revenge on all fruit.

"No session with little Ms. Doss," he said. "Swami Milo knows because Ms. Doss came over to Daddy's office right around the time she was supposed to be with you. Right when I'd started talking to Daddy. Something about her brother. Looks like he's run away."

"From Stanford?"

"From Stanford. Doss moved my eleven up to ten and I'd just gotten into his sanctum sanctorum—ever been there?"

I shook my head.

"Penthouse suite with an ocean view, executive trappings plus your basic private museum. Antiques, paintings, but mostly walls of Oriental breakables—hundreds of bowls, vases, statues, little incense burners, whatever. These glass shelves that make it look as if everything's floating. Had me worried about breathing too hard, but maybe that's the point. Maybe throwing me off balance is why he changed the time. He left the message at midnight, it was only by luck that I got it. I figure the plan was I wouldn't, would show up at eleven, and he'd tell me aw shucks. Anyway, I made it, waited, finally got ushered in, Doss is sitting behind this ultrawide desk, so big that I've got to reach over and kill my back to shake his hand—the guy thinks everything out, doesn't he, Alex?"

I remembered my stretch for the photos. "So what happened?"

"My butt's just hitting the chair and his intercom burps. 'Stacy's here.' *That* throws *Doss*. Before he puts down the phone, the kid runs in, like she's about to blurt something to Daddy. Then she sees me, gives Daddy one of those we-have-to-talk-in-private looks, Doss asks me to please leave for a second. I head back for the waiting room, but the secretary's on the phone, has her back to me, so I keep the door open a crack, I know it's naughty, but . . ."

Detective's grin, ripe with suspicion and worst-case glee.

"Mostly what I heard was a helluva lot of anxiety. A few 'Stanford's, bunch of 'Eric's, so I knew it had something to do with her brother. Then Doss starts asking her questions—'When?' 'How?' 'You're sure?' Like what's going on is her fault. At that point, the secretary gets off the phone, turns around, shoots me a murderous look and closes the door. I wait out there another ten minutes."

He chomped the peach, ripping golden flesh away from the pit. Went for the milk, holding the spout inches from his mouth. White liquid arced down his gullet. His throat muscles pulsed. Lowering the empty carton, he crushed it, said, "Ahhh, does a body good."

"What else?" I said.

"A few minutes later, Stacy comes out looking very uptight and leaves. Then Doss emerges, tells me he can't talk, family emergency. I do the old protect-and-serve: Any way I can be of service, sir? Doss looks at me like, Who are you kidding, moron. Then he tells me to make another appointment with the secretary, goes back inside the Porcelain Palace. The secretary looks at her book, says, Nothing tomorrow, how about Thursday? I say fine. When I'm back down in the parking garage, I ask the attendant to show me Doss's car. Black-on-black BMW 850i, chrome wheels, illegally tinted windows, custom spoiler. Shiniest damn thing I've ever seen, like he dipped it in glass. There's only one exit from the garage, so I wait down the block. But Doss never comes out, so whatever the problem is, he's handling it by phone. One thing I did think of, though: a dark BMW. What Paul Ulrich saw parked on the road the morning of Mate's murder."

"Lots of those on the Westside."

"True." Jumping up, he made it back to the fridge with two giant steps, grabbed a new quart of orange juice, popped the seal, began gulping. "But I'm still curious, so I call Stanford, locate Eric's dorm, talk to his roommate, some kid named Chad Soo. What I manage to get out of him is that Eric was looking real depressed for a few days, then he didn't come back to his room for a couple of days after that."

"When?"

"Yesterday, but Chad didn't call till this morning. Didn't want to get Eric in trouble, but Eric had a big test he didn't show up for and that wasn't like Eric, so after the second day he thought maybe he should tell someone. He called the house, talked to Stacy."

"He told you all this?"

"He was under the misconception that I was Palo Alto PD. So how come the kid gets depressed now, Alex? Nine months since his mother dies, but a week after Mate gets killed?"

"Mate's death could've brought up memories," I said.

"Yeah, well . . . that's how I knew your morning was gonna be quiet. So Stacy never called?"

"I'm sure she will when things settle down."

He drank more juice. I said, "Regarding the BMW, Ulrich said he saw a smaller model, like his."

"Yes, he did."

I got up. "I'm going to try to reach Stacy. From my office."

"Meaning I'm kicked out."

"Meaning feel free to stay in the kitchen."

"Fine," he said. "I'll wait."

"Why?"

"Something about this family bugs me."

"What?"

"Too secretive, too evasive. Doss has no reason to play games with me unless he's got something to hide."

I headed for the office. He called out, "Make sure you close the door all the way."

Richard's secretary used her boss's very busy schedule as a weapon: the chance of talking to him today was less probable than the sudden achievement of world peace.

"I'm calling about Stacy," I said. "Any idea where she might be?"

"Is there a problem, sir?"

"She didn't show up for her appointment at eleven," I said.

"Oh?" But she didn't sound surprised. "Well, I'm sure there's an explanation. . . . May I assume you'll be billing us anyway, Doctor?"

"That's not the issue. I want to make sure everything's okay."

"Oh . . . I see. Well, as I said, Mr. D.'s not here now.

But I did see Stacy a while back and she's fine. She didn't mention the appointment."

"Richard made it. Perhaps he forgot to tell her. Please have him call me."

"I'll give him the message, sir, but he's traveling on business."

"Business as usual?" I said.

Pause. "We will honor your bill, Dr. Delaware. Bye now."

Returning to the kitchen, I found myself hoping something—a sudden lead, anything—had spirited Milo away and I wouldn't have to wear my calm mask. But he was still sitting at the table, finishing the juice, looking too damn smug for someone working a whodunit with no clues.

"Bellyful of double-talk?" he said.

I shrugged. "So what's next?"

"More of the same, I guess. . . . Doss is an interesting one. Little man behind a gigantic desk, his chair's elevated on some kind of pedestal. I'll bet he's one of those guys who believes intimidation is the ultimate orgasm. The power of positive domination. Yeah, I've definitely got to take a closer look at him."

"What about Roy Haiselden and Donny Mate?"

"Still looking for them, too. I lucked out and found Haiselden's gardener mowing the lawn. Haiselden didn't tell him to stop showing up."

"Keeping up appearances," I said.

"The utilities are also still on. Only the mail's been cut off. Waiting in the Westwood branch, general delivery. And Alice Z. was telling the truth about Haiselden being into laundromats. He's the registered owner of six, mostly on the Eastside—El Monte, Artesia, Pasadena."

"Collecting coins can be a dangerous business. Did he do it himself?"

"Don't know yet. All I've got is his business registration. Roy Haiselden d.b.a. Kleen-U-Up, Inc. As far as Donny Mate goes, there was no parole, he served his full sentence, was let straight out. Petra's asking about him. Thanks for brunch."

His hand landed on my shoulder. Lightly, very lightly, then he began to leave.

"Happy hunting," I said.

"I'm always happy when hunting."

CHAPTER
15

STACY'S CALL CAME at four P.M. The connection was grainy and I wondered where she was. Had Richard given her her own little silver phone?

"Sorry for the inconvenience," she said, not sounding apologetic at all. Cool. The detachment was back.

"What happened, Stacy?"

"Don't you already know?" From cool to cold.

"Eric," I said.

"So my father was right."

"About what?"

"The cop who was here to talk to him. My father said he's your friend. He informs you, you inform him. Didn't you think that would be a *problem*, Dr. Delaware?"

"Stacy, I spoke to your father about that and he—"

"You didn't speak to *me* about it."

"We haven't spoken at all. I was planning to bring it up when you arrived."

"And if I told you I didn't like it?"

"Then I'd drop off the Mate investigation. That's exactly what I planned to do until your father asked me not to. He wanted me to continue."

"Why would he want that?"

"You'd have to ask him, Stacy."

"He told you to continue?"

"In no uncertain terms. Stacy, if it's a matter of trust—"

"I don't get it," she said. "When he told me about the cop, he seemed angry."

"At something Detective Sturgis did?"

"At being questioned like a criminal. And he's right. After all we went through with my mother, to be harassed by the police. And now I find out *you're* working *with* them. It just seems . . . wrong."

"Then I'm off the investigation."

"No," she said. "Don't bother."

"You're my patient, you come first."

Pause. "That's the other thing. I'm not sure I want to be your patient—nothing to do with you. I just don't see why I need therapy again."

"So the appointment was all your father's idea?"

"Same as all the other appointments—no, I don't mean that. Before, once I got into it, it was good. Great. You helped me. I'm coming across so rude, I'm sorry. I just don't see that I need any more help."

"Maybe not," I said. "But can we at least sit down once to discuss it? I've got time right now if you can make it over."

"I—I don't know. Things are pretty intense—what exactly did your cop friend tell you about Eric?"

"That Eric hadn't returned to his dorm for a couple of days. That he'd missed a test."

"More like a day and a half," she said. "It's probably no big deal, he was always going off on his own."

"Back when he was living at home?"

"Back to ninth or tenth grade. He'd cut school without explanation, take his bike somewhere, disappear all day. Later, he told me he used to check out used-book stores, play pool on the pier, or go over to the Santa Monica courts and listen to trials. The school used to phone, but Eric always got away with it because his grades were so much higher than anyone else's. Once he got his driver's license, he'd go away overnight, not come home till morning. *That* got to my father. Waking up in the morning and finding Eric's bed still made and Eric gone. Then Eric would drive up at breakfast time, start toasting Pop-Tarts, and the two of them would get into hassles, my father demanding to know where Eric had been, Eric refusing to say."

"Did your mother get involved?"

"When she was still healthy, she'd take my father's side. But Dad's always been the main one."

"Was Eric ever punished?"

"Dad made threats—kept warning he'd take away Eric's car keys, but Eric shined him on. Everyone knew he wouldn't follow through."

"Why not?"

"Because Eric's his golden boy. Any time Dad complains about him, all Eric has to say is, 'What? Aren't straight A's good enough? Want me to get higher than sixteen hundred on the SAT?' Same for Pali Prep. He was their big advertisement. Perfect GPA, Bank of America Award winner, National Merit Scholar, Prudential Life Scholar, Science Achievement winner, hockey team, fencing team, baseball team. When he interviewed for Stanford, the interviewer called our headmaster and told him he'd just encountered one of the great minds of the century. So why would they want to tick him off?"

"So you're not worried about him," I said.

"Not really . . . The only thing that does bother me is his missing an exam. Eric always took care of business, academically speaking. . . . Maybe he just decided to hike."

"Hike?"

"Back when he was living at home and stayed out all night, he'd sometimes come home with mud on his shoes, looking pretty dusty. At least one time I'm sure he was out camping. This was maybe a year ago, when he was home taking care of Mom. Our rooms are next to each other, and when he came in I woke up, went to see what was going on. He was folding up this nylon tent, had this backpack, bag of potato chips and candy, pepperoni sticks, whatever. I said, 'What's all this, some kind of loner-loser picnic?' He got angry and kicked me out of his room. So maybe that's what he did last night—went out hiking. There are lots of nice places around Palo Alto. Maybe he just wanted to get away from the city lights so he could look up at the stars. He used to love astronomy, had his own telescope, all these expensive filters, the works."

I heard her breath catch.

"What is it, Stacy?"

"I was just thinking . . . We had a dog, this yellow mutt named Helen that we got from the pound. Eric would take her with him on long walks, then she got old and lost the use of her legs and he built her a little wagon thingie and pulled her around—pretty funny-looking, but he took it seriously. She died—a year before Mom. Eric stayed out all night with her. That's got to be what happened. When I asked him about it, he said he did his best thinking late at night, up in the mountains. So that's probably it, he's a little stressed, decided to try that. As far as the test, he probably figured he could talk his professor into a makeup—Eric can talk his way into anything."

"Why's he stressed?"

"I don't know." Long silence. "Okay, to be honest, Eric's having a *real* hard time. With Mom. He had a terrible time with it right from the beginning. Took it much worse than I did. Bet that's not what my father told you, though. Right?"

My son deals with his anger by organizing. . . . I think it's a great way of handling stress. . . . Get in touch with how you feel, then move on.

"We didn't discuss Eric in detail," I said.

"But I know," she said. "Dad thinks I'm the screwed-up one. Because I get low, while Eric does a great job of looking okay on the surface—keeping up his grades, staying achievement-oriented, saying the right things to my father. But I can see through that. *He's* the one who took it really hard. By the time my mother died, I'd already done my years of crying, but Eric kept trying to pretend nothing was wrong. Saying she'd get better. Sitting with Mom, playing cards with her. Acting happy, like nothing was any big deal. Like she just had a cold. I don't think he ever dealt with it. Maybe hearing about Dr. Mate brought the memories back."

"Did Eric talk about Mate?"

"No. We haven't talked at all, not for weeks. Sometimes he e-mails me, but I haven't heard from him in a while. . . . One time—toward the end of my mother's . . . a few days before she died, Eric came into my room and found me crying, asked what was the matter. I said I was sad about Mom and he just *lost* it, started screaming that I was stupid, a wimp and a loser, that falling apart would accomplish nothing, I shouldn't be so selfish, thinking about my own feelings—*wallowing* in my feelings was the phrase he used. It was Mom's feelings I should be concentrating on. We all needed to be positive. To never give up."

"He was tough on you," I said.

"No big deal. He yells at me all the time, that's his

style. Basically, he's this big huge brain machine with the emotions of a little kid. So maybe he's having some sort of delayed reaction, doing what he used to do when he got uptight. Do you think I *should* be worried about him?"

"No, but I think you did exactly the right thing by calling your father."

"Walking in on that detective . . . Guess what my father did? Chartered a plane and flew up to Palo Alto. He looked worried. And *that* bothers me."

"He doesn't get worried too often?"

"Never. He says anxiety is the province of fools."

I thought: The lack of anxiety is the province of psychopaths. Said, "So you're alone in the house."

"Just for a couple of days. I'm used to it, my father travels all the time. And Gisella—the maid—comes every day."

The phone cut in and out during the last sentence.

"Where are you, Stacy?"

"At the beach, some big parking lot on PCH. I must have driven here from Dad's office." She laughed. "Don't even remember. *That's* weird."

"Which beach?" I said.

"Um, let's see . . . There's a sign over there, says . . . Topanga . . . Topanga Beach. Kind of pretty out here, Dr. Delaware. Plenty of traffic on the highway, but no one on the sand—except for one guy walking around near the tide line . . . seems to be looking for something . . . he's holding some kind of a machine . . . looks like a metal detector . . . I know this place, you can see it from Dad's office."

Her voice had softened, turned dreamy.

"Stay right there, Stacy. I can be there in twenty, twenty-five minutes."

"There's no need," she said. It sounded like a policy statement.

"Humor me, Stacy."

Silence. Crackle. For a moment I thought I'd lost her. Then: "Sure. Why not? Got nowhere else to go."

I drove too fast, thinking about Eric. A brilliant, impetuous loner, used to getting his way. The one person who seemed able to elude Richard's dominance. Working hard at maintaining control, but powerless over what had mattered most: his mother's survival.

Close to his father, and his father despised Mate, expressed his hatred openly.

Eric. A hiker who disappeared when he wanted to, liked the mountains, knew the terrain. Dark, hidden places, like the dirt road stretch of Mulholland.

Impetuous enough to get violent? Smart enough to clean up thoroughly?

How far had filial devotion taken him?

After Joanne's death, Richard had tried to contact Mate, but the death doctor hadn't called back. Had Joanne warned Mate about Richard? Knowing Richard would fight her decision—that's why she'd kept it from him. From her children, as well.

But what if Mate *had* answered a call from Eric?

Poor, distraught kid wanting to talk about his mother's final passage. Had there been enough of the physician left in Mate to respond to a cry for help?

Dark BMW parked down the road.

Borrowing Daddy's car . . .

I kept racing west on Sunset, turning it over and over. Pure speculation, I'd never breathe a word to Milo or anyone else, but there was nothing that *didn't* fit.

A red light at Mandeville Canyon stopped the Seville, but my mind kept revving.

Stacy had offered a sibling's eloquence: a big brain machine combined with emotional immaturity.

Combined with boiling, adolescent rage. Perfect for the meld of compulsive planning and reckless daring that had transformed the brown van into a charnel house on wheels.

Broken stethoscope . . . *Beowulf. Happy Traveling, You Sick Bastard.*

Slaying the monster, as if it were just another myth—just another video game.

There was an adolescent feel to the phony book. To sneaking into Mate's flat and leaving a note. The message itself. Primitive gamesmanship, but backed up by an intellect that was starting to scare the hell out of me.

Where had Eric been last Sunday? The trip from Stanford to L.A. was no big deal, shuttles from San Francisco ran all day. Easy enough for a college student with a credit card. Do your business, jet back to school, show up for class as if nothing had happened.

But now the perfect student had missed a test for the first time. Unable to run from what he'd done? Or had some other stress worked apart the fissures that had spidered their way across the perfect porcelain image of the Doss family?

Richard jetting up to Stanford, leaving Stacy alone, sitting at the beach, oblivious . . . I sensed she'd always been alone. Squeakless wheel not getting any grease.

A car horn honked. The light had turned green but I'd sat there—obliviousness was contagious.

I shot forward, warning myself not to get caught up in it. Not good for the soul, all this hypothesizing. Besides, Milo had other suspects.

Roy Haiselden. Donny Mate.

Richard Doss.

None of the above? None of my business. Time to concentrate on what the state said I was qualified to do.

Stacy was easy to spot. Little white Mustang coupe facing the water, one of the few cars stationed in the city lot that paralleled the beach. Low tide, miles of beige kissing Wedgwood-blue water, all of it topped by the same clear sky as inland. The ocean was pretty but roiling. As I hooked across the highway and pulled onto the asphalt beside her, I saw the man with the metal detector, a hundred feet past Stacy's car, knees bent, hunched over a find.

Stacy's windows were closed. As I got out of the Seville, the driver's panel rolled down. She glanced at me, both hands on the steering wheel. Her face was thinner than six months ago. Deepened hollows around the cheeks, darkened flesh beneath the eyes, a few more pimples. No makeup. Her black hair was tied back in a ponytail, bound by a red rubber band.

"Didn't know doctors still did house calls." Weak smile. "Beach calls. I must have sounded pretty screwed up for you to drive all the way here. I'm sorry."

The man with the metal detector straightened, turned and faced us. As if he could hear our conversation. But of course he couldn't. Too far away and the ocean was roaring.

Before I could answer, Stacy said, "Why'd you come, Dr. Delaware? Especially after I snotted off to you like that."

"I wanted to make sure you were okay."

"You thought I'd do something stupid?"

"No," I said. "You sounded worried about Eric.

You're by yourself. If there's some way I can help, I want to."

Her eyes faced forward and her hands whitened around the wheel. "That's . . . very sweet, but I'm fine. . . . No, I'm not. I'm screwed up, aren't I? Even our dog was screwed up."

"Helen."

She nodded. "Two legs that couldn't move, and Eric pulled her around. That's why you drove all the way—you think I'm cracking up."

"No," I said. "I think you've got good insights."

She whipped around, stared at me. Laughed. "Maybe I should be a psychologist, then. Like Becky—not that she'd ever get to be one. Talk is, she's barely passing. That's got to be making Dr. Manitow and the judge real happy. . . ."

"You sound angry at them," I said.

"I do? No, not at all. I'm a little resentful of *Becky*, turning into a total snob, never even saying hello. Maybe she's getting back at me for Eric. He and Allison Manitow were dating and Eric dumped her . . . but that was a long time ago. . . . Why am I talking about this?"

"Maybe it's on your mind."

"No it's not. Helen is. After I told you about her on the phone, I started thinking about her." Laughter. "She had to be the dumbest mutt ever put on this earth, Dr. Delaware. Thirteen years old and she was never completely housebroken. When you gave her a command, she just sat there and stared at you with her tongue hanging out. Eric called her the Ultimate Canine Moron Alien from the Vortex of Idiocy. She used to jump on him and paw him and lick him and he'd say, Get a brain, bitch. But he ended up feeding her, walking her, cleaning up her poop. 'Cause Dad was too busy and Mom was too passive. . . . That stupid little wagon he rigged up, it kept her alive. My father wanted to put her to sleep, but Eric wouldn't hear of it. Eventually, even with the wagon, she started failing. Toward the end, he was carrying her outside to poop, cursing the whole time. Then one night, he took her with him on one of his overnights. She looked awful—rotting gums, her hair was falling out in clumps. Even so, when Eric wheeled her out she looked thrilled—like, Oh boy, another adventure. They were out all night. The next morning Eric came home by himself."

She turned to me. "No one talked about it. A few weeks later, Mom died."

Her fingers snapped away from the steering wheel, as if shoved by an unseen demon, flew to her face, grabbing, concealing. She bent forward, touched her brow to the steering wheel. The ponytail bounced, black curls fibrillating. She shook like a wet puppy, and when she cried out the ocean blocked nearly all the sound. The man with the metal detector had moved fifty yards up the beach, back in his own world, hunched, probing.

When I reached through the window and placed a hand on Stacy's shoulder, she shivered, as if repulsed, and I withdrew.

All those years listening to people in pain and I can do it like a pro, but I've never stopped hating it. I stood there and waited as she sobbed and shuddered, voice tightening and rising in pitch until she was letting out the raw keen of a startled gull.

Then she stopped shaking, went silent. Her hands flipped upward, like visors, exposing her face, but she kept her head low, mumbled at the steering wheel.

I bent forward, heard her say, "Disappearing."

"What is?"

She shut her eyes, opened them, turned toward me. Heavy, labored movements.

"What?" she said sleepily.

"What's disappearing, Stacy?"

She gave a casual shrug. "Everything."

I didn't like the sound of her laughter.

Eventually, I convinced her to get out of the car and we strolled north on the asphalt, following the shoreline, not talking. The man with the metal detector was a pulsating speck.

"Buried treasure," she said. "That guy believes in it. I saw him up close, he's got to be seventy, but he's digging for nickels—Listen, I'm sorry for making you come all the way out here. Sorry for being bratty over the phone. For hassling you because you're working with the cops. You're entitled to do whatever work you want."

"It had to be confusing," I said. "Your father okayed it, but he didn't tell you. If he changed his mind, he didn't tell me."

"I don't know that he did. He was just getting peevy because the cop came to question him and he doesn't like not being in charge."

"Still," I said, "I think it's best that I drop off the—"

"No," she said. "Don't do it on my account. I don't care—it really doesn't matter. Who am I to take away your income?"

"It's no big deal, Stacy—"

"No. I insist. Someone killed that man and we should be doing everything we can to find out who it was."

We.

"For justice," she said. "For society's sake. No matter who he was. People can't get away with that kind of thing."

"How do you feel about Dr. Mate?"

"Don't feel much, one way or the other. Dr. Delaware, all those other times we talked, I was never really honest with you. Never talked about how screwed up our family is. But we are—no one really communicates. It's like we live together—exist together. But we don't . . . connect."

"Since your mother got sick?"

"Even before then. When I was young and she was healthy, we must have had fun together, but I don't remember. I'm not saying she wasn't a good mother. She did all the right things. But I never felt she . . . I don't know, it's hard to express. It's like she was made of air— you couldn't get hold of it. . . . I just can't resolve what she did, Dr. Delaware. My dad and Eric blamed Mate, it was this big topic in our house, what a monster he was. But that's not true, they just can't deal with the truth: it was *her* decision, wasn't it?"

Turning to me. Wanting a real answer, not therapeutic reflection.

"Ultimately it was," I said.

"Mate was just the vehicle—she could have chosen anyone. She left because she just didn't care enough to keep trying. She made a *decision* to leave us, without saying good-bye."

Snapping her arms across her bust, she drew her shoulders forward, as if bound by the straps on a straitjacket.

"Of course," she said, "there was the pain, but . . ." She chewed her lip. Shook her head.

"But what?" I said.

"With all that pain, she kept eating—she used to have such a good figure. That was always a big thing in the house—her figure, my father's physique. They both used to wear the skimpiest bathing suits. It was embarrassing. I remember once, the Manitows were over for a swim party and Mom and Dad were in the pool . . . groping each other. And Dr. Manitow was just staring. Like, how tasteless—I guess that was good, though. Right? The fact that they were attracted to each other. My father would always talk about how they didn't age as quickly as everyone else, they'd always be kids. And then Mom just . . . *inflated* herself."

She took a step, put her foot down heavily, stopped again, fought back tears. "What's the use of going on and on about it? She did it, it's over, whatever. . . . I have to keep thinking of the good memories, don't I? Because she *was* a good mother. . . . I know that."

She edged closer to me. "Everyone talks about getting closure, moving on. But where do I go *to*, Dr. Delaware?"

"That's what we need to find out. That's why I'm here."

"Yes. You are." She surged forward, threw her arms around me. Her hands dug into my coat. Curly, shampooed hair—too-sweet shampoo, heavy with apricots—tickled my nose.

Someone watching from a distance would have thought, Romance on the beach.

The professional thing would be to pull away. I compromised, avoiding a full embrace by keeping one arm at my side. Patting her back lightly with the other.

What used to be called therapeutic touch, before the lawyers got involved.

I held her for the shortest possible period, then gently drew away.

She smiled. We resumed walking. Walked in step. I kept enough distance between us to avoid the accidental graze of hand against hand.

"College," she said, laughing. "That's what we were supposed to be talking about this morning."

"College isn't all of your future, but it's part of it," I said. "Part of where to *go*."

"A small part. So no big deal, I'll make Dad happy, apply to Stanford. If I get in, I'll go. Why not? One place is the same as another. I'm not some spoiled brat. I know I'm lucky my dad can afford a place like that. But there are other things we need to talk about, right? If you trust me not to flake out, I can come in tomorrow—if you've got time."

"I've got time. How about after school—five P.M."

"Yes," she said. "Thank you so, so much. . . . I'd better get back home, see if Dad called, maybe he found Eric—he'll probably just blow into the dorm and scream at my father for flying up."

We turned around.

Back at the Mustang, she said, "And I meant what I said—please don't stop working with the cops. Take care of *yourself*."

Nice kid.

I watched her drive away, eased onto PCH feeling pretty good.

CHAPTER

16

WHEN I GOT home, Robin was in the kitchen stirring a pot—one of those big blue things flecked with white. Spike was off in a corner, making rapturous overtures to a delicious-looking bone.

"You look tired," she said.

"Bad traffic." I kissed her cheek and looked inside the pot. Chunks of lamb, carrots, prunes, onions. My nose filled with cumin and cinnamon and heat, and my eyes watered.

"Something new," she said. "A tajine. Got the recipe from the guy who sells me maple."

I dipped the spoon, blew, tasted. "Fantastic, thank you, thank you, thank you."

"Hungry?"

"Starving."

"No sleep, no food." She sighed. "Bad traffic, where?"

I told her about having to meet a patient at the beach.

"Emergency?"

"Potentially, but it resolved." I placed my arms under her rear, lifted her, deposited her on the counter.

"What is this?" she said. "Passion amid the pots and pans, one of those male-fantasy things?"

"Maybe later. If you behave yourself." I went to the

fridge, found some leftover white wine, sniffed the bottle, poured two glasses. "First we celebrate."

"What's the occasion?"

"No occasion," I said. "That's the point."

The rest of the evening passed quietly. No calls from Milo or anyone else. I tried to imagine what life would be like without a phone. We ate too much lamb, drank enough wine to get silly. The idea of making love seemed remote, more of a scripted segment than passion; both of us seemed content just to be.

So we just sat on the couch, holding hands, not moving, not talking. Would it be like this when we grew old? That prospect seemed suddenly glorious.

Eventually, something changed in the air, and we began touching each other, stroking, kissing, risking exploration. Eventually, we were naked, intertwined, moving from the couch to the floor, enduring chafed knees and elbows, strained muscles, ridiculous postures.

We ended up in bed. Afterward, Robin showered off, then announced she was going to do a bit of carving, did I mind?

After she left for the studio, I slouched in my big leather chair reading journals, Hawaiian slack-key guitar music droning in the background. For a while I did a pretty good job of forgetting. Then I was thinking about Stacy again. Eric. Richard. The deterioration of Joanne Doss.

I considered calling Judy Manitow, tomorrow, to find out if she'd come up with any new insights since the original referral. Bad idea. Stacy might find that intrusive. And Stacy had told me enough for me to see that the Dosses and the Manitows had been entangled beyond mere neighborliness. Joanne tutoring Becky, Eric dumping Allison, Becky and Stacy drifting apart.

Bob regarding Richard and Joanne's displays of affection with distaste.

Judy and Bob, dealing with Becky's problems. Yet they'd cared enough about Stacy to pressure Richard to contact me.

Me, not Becky's therapist, because they'd been guarding their privacy—keeping Stacy's issues at arm's length from Becky's? Or had it been Becky's choice—Stacy had just told me Becky had distanced herself, barely spoke to her. Whatever the details, it was best to avoid further complications.

I got up and poured a finger of Chivas. Added to the wine, that put me way past my usual alcohol consumption. Some Hawaiian virtuoso let forth a glissando in C-wahine tuning and I thought about palm trees.

I finished the scotch and had another.

On Wednesday morning, I woke up with a well-deserved headache, an agreeably moldy tongue, sandpaper eyes. Robin was already out in back. I couldn't smell the coffee she'd put on.

I took a one-minute shower and got dressed without falling over, looked for the morning paper. Robin had been so eager to work that she hadn't taken it in. I went outside and retrieved it.

The front page screamed at me.

The Mysterious Portrait of Dr. Death

Sudden Appearance of Painting Raises
New Questions About Eldon Mate's Murder

SANTA MONICA. When Grant Kugler, owner of the Primal Images art gallery on Colorado Avenue, showed up last night to unpack an installation, he

found a surprise donation propped against the rear
door. A package, wrapped in brown paper, containing an original, unsigned oil painting described
as a copy of Rembrandt's "The Anatomy Lesson."
Only this version deviated from the original in that
it depicted murdered "death doctor" Eldon Mate in
a double role, as dissector and cadaver.

"Not the work of a master," opined Kugler. "I'd
rate it competent. Why it ended up at my door,
I can't say. I'm not one for representational art,
though I can be amused by social commentary."

The article went on to quote "police sources who
spoke on condition of not being named," and attested to
"intriguing similarities between the painting and details
of the Eldon Mate crime scene, raising questions about
the identity of the artist and the motivations for aban-
doning the portrait. The picture has been taken into
custody."

That conjured images of burly men trying to figure out
a way of handcuffing the frame. I wondered how long it
would take Milo to get in touch. I'd finished half a cup of
coffee when the phone screeched.

"I assume you read," he said.

"Sounds like Zero Tollrance is in town."

"Tried to do some follow-up on that Colorado article
you gave me. No one knows Tollrance, there was no
lease on the building he used for his show because he
was squatting in it, one of those big industrial shells full
of lowlifes. I don't know if Tollrance was even living
there. Denver PD never heard of him, and the critic who
wrote up the show doesn't remember much other than
Tollrance looked like a bum and didn't answer his
questions—didn't talk at all, just pointed to his canvases

and stomped away. He figured him for a nut. That's why he called it 'outsider art.' "

"A bum."

"Long hair and a beard. Mr. Critic said he had some 'primitive talent.' Said the same thing the gallery owner did—representation's not his thing. Which I guess means in the art world, if you know how to draw, you suck."

"So why'd he go to Tollrance's show?"

"Cuuuuurious. *Intriiiiigued.* Couldn't even get out of him how he found out about the show. Maybe Tollrance faxed him an announcement, maybe not. He said there hadn't been much of a crowd, no one buying. He never heard from Tollrance again, has no idea what happened to the paintings."

"Well, we know where one is," I said. "A bearded bum could be the same guy Mrs. Krohnfeld chased away. Could be Donny Salcido Mate."

"It crossed my mind," he said.

"Any idea where Donny was at the time of the show?"

"No, but it wasn't prison. He didn't get busted till four months later."

"His mother said by then he was living on the street," I said. "He could've drifted east, ended up in Colorado, found himself a vacant building to pursue his art. Funny, his mother never mentioned any talent. Then again, she didn't want to talk about him at all."

"I called her at the motel. She checked out yesterday. You're thinking Donny painted Daddy getting sliced up, then maybe decided to act it out?"

"The paintings could've been yet another attempt to establish a bond with Daddy. Selling *himself.* Maybe he tried to show off to Mate and got rebuffed again."

"Why deliver the painting to the gallery?"

"He's an artist. He wants recognition. And look at the

painting he delivered. All the others were straight portraits of Mate. *The Anatomy Lesson* put Mate on the dissecting table."

"*Look what I did to Daddy.* Showing off."

"Just like the note. And the broken stethoscope."

"On the other hand," he said, "Tollrance could just be another starving artist, and this is a pure publicity stunt—taking advantage of Mate's murder to breathe some life into a dead career. If so, it worked—here he is on the front page, making my life difficult. If he shows up tomorrow on TV with an agent and a publicist, scratch the whole psychological scenario."

"Maybe," I said. "This *is* L.A. But if he doesn't surface, that says something, too."

Three beats of silence. "Meanwhile, the painting's resting comfortably in our evidence room. Care to see it?"

"Sure," I said. "Representation *is* my thing."

CHAPTER

17

"NOT HALF BAD, but no Rembrandt," I said.

Milo ran his finger along the top of the canvas. We were in the Robbery-Homicide room, second story at West L.A. Half a dozen detectives hunched at their desks, a few sidelong stares as Milo propped the painting on his chair.

Zero Tollrance's masterpiece was all browns and blacks and muted light, just the merest wash of pink where the left arm of the man on the dissecting table had been reduced to tendons and ligaments.

Cadaver with the fussy, soft face of Eldon Mate. Even Tollrance's middling talent made that clear. Seven men, extravagantly robed and ruffed and goateed, surrounded the dissecting table, gazing down at the corpse with academic detachment. The dissector—another Mate—was clad in a black robe, white lace collar, tall black hat, probing the shredded arm with a scalpel, wearing a look of boredom.

In the original, the artist's genius had distracted from the cruelty of the scene. Tollrance's cartoon drove it home. Angry swirling brushstrokes, pigments laid on thickly to the point of impasto, sharp peaks of paint stabbing up from the surface of the canvas.

A smallish canvas—twenty-four by eighteen inches. I'd expected something far more grand.

Reducing Mate to size?

Milo lifted a stack of message slips, let them fall to the desk in disarray. "Kugler, the art dealer, has been bugging me all day. All of a sudden, he likes realism."

"Probably got an offer," I said. "Same guy who'll pay big bucks for a stained blue dress."

Phones rang, keys clicked, someone laughed. The room smelled of scorched coffee and gym sweat. "Got sleazeball talk shows wanting to interview me, too. And a six A.M. memo from the brass reminding me to keep my mouth shut."

"Tollrance has bought himself some celebrity, too," I said. "I wonder how long that'll satisfy him."

"Meaning he'll want true realism?"

I shrugged.

"Well," he said, "so far, he hasn't made any slipups." He tapped the upper edge of the painting. "Not a single print. Maybe you're right, a careful head case." He angled the painting toward me. "Does seeing this give you any other ideas?"

"Not really," I said. "Rage toward Mate. Ambivalence about Mate. You don't need me to tell you that."

His phone rang. "Sturgis—Oh yeah, hi." His expression brightened, as if an internal filament had ignited. "Really? Thanks. When? . . . Sure, that would be better than convenient. I've got Dr. D. with me— Yeah, sure, great.

"Talk about karma," he said, hanging up. "That was Petra. Seems she came up with some stuff on Donny. She's on her way to a trial at the Santa Monica courthouse, will stop by in ten minutes. We'll meet her out in front."

* * *

We waited by the curb. Milo paced and smoked a Tiparillo and I thought about the Doss family. A few moments later, Petra Connor drove up in a black Accord, parked in the red zone, and got out with her usual economy of movement. I'd never seen her when she wasn't wearing a black pantsuit. This time it was a slim-cut thing with indigo overtones, some kind of slinky wool that flattered her long, lean frame and looked beyond a D-II's budget. On her feet were medium-heeled black lace-ups. Her black hair was cropped in the usual no-nonsense wedge cut, and slung across her shoulder was a black leather bag the texture of a wind-whipped motorcycle jacket. No gun visible beneath the tailored jacket, so she was probably toting it in the bag.

The bad September light was somehow kind to her ivory skin, setting off her tight jaw, pointed chin, ski-slope nose. Pretty, in a taut way, but something about her always warned, Keep Your Distance. The dedication with which she'd followed Billy Straight's recovery told me there was warmth tucked behind the searching brown eyes. But that was inference on my part; she was all business, never talked about herself. I figured she'd jumped high hurdles to get where she was.

"Hi," she said, flashing a cool smile, and I knew what I was supposed to ask.

"How's our guy?"

"Doing great from what I can tell. Straight A's, and he tested out a full grade ahead—amazing, considering most of what he knows is self-taught. A true intellectual, just like you said at the beginning."

"What about his ulcer?" I said.

"Clearing up slowly. He fusses about taking his medicine, but for the most part he's compliant. He's also making some friends. Finally. Other 'creative' types, quoth the principal. Mrs. Adamson's big worry is he doesn't want to do much other than study and read and play with his computer."

"What would she prefer him to do?"

"I'm not sure there's anything specific—she just seems to be nervous. About doing everything right. I think she feels she needs to report to me. She calls me once a week."

"Hey, you're the long arm of the law," I said.

Small smile. "I know she really cares about him. I tell her not to worry, he'll be fine."

She blinked, wanting confirmation.

"Good advice," I said.

Rosy coins appeared on her cheeks. "All in all he's getting plenty of attention. Maybe too much, considering that he's basically a loner? Sam shows up like clockwork on Friday, takes him to Venice on weekends. San Marino all week, then the freak scene. How's that for contrast?"

"Multicultural experience. I'm sure he can handle it."

"Yes—good. If any problems come up, I assume it's okay to call you."

"Anytime."

"Thanks." She turned to Milo. "Sorry, I know you're waiting for this." Out of the leather bag came a folder. "Here's the info on your Mr. Salcido. Turns out he's a known quantity to us. Because of the Hollywood redevelopment thing, Councilwoman Goldstein's office ordered us to keep tabs on transients—the Bum Squad, we called it, lasted a month. Salcido's name came up in one Bum Squad file. No arrest, all they did was canvass squats, find out what the squatters were up to. If they saw drugs or any other crime, they could make an arrest, but basically it was to appease Councilwoman Goldstein."

Milo flipped the chart open. Petra said, "Salcido was living in an abandoned building near Western and Hollywood—the one with the big frieze in front, I think Louis B. Mayer or some other film type built it. Later, the Bummers found out he had a felony record and noted it accordingly."

"Our tax dollars at work." Milo thumbed the pages of the file. "Was he living alone?"

"Unless a known associate is noted, he probably was."

"Says they found him in 'a room full of garbage.'"

"As you see, he claimed to be gainfully employed but couldn't produce backup. The squad pegged him as mentally ill, probably a dope fiend, suggested he seek some help at a community MH center. He refused."

"Why didn't the squad evict him?"

"Without a complaint from the owner, no grounds. I stopped off at the building this morning but he's gone, everyone is. Just construction workers, big remodeling project. Sorry it's not more."

"Hey, it's something—thanks for taking the time," said Milo. "Squatting by himself . . ."

I knew he was thinking about the abandoned building in Denver. He turned a page. "No mug shot?"

"The Bummers didn't carry cameras. But look at the back page, I got a booking photo faxed down from Marin County Jail, not terrific quality."

Milo found the shot, studied it, showed it to me.

Eldon Salcido Mate, freshly inducted to penal custody, numbered plaque dangling from a chain around his neck, the mandatory sullen stare leavened by a hard, hot light in the eyes that might've been madness, or just the glare of the room.

Long, stringy hair but clean-shaven. Light-complected, as Guillerma Salcido had said. Round face, weak around the jowls. Small, prissy features that could've made incarceration a greater-than-usual challenge. Premature wrinkles. A young man aging too fast.

Striking resemblance to a face on a dissecting table; Guillerma Salcido Mate had been right. Donny was his father's son.

Milo read some more. "Says here he claimed to be working in a tattoo parlor on the Boulevard, didn't remember which one."

"I tried a few places, no one knows him. But the jailer up in Marin said Salcido had done some skin work on other inmates, that was probably what kept him safe."

"Safe from what?" I said.

"The jail's organized along gang lines," she said. "Someone without affiliation is fair prey unless they've got something to offer. Salcido sold his art, but the jailer said no one wanted him in their group because he was seen as a mental case."

"Tattoos," said Milo. "The boy likes to draw."

Petra nodded. "I read about the painting. You're thinking it's him?"

"Seems like a good bet."

"What's the painting like?"

"Not what I'd want in my dining room." Milo shut the file. "You're an artist, aren't you?"

"Not hardly."

"Come on, I've seen your stuff."

"My past life," she insisted.

"Want to see it?"

She looked at her watch. "Sure, why not?"

* * *

She held it at arm's length. Squinted. Turned it around, inspected the sides. Placed it on the floor and backed away ten feet before returning to get another close look.

"He really slapped on the paint," she said. "Looks like he worked quickly here—probably a palette knife as well as a brush . . . here, too . . . fast but not sloppy, the composition's actually pretty good—he got the proportions just about right."

She turned away from the painting. "This is only a guess, but what I see here is someone alternating between careful draftsmanship and abandon—at some point he planned meticulously, but once he got into the groove he gave himself over to it."

Milo frowned, then glanced at me.

"Anyway," said Petra. "So much for art criticism."

"What does that mean?" Milo asked her. "Being careful and then cutting loose."

"That he's like most artists."

"You see any talent here?"

"Oh sure. Nothing staggering, but he can render. Plenty of ambition, too—redoing Rembrandt."

"Rembrandt and tattoos," said Milo.

"If Salcido did tattoos well enough to keep himself out of trouble in prison, he's got to be pretty good. Skin work's challenging, you have to get a feel for the changing density of the epidermis, movement, resistance to the needle."

Now she was flushed pink.

Milo smiled. "I'm not even going to ask."

She smiled back. "High school. Anyway, got to run. Hope it helps."

"I owe you, Petra."

"I'm sure I'll find a way to collect." Shifting her bag to her other shoulder, she moved toward the stairs. "I wish I could tell you we'll have our eyes peeled for Salcido, Milo, but you know how it is—sorry to run."

"Good luck in court," said Milo.

"Hopefully I won't need luck. No-brainer shooting that got transferred to SM because downtown's back-logged with potential three-strikers. Unattractive defendant, inexperienced public defender with a caseload as long as *The English Patient.* Today I will triumph! Nice to see you, Doctor—let's keep rooting for Billy."

Back to Milo's desk. During the time we'd spent with Petra, a new message slip had been added to the stack.

"Special Agent Fusco again. The painting probably heated up *his* attention-seeking blood." He tossed the slip, looked across the room.

Detectives Korn and Demetri were headed our way. They stopped at the desk, glaring, as if it were a barrier to freedom. Milo made the introductions. They nodded stiffly, didn't offer their hands. Demetri's eyeglasses were slightly askew and his bald head was sunburned and peeling.

"What's up, gentlemen?"

"Nothing," said Demetri. He had one of those voices so low it sounded electronically manipulated. "That's the problem."

Korn ran his finger under his collar. His blow-dried hair seemed an affront to his partner's tonsure. "Nothing with *whipped* cream and a cherry," he said. "We spent all morning at Haiselden's neighborhood. Found the gardener, big deal. Haiselden's paid up for the month, guy has no idea where señor is, couldn't give a *shit* where señor *went.* Haiselden's mail is piling up at the Westwood post office, but we can't get hold of it without a warrant. You want us to do that?"

"Yes," said Milo.

"Figures."

"Problem, Steve?"

"No. No problem at all." Korn played with his collar again. Demetri removed his glasses and wiped them on a corner of his sport coat.

"Don't lose heart, boys," said Milo. "Haiselden's mail stop shows he definitely rabbited. So keep on him—who knows, you might solve this one."

A glance passed between the two detectives. Demetri shifted his weight to his left leg. "That's assuming Haiselden has anything to do with Mate. We discussed it and we're not convinced he does."

"Why's that, Brad?"

"There's sure no evidence in that direction. Besides, it doesn't make sense. Haiselden made money from Mate. Why would he off his meal ticket? We figure he just went on a vacation—probably got depressed *because* he lost his meal ticket."

"Taking some time off to reflect," said Milo.

"Right."

"Diagnosis of depression, he decided to deal with his feelings on some sunny beach."

Demetri looked at Korn for support. Korn said, "Makes sense to me." His jaw tightened. "With all the publicity over Mate, maybe Haiselden wants time to sort things out. Face it, you've got nothing on his being dirty."

"Nothing at all," said Milo. "Except for the fact that he was a damn publicity hound who rabbited during what has to be the most public moment of his life."

Neither of the younger men spoke.

"Okay then," said Milo. "So how about you write up that warrant for his mail, see if you can get hold of his credit card bills, too. Maybe there'll be a travel agent charge somewhere in there and you can verify your vacation hypothesis."

Another passed glance. Demetri said, "Yeah, sure, whatever you say. We figured we'd hit the gym first. All the hours we've been puttin' in, we haven't had a chance to work out."

"Sure. Get yourselves a coupla Jamba Juices afterward—make sure they put plenty of enzymes in them."

"Something else," said Demetri. "That painting, we just saw it. Real piece of shit, if you ask me."

"Everyone's a critic," said Milo.

CHAPTER

18

"WHAT NOW?" I said.

"If those two manage to write a decent warrant application, I'll have a look at Haiselden's mail. More likely, I'll be correcting their grammar. Meantime, I'm gonna check out art galleries, tattoo parlors, see if anyone else knows Donny, as himself or Tollrance. The fact that he chose a Santa Monica gallery might mean he left Hollywood and is squatting somewhere on the Westside. There are a few abandoned buildings in Venice I want to take a look at."

"Are you liking him better than Haiselden because of the painting?"

"That, his felony record, and what Petra said about the combination of cleverness and psychosis—your hypothesis. With Haiselden, all I've got is his rabbiting, for all I know those two La-Z-Boys could be right and it's one big goose chase, but let them prove it to me." He stood. "As good a time as any to heed the call of nature. 'Scuse me."

He loped toward the men's room and I used his phone to call in for messages.

Two requests for consults from judges that had come in during my ride to the station, and Richard Doss's office wanting me to call—that one was less than five minutes old.

Richard's secretary—the same woman who'd treated me like hired help yesterday—thanked me for getting back *so* soon and asked me to *please* hold for just *one* second. Before her words had faded, Richard came on.

"Thank you," he said, in a tone I'd never heard. Hoarse, faltering, tentative. Both volume and tone controls switched to low.

"What's up, Richard?"

"I found Eric. This morning, four A.M., on campus, he never left, was sitting in an out-of-the-way spot, under a tree. He'd been there for a long time, just sitting, won't say why. He refuses to talk to me at all. I did manage to get him back on the plane, brought him back to L.A. He's missing all kinds of exams, but I don't give a goddamn about that. I'd like you to see him. *Please.*"

"Does Stacy know about this?"

"I knew you'd be concerned about sibling rivalry, or whatever, so I asked her if you could see Eric and she said sure—if you want to verify that, I'll get her on another line."

Voice straining—a man racing against something inexorable.

"No, that's all right, Richard," I said. "Have you had Eric examined medically?"

"No, there wasn't a scratch on him. It's his psychological status I'm worried about. Let's do it sooner rather than later, okay? This isn't Eric. He's always been the— Never lost his productivity. Whatever the hell's going on, I don't like it. When should we set it up?"

"Bring him by this afternoon. But please have a physician check him out first. Just to make sure we're not missing something."

Silence. "Sure. Whatever you say. Are there any particular tests you want?"

"Check for head trauma, fever, acute infection."

"Fine, fine—what time?"

"Let's plan on four."

"That's nearly four hours from now."

"If the doctor finishes sooner, call me. I'll stay close. Where's Eric now?"

"Right here, in my office. I've got him in the conference room. One of my girls is keeping him company."

"He hasn't said anything since you found him?"

"Not a word, just sitting there—this is so damn neurotic, but I can't help thinking this is what Joanne did. The way she started. Pulling away."

"When you touch Eric or move him, how's his muscle tone?"

"Fine, it's not like he's catatonic or anything. He looks me in the eye, I can tell he's all there. He just won't talk to me. Shutting me out. I don't like this one damn bit. One more thing: I don't want Stanford to know about this, see him as damaged goods. The only one who knows so far is that Chinese kid, the roommate, and I let *him* know it would be in all our interests to keep this close to the vest."

Click.

Milo entered the room. Before he reached the desk, another detective pulled a sheet out of the fax machine and handed it to him.

"Look at this," he said, bringing it over. "Further communication from Agent Fusco. Persistent little civil servant, ain't he?"

He placed the fax on the desk. Reprint of a news item, dated fifteen months earlier, datelined Buffalo, New York.

Doctor Suspected in Attempted Murder

An emergency room physician who allegedly laced
the drink of a former supervisor with poison is
being sought by police. Michael Ferris Burke, 38, is
suspected of concocting a lethal combination of
toxic materials in an attempt to murder Selwyn Rabinowitz, chairman of the Department of Emergency Medicine at Unitas Critical Care Center in
Rochester. Burke had recently been placed on suspension by Rabinowitz due to "questionable medical
practices" and had made veiled threats to his superior. Rabinowitz drank one sip of the doctored
coffee and grew ill almost immediately. Suspicion
fell on Burke because of the threats and due to the
fact that the suspended doctor had left town. Several syringes and vials were recovered from a locker
in the physicians' lounge at Unitas, but police refuse
to say if they belonged to Burke. Rabinowitz remains hospitalized in stable condition.

Below the article, a few lines of neat, upright
handwriting:

Detective Sturgis:
You might want to know more about this.
Lem Fusco

"So what's he saying?" said Milo. "This has something to do with Mate?"

"Burke," I said. "Why's that name familiar?"

"Hell if I know. I'm getting to the point where everything sounds familiar."

I gave the clipping another read. Something came into
focus. "Where's the material I pulled off the Internet?"

He opened a drawer, searched for a while, pulled out more papers, produced the printouts. I found what I was looking for right away. "Here you go. Another upstate New York story. Rochester. Roger Sharveneau, the respiratory tech who confessed to poisoning ICU patients, then recanted. Months later, he claimed to have been under the influence of a Dr. Burke, whom no one had ever seen. No sign anyone followed up on that, probably because Sharveneau's pattern of confessing and recanting led them to believe he'd made it all up. But *this* Dr. Burke was working in Buffalo, sixty, seventy miles away, and getting into mischief. Poison mischief, and Sharveneau died of an overdose."

Milo exhaled. "Okay," he said. "I give in. S.A. Fusco gets his meeting. Want to come?"

"If it's soon," I said. "I've got an appointment at four."

"Appointment for what?"

"What they sent me to school for."

"Oh yeah, you do that occasionally, don't you." He punched the number Fusco'd listed on the fax, got through, listened.

"Taped message," he said. "Hey, personalized for me . . . If I'm interested, meet him at Mort's Deli on Wilshire and Wellesley in Santa Monica. He'll be the one with the boring tie."

"What time?"

"He didn't specify. He knew I'd call after I got the fax, is confident I'll show up. I just love being played." He put on his jacket.

"What key?" I said.

"D minor. As in detective. As in dumb. But why the hell not, the deli's not far from those squats in Venice. How about you?"

"I'll take my own car."

"Sure," he said. "That's how it starts. Soon you'll be wanting your own dish and spoon."

CHAPTER

19

THE EXTERIOR OF Mort's Deli was a single cloudy window over a swath of brown board below red-painted letters proclaiming lunch for $5.99. The interior was all yellows and scarlets, narrow black leatherette booths, wallpaper that looked inspired by parrot plumage, the uneasily coexisting odors of fried fish, pickle brine and overripe potatoes.

Leimert Fusco was easy to spot, with or without neck-wear. The only other patron was an ancient woman up in front spooning soup into a palsying mouth. The FBI man was three booths back. The tie was gray tweed—same fabric and shade as his sport coat, as if the jacket had given birth to a nursing pup.

"Welcome," he said, pointing to the sandwich on his plate. "The brisket's not bad for L.A." In his fifties, the same gravel voice.

"Where's the brisket better?" said Milo.

Fusco smiled, showed lots of gum. His teeth were huge, equine, white as hotel sheeting. Short, bristly white hair rode low on his brow. Long, heavily wrinkled face, aggressive jaw, big bulbous nose. The tail end of his fifties. The saddest brown eyes I'd ever seen, nearly hidden by crepey folds. He had broad shoulders and wide hands. Seated, he gave the impression of bulk and frustrated movement.

"Meaning, where am I from?" he said. "Most recently Quantico. Before that, all kinds of places. I learned about brisket in New York—where else? Spent five years at the main Manhattan office. Those qualifications good enough for you to sit down?"

Milo slid into the booth and I followed.

Fusco looked me over. "Dr. Delaware? Excellent. My doctorate's not in clinical. Personality theory." He twisted the tweed tie. "Thanks for coming. I won't insult your intelligence by asking how you're doing on Mate. You're here because even though you think it's a waste of time, you're not in a position to refuse data. Want to order something, or is this going to remain at the level of testosterone-laden watchfulness?"

"So how do you really feel about life?" said Milo.

Fusco gave another toothy grin.

"Nothing for me," Milo said. "What's with this Burke?"

A waitress approached. Fusco motioned her away. Next to his sandwich was a tall glass of cola. He sipped, put the glass down silently.

"Michael Ferris Burke," he said, as if delivering the title of a poem. "He's like the AIDS virus: I know *what* he is, know what he *does*, but I can't get hold of him."

Gazing pleasantly at Milo. I wondered if the AIDS reference went beyond general metaphor.

Milo's expression said he thought it did. "We've all got our problems. Want to fill me in, or just bitch?"

Fusco kept smiling as he reached down to his left and produced a brick-red accordion file folder, two inches thick and fastened with string.

"Copy of the Burke file for your perusal. More accurately, the Rushton file. He went to med school as Michael Ferris Burke, but he was born Grant Huie Rushton. There are a few other monikers in between. He likes to reinvent himself."

"So now he can get a job in Hollywood," said Milo.

Fusco pushed the file closer. Milo hesitated, then pulled it over and placed it on the seat between us.

Fusco said, "If you want a capsule summary, I'll give you one."

"Go ahead."

The muscles of Fusco's left eyelid twitched before settling. "Grant Huie Rushton was born forty years ago in Queens, New York. Flushing, to be exact. Full-term birth, no complications, only child. The parents were Philip Walter Rushton, a tool-and-die maker, age twenty-nine, and Lorraine Margaret Huie, twenty-seven, a housewife. When the boy was two, both parents were killed in an accident on the Pennsylvania Turnpike. Little Grant was shipped off to Syracuse to be raised by his maternal grandmother, Irma Huie, a widow with a history of alcoholism."

Fusco's hands rubbed together. "Logic and psychology tell me Rushton's problems had to begin early, but getting hold of childhood records that document his pathology has been difficult because he never received professional help. I located some grade-school reports that note 'disciplinary problems.' He wasn't a sociable child, so locating peers who remember him clearly has been a problem. A trip I made to his Syracuse neighborhood several years ago unearthed some people who remember the boy as bright and talented and major-league mean—'malicious' is the word that keeps cropping up."

He ticked his left index finger with its right-hand

counterpart. "Cruelty to animals, bullying other kids, suspicions of neighborhood pranks and thefts and burglaries. The grandmother was an inept parent, and Grant had free rein. He was smart enough to avoid getting caught, has no juvenile record that I can find. His high-school yearbook entry—a copy's in there—lists no extracurricular activities or honors. He graduated with a B average, which for him was no challenge, he could've done that in his sleep. A few Unsatisfactories in conduct but no suspensions or expulsions." To me: "You know the data on psychopaths, Doctor. High IQ can be protective. Grant Rushton knew how to keep his impulses under control, even back then. Precisely when he went all the way is unclear, but when he was eighteen, a fourteen-year-old girl—a neighbor—disappeared. Her body was found two months later in a forested area on the outskirts of town. Decomposition was advanced and precise cause of death was never determined, but the autopsy did reveal head trauma and neck wounds and sexual exploration without actual rape. The investigation never got very far and no suspects were ever named."

"Was Rushton questioned?" said Milo.

"No. After the girl—Jennifer Chapelle—was found, Rushton graduated and joined the navy. Basic training in California—Oceanside. Honorable discharge after only two months. Military records have proven to be less than precise. All I've been able to learn is that he went AWOL once and they let him go."

"That merits honorable?" I said.

"In a volunteer military, sometimes it does. During the time he was stationed at Oceanside, a prostitute named Kristen Strunk was chopped up and dumped a mile from the base. Another unsolved."

"Same question," said Milo. "Was Rushton ever considered a suspect?"

Fusco shook his head. "Bear with me. After his discharge, Grant Rushton died: single-car crash off the old Route 66 in Nevada. Burned-up auto, charred corpse."

"Same death as his parents," I said.

Fusco's sad eyes glowed.

Milo said, "What are you saying? A body switch?"

"The corpse was never examined closely—we're talking french fry. It wasn't till years later, when I matched Rushton's navy prints to those of Michael Burke, that I came across the switch. By that time, it was too late to learn anything about who really got burned. The owner was an accountant from Tucson, driving to Vegas with his wife. The car was hot-wired while they sat at a truck-stop eating burgers."

"Any idea who got burned?" said Milo.

Fusco shook his head and looked over his shoulder again. "No sign of Rushton for a year and a half. I figure he copped one or more false identities and traveled around for a while. The next time I can tag him he was living in Denver and going by the name of Mitchell Lee Sartin, a student at Rocky Mountain Community College, majoring in biology. The print backtrack verifies Sartin as Rushton. He applied for a job as a security guard, got his fingers inked. The Sartin I.D. was one of those graveyard switcheroos—the real Mitchell was buried twenty-two years before, in Boulder. Sudden infant death, three months old."

"And no reason for the security firm to cross-reference with the navy," said Milo.

"Not hardly. Those guys have been known to hire schizophrenics. The prints were checked with local felony files, where, of course, they didn't show up. Sartin got a job patrolling a pharmaceutical company at night. By day, he attended classes. He lasted one semester—straight A's. Life sciences and a course in human figure drawing."

"Drawing," I said. "Is that what you meant by talented?"

Fusco nodded. "A couple of his former schoolmates remember him as a great doodler—cartoons, mostly. Obscene stuff, making fun of teachers, other authority figures. He never worked for the school paper. Never chose to *affiliate*."

He took a long drink of cola. "During Sartin's enrollment at Rocky Mountain CC, two female students went missing. One was eventually found up in the mountains, dead, sexually abused and mutilated. The other girl's whereabouts remain unknown. This was the first time Grant Rushton/Mitchell Sartin attracted any attention from law enforcement. He was among several individuals questioned by the Denver police because he'd been seen talking to one of the girls in the college cafeteria the day before she disappeared. But it was just a routine interview, no reason to check further. Sartin didn't reenroll, left town. Disappeared."

"All this within two years of high-school graduation?" I said. "He was only twenty?"

"Correct," said Fusco. "Precocious lad. The next few years are another cloudy area. I can't prove it, but I know he returned to Syracuse to visit Grandma a year later. Though no one remembers seeing him."

"Something happened to Grandma," said Milo.

Fusco's lips curled inward. He ran a hand over the white bush atop his head. "One of those Syracuse winters, late at night, Grandma drove her car into a tree on a rural road and went through the windshield. Her blood alcohol was just over the limit and an empty brandy bottle was found on the front seat. By the time they found her body, it was frozen stiff. No reason to think it was anything other than a single-driver DUI thing, except for the fact that Grandma was a stay-at-home drinker, never went out at night. Rarely drove, period. No one could explain why she'd taken the car out in a freezing storm or why she was out in the sticks, a good fifteen miles from her house. No one also thought to question why, with that kind of impact, the bottle would be right there on the seat. Irma Huie didn't leave much of an estate—her place was rented, she kept no bank accounts. The police didn't find any money, not a penny in the cookie jar. Which I find curious because she'd lived on pension money from her husband and Social Security income, and her landlord said she kept cash around, he'd seen wads of bills bound by rubber bands. A year later, Mitchell Sartin surfaced as Michael Ferris Burke and enrolled in City University of New York as a sophomore pre-med major. He presented a transcript—later shown to be forged—from Michigan State University, claiming a year of courses, GPA of 3.8. CUNY bought it. Burke gave his age as twenty-six—to match the stats on another I.D. he'd cribbed, this time from a dead baby in Connecticut. But he was only twenty-two."

"He bought himself some time with Grandma's money?" I said. "But he made no attempt to claim the pension or the Social Security payments."

"He knows how to be careful," said Fusco. "That's why there are periods in his life I just can't tag, and a lot of what I'm going to tell you won't go beyond theory and guesses. But have I said anything, so far, that doesn't make sense from a psychological standpoint, Doctor?"

"Go on," I said.

"Let me backtrack. During the year between Irma Huie's death in Syracuse and Michael Burke's enrollment at CUNY, two clusters of mutilation murders occurred that bear marked similarities to the particulars of the Denver victim. The first popped up in Michigan. Beginning four months after Mitchell Sartin left Colorado, three coeds were attacked in Ann Arbor. All were jogging at night on pathways near the University of Michigan campus. Two were ambushed from behind by a man wearing a ski mask, knocked to the ground, punched in the face till semiconscious, then raped, stabbed and slashed with a sharp knife—probably a surgical scalpel. Both escaped with their lives when other joggers happened upon the scene, and the assailant fled into the bushes. The third girl wasn't so lucky. She was taken three months later, by that time some of the campus panic generated by the first two attacks had died down. Her body was found near a reservoir, badly mutilated."

"Mutilated in what way?" I said.

"Extensive abdominal and pelvic cutting. Wrists and ankles bound to a tree with a thick hemp rope. Breasts removed, skin peeled from the inner thighs—your basic sadistic sexual surgery. Subdural hematomas from head wounds that might've eventually proven fatal. But arterial spurts on the tree said she'd been alive while being cut. The official cause of death was bleeding out from a jugular slash. Shreds of blue paper were found nearby and the Ann Arbor investigators matched it, eventually, to disposable surgical scrub suits used at that time at the University of Michigan Medical Center. That led to numerous interviews with med-school staff and students, but no serious leads developed. The surviving girls could only give a sketchy description of the attacker: male Caucasian, medium-size, very strong. He never spoke or showed his face, but one of them remembers seeing white skin between his sleeve and his glove. His modus was to throw a choke hold on them as he hit them from behind, then flip them over and punch them in the face. Three very hard blows in rapid succession." Fusco's fist smacked into an open hand. Three loud, hollow reports. The old woman drinking soup didn't turn around.

" 'Calculated,' one of the surviving victims called it. A girl named Shelly Spreen. I had the chance to interview her four years ago—fourteen years after the attack. Married, two kids, a husband who loves her like crazy. Reconstructive facial surgery restored most of her looks, but if you see pre-attack pictures, you know it didn't do the trick completely. Gutsy girl, she's been one of the few people willing to talk to me. I'd like to think talking about it helped her out a little."

"Calculated," I said.

"The way he hit her—silently, mechanically, methodically. She never felt he was doing it out of anger, he always seemed to be in control. 'Like someone going about his business,' she told me. Ann Arbor did a competent job, but once again, no leads. I had the luxury of working backward—focusing on young men in their twenties, possibly security guards, or university employees who'd left town shortly after, then dropped completely out of sight. The only individual who fit the bill was a fellow named Huey Grant Mitchell. He'd worked at the U. Mich medical school, as an orderly on the cardiac unit."

I said, "Grant Huie Rushton plus Mitchell Sartin equals Huey Grant Mitchell—wordplay instead of a graveyard switch."

"Exactly, Doctor. He loves to play. The Mitchell I.D. was created out of whole cloth. The job reference he gave—a hospital in Phoenix, Arizona—turned out to be bogus, and the Social Security number listed on his employment application was brand-new. He paid for his Ann Arbor single with cash, left behind no credit card receipts—no paper trail of any kind, except for a single employment rating: he'd been an excellent orderly. I think the switch from graveyard hoax to brand-new I.D. represents a psychological shift. Heightened confidence."

Fusco pushed his Coke glass away, then the half-eaten sandwich. "Something else leads me to think he was stretching. Craving a new game. During the time he worked the cardiac floor, several patients died suddenly and inexplicably. Sick but not terminally ill patients who could've gone either way. No one suspected anything—no one realizes anything, to this day. It's just something that turned up when I was digging."

"He cuts up girls and snuffs ICU patients?" said Milo. "Versatile."

Any trace of amiability left Fusco's face. "You have no idea," he said.

"You're talking nearly two decades of bad stuff and it's never come out? What, one of those covert federal things? Or are you out to write a book?"

"Look," said Fusco, jawbones flexing. Then he smiled, sat back. Let his eyes disappear in a mass of folds. "It's covert because I've got nothing to go overt. Air-sandwich time. I've only been on it for three years."

"You said two clusters. Where and when was the second?"

"Back here, in your Golden State. Fresno. A month after Huey Mitchell left Ann Arbor, two more girls were snagged off hiking trails, two weeks apart. Both were found tied to trees, cut up nearly identically to the Colorado and the Michigan vics. A hospital orderly named Hank Spreen left town five weeks after the second body turned up."

"Spreen," I said. "Shelly Spreen. He took his *victim's* name?"

Fusco grinned horribly. "Mr. Irony. Once again, he got away with it. Hank Spreen had worked at a private hospital in Bakersfield specializing in cosmetic work, cyst removals, that kind of thing. It was a big surprise when three post-op patients had sudden reversals and died in the middle of the night. Official cause: heart attacks, idiopathic reactions to anesthesia. That happens, but not usually three times in a row over a six-month period. The publicity helped close the hospital down, but by then Hank Spreen was long gone. The following summer, Michael Burke showed up at CUNY."

"Long body list for a twenty-two-year-old," I said.

"A twenty-two-year-old smart enough to make it through pre-med and med school. He worked his way through by holding down a job as a lab assistant to a biology professor—basically a nighttime bottle washer, but he didn't need much income, lived in student housing. Had Grandma's dough. Pulled a 3.85 GPA—from what I can tell, he really earned those grades. Summers, he worked as an orderly at three public hospitals—New York Medical, Middle State General and Long Island General. He applied to ten med schools, got into four, chose the University of Washington in Seattle."

"Any coed murders during his pre-med period?" said Milo.

Fusco licked his lips. "No, I can't find any definite matches during that time. But there was no shortage of missing girls. All over the country, bodies that never showed up. I believe Rushton/Burke kept on killing but hid his handiwork better."

"You believe? This joker's a homicidal psychopath and he just changes his ways?"

"Not his ways," said Fusco. "His mode of expression. That's what sets him apart. He can let loose his impulses along with the bloodiest of them, but he also knows how to be careful. Exquisitely careful. Think about the patience it took to actually become a doctor. There's something else to consider. During his New York period, he may have diverted his attention from rape/murder to the parallel interest he'd developed in Michigan and continued in Bakersfield: putting hospital patients out of their misery. I know they seem like different patterns, but what they've got in common is a lust for power. Playing God. Once he learned all about hospital systems, playing ward games would've been a snap."

"How is he supposed to have killed all those patients?" said Milo.

"There are any number of ways that make detection nearly impossible. Pinching off the nose, smothering, fooling with med lines, injecting succinyl, insulin, potassium."

"Any funny stuff go down at the three hospitals where Burke spent his summers?"

"New York's the worst place to obtain information. Large institutions, lots of regulations. Let's just say I have learned of several questionable deaths that occurred on wards where Burke was assigned. Thirteen, to be exact."

Milo pointed down at the file folder. "All this is in here?"

Fusco shook his head. "I've limited my written material to data, no supposition. Police reports, autopsies, et cetera."

"Meaning some of your stuff was obtained illegally, so it can never be used in court."

Fusco didn't reply.

"Pretty dedicated, Agent Fusco," said Milo. "Cowboy stuff's not exactly what I'm used to when dealing with Quantico."

Fusco flashed those big teeth of his. "Pleased to bust your stereotype, Detective Sturgis."

"I didn't say *that*."

The agent leaned forward. "I can't stop you from being hostile and distrustful. But, really, what's the point of playing uptight-local-besieged-by-the-big-bad-Fed? How many times does someone offer you this level of information?"

"Exactly," said Milo. "When something seems to be too good to be true, it usually is."

"Fine," said Fusco. "If you don't want the file, give it back. Good luck chipping away at Dr. Mate. Who, by the way, began his own little death trip around the same time Michael Burke/Grant Rushton decided to seriously pursue a career in medicine. I believe Burke took note of Mate. I believe Mate's escapades and the resulting publicity played a role in Michael Burke's evolution as a ward killer. Though, of course, Michael had begun snuffing out patients earlier. Michael's main objective *was* killing people." To me: "Wouldn't you say that applied to Dr. Mate, as well?"

Calling Burke by his first name. The hateful intimacy born of futile investigation.

Milo said, "You see Mate as a serial killer?"

Fusco's face went pleasantly bland. "You don't?"

"Some people consider Mate an angel of mercy."

"I'm sure Michael Burke could manipulate some people to say the same of him. But we all know what was really going on. Mate loved the ultimate power. So does Burke. You know all the jokes about doctors playing God. Here're a couple who put it into practice."

Milo rubbed the side of the table as if cleaning off his fingertips. "So Mate inspires Burke, and Burke goes up to Seattle for med school. He moves around a lot."

"He does nothing *but* move," said Fusco. "Funny thing, though: until he showed up in Seattle and purchased a used VW van, he'd never officially owned a car. Like I said, a retrovirus—keeps changing, can't be grabbed hold of."

"Who died in Seattle?"

"The University of Washington hasn't been forthcoming with its records. Au contraire, officially none of their wards have experienced a pattern of unusual patient deaths. But would you take that to the bank? There's certainly no shortage of serials up there."

"So now Burke's back to girls? What, he's the Green River Killer?"

Fusco smiled. "None of the Green River scenes match his previous work, but I know of at least four cases that do bear further study. Girls cut up and left tied to trees in semirural spots, all within a hundred miles of Seattle, all unsolved."

"Burke's fooling with I.V. lines by day, cutting up girls in his spare time, somehow working in med school."

"Bundy killed and worked while in law school. Burke's a lot smarter, though like most psychopaths he tends to slack off. That almost cost him his MD. He had to spend a summer making up poor basic-science grades, received low marks for his clinical skills, graduated near the bottom of his class. Still, he finished, got an internship at a V.A. clinic in Bellingham. Once again, I can't get hold of hospital records, but if someone finds an unusual number of old soldiers expiring under his watch, I'm not going to faint from shock. He finished an emergency medicine residency at the same place, got a six-figure job with Unitas, moved back to New York, and added another car to his auto arsenal."

"He held on to the van?" I said.

"Most definitely."

"What kind of car?" said Milo. I knew he was wondering: BMW?

"Three-year-old Lexus," said Fusco. "The way I see it, emergency medicine's perfect for a twisted loner—plenty of blood and suffering, you get to make life-and-death decisions, cut and stitch, the hours are flexible—work a twenty-four-hour shift, take days off. And important: no follow-up of patients, no long-term relationships, office or staff. Burke could've gone on for years, but he's still a psychopath, has that tendency to screw up. Finally did."

Milo smiled. He'd been living with an E.R. doctor for fifteen years. I'd heard Rick praise the freedom that resulted from no long-term entanglements.

"Poisoning the boss," Milo said. "The article said he'd been suspended for bad medicine. Meaning?"

"He had a habit of not showing up at the E.R. when he was supposed to. Plus poor doctor-patient relations. The boss—Dr. Rabinowitz—said sometimes Burke could be terrific with patients. Charming, empathetic, taking extra time with kids. But other times he'd turn—lose his temper, accuse someone of overdramatizing or faking, get really nasty. He actually tried to kick a few patients out of the E.R., told them to stop taking up bed space that belonged to sick people. Toward the end, that was happening more and more. Burke was warned repeatedly, but he simply denied any of it had ever happened."

"Sounds like he was losing it," said Milo. He looked at me.

"Maybe heightened tension," I said. "The pressure of working a tough job when his qualifications were marginal. Being scrutinized by people who were smarter. Or some kind of emotional trauma. Has he ever had an outwardly normal relationship with a woman?"

"No long-term girlfriend, and he's a nice-looking guy." Fusco's eyes drooped lower. His hands balled. "That brings me to another pattern. A more recent one, as far as I can tell. He developed a friendship with one of his patients up in Seattle. Former cheerleader with bone cancer. Burke was circulating through as an intern, ended up spending a lot of time with her."

"Thought you couldn't get hospital records," said Milo.

"I couldn't. But I did find some nurses who remembered Michael. Nothing dramatic, they just thought he'd spent too much time with the cheerleader. It ended when the girl died. A couple of weeks later, the first of the four unsolved cutting vics was found. Next year, in Rochester, Burke got close to another sick woman. Divorcée in her early fifties, onetime beauty queen with brain cancer. She came into the E.R. in some sort of crisis, Burke revived her, visited her during the four months she spent as an inpatient, saw her at home after she was discharged. He was at her side when she died. Pronounced her dead."

"Died of what?" said Milo.

"Respiratory failure," said Fusco. "Not inconsistent with the spread of her disease."

"Any mutilation clusters after that?"

"Not in Rochester, per se, but five girls within a two-hundred-mile radius have gone missing during Burke's two years at Unitas Hospital. Three of them after Burke's lady friend died. I agree with Dr. Delaware's point about loss and tension."

"Two hundred miles," said Milo.

Fusco said, "As I've pointed out, Burke has the means to travel. And plenty of privacy. In Rochester, he lived in a rented house in a semirural area. His neighbors said he kept to himself, tended to disappear for days at a time. Sometimes he took along skis or camping equipment—both the van and the Lexus had roof racks. He's in good shape, likes the outdoors."

"These five cases are missing only, no bodies?"

"So far," said Fusco. "Detective, you know that two hundred miles is no big deal if you've got decent wheels. Burke kept his vehicles in beautiful shape, clean as a whistle. Same for his house. He's a lad of impeccable habits. The house reeked of disinfectant, and his bed was made tight enough to bounce a hubcap."

"How'd he get tagged for poisoning Rabinowitz?"

"Circumstantial. Burke kept screwing up, and Rabinowitz finally put him on suspension. Rabinowitz said the look in Burke's eyes gave him the creeps. A week later, Rabinowitz got sick. It turned out to be cyanide. Burke was the last person to be seen in the vicinity of Rabinowitz's coffee cup other than Rabinowitz's secretary, and she passed the polygraph. When the locals tried to question Burke and put him on the machine, he was gone. Later, they found needles and a penicillin ampule in a locker in the physicians' lounge, traces of cyanide in the ampule. Rabinowitz is lucky he took a small sip. Even with that, he was hospitalized for a month."

"Burke left cyanide in his locker?"

"In another doctor's locker. A colleague Burke had had words with. Fortunately for him, he was alibied. Home sick with the stomach flu, never left his house, lots of witnesses. There was some suspicion he'd been poisoned, too, but it turned out to just be the flu."

"So all you've really got on the poisoning is Burke's rabbit."

"That's all Rochester's got. I've got *that*." Pointing toward the still-unopened file folder. "I've also got Roger Sharveneau, certified respiratory tech. Buffalo police never checked out his Burke story, but Sharveneau worked at Unitas for three months, same time Burke was there. Sharveneau mentions Burke, and a week later *he's* dead."

"Why didn't Buffalo check out the Burke lead?" said Milo.

"To be charitable," said Fusco, "Sharveneau came across highly disturbed and lacking credibility. My guess would be severe borderline personality, maybe even a full-blown schizophrenic. He jerked Buffalo PD around for a month—confessing, recanting, then hinting that maybe he'd killed some of the patients but not all of them, calling press conferences, changing lawyers, acting goofier and goofier. During the time he was locked up he went on a hunger strike, went mute, refused to talk to the court-appointed psychiatrists. By the time he gave them the Burke story, they were fed up with him. But I believe he did know Michael Burke. And that Burke had some kind of influence on him."

I said, "Why would Burke put himself in jeopardy by confiding in someone as unstable as Sharveneau?"

"I'm not saying he confided in Sharveneau, or gave Sharveneau direct orders. I'm saying he exerted some kind of influence. It could very well have been subtle—a remark here, a nudge there. Sharveneau was unstable, passive, highly suggestible. Michael Burke's the peg that fits that hole: dominant, manipulative, in his own way charismatic. I believe Burke knew what buttons to push."

Milo said, "Dominant, manipulative, and he gets away with bad stuff. So what's next, he runs for public office?"

"You don't want to see the profiles of the people who run the country."

"The Bureau's still doing that J. Edgar stuff, huh?"

Fusco smiled.

Milo said, "Even if your boy really is the ultimate purveyor of evil, what's the connection to Mate?"

"Tell me about Mate's wounds."

Milo laughed. "How about you tell me what you think they might be."

Fusco shifted in the booth, leaned to his left, stretched his left arm across the top of the seat. "Fair enough. I'd guess that Mate was rendered semiconscious or totally unconscious, probably with a strong blow to the head that came from behind. Or a choke hold. The papers said he was found in the van. If that's true, that's at odds with Burke's tree-propping signature. But the wooded site fits Burke's kills. More public than Burke's previous dumps, but that fits the pattern of increased confidence. And Mate was a public figure. I suspect Burke conned Mate into arranging a meeting, possibly by feigning interest in

Mate's work. From what I've seen of Mate, an appeal to his ego would be most effective."

He stopped.

Milo said nothing. His hand had come to rest atop the file folder. Touching the string. Unfurling it slowly.

Fusco said, "However the meeting was arranged, I see Burke familiarizing himself with the site beforehand, learning the traffic patterns, leaving a getaway vehicle within walking distance of the kill-spot. Which in his case, could be miles. Probably to the east of the kill-spot, because the east affords multiple avenues of escape. Living in L.A., Burke needs wheels, so I'm sure he's obtained registration under a new identity, but whether he used his own car or a stolen vehicle, I couldn't say."

"I assume you've combed DMV, done all the combinations of Burke, Rushton, Sartin, Spreen, whatever."

"You assume correctly. No good hits."

"You were going to speculate about the wounds."

" 'Speculate.' " Fusco smiled. "Brutal but precise, carved with a surgical-grade blade or something equally sharp. There may also have been some geometry involved."

"What do you mean by geometry?" said Milo, sounding casual.

"Geometrical shapes incised into the skin. He began that in Ann Arbor, the last victim, diamonds snipped out of her upper pubic region. When I first saw it, I thought: his idea of a joke—the irony again, diamonds are a girl's best friend. But then he changed shapes with one of the Fresno vics. Circles. So I won't tell you I know exactly what it means, just that he likes to play around."

"There were two Fresno victims," I said. "Was only one incised geometrically?"

Fusco nodded. "Maybe Burke had to hurry away from the other kill."

"Or maybe," said Milo, "both victims weren't his."

"Read the file and decide for yourself." Fusco drew his glass nearer, touched the corner of his sandwich.

"Anything more you want to say?"

"Just that you probably didn't find much trace evidence, if any. Burke loves to clean up. And killing Mate would represent a special achievement for him: synthesis of his two previous modes: bloody knife work and pseudo-euthanasia. The papers said Mate was hooked up to his own machine. That true?"

"Pseudo-euthanasia?"

"It's never real," said Fusco with sudden heat. "All that talk about right to die, putting people out of their misery. Until we can crawl into a dying person's head and read their thoughts, it'll never be real." Forced smile, more of a snarl, really: "When I heard about the painting, I knew I had to be more assertive with you. Burke loves to draw. His house in Rochester was full of art books and sketch pads."

"How good is he?" I said.

"Better than average. I took some photos. It's all in there. But don't hold me to any specific guess, look at the overall picture. I've done hundreds of profiles, most of the time I miss something."

"What you've done with Burke goes beyond profiling," I said.

He stared at me. "Meaning what?"

"Sounds as if you've made him your project."

"Part of my current job description is depth research on cold cases." To Milo: "You'd know something about that."

Milo uncoiled the string and opened the file. Inside

were three black folders, labeled I, II, and III. He removed the first, opened it to a page containing five photocopied head shots.

In the upper left: a color school photo of ten-year-old T-shirted Grant Huie Rushton. Button nose, blond crew cut, Norman Rockwell cute, except this kid hadn't smiled for the camera. Had looked away from it, set his mouth in a horizontal line that should've been merely noncommittal, but wasn't.

Anger. Cool anger, backed by . . . wariness? Emotional unsteadiness? Furtive, wounded eyes. Norman Rockwell meets Diane Arbus. Or was I interpreting because of what Fusco had told me?

Next: a high-school graduation shot. At eighteen, Grant Rushton looked more relaxed. Pleasant-looking young man wearing a plaid shirt, face broadened by puberty, the features symmetrical, tending a bit toward pug. Clear complexion but for sprinkles of pimples in the folds between nostril and cheek. Strong, square chin, mouth shut tight but uplifted at the corners. Teenage Grant's hair was several shades darker but still fair, worn to his shoulders with thick bangs. This time, he confronted the lens, full-face—confident—more than that: brash. By then, Fusco claimed, Rushton had murdered and gotten away with it.

Below the childhood shots was Huey Mitchell's bearded face on a Great Lakes Security badge. The beard was thick, spade-shaped, a mink brown that contrasted with Mitchell's dirty-blond head hair. Running from atop the cheekbones to his first shirt button in an uninterrupted swath broken only by a mouth slit, it rendered any comparison to the other photos useless. Mitchell wore his hair even longer, drawn back tight into a ponytail that dangled over his right shoulder.

The pale eyes narrower, harder. My flash impression would have been blue-collar resentment. Vital statistics: five-ten, one eighty, blond hair, blue eyes.

The bottom row featured two pictures of Michael Burke, MD. In the first, taken from a New York driver's license, the beard remained, this time clipped and barbered to an inch of dark pelt that served the now powerful-looking head well. So did Burke's haircut—razor-layered, blow-dried, worn just above the ears. By his early thirties, Burke's face had begun to reveal the advent of middle age: thinner hair, wrinkles around the mouth, puffiness under the eyes. Overall, a pleasant-looking man, wholly unremarkable.

This time the stats said five-nine, one sixty-five.

"He shrank an inch and lost fifteen pounds?" I said.

"Or lied about it to Motor Vehicles," said Fusco. "Doesn't everyone?"

"People reduce their weight, but they don't generally claim to be shorter."

"Michael isn't people," said Fusco. "You'll also notice that the license says brown eyes. His true color's green-blue. Obviously, Burke jerked them around—either because he was hiding something or just having fun. On his Unitas I.D., he's back to blue."

I examined the last photo.

Michael F. Burke, MD, Dept. of Emergency Medicine.

Clean-shaven. Square-jawed, even fuller, the hair thinner but worn slightly longer, flatter. Burke had been content with a decent comb-over.

I compared the last shot with Grant Rushton's high-school photo, searching for some commonality. Similar bone structure, I supposed. The eyes were the same shape, but even there, gravity had tugged sufficiently to prevent immediate identification. Huey Mitchell's beard obscured everything. Rushton's bang-shadowed brow and Burke's clear forehead gave the rest of their faces entirely different appearances.

Five faces. I'd never have linked any of them.

Milo shut the folder and placed it back in the file. Fusco had been waiting for some kind of response and now he looked unhappy, curled his fingers around his glass.

"Anything else?" said Milo.

Fusco shook his head. Unfolding a paper napkin, he wrapped the half-eaten brisket sandwich and stashed it in a pocket of his sport coat.

"You bunked down at the Federal Building?" said Milo.

"Officially," said Fusco, "but mostly I'm on the road. I wrote down a number in there that routes automatically to my beeper. My fax runs twenty-four hours a day. Feel free, anytime."

"On the road where?"

"Wherever the job takes me. As I said, I've got projects other than Michael Burke, though Michael does tend to occupy my thoughts. Tonight, I'll be flying up to Seattle, see if I can get U. Wash to be a bit more forthcoming. Also, to look into those unsolveds, which is a mite touchy. With all the publicity about the Pacific Northwest being the serial-killer capital of the world and no resolution on Green River, they don't like being reminded of loose ends."

Milo said, "Bon voyage."

Fusco slid out of the booth. No briefcase. His jacket bulged where he'd stuffed the sandwich. Not a tall man, after all. Five-eight, tops, with a big torso riding stumpy, bowed legs. His jacket hung open and I saw several black pens lined up in his shirt pocket, the beeper and a cell phone hitched to his belt. No visible weapon. Fingering his white hair, he left the restaurant, limping. Looking like a tired old salesman who'd just failed to make his quota.

CHAPTER

20

MILO AND I stayed in the booth.

The waitress was leaning protectively over the old woman. He waved for her. She held up a finger.

He said, "Just like the Feds—we get stuck for the check."

"He liked the brisket, but didn't eat much of it," I said. "Maybe his gut's full of something else."

"Like what?"

"Frustration. He's been on this for a while—got a bit touchy when I called Burke his project. Sometimes that can lead to tunnel vision. On the other hand, there's a lot that seems to match."

"What—'geometry'?"

"A killer with a medical background and artistic interests, the combination of 'euthanasia' and lust-murder. And he was awfully close when he described the details of Mate's murder, down to the blitz attack and the cleanup."

"That he could've gotten from a departmental leak."

The waitress came over. "It's been taken care of, sir. The white-haired gentleman."

"And a gentleman he is." Milo handed her a ten.

"The tip's also been taken care of," she said.

"Now it's been taken care of twice."

She beamed. "Thanks."

When she was gone, I said, "See, you judged him too harshly."

"Force of habit . . . Okay, so some of my income tax came back to me. . . . Yeah, there are similarities, there often are with psycho killers, right? Limited repertoire: you bludgeon, you shoot, you cut. But it's far from a perfect match. Starting with the basics: Mate's not a young girl and he wasn't tied against a tree. Fusco can fudge all he wants, but, PhD or not, in the end it comes down to his *feelings*. And where does making Burke a suspect lead *me*? Trying to chase down some phantom the Bureau hasn't been able to snag for three years? I've already got prospects close to home."

His hand grazed the file folder. "If I don't cooperate eventually, he'll call the brass and I'll be stuck with task-force bullshit. For the moment, he's trying cop-to-cop."

A couple of multiple-pierced kids dressed in black entered the deli and took a booth at the front. Lots of laughter. I heard the word "pastrami" used as if it was a punch line.

"Nitrites for the night crawlers," Milo muttered. "Wanna do me a big favor? One that won't put you in conflict of interest?" Tapping the file. "Go over this for me. You come up with something juicy, I take it more seriously. . . . Artistic. Burke draws, he doesn't paint. We've already got a good idea who did that masterpiece. . . . So, you mind?"

"Not at all."

"Thanks. That frees me up for the fun stuff."

"Which is?"

"Scrounging through putrid squats in Venice. Cop's day at the beach."

He hoisted himself out of the booth.

"Feds with PhDs," he said. "Bad guys with MDs. And *moi* with a lowly master's—it's not pretty, being outclassed."

I brought the file home just after three. Robin's truck was gone and the day's mail was still in the box. I collected the stack, made coffee, drank a cup and a half, brought the file to my office and called my service.

Richard Doss's secretary had phoned to let me know Eric would be a half hour early for his four o'clock appointment. The boy had been examined by Dr. Robert Manitow; if I had time, please call the doctor.

She'd left Manitow's number and I punched it. His receptionist sounded harried and my name evoked no recognition. She put me on hold for a long time. No music. Good.

I'd never met Bob or talked to him, knew him only from silver-framed family photos on a carved credenza in Judy's chambers.

A clipped voice said, "Dr. Manitow. Who's this?"

"Dr. Delaware."

"What can I do for you?" Curt. Had his wife never mentioned working with me?

"I'm a psychologist—"

"I know who you are. Eric's on his way over to see you."

"How's he doing physically?"

"He's doing fine. It was your idea to have me check him out, wasn't it?" Each word sounded as if it had been dragged over broken glass. No mistaking the accusatory tone.

I said, "I thought it would be a good idea, seeing what he's gone through."

"What exactly is he supposed to have gone through?"

"Beyond the long-term effects of losing his mom, his behavior was unusual, according to his father. Disappearing without explanation, refusing to talk—"

"He talks fine," said Manitow. "He just talked to me. Told me this whole thing was bullshit, and I heartily concur. He's a *college* student, for God's sake. They leave home and do all kinds of crazy things—didn't you?"

"His roommate was concerned enough to—"

"So the kid decided not to be perfect, for once. Of all people, I thought you'd evaluate the source before getting sucked into all this hysteria."

"The source?"

"Richard," he said. "Everything in Richard's life is one big goddamn production. The whole family's like that—nothing's casual, everything's a big goddamn deal."

"You're saying they overdramatize—"

"Don't do that," he said. "Don't bounce my words back to me like I'm on the couch. Hell yes, they overdramatize. When they built that house of theirs, they should've included an amphitheater."

"I'm sure you know them well," I said, "but given what happened to Joanne—"

"What happened to Joanne was hell for those poor kids. But the truth is, she was screwed up psychologically. Pure and simple. Not a damn thing wrong with her other than she chose to drop out of life and eat herself to death. She discarded her good sense. That's why she called that quack to finish the job. Nothing more than depression. I'm no shrink, and *I* could diagnose it. I told her to get psychiatric help, she refused. If Richard had listened to me in the first place and had her committed, they could've put her on a good tricyclic and she might be alive today and the kids could've been spared all the shit they went through."

He wasn't talking loud but I found myself holding the phone away from my ear.

He said, "Good luck with the kid. *I've* got to run."

Click. His anger hung in the air, bitter as September smog.

Yesterday, after viewing Stacy's pain as we walked along the beach, I'd decided not to call Judy, wondering about entanglements between the Manitows and the Dosses, something that went beyond Mommy and Me, country-club tennis, Laura Ashley bedrooms. Now my curiosity took off in a whole new direction.

Her Eric, my Allison, then Stacy and Becky . . .

Becky having trouble in school—tutored by Joanne, then dropping back down to D's when Joanne could no longer see her . . . Was Bob's anger a reaction to perceived rejection?

Becky getting too skinny, entering therapy, trying to play therapist with Stacy, then cooling off.

Eric dumping Allison. Yet another rejection?

Bob Manitow smarting at his daughter's broken heart? No, it had to be more than that. And his resentment of the Dosses' problems wasn't shared by his wife. Judy had referred Stacy to me because she cared about the girl. . . . Just another case of male impatience versus female empathy? Or had Bob's empathy been trashed by his inability to rouse Joanne from what he saw as "nothing more than depression"? Sometimes physicians get angry at psychosomatic illness . . . or maybe this physician was just having a really bad day.

I thought of something else: Stacy's tale of how Bob had stared with distaste as Richard and Joanne groped each other in the pool.

A prudish man, offended? Perhaps his resentment at having to confront the Dosses' tribulations was *emotional* prudishness. I'd seen that most often in those running from their own despair, what a professor of mine had called baloney fleeing the slicer.

No sense speculating, the Manitows weren't the issue; I'd allowed Bob Manitow's anger to take me too far afield. Still, his reaction had been so intense—so out of proportion—that I had trouble letting go of it, and as I waited for Eric my thoughts kept drifting back to Judy.

Pencil-thin Judy in her chambers. Impeccable office, impeccable occupant. Tanned, tight-skinned, strong-boned good looks. Hanging her robe on a walnut valet, revealing the body-hugging St. John Knits suit underneath.

The room perpetually ready for a photo shoot: polished furniture, fresh flowers in crystal vases, soft lights, gelid convexities. No hint that the fury and tedium of Superior Court waited just beyond the door.

Those family photos. Two lithe blond girls with that same strong-boned beauty. Thin, very thin. Dad in the background . . . Had any of them smiled for the camera? I couldn't remember, was pretty sure Bob hadn't.

Stick-mom and a pair of stick-daughters, Becky carrying it too far. Did Judy's attention to detail manifest as pressure upon her kids to look, sound, act, *be* faultless? Had the Dosses and their problems somehow become enmeshed with their neighbors?

Maybe I was indulging myself in speculation because the family was far less unpleasant than the file I'd taken from the deli. *Geometry.*

Finally, the red light flashed.

Richard and Stacy at the side door. Eric between them.

Richard in his usual black shirt and slacks, the little

silver phone in one hand. Looking a bit haggard. Stacy's hair was loose and she wore a sleeveless white dress and white flats. I thought of a little girl in church.

Eric gave a disgusted look. His father and his sister had spoken about him in a way that connoted a huge presence. But when it came to physical stature, Doss DNA hadn't faltered. He was no taller than Richard, and a good ten pounds lighter. A dejected slump bowed his back. Small hands, small feet.

A frail-looking boy with enormous black eyes, a delicate nose, and a soft, curling mouth. Rounder face than Stacy's, but that same leprechaun cast. Copper skin, black hair clipped so short the curls had diminished to fuzz. His chambray shirt was oversize, and it bagged over the sagging waistband of dirt-stained baggy khakis wrinkled to used-Kleenex consistency. The cuffs accordioned atop running shoes encrusted with gray dried mud. Skimpy beard stubble dotted his chin and cheeks.

He looked everywhere but at me, his fingers flexed against his thighs. Delicate hands. Blackened, cracked nails, as if he'd been clawing in the dirt. His father hadn't tried to clean him up. Or maybe he'd tried and Eric had resisted.

I said, "Eric? Dr. Delaware," and extended my hand. He ignored the gesture, stared at the ground. The fingers kept flexing.

Good-looking kid. On a certain kind of sweet, convincing, college night, girls attracted to the brooding, sensitive type would be drawn to him.

Just as I began to retract my hand, he gripped it. His skin was cold, moist. Turning to his father, he grimaced, as if bracing for pain.

I said, "Richard, you and Stacy can wait out here or

walk around in the garden. Check back in an hour or so."

"You don't need to talk to me?" said Richard.

"Later."

His lips seemed on the verge of a retort—making a point—but he thought better of it. "Okay then, how about we get coffee or something, Stace? We can make it into Westwood and back in an hour."

"Sure, Daddy."

I caught Stacy's eye. She gave a tiny nod, letting me know seeing her brother was okay. I nodded back, the two of them left, and I closed the door behind Eric and myself and said, "This way."

He followed me into the office, stood in the center of the room.

"Make yourself comfortable," I said. "Or at least as comfortable as you can be."

He moved to the nearest chair and lowered himself slowly.

"I can understand your not wanting to be here, Eric. So if—"

"No, I want to be here." A big man's voice flowed out of the cupid's mouth. Richard's baritone, even more incongruous. He flexed his neck. "I deserve to be here. I'm fucked up." He fingered a shirt button. "That's absurd, isn't it?" he said. "The way I just phrased that. The way we use 'fuck' as a pejorative. Supposedly the most beautiful act in the world and we use it that way." Sickly smile. "Scroll back and edit: I'm *dysfunctional*. Now you're supposed to ask in what way."

"In what way?"

"Isn't your job finding out?"

"Yup," I said.

"Good deal, your job," he said, looking around the

office. "No need for any equipment, just your psyche and the patient's encountering each other in the great affective void, hoping for a collision of insight." The briefest smile. "As you can see, I've had intro psych."

"Did you enjoy it?"

"Nice relief from the cold, cruel world of supply and demand. One thing did bother me, though. You people put so much emphasis upon function and dysfunction but pay no attention to guilt and expiation."

"Too value-free for you?" I said.

"Too *incomplete*. Guilt's a virtue—maybe the *cardinal* virtue. Think about it: what else is going to motivate us bipeds to behave with proper restraint? What else prevents society from sinking into mass, entropic fuckupedness?"

His left leg crossed over his right and his shoulders loosened. Using big words relaxed him. I imagined his first, precocious utterances, met with astonishment, then cheers. Achievements piling up, expectations exceeded.

I said, "Guilt as a virtue."

"What other virtue *is* there? What else keeps us civilized? Assuming we *are* civilized. Highly open to debate."

"There are degrees of civilization," I said.

He smiled. "You probably believe in altruism for its own sake. Good deeds carried out for the intrinsic satisfaction. I think life's essentially an avoidance paradigm: people do things to avoid being punished."

"Does that come from personal experience?"

He shifted back in the chair. "Well, well, well. Isn't that a bit *directive*, considering I've been here all of five minutes and it's not exactly a voluntary transaction?"

I said nothing.

He said, "Get too pushy and I could revert to the treatment I gave my father when he chanced upon my meditation spot."

"Which is?"

"Total freeze-out—what you guys call elective mutism."

"At least it's 'elective.' "

He stared at me. "Meaning?"

"Meaning you're in control," I said.

"Am I? Is there really any such thing as volition?"

"Without volition, why the need for guilt, Eric?"

He frowned for less than a second. Wiped away consternation with a smile. "Aha!" Fingering a button of his wrinkled shirt. "A philosopher. Probably an Ivy League guy—let's take a look at those diplomas. . . . Oh. Sorry, the U. Native son?"

"Midwesterner."

"Corn and cows and yet you're philosophical—this could start sounding like *My Dinner with Andre.*"

"Favorite movie of yours?" I said.

"I liked it, considering the chattiness level. *Lethal Weapon*'s more to my taste."

"Oh?"

"The comfort of simplicity."

"Because life's complicated."

He began to reply, checked himself, scanned my diplomas again, resumed studying the carpet. Neither of us spoke for a minute or so, then he looked up. "Waiting me out? Technique Number Thirty-six B?"

"It's your time," I said.

"Your job requires patience. I'd be lousy at it. I've been told I don't suffer fools well."

"Told by whom?"

"Everyone. Dad. He meant it as a compliment. He's

rather proud of me and displays it with ostentatious shows of support—there's a case of constructive guilt for you."

"What's your father guilty about?" I said.

"Losing control. Raising his kiddies by himself when all three of us know what he'd really rather be doing is flying all over the country amassing real estate."

"It's not as if it was his decision."

"Well"—the curling lips twisted upward—"Dad's not always rational. But then, who is? To understand the root of his guilt, you'd need to know something about his background—do you?"

"Why don't you fill me in."

"He's your basic self-made man, the cream of immigrant stock. His father's Greek, his mother's Sicilian. They ran a grocery in Bayonne, New Jersey, can't you just smell the Kalamata olives? In that world, family means mama, papa, kiddies, grape leaves, farting after too much soup, the usual Mediterranean accoutrements. But poor Dad's stuck with no mama in *his* family—he didn't save his wife."

"Was that within his power?"

His face flushed and his hands rolled into fists. "How the fuck should *I* know? Why even ask that kind of question when it's structurally *unanswerable*? Why should I have to answer *any* of your questions?"

He looked at the door, as if considering escape, muttered, "What's the use?" and slumped lower.

"The question bothered you," I said. "Have you been asked it by someone else?"

"No," he said. "And why would I give a *fuck* about anyone else? Why the *fuck* would I give a *fuck* about the fucking *past*, period? It's what's happening now that's . . . Forget it, there's clearly no point discussing this. Don't start feeling all triumphant because the first time I meet you I exhibit emotion. If you knew me, you'd know that's no big deal. I'm *Mr.* Emotion. I think it, I say it, in the brain, out the mouth. I'll emote to a fucking *stranger* if the mood strikes me, so this isn't progress."

More sotto voce swearing.

"The only reason I let Dad get me into this is . . ."

Silence.

"Is what, Eric?"

"He caught me in a weak moment. The moon was full and I was full of shit. Believe me, it won't happen again. First item of business: back to Palo Alto tonight. Second item: get a new roommate who won't rat me out if I decide to deviate from routine. This is *bullshit*, understand? I know it, Dr. Manitow knows it and if you earned all that paper on the wall, you should know it."

"Much ado about nothing," I said.

"It sure isn't *A Midsummer Night's Dream*—no comedy in my life, *dottore*, I'm a po', po' child of tragedy. My mother came to a horrible end, I'm entitled to be obnoxious, right? Her death bought me *leeway*." His hands pressed together prayerfully. "Thank you, Mom, for miles of leeway."

He slid down so that he was nearly lying in the chair. Smiled. "Okay then, let's talk about something a bit cheerier—how about them Dodgers?"

I said, "Seeing as you're going back to Stanford and I'll probably never talk to you again, I'm going to incur your wrath by suggesting you find someone there to talk to— Hear me out, Eric. I'm not saying you're dysfunctional. But you have been through something terrible and—"

"You are so full of shit," he broke in. Discomfortingly mild tone. "How can you sit there and judge my experience?"

"I'm not judging, I'm empathizing. I was older than you when my father died, but not much older. He brought on his own death, too. I was a good deal older when my mother died, but the loss was more profound because I was closer to her and now I was an orphan. There's something about that—the aloneness. My father's death was a big blow to my sense of trust. The fact that something so important can be taken away from you, just like that. The powerlessness. You view the world differently. I think that's worth talking about to someone who'll really listen."

The black eyes hadn't moved from mine. A vein in his neck pulsed. He smiled. Slouched. "Nice speech, bro. What's that called? Constructive self-disclosure? Technique Number Fifty-five C?"

I shrugged. "Enough said."

"Sorry," he said in a small, hurried voice. "You're a nice guy. Problem is, *I'm* not. So don't waste your time."

"You seem heavily invested in that," I said.

"In what?"

"Being the quirky, obnoxious genius. My guess is that somewhere along the line you were taught to associate smarts with having an edge. But I've met some really bad people and you don't qualify for that club."

His face went scarlet. "I apologized, man. No need to twist the fucking *knife*."

"No need for apologies, Eric. This is about you, not me. And yes, you're right, that was constructive self-disclosure. I chose to expose part of myself in the hope it might spur you to get some help."

He turned away from me. "This *is* bullshit. If Dad

hadn't been a fucking old maid and freaked out, none of this would be happening."

"That wouldn't change the reality."

"Give me a break."

"Forget philosophy, Eric. Forget intro psych. *Your* reality is what you're experiencing. Most people your age don't have to endure what you've endured. Most aren't concerned with guilt and expiation."

His shoulders jerked as if I'd shaken him. "I. Was. Talking. Abstractly."

"Were you?"

He seemed poised to leap from the chair. Settled back down. Laughed. "So you've met a lot of bad guys, have you?"

"More than I'd care to."

"Killers?"

"Among others."

"Serial killers?"

"That, too."

Another laugh. "And you don't think I'd qualify?"

"Let's call it an educated guess, Eric. Though you're right: I don't really know you. I'm also guessing guilt's more than an abstraction for you. Your father and your sister both told me how much time you spent with your mother during her illness. Taking the semester off—"

"So, now I get punished for it? Have to listen to all this fucking *shit*?"

"Being here's not punishment."

"It is if it's against your will."

"Could your father really have forced you?" I said.

He didn't answer.

"It's your choice," I said. "Your volition. And since this is a one-shot deal, the best I can do is give you some advice and let you run with it."

"*My* advice is forget it—don't waste your midwestern time. I shouldn't be here in the first place. I shouldn't be horning in on Stacy's therapy."

"Stacy's okay with it—"

"That's what she says. That's the way she always starts out, path of least resistance, everything's fine. But, believe me, she'll get pissed about it, it's just a matter of time. Basically, she hates me. I'm a shadow in her life, the best thing that ever happened to her was my going away. Stanford's the last place she should go, but with Dad leaning on her, she'll comply once again—the path of least resistance. She'll come up there, want to hang out with me, start hating me again."

"She stops hating you when you're apart?"

"Absence makes the heart grow fonder."

"Sometimes absence makes the heart grow hollow."

"Profound," he said. "All this fucking profundity so early in the day."

"You really think Stacy hates you."

"Ah *knows* she duz. Not that I can do anything about it. Birth order's birth order, she'll just have to deal with being number two."

"And you have to deal with being number one."

"The burdens of primacy." He peeled back a sleeve. "Oh man, left my watch back in my dorm room . . . Hopefully no one swiped it—I've really got to get back, take care of business. How much more time do we have?"

"Ten more minutes."

He examined the room some more, saw the play corner, the bookcase stacked with board games. "Hey, let's play Candy Land. See who gets to the top of that big rock-candy mountain first."

"Nothing wrong," I said, "with having a sweet life."

He wheeled, gaped at me. I never saw the tears in his eyes but the frantic way he swiped at them told me they were there. "Everything's a punch line with you— making your fucking point. Well, thanks for all the fucking *insight*, Doc."

The bell rang. Eight minutes early. Richard, overeager?

I picked up the phone, punched the intercom button for the side door.

"It's me," said Richard. "Sorry for interrupting, but we've got a bit of a problem out here."

Eric and I hurried over. Richard stood on the porch along with Stacy. Two tall men behind them.

Detectives Korn and Demetri.

Richard said, "These gentlemen want me to accompany them to the police station."

Korn said, "Hey, Doc. Nice place."

Richard said, "You *know* them?"

"What's going on?" I said.

Korn said, "Like Mr. Doss said, his presence is requested at the station."

"For what?"

"Questioning."

"In regard to?"

Demetri stepped forward. "That's not your business, Doctor. We allowed Mr. Doss to call you because his children are present and one of them's a minor. The boy's twenty, right? So he can drive both of them home in Mr. Doss's car."

He and Korn moved closer to Richard. Richard looked scared.

Stacy said, "Daddy?" Her eyes were wide with terror.

Richard didn't answer her. Nor did he ask what it was all about. Not wanting his children to hear the answer?

"You ride with us, sir," said Demetri.

"First I'm calling my lawyer."

"You're not being arrested, sir," said Korn. "You can call from the station."

"I'm going to call my lawyer." Richard brandished the silver phone.

Korn and Demetri looked at each other. Korn said, "Fine. Tell him to meet you at the West L.A. station, but you're coming with us."

"What the fuck," said Eric, moving toward the detectives.

Demetri said, "Stand back, son."

"I'm not your fucking son. If I was, my knuckles would be scraping the ground."

Demetri reached inside his jacket and touched his gun. Stacy gasped and Eric's eyes got wide.

I placed my hand on his shoulder, bore down. He was trembling.

Richard stabbed the keypad of the silver phone. Eric got next to Stacy, put his arm around her. She threw her arm across his chest. Her lips quivered. Eric's were still but the neck vein was racing. Both of them watched their father as he held the phone to his ear.

Richard's foot tapped impatiently. No more fear in his eyes. Calm under fire, or not totally surprised?

"Saundra? Richard Doss. Please get Max on the phone. . . . What's that? When? . . . Okay, listen, it's really important that I talk to him . . . I'm in a bit of a jam . . . no, something different, I can't get into it right now. Just reach him in Aspen. ASAP. I'll be at the West L.A. police station—with some detectives. . . . What're your names?"

"Korn."

"Demetri."

Richard repeated that. "Reach him, Saundra. If he can't jet back, at the very least I need the name of someone who can help me. I'm on cellular. I'm counting on you. Bye." He clicked off the phone.

"On our way," said Demetri.

Richard said, "Demetri. Greek?"

"American," said Demetri, too quickly. Then: "Lithuanian. A long time ago. Let's get going, sir."

No one can make "sir" sound like an insult the way a cop can.

Stacy started to cry. Eric held her tight.

Richard said, "I'll be okay, kids, you just hold on—I'll see you for dinner. Promise."

"Daddy," said Stacy.

"It'll be fine."

"Sir," said Korn, taking hold of Richard's arm.

"Hold on," I said. "I'm going to call Milo."

Both detectives grinned, as if on cue. I was the perfect shill.

Demetri moved behind Richard as Korn kept his grip. The two of them shadowing the much smaller man.

"*Milo,*" Demetri said, "knows."

CHAPTER
21

THE BIG, PALE palm of a hand hung inches from my face, a fleshy cloud.

"Don't," said Milo, barely audible. "Don't say a thing."

It was 5:23. I was in the front reception area of the West L.A. station and he'd just come down the stairs.

I wanted to knock his hand away, waited as it lowered. His jacket was off but his tie was tight—too tight, reddening his neck and face. What did *he* have to be angry about?

I'd been waiting in the lobby for over an hour, most of it alone with the civilian clerk behind the desk, a pasty, overly enunciative man named Dwight Moore. I knew some of the clerks. Not Moore. The first time I'd approached, he'd looked wary, as if I had something to sell. When I asked him to reach Milo upstairs, he took a long time to put the call through.

For the next sixty-three minutes I used every anger-reduction trick I knew while warming a hard plastic chair as Moore answered the phone and moved paper around. Twenty minutes into the wait, I stepped up to the desk and Moore said, "Why don't you just go home, sir? If he really does know you, he's got your number."

My hands clenched below the counter. "No, I'll wait."

"Suit yourself." Moore got up, walked into a back room, returned with a large cup of coffee and a glazed bear claw. He ate with his back to me, taking very small bites and wiping his chin several times. Minutes dripped by. A few blues came and went, some of them greeting Moore, none with enthusiasm. I thought of Stacy and Eric watching their father taken away by LAPD's finest.

At five-fifteen, an elderly couple in matching green cardigans walked into the station and asked Moore what could be done about their lost dog. Moore adopted a skeptical look and gave them the number for Animal Control. When the woman asked another question, Moore said, "I'm not Animal Control," and turned his back.

"What you are," said the old man, "is a little prick."

"Herb," said his wife, easing him toward the door.

As they left, he told her, "And they wonder why no one likes them."

Five-twenty. Eric and Stacy were nowhere in sight. If they'd made it, I assumed they'd been allowed upstairs, but Moore wouldn't confirm it.

I'd sped over in the Seville, following Richard's black BMW as Eric gunned it down from the glen and wove through Westwood traffic. Easy to follow: the car was a blade of onyx cutting through dirty air. The car that I'd wondered about as the match to the vehicle Paul Ulrich had spotted on Mulholland. Richard, Eric . . .

The boy drove much too fast, took foolish chances. At Sepulveda and Wilshire, he ran a red light, nearly collided with a gardener's truck, swerved into the center lane, sped away from a chorus of honks. I was two cars back, got caught at the light, lost sight of him. By the time I reached the station, I couldn't find the BMW on the street. No parking space for me in the police lot this time. I circled several times, finally grabbed a spot two blocks away. Jogging the distance, I arrived huffing.

Remembering the fear in Stacy's eyes as Korn and Demetri placed their father in the back of a dung-brown unmarked. Tears striping her face. As Korn slammed the door of the police car, she mouthed, "Daddy." Eric dragged her to the BMW, opened her door, nearly shoved her into the passenger seat. Flashing me one furious look, he ran to the driver's side, started the car up hard, shoved the RPMs to a defiant whine. Fishtailing and burning rubber, he took off.

"Where are the kids?" I asked Milo.

Something in my voice made him wince. "Let's talk upstairs, Alex."

The use of my name made Moore look up. "Hey there, Detective Sturgis," he said. "This gent's been waiting for you."

Milo grunted and led me to the stairs. We climbed quickly to the second floor, but instead of exiting, he stopped at the fire door and leaned against it. "Hear me out. This was not my decision—"

"You didn't send those two—"

"The command to pick up and question Doss came from downtown. *Command*, not request. Downtown claims they tried to reach me. I was out in Venice, and instead of trying harder they went around me and gave the order to Korn."

"Demetri said you knew."

"Demetri's an asshole." Neck bulging against the collar. Unhealthy flush. I was three steps below him and he probably didn't mean to glare down at me. But the effect was there—looming bulk, volcanic rage. The stairwell was hot, gray, soupy with the steel-and-sweat pungency of a high-school corridor.

"Would I have done the same thing?" he said. "Yes, it was a command. But not at your house. So please. I've got plenty to deal with."

"Fine," I said, not sounding fine at all. "But cut me some slack, too. I saw the looks on those kids' faces. What the hell's the emergency? What's Richard done?"

He exhaled. "Upsetting his kids is the least of his problems. He's in serious trouble, Alex."

My stomach lurched. "On Mate?"

"Oh yeah."

"What the hell changed in two hours?" I said.

"What changed is we've got *evidence* on Doss."

"What kind of evidence?"

He ran a finger under his collar. "If you breathe a word of it, you're essentially decapitating me."

"Heaven forbid," I said. "Without a head, you couldn't eat. Come on, what do you have?"

He stretched a leg, sat on the top step. "What I have is a pleasant fellow named Quentin Goad, locked up at County, waiting trial on an armed robbery beef."

He fished a mug shot out of his pocket. Heavyset white man with a shaved head and black goatee.

"Looks like an overweight Satan," I said.

"When Quentin's not holding up 7-Elevens, he works construction—roofing and sheet-metal work. He's done a lot of work for Mr. Doss—apparently Mr. Doss likes to hire cons, pays them under the table to avoid taxes, which tells you something about *his* character. The way Goad tells it, two months ago he was roofing a project out in San Bernardino—some big shopping center Doss bought cheap and was refurbishing—when Doss approached him and offered him five thousand bucks to kill Mate. Told him to make it nasty and bloody so everyone would think it was a serial killer. Gave Goad a thousand up front, promised four when the job was finished. Goad says he took the dough but never intended to follow through, saw it as a perfect way to con Doss and cut town with a grand. He'd been wanting to move to Nevada anyway, because he had two strikes against him in California and it made him nervous."

"Don't tell me," I said. "Before he left, he decided to give himself a going-away party."

"A month ago, hamburger joint in San Fernando, late at night, just before closing time. Mr. Goad, a .22, a paper bag. Eight-hundred-buck haul. Goad already had the counter boy facedown on the floor and the money in the bag when the security guard appeared out of nowhere and took him down. Gunshot to the leg. Flesh wound. Goad spent two weeks at County Gen getting free medical care, and then they moved him to the Twin Towers. The .22 wasn't even loaded."

"So now he's facing three strikes and he's trying to deal by selling out Richard. He's claiming Richard gave him money two months ago and didn't mind no follow-through. The Richard I know isn't high on patience."

"Richard bugged him, all right. About three weeks in, wanting a progress report. Goad told him he needed to plan it just right, was watching Mate, waiting for the perfect opportunity."

"Was he?"

"He says no. The whole thing was a scam."

"Come on, Milo, however you look at it, this guy's a liar and a—"

"Low-life moke. And if it was only Goad's story, your pal would be facing a much brighter future. Unfortunately, witnesses saw Doss and Goad meet at one of Goad's hangouts—ex-con bar in San Fernando, only a block from the hamburger joint he tried to rip off, which tells you how smart Goad is. The thing is, Doss didn't act too smart, either. We've got three drinkers and the bartender who saw the two of them having a serious head-to-head. They remember Doss because of the way he dressed. Fancy black duds, he didn't fit in. The waitress saw Doss pass an envelope to Goad. Nice, fat envelope. And she's got no reason to lie."

"But she never actually saw money changing hands."

"What?" he said. "Doss was passing him Halloween candy?"

"Goad claims Richard passed him cash, right out in the open?"

"The bar's a con hangout, Alex. Dark dive. Maybe Doss figured no one was watching. Or that it wouldn't come back to haunt him. For all I know, this isn't the first time Doss paid a con to do dirty work for him. We've also recovered some of the money. Doss paid Goad ten hundreds, Goad spent eight but two bills are left. We just printed Doss, should know soon if anything shows up. Want to take bets on that?"

"A dumb psychopath like Goad actually held on to loose cash?"

"He says it was Greyhound money. Something to tide him over until he pulled off the hamburger heist. What's the alternative explanation, Alex? Everyone in the bar's lying? Some grand conspiracy to frame poor Richard because maybe one time he played golf with O.J.? Come on, this is crime as I know it: tawdry, predictable, stupid. Doss may be a hotshot businessman but he was out of his element and he screwed up. He's been on my list, along with Haiselden and Donny. Now he's moved up to number one man."

"Does Goad claim Richard gave him a reason to kill Mate?"

"Goad says Richard told him Mate had murdered his wife. That she wasn't really sick, that as a doctor Mate should have known that, should have tried to talk her out of it. He told Goad he'd be doing a public service by getting rid of the guy. As if Goad cared about doing good—your boy thinks he's street-smart but that shows how out of his element he was. Mr. Brentwood slumming with the lowlife . . . It sounds damn real to me, Alex."

"Even if you do find Richard's prints on the money, what would that prove?" I said. "Goad worked for Richard and you just said he paid his workers under the table."

He looked up at me wearily. "All of a sudden you're a defense attorney? In my humble opinion, your time would be better spent dealing with those two kids than constructing excuses for their daddy. I'm sorry for you that it worked out this way, but as the guy who's been slogging this case, I'm happy as hell to have a real lead."

He didn't look happy.

I said, "Once more with feeling: where are the kids now?"

He hooked a thumb at the door. "I put them in a victim's family room. Assigned them a nice, sensitive female D to keep them company."

"How're they doing?"

"Don't know. Frankly, I've been spending my time on the phone with my alleged superiors and trying to talk to Daddy—who's clammed till his attorney gets here. I can't promise you the kids won't be interviewed eventually, but right now they're just waiting. Want to see them?"

"If they'll see me," I said. "Having the gruesome twosome show up at my door didn't do much for my credibility."

"I'm *sorry*, Alex. Goad's PD called Parker Center direct, ready to deal, and a big brass hard-on developed. Try to forget the kids for a second and see this for what it is: major unsolved homicide going nowhere and along comes credible evidence of a prior threat against the victim from someone with means and motive. At the very least, we've got Doss on conspiracy to solicit murder, which might be enough to hold him while we go looking for goodies."

"How'd Korn and Demetri figure out where he was?"

"Dropped in on his secretary." He chewed his cheek. "Saw your name in the appointment book."

"Great."

"You of all people should know it's not a pretty job, Alex."

"When's Richard's lawyer due?"

"Soon. Big-time mouthpiece named Safer, specializes in getting the upper crust out of scrapes. He'll advise Doss to stay clammed, we'll try to hold your boy on conspiracy. Either way, it'll take a long time clearing the paperwork, so figure on his being here overnight, at least."

He stood, stretched his arms, said, "I'm stiff, too much sitting around."

"Poor baby."

"You want me to apologize again? Fine, mea culpa, culpa mea."

I said, "What about Fusco's file? What about the painting? What does Doss have to do with that?"

"Who's to say the painting has anything to do with the murder? And no, nothing's forgotten, just deferred. If you can still bring yourself to do it, read the damn file. If not, I understand."

He shoved at the door and walked out into the hall.

The victim's family room was a few doors up. A

young, honey-haired woman in a powder-blue pantsuit stood a few feet away.

"Detective Marchesi, Dr. Delaware," said Milo.

"Hi," she said. "I offered them Cokes but they refused, Milo."

"How're they doing?"

"Can't really say, because I've been out here the whole time. They insisted—the boy insisted—that they be by themselves. He seems to be the boss."

"Thanks, Sheila," said Milo. "Take a break."

"Sure. I'll be at my desk if you need me."

Marchesi made her way to the detective's room. Milo said, "All yours," and I turned the handle.

The room wasn't much different from an interrogation cell, had probably been converted from one. Tiny, windowless, hemmed by high-gloss mustard walls. Three chairs upholstered in mismatched floral cotton prints instead of county-issue metal. In place of the steel table with the cuff bolts was a low wooden slatted thing that resembled a picnic bench with the legs cut off. Magazines: *People, Ladies' Home Journal, Modern Computer.*

Eric and Stacy sat in two of the chairs.

Stacy stared at me.

Eric said, "Get out."

Stacy said, "Eric—"

"He's the fuck out of here—don't argue, Stace. He's obviously part of this, we can't trust him."

I said, "Eric, I can understand your thinking—"

"No more bullshit! The fat cop's your pal, you set my dad up, you fuck!"

I said, "Just give me—"

"I'll give you dick!" he shouted. Then he rushed me as Stacy cried out. Suffused blood darkened his skin to chocolate. His eyes were wild and his arms were churning and I knew he'd try to hit me. I backed away, got ready to protect myself without hurting him. Stacy was still shouting, her voice high and feline and frightened. I'd made it out the door when Eric stopped, stood there, waved his fist. Spittle foamed at the corners of his mouth.

"Get out of our lives! We'll take care of *ourselves*!"

Over his shoulder, I saw Stacy, bent low, face buried in her hands.

Eric said, "You're off the case, you fucking loser."

CHAPTER

22

I DROVE HOME, cold hands strangling the steering wheel, heart punching against my chest wall.

Try to forget the kids, they are no longer my affair. Concentrate on facts.

Milo was right. The facts fit. His instincts had aimed him at Richard. Time to be honest: so had mine. The first time I'd heard about Mate's death, Richard had popped into my head. I'd run from the truth, hidden behind the complexities of ethical conflict, but now reality was spitting in my face.

I recalled Richard's gloating after bringing up Mate's death: *Festive times. The sonofabitch finally got what he deserved.*

Finally. Did that mean he'd turned to someone else when Goad had failed to follow through?

Means, motive. Vicarious opportunity. Ready with an alibi. Milo had pegged it right away. People like Richard didn't do their own dirty work.

For all my theories about co-optation and irony, did the van butchery boil down to stupid, bloody revenge?

But why? What could lead someone as bright as Richard to risk so much over a man who'd been no more than an accomplice to his wife's last wishes? Was he one of those skillful psychopaths bright enough to channel his drives into high finance?

Distressed properties. A man who profited from the distress of others. Had Richard been running from a truth of his own? The fact that Joanne had frozen him out of her life, shut him out completely, chosen death in a cheap motel room over a life with him in the Palisades?

Dying in the company of another man . . . the intimacy of death. The feminist journal—*S(Hero)*—wondered about the preponderance of female travelers, speculated about the sexual overtones of assisted suicide. Had Richard seen Joanne's last night as the worst kind of adultery? I supposed it was possible, but it still seemed so . . . clumsy.

Was Richard behind the phony book and the broken stethoscope? *You're out of business, Doc?*

A sick uneasiness slithered over me. *Happy Traveling, You Sick Bastard.* . . . Why had Richard contacted me within a week of the murder? Stacy's college future, as he'd claimed, or, knowing that Quentin Goad had been arrested, was he preparing himself for exactly what had happened?

Asking me to see Eric, too.

Take care of the kids while I'm gone. . . . Look how *that* had turned out.

Then I thought of something much worse. Eric, all that talk of guilt and expiation.

The *directed* child, the gifted firstborn who'd dropped out to tend to his mother, had seemed to be adjusting. Suddenly leaving his dorm room, sitting up all night . . . obsessed with guilt because guilt was all he felt?

Involved. Had his father been cruel enough, crazy enough to get him *involved*?

I'd allowed myself to wonder if Eric had been Mate's

slayer. Now that I'd seen his anger at work, those speculations took on weight.

Richard's deal with Goad peters out, so he keeps it in the family.

Dad in San Francisco, son down in L.A. for a couple of days with the keys to Dad's car.

I wanted to think Richard was—if nothing else—too smart for that, but if he'd been willing to risk his family by passing cash in a con bar, was there any reason to trust his judgment?

Something—a fissure—had forced its way through this family. Something to do with Joanne's death—the how, the why. Bob Manitow claimed her deterioration was all due to depression, and maybe he was right. Even so, that kind of emotional collapse didn't manifest overnight. What had led a woman with two PhDs to destroy herself slowly?

Something long-standing . . . something *Richard* had reason to feel guilty about? A guilt so crushing it had caused him to displace his feelings onto Mate?

Kill the messenger.

Make it bloody.

Father and son. And daughter.

Stacy sitting alone at the beach. Eric sitting alone under a tree. Everyone isolated. Driven apart . . . something that Mate's murder had brought to a head? Here I was again, guessing. Obsessing.

Once, when I was nine, I went through a compulsive phase, labeling my drawers, lining my shoes up in the closet. Unable to sleep unless I pulled the covers over my head in a very special way. Or maybe I'd just been trying to shut out the sound of my father's rage.

I turned off Veteran onto Sunset, raced up the glen, was still groping and supposing when the road to my house appeared so suddenly I nearly missed it. Hooking onto the bridle path, I sped up the hill, drove through the gateposts, parked in front of my little chunk of the American dream.

Home sweet home. Richard's was being torn down, brick by brick.

Robin was in the living room, straightening up. No sign of Spike.

"Out in back," she said. "Doing his business, if you must know."

"A businessman."

She laughed, kissed me, saw my face. Looked at the file. "Looks like you've got business, too."

"Things you don't want to know about," I said.

"More on Mate? The news said they arrested someone."

"Did they." I told her about Korn and Demetri's drop-in.

"*Here?* Oh my God."

"Rang the bell and took him away in front of his kids."

"That's horrible—how could Milo *do* that?"

"Not his decision. The brass went around him."

"That's just horrible—must have been hell for *you*."

"A lot worse for the kids."

"Poor things . . . The father, Alex, is he capable of that? Sorry, they're still your patients, I shouldn't be asking."

I said, "I'm not sure they are. And I don't have a good answer to that."

But I'd answered her as clearly as if I'd spelled it out. *Sure, he's capable.*

"Honey?" she said, cupping her hand around the back

of my neck. She stood on her tiptoes, pressed her nose to mine. I realized I'd been standing there for a long time, silent, oblivious. The file felt leaden. I hoisted it higher.

She put her arm around my waist and we entered the kitchen. She poured iced tea for both of us and I sat at the table, placing Fusco's opus out of my field of vision. Fighting the urge to walk away from her, throw myself into the FBI man's crusade. Wanting to build up faith in Fusco's project, discover some grand, forensic *aha!* that would exonerate Richard, make me a hero in Stacy's eyes. Eric's, too.

Instead, I sat there, reached for the remote control, flicked on TV news. A red UPDATE! banner filled a corner of the screen. A very happy reporter clutched his microphone and warbled, ". . . in the murder of death doctor Eldon Mate. Police sources tell us that the man being questioned is Richard Theodore Doss, forty-six, a wealthy Pacific Palisades businessman and former husband of Joanne Doss, a woman whose suicide Dr. Mate assisted nearly a year ago. Reports of a possible murder-for-hire scheme have not been confirmed. A few minutes ago Doss's attorney arrived at the West Los Angeles police station. We'll update you on this story as it unfolds. Brian Frobush for On-the-Scene News."

In the background was the building I'd just left. The news crew must have showed up moments after I drove away.

I pressed OFF. Robin sat down next to me.

We touched glasses. I said, "Cheers."

I endured ten more minutes of togetherness. Then I told her I was sorry, picked up the file, and left.

Wounds.

Fissures. Real ones.

It was well after midnight. Robin had been asleep for over an hour and I was pretty sure she hadn't heard when I'd left the bed and made my way to the office.

I'd started with the file, but she'd come after me. Convincing me to bathe with her, take a walk, a long walk. Drive into Santa Monica for an Italian dinner. Come home and play Scrabble, then gin, then sit side by side in bed collaborating on the crossword puzzle.

"Like normal folks," I said, when she said she was sleepy.

"Acting. Genius."

"I love you—and see, I said it without making love first."

"Hey, a new pattern."

"What do you mean?"

"Saying it before. How nice." She reached for me.

Now here I was, throwing on a robe, making my way through the dark house, feeling like a burglar.

Back in the office. Switching on the green-shaded desk lamp and casting a hazy beam on the file.

The room was cold. The house was cold. The robe was old terry cloth, worn to gauze in spots. No socks. The chill took hold in the soles of my feet and worked its way up to my thighs. Telling myself that was appropriate for the task at hand, I drew the file close and untied the string.

Fusco had spared no detail in his study of Grant Rushton/Michael Burke.

Everything neat, organized, subheaded, three-hole-punched. The detached precision of postmortem reports, the weights and measures of degradation.

Page after page of crime-scene description—Fusco's

summaries and analyses as well as some of the original police reports. The agent's prose was more erudite than the typically stilted cop-write, but still far from Shakespeare. He seemed to like dwelling on the nasty stuff, or maybe that was my fatigue and the cold talking.

I stuck with it, found myself entering a state of hyperawareness as I sucked up page after page of small print, photographs, crime-scene Polaroids. Autopsy shots. The beautiful, hideous, lurid hues of the human body imploded, debased, exploited like a rain forest. Sternumcracking, face-peeling, skin-flaying, all in the name of truth. The framing of flesh-tunnels in three-by-five universes, blossoming orchids of ruptured viscera, rivers of hemoglobin syrup.

Dead faces. *The look*. Extraction of the soul.

A realization strobed my brain: Mate would've liked this.

Had he sensed what was happening to him?

I returned my eyes to the pictures. Women—things that had once been women—propped up against trees. A page of abdominal close-ups, gashes and gapes on skin transmuted to plum-colored shapes sketched on gray paper. Precisely excised wounds. The geometry.

The chill found my chest. Inhaling and letting the breath out slowly, I studied the shapes and tried to recall the death shots of Mate that Milo had showed me up on Mulholland.

Craving equivalence between all of this and the concentric squares engraved in Mate's flabby white belly.

Some concordance, I supposed, but once again Milo was right. Lots of killers like to carve.

Skin art . . .

Where was Donny Salcido Mate, self-proclaimed

Rembrandt of the flesh? *The Anatomy Lesson.* Let us carve and learn.

Let us carve Daddy? 'Cause we hate Daddy but want to be him? The art of death . . . Why couldn't it be him? It *should* be him.

Then I thought of Guillerma Mate, the way she'd stood at the closet of that dingy little motel room, frozen, as I asked about her only child. Maybe faith was its own reward, but still, hers had to be a lonely life: a single mom, abandoned by her husband, disappointed by her only child.

She prayed regularly, offered thanks.

Casting her eye upon some grand world to come, or had she truly found peace? Her bus trip to L.A. said she hadn't.

Richard and his kids, Guillerma and her boy.

Alone, everyone alone.

CHAPTER

23

THREE HOURS INTO Thursday.

Three twenty-two A.M. and I'd finished every word in Fusco's omnibus. No thunderous conclusions. Then I went over the photos a second time and saw it.

Crime-scene shot from a Washington State unsolved—one of the four victims murdered during Michael Burke's term as a medical student. Four killings Fusco saw as consistent with Burke's technique because the victims had been left propped against or near trees.

The girl was a twenty-year-old waitress named Marissa Bonpaine, last seen serving shrimp cocktail at a stand in the Pike Place Market in Seattle, found a week later splayed in front of a fir in a remote part of the Olympic National Forest. No footprints near the scene; the build-up of pine needles and decaying leaves on the forest floor was a potentially fertile nest for forensic data, but nothing had been found. Add eleven days of rain to that, and the scene was as clean as the operating room the killer had intended it to be.

Marissa Bonpaine had been savaged in a manner I now found uncomfortably familiar: throat slash, ab-dominal mutilations, sexual posturing. A single, deep trapezoidal wound just above the pubic bone could be considered geometrical, though the edges were rough. Death from shock and blood loss.

No blunt-force head wound. I supposed Fusco would attribute that to the killer's escalating confidence and the seclusion of the spot: wanting Bonpaine conscious, wanting her to watch, to suffer. Taking his time.

I checked the girl's physical dimensions. Four-eleven, one hundred one. Tiny, easy to subdue without knocking her out.

What caught my eye wasn't any of that; after three hours of wading in gore and sadism, I'd grown sadly habituated.

I'd noticed something glinting against the brown cushion of forest detritus, several feet to the right of Marissa Bonpaine's frail left hand. Something shiny enough to catch the miserly light filtering through the dense conifer ceiling and bounce it back. I flipped pages till I found the police report.

A hiker had found the body. Forest rangers and law enforcement personnel from three departments had conducted a two-hundred-yard grid search and listed their findings under "Crime Scene Inventory." One hundred eighty-three retrieved items, mostly trash—empty cans and bottles, broken sunglasses, a can opener, rotted paper, cigarette butts—tobacco and cannabis—animal skeletons, solid lead buckshot, two copper-jacketed bullets ballistically analyzed but deemed unimportant because Marissa Bonpaine's body bore no gunshot wounds. Three pairs of insect-infested hiking boots and other discarded clothing had been studied by the crime lab and dated well before the murder.

Halfway down the list, there it was:

C.S.I. Item #76: *Child's toy hypodermic, manu. Tommi-Toy, Taiwan, orig. component of U-Be-the-Doctor*

Kit, imported 1989–95. Location: ground, 1.4 m from victim's l. hand, no prints, no organic residue. ·

No residue might have indicated recent placement, but the rain might have just washed any residue away. I read the rest of the Bonpaine documents. No sign anyone had considered the toy. A review of all the other Washington cases revealed no other medical toys.

Marissa Bonpaine was the last of the Washington victims. Her body had been found July 2, but the abduction was believed to have occurred around June 17. More page-flipping. Michael Burke had received his MD on June 12.

Graduation party?

I'm a doctor, here's my needle!

I'm *the* doctor!

Stethoscope, hypodermic. One broken, the other intact. I knew what Milo would say. Cute, but so what?

Maybe he was right—he'd been too damn right, so far—and the injector was nothing more than a piece of trash left by some kid who'd hiked through the forest with his parents.

Still, it made me wonder.

A message . . . always messages.

To Marissa: I'm the doctor.

To Mate: I'm the doctor and you're not.

I reread Fusco's notes. No mention of the toy.

Maybe I'd mention it to Milo. If he and I had the chance to talk soon.

I flipped back to the front of the first volume, the various incarnations of Michael Burke, studied every feature of every photo. A song danced through my head—*Getting to know you, getting to know all about you*—but Burke remained a stranger.

High-IQ psychopath, lust-killer, master euthanist. Comforter of terminally ill women, brutalizer of healthy females. Compartmentalizing. It helped in murder as well as politics.

Maybe in real estate, as well. The world of distressed properties.

Milo had his prime witness and I had two toys. Still, the wounds fit. And Milo had asked me to study the files.

You're out of business, I'm in.

When we'd questioned Alice Zoghbie, we'd asked her about confederates, and she'd just about admitted they existed but refused to go further, pooh-poohed the chance anyone close to Mate could have savaged him.

Eldon was brilliant. He wouldn't have trusted just anyone.

But Mate would've *loved* the idea of the MD sidekick. Another boost to his respectability—supervising an internship in cellular cessation.

Zoghbie was worth another try. She'd worshiped Mate, would want to punish his murderer. Now I had a name to throw her, a general physical description, could observe her reaction. What risk was there? I'd call her later this morning. Worst case, she'd tell me to go to hell.

Best case, I'd learn something, maybe make some progress revealing a new suspect.

Someone other than Richard. *Anyone* but Richard.

Stretching out on the old leather sofa, I covered myself with a woolen throw, stared up at the ceiling, knowing I'd never fall back asleep.

When I awoke, it was just after seven and Robin was standing over me.

"What a guy," she said, "moves out to the couch even when he hasn't misbehaved." She sat perched on the edge of the cushion, smoothed my hair.

"Morning," I said.

She looked at the file. "Cramming for the big test?"

"What can I say? Always been a grind."

"And look where it's gotten you."

"Where?"

"Fame, fortune. Me. Rise and shine. Fix yourself up so I can take care of you—I seem to be doing that a lot, lately, don't I?"

Showering and shaving provided a veneer of humanness, but my stomach recoiled at the idea of breakfast and I sat watching as Robin ate toast and eggs and grapefruit. We shared a pleasant half hour and I thought I pulled off amiable pretty well. When she left for the studio, it was eight and I turned on the morning news. Recap of the Doss story but no new facts.

At 8:20, I phoned Alice Zoghbie and heard the taped greeting from her machine. Just as I hung up, my service rang in.

"Morning, Dr. Delaware. I have a Joseph Safer on the phone."

Richard's lawyer. "Put him on."

"Doctor? Joe Safer. I'm a criminal-defense attorney representing your patient Richard Doss."

Mellow baritone. Slow pace but no faltering. The voice of an older man—deliberate, grandfatherly, comforting.

"How's Richard doing?" I said.

"We-ell," said Safer, "he's still incarcerated, so I don't imagine he's doing too well. But that should be resolved by this afternoon."

"Paperwork?"

"Not to be paranoid, Doctor, but I do wonder if the boys in blue haven't slowed things down a bit."

"God forbid."

"Are you a religious man, Doctor?"

"Doesn't everyone invoke God when times get rough?"

He chuckled. "How true. Anyway, the reason I'm calling is once Richard does get out, he would like to speak with you about his children. How to best get them through this."

"Of course," I said.

"Terrific. We'll be in touch." Cheerful. As if planning a picnic.

"What's in store for him, Mr. Safer?"

"Call me Joe. . . . We-ell, that's hard to say . . . we both enjoy the privilege of confidentiality here, so I'll be a bit forthcoming. I don't believe the police have anything one might judge as seriously incriminating. Unless something turns up during the search, and I don't expect it will . . . Doctor, you've got more latitude than I in terms of your confidentiality."

"What do you mean?"

"Unless your patient poses a Tarasoff risk, you're not obligated to divulge anything. I, on the other hand . . . There are questions I don't ask."

Letting me know he didn't want to know if his client was guilty. That I should keep my mouth shut if I knew.

"I understand," I said.

"Splendid . . . Well, then talk about Stacy and Eric for a moment. They seem like nice children. Bright, extremely bright, that's evident even under the circumstances. But troubled—they'd have to be. I'm glad you're on board if therapy's called for."

"There may be a problem with that. Eric's furious with me, convinced I'm aligned with the police. I can understand that because I am friends with one of the—"

"Milo Sturgis," said Safer. "A very effective investigator—I'm well aware of your friendship with Mr. Sturgis. Commendable."

"What is?"

"A heterosexual man enjoying a friendship with a homosexual man. One of my sons was gay. He taught me a lot about having an open mind. I didn't learn quickly enough."

Past tense. His voice had dropped in pitch and volume. "Impetuous youth," he continued. "I'm referring to Eric. I have five of my own, thirteen grandchildren. Four of my own, to be truthful. My boy Daniel passed on last year. His diagnosis sped up my learning curve."

"I'm sorry."

"Oh it was terrible, Doctor, your life's never the same . . . but enough of that. In terms of Eric's recalcitrance, I'll have a talk with the boy. As will Richard. What about Stacy? I don't have as much of a feel for her. She sits there while Eric does all the talking. Reminds me of my Daniel. He was my firstborn, always a peacemaker—his siblings' ambassador to their mother and me when things got rough."

I heard him sigh.

"Stacy's a good kid," I said. "My primary patient in the family. I had only one session with Eric, and not a complete one. The police showed up before we were through and took Richard away."

"Yes. Dreadful. Rather cossacklike behavior . . . We-ell, thank you for your time, Dr. Delaware. Take care of yourself. You're needed here."

CHAPTER

24

THURSDAY AT 8:45 A.M. I called Alice Zoghbie, got the same taped message. Fifteen minutes later, I caught a newsbreak. Different reporter, same I've-got-a-scoop smile. Another backdrop that I recognized.

". . . the woman, Amber Breckenham, claims that in addition, Haiselden regularly abused her and her daughter during their relationship. We're here at Haiselden's house, where neighbors say he hasn't been seen for well over a week. At the moment this remains a civil case, and no word has come down from LAPD as to whether a criminal investigation will be pursued. From Westwood, with another bizarre twist on the murder of death doctor Eldon Mate, I'm Dana Almodovar, On-the-Spot News."

Shift to the weather report. Hazy skies, low sixties to mid-seventies, for the fortieth day in a row. I played with the remote, finally found a complete story on one of the networks specializing in lurid.

Amber Breckenham, thirty-four, the manager of one of Roy Haiselden's laundromats, in Baldwin Park, had filed a civil suit against her former boss. A shot of Breckenham walking into court with her attorney showed a tall, thickly built bleached blonde. Holding her hand was a dark-haired girl, eleven or twelve. The child kept her head down, but someone called her name—

"Laurette!"—and she looked up just long enough for the camera to capture a glimpse of pretty African features and straightened hair brushed back from a high, smooth brow.

Breckenham's story was that she'd had a seven-year affair with Haiselden, during which time he'd claimed to be investing her money but had, in fact, embezzled. Furthermore, he'd abused her physically and intimidated Laurette psychologically. The suit was for five million dollars, most of it punitive damages.

Haiselden's reason for cutting town? Scratch one murder suspect?

But if Amber Breckenham's charges were true, it indicated Mate had been less than a sterling judge of character. Had he misjudged fatally?

Or had choosing Joanne Doss been his big mistake?

And what had been *Joanne*'s mistake—the sin, if there was one, that had caused her to turn herself into the creature in Eric's Polaroid?

I left the house, drove to the U. for my second trip to the research library in as many days.

Only one reference to Joanne's death, a page-20 story in the *Times*:

Body Found in Desert Motel
Attributed to Dr. Mate's Machine

LANCASTER. A motel maid entering to clean a room at the Happy Trails Motel on the outskirts of this high desert community discovered the fully clothed body of a Pacific Palisades woman early yesterday morning. While no sightings of "death doctor" Eldon Mate's van in the vicinity have been reported, toxicologic analysis of the blood of Joanne Doss, 43, indicating the presence of two drugs used consistently by the self-styled euthanist, as well as puncture marks suggesting intravenous injection, and the absence of forced entry or struggle, have led Sheriff's detectives to suspect assisted suicide.

Lead investigator David Graham stated, "She looked peaceful. Classical music was playing on the radio and she'd eaten a last meal. From what I understand, Dr. Mate encourages his patients to listen to music."

Ms. Doss, married to a businessman and the mother of two, was reported to have suffered from deteriorating health, and would be the forty-eighth person whose death Mate has facilitated. Given Mate's success in avoiding conviction, and most recently, his indictment, authorities say it is unlikely criminal charges will be filed.

No follow-up, not even an obituary for Joanne.

No attempt by Mate to claim credit. Maybe I'd missed something. I spent another half hour combing the data banks. Not a single additional line on Joanne Doss's final night. Because by victim number forty-eight, Mate and the Humanitron were no longer news?

Mate had hooked two additional travelers to his machine before ending up in the van himself.

The van. When had he stopped using motels?

Using Mate's name as a keyword and limiting my search to three months before and after Joanne's death, I pulled up three references.

Traveler forty-seven, seven weeks before Joanne: Maria Quillen, sixty-three, terminal ovarian cancer, her body deposited at the front door of the County Morgue wrapped in a frilly pink comforter. Mate's business card tucked into the folds. Driven in the rented van where Mate had helped her die.

Mate informed the press of the details.

Number forty-nine, one month after Joanne. Alberta Jo Johnson, fifty-four, muscular dystrophy. A black woman, the papers specified. Mate's first African American. As if her death represented a new variant of affirmative action. Her corpse had been left at the Charles Drew Medical Center in South L.A., similarly wrapped.

Another van job. Another statement by Dr. Mate.

Now my pulse was racing. I found the fiftieth traveler, a man named Brenton Spear. Lou Gehrig's. Van. Press conference.

Three people with definitive diagnoses. Three van jobs, three public statements—Mate chasing the press because, I was right, he loved the attention.

No word out of him on Joanne. No van.

Joanne's death didn't fit.

I kept searching till I found the last time he'd used a motel.

Number thirty-nine, a full two years before Joanne. Another Lou Gehrig's patient, Reynolds Dobson, dispatched in a Cowboy Inn up near Fresno.

I reread the account of Joanne's final night. No sightings of Mate in the vicinity. *Attribution* to Mate because circumstances had pointed to him.

Cheap motel, the risk of a traumatized maid. After nearly a year's success with motor vehicles, it didn't make sense.

Mate hadn't taken credit for Joanne, because he knew he didn't deserve it.

Then why hadn't he come out and denied his involvement?

Because that would have made him look foolish. *Displaced.*

Someone horning in, a new Dr. Death, just as I'd guessed.

Broken stethoscope. Someone—Michael Burke?—making his grand entry by bathing himself in the blood of his predecessor. Hacking off Mate's manhood—you could deny Freud had ever existed and still understand *that.*

But how had Joanne gotten in contact with the person who'd accompanied her to the Happy Trails Motel?

Maybe I had it all wrong and Mate *had* known. Had allowed his apprentice to strike out on his own.

I considered that. Joanne, ready to die, calling Mate and talking instead to an underling—let's say Burke. Mate supervising, judging Burke's readiness. Unaware Burke was already an expert in the fine art of cellular cessation.

Then I remembered Michael Burke's affinity for older, seriously ill women—patients he met in hospitals—and a whole different scenario flashed.

Joanne, shuffled from doctor to doctor, enduring batteries of medical tests. MRIs, CAT scans, lumbar punctures. Procedures carried out in hospitals.

I pictured her, bloated, pain-racked, regressed to silence, waiting in yet another antiseptic waiting room for the next round of indignities, as people in white coats hurried by, no one noticing her.

Then someone did. A charming, helpful young man. MD on his badge, but he took the time to talk. How wonderful to finally encounter a doctor who actually *talked*!

Or perhaps Burke had been more than a drop-in. Maybe he'd actually carried out some of the tests.

Working as a *technician*, because he hadn't figured out a way, yet, to bogus a new medical diploma but was well-qualified to obtain a paramedical job.

Either way, I needed to learn where Joanne had been evaluated. Richard could tell me, but Richard was indisposed. Bob Manitow would also know, but there was no reason to think he'd even take my call. Whatever the reason for his antipathy, his wife didn't share it.

I'd phone Judy, find some pretense for asking about Joanne's hospital experiences—wanting to know more so I could help the kids. Especially now that Richard was in jail. I'd also try to learn more about the stress fractures that had worked their way through the Doss family. Maybe her family, as well. About why *her* husband was so angry.

Better a face-to-face, a chance to read nonverbal cues. Could I get Judy out of chambers long enough? She and I had always been cordial, and I'd come through for her on lots of tough cases. Now she'd landed me in the toughest one of all and I was ready to tell her so.

I called her number at Superior Court, expecting someone to tell me the judge was in trial. Instead, she picked up herself. "You're calling about Richard."

"The police took him away at my house. Eric and Stacy were there."

"You're kidding. Why would they do that?"

"Orders from above," I said. "They see Richard as a prime suspect for Mate. Have you heard anything around the courthouse?"

"No," she said, "just what was on the news. Bob and I were in Newport for the evening, never looked at the TV, didn't find out about it till last night when we drove home and saw the police cars at Richard's house. I just can't believe this, Alex. It makes no sense."

"Richard as a murderer."

Pause. "Richard doing something so stupid."

"On the other hand," I said, "he did despise Mate. Wasn't shy about expressing it."

"You think he's *guilty*?"

"Just playing devil's advocate."

"I don't allow those in my court— Seriously, Alex, if Richard was up to no good, why would he advertise it? All that tough talk was just Richard being Richard. Spouting off, attributing blame. He's always been a big blamer."

"Who else did he blame besides Mate?"

"No one in particular—it's just his overall style. Being dominant. The truth is, Richard's always been a difficult person—and yes, he does have a vindictive streak. You should hear him talk about how he destroys business rivals. But this? No, it just doesn't make sense. He has too much to lose— Hold on. . . ." Fifteen-second hold. "Alex, they're waiting for me, got to go."

"Could we talk more, Judy?"

"What about?"

"Eric and Stacy. With all this going on, I really need all the data I can get. If you could spare me an hour, I'd greatly appreciate it."

"I . . . I just don't know what I can tell you that hasn't already been said." Brittle laughter. "Some referral, huh? I'll bet from now on you're not going to return my calls quite so quickly."

"I'll always take your referrals, Judy."

"Why's that?"

"Because you give a damn."

"Oh come on," she said. "Don't get all sugary on me. I'm just a judicial hack, putting in my time."

"I don't think so."

"That's very kind of you." Now she sounded sad. "Just an hour?"

"Use that egg timer you pull out when attorneys go on too long."

She laughed again. "You've heard about that."

"I've seen it. The Jenkins case."

"Oh yeah, good old Mr. and Mrs. Jenkins. That one deserved an egg timer with a sonic alarm— Okay, let me check my calendar, here . . . there's so much scrawl I can barely make it out."

"Sooner rather than later if possible, Judy."

"Hold again . . ." Another female voice in the background. Her clerk Doris's contralto. Judy's soprano reply. "The husband's lawyer is trying to pull shtick, time to whip him into shape. . . . Okay, how about dinner tonight? I've got a ton of reports to do, will be working late, anyway. Bob's taking Becky to the Cliffside, so I'm flexible. How about someplace on my way home—Grun!, in Westwood. That's not far from you—eight-thirty tonight."

"Grun! it is. Thanks, Judy. I really appreciate it."

"Oh yes," she said, "I'm quite the saint."

CHAPTER

25

WESTWOOD VILLAGE, AS those who live nearby are quick to point out, used to be a nice place.

Once a high-end shopping district for a high-end residential area, a twist of charmingly curving streets lined with single-story brick buildings, the Village has devolved into a confused tangle of neon and chrome, weekends pulsating with noise, fast-food joints ejaculating gusts of grease and sugar.

Some of that was inevitable. Dominating the north end of the Village is the land-grant sprawl of the U., perched like a hungry bear. The encroachment stretches beyond campus borders, as the university pounces on vacant offices and builds parking lots. Student sensibilities means multiplex theaters, U-print T-shirt shops, discount record stores, jeans emporiums. Student budgets means burgers, not beluga. When a grizzly lolls near a trout stream, guess who gets eaten?

But there are other beasts at work. Developers, aiming to squeeze every dollar out of dirt. Building up, up, up, beyond, beyond, beyond. Lunching and boozing and bribing their way past zoning restrictions. People like Richard.

As token appeasements to the neighbors, some of the high-rise barons bring in pricey restaurants. Grun! was one of those, set on the top floor of a heartless black glass rhomboid on the north end of Glendon. The latest creation of a German celebrity chef with his own brand of frozen dinners.

I'd been there once, the lunch guest of an overeager personal-injury lawyer. Allegedly healthful dining formed of unlikely ethnic melds, prices that kept out the middle class. Waiters in pink shirts and khakis who launched into a world-weary, robotic recitation of the daily specials as if it were another audition. What happened to all the kids who didn't break into pictures?

I drove down Hilgard, passing sorority houses to the west, the U.'s botanical garden to the east, made it to the restaurant in ten minutes. I live close to the Village, but I rarely venture into the cacophony.

A red-jacketed valet lounged by the curb. I squeezed in between two Porsche Boxsters, and the attendant examined the Seville as if it were a museum piece.

I was inside by eight-thirty on the nose. The hostess was a hollow-cheeked, lank-haired brunette working hard on a Morticia Addams act. Judy Manitow hadn't arrived. It took a while to get Tish's attention and figure out that the JTJ in the reservation book stood for Judy the Judge. Tish directed me to the bar. I looked over her shoulder at the half-empty dining room and gave my best boyish grin. She sighed and fluttered her lashes and allowed me to trail her to a corner table.

Half-empty but noisy, sound waves caroming against bleached wood walls, ostentatiously distressed plank floors and mock-wormwood ceiling beams. Where plaster had been applied, it was an unhealthy sunburn pink. Iron tables covered in rose linen, chairs sheathed in dark green suedette.

Tish stopped midway in our trek. Sighed again.

Turned. Rotated her neck, as if warming up for a work-out. "I just love the way the light hits the room from this spot."

"Fantastic." Lights, camera, action. *Cut.*

The table was barely big enough for solitaire. A couple of waiters loitered nearby but neither made a move toward me. Finally, a Hispanic busboy came over and asked if I wanted something to drink. I said I'd wait and he thanked me and brought water.

Ten minutes later, Judy breezed in looking harried. She wore a formfitting, plum-colored knit suit, the skirt ending two inches above her knees, and matching pumps with precarious heels. Her cream-colored handbag had a sparkly clasp that functioned like a headlight, and as she approached at power-walk speed I thought of a little hot rod.

She looked even thinner than I remembered, facial bones expressing themselves sharply under an ash-blond, tennis-friendly cap of hair. Sparkles flashed at her neck, too, and on both hands. As she got closer, she saw me, wiggled two fingers, and picked up speed, playing a castanet solo on the plank floor, hips swiveling, calves defined. The waiters exchanged appreciative glances as they followed her and I wondered if they thought they had her figured out.

Good-looking, wealthy woman out for a night on the town. Little chance she'd be pegged as a presiding Superior Court judge.

I stood to greet her and she pecked my cheek. When I held her chair, she acted as if she was used to it.

"Good to see you again, Alex. Though I'm sure we'd both rather it be under different circumstances."

One of the loitering waiters came over, smiled at Judy,

opened his mouth. Before he could speak, she said, "Gin and tonic. Sapphire gin. And no bruising. Please."

He pouted and his eyes found their way over to me. "Sir?"

"Iced tea."

"Very good."

As he walked away, Judy said, "Veddy *good*. I'm so glad the children approve." She laughed. Too loud, too much edge. "I don't know why I suggested this place, Bob and I never come anymore. . . . Pardon me, Alex, I'm feeling mean, need time to wind down and get human. That's one good thing about the drive from downtown. If you don't succumb to road rage, there's plenty of time to decompress."

"Rough day in court?" I said.

"Is it ever sweetness and light? No, nothing extraordinary, just the usual parade of people with unsolvable problems. When things are fairly calm on the outside, I have no problem with any of it. But today . . ." She fingered a diamond ring on her left hand. Big, round solitaire in a platinum setting. Her right hand sported a cocktail piece—yellow diamonds and sapphires formed into a marigold. "I still can't believe this mess with Richard. Did you have a chance to see Eric and Stacy after they took him away?"

"I saw them briefly at the station but didn't have a chance to talk to them. Richard's lawyer—Joseph Safer—called me this morning and told me he expected to get Richard out by today and that Richard would be calling me to talk. I'm still waiting."

It had been a day for waiting. And guesswork. If a hypothesis is formed in the forest and no one's there to . . . After returning from the library, I'd gone over Fusco's file again, no new insights. No new messages from anyone. I hadn't run for a couple of days, forced myself to do it, ended up in the mountains for a long time, got home still wired, did some push-ups, showered, drank water.

At six, despite the dinner appointment with Judy, I broiled two steaks and baked a couple of Idahos. Steak with Robin. I figured on a salad with Judy. Light and healthful me, what a social butterfly.

The drinks came. Judy raised her glass, inspected the contents and sipped. "Joe Safer is a prince—I'm not being sarcastic. The ideal defense attorney: kindly demeanor combined with the single-mindedness of a psychopath. If I were in trouble, I'd want him to talk for me." Her blue eyes clouded for a moment. She drank some more and they seemed to clear.

"Ah," she said. "This hits the spot. I don't ingest enough poison."

"Too temperate?"

"Too weight-conscious."

"You?"

She smiled. "When I was sixteen I weighed a hundred and ninety-seven pounds. In high school, I was a total slug. To be accurate, I was *repugnant*. Walking two steps exhausted me." Another sip. "I guess that's why I could empathize with Joanne . . . up to a point."

"Up to a point?" I said.

"Only up to a point." Angry squint. "Let's just say that where she ended up was a whole different planet." She drank more, licked her lips.

"It's hard to imagine someone deciding to eat herself into a stupor."

"Oh," she said, "Joanne was full of surprises."

"Such as?"

Another squint. "Just that. And unlike me, she started off thin."

Her voice had filled with anger and I decided to veer away. When in doubt, show personal interest.

"How'd you take off the weight?" I said.

"The old-fashioned way: deprivation. Self-denial has become my lifestyle, Alex." She ran her finger around the rim of the glass. "There's no other way, is there?"

"Self-denial?"

"Fighting," she said. "Most people lack the will. That's why we spend gazillions on the so-called war on drugs, preach about smoking and eating too much fat, but never make any progress. People will never stop getting high. People will take comfort where they find it." Another laugh. "Some talk for a judge, huh? Anyway, I take care of myself. For health, not cosmetics. I keep my family healthy."

"Your girls are pretty athletic, aren't they?"

"What makes you say that?"

"I seem to recall pictures in your office—outdoor sports?"

"My, what a memory," she said. "Yes, Ali and Becky like to sail and ski and they're trim now, but both of them have a tendency to pudge. Lousy genetics: Bob and I were both lumpy kids. I stay on them. It's easier now that they've discovered boys." She sat back. "They both have, thank goodness. Does that sound terrible? Perfectionistic mom?"

"I'm sure you care about them."

"That was shamelessly nonjudgmental, Alex. We're diametric opposites, aren't we? I get paid to do precisely what you avoid."

The waiter approached and asked if she wanted a refill.

"Not at this point," she said. "The doctor here will have a look at the menu, but I know what I want. The

Tender Greens Salad, everything chopped very fine, no dried apricots or olives or nuts, dressing on the side."

"I'll have the same," I said, "but leave in the nuts."

The waiter glanced at his list of specials and walked away looking miffed. Judy said, "Leave in the nuts? Funny. . . . So—you have no idea how Eric and Stacy are coping?"

"I'm sure it's rough for them. Any further thoughts about Richard?"

"Do I think he's capable of soliciting murder? Alex, you know as well as I do that no one can ever really fathom what goes on in someone's head. So yes, I suppose it's theoretically possible that Richard tried to have Mate killed. But the way they said he did it sounds so damn stupid, and Richard's anything but."

"Joanne was brilliant, too."

Her face tightened. Tiny lines, softened by makeup and indirect lighting, appeared all over the surface of her skin. A woman cracking.

"Yes, she was. I won't profess to understand why she did the things she did."

I waited for the stress lines to fade. They didn't. She was gazing into her gin and tonic, playing with the stirrer.

"I guess we never really understand anyone, do we?"

I said, "Let's assume—for argument's sake—that Richard did pay Quentin Goad. Why would he hate Mate that much?"

She touched a finger to her upper lip, massaged, looked up at the ceiling. "Perhaps he saw Mate as taking away something that belonged to him. Richard likes his possessions."

"Was he especially possessive when it came to Joanne?"

"More than any other alpha male? He's a middle-aged *man*, Alex. He's from a certain generation."

"So he saw Joanne as his."

"Bob sees me as his. If you're asking was Richard pathologically jealous, I never saw it."

"And Joanne chose to exclude him from the most important decision of her life."

She swiped her lips with her napkin. "Meaning?"

"Meaning I don't understand much about this family, Judy."

"Neither do I," she said, very softly. "Neither do I." The restaurant din nearly blocked out the sound and I realized I was reading her lips.

"Have you ever met Richard's parents?"

"No," she said. "They never visited, as far as I know, and Richard never talked about them. Why?"

"Grabbing any fact I can. Eric told me he's Greek-Sicilian."

"I suppose I was aware of that—Joanne must've said something, or one of the kids did. But I can't recall Richard ever making a thing about it. I never saw grape leaves in the house, or anything like that."

She looked and sounded tired, as if talking about the Doss family drained her.

I said, "As friends and neighbors, they must have been a challenge."

"What do you mean?" she said, in the same sharp tone I'd heard her use on an errant lawyer.

"They're the kind of people to whom things happen. When I spoke to Bob about Joanne's diagnosis, he sounded pretty frustrated about Joanne's condition—"

"Did he?" she said absently. She gazed around the room. A few more tables had filled. "That's just Bob being Bob. He prides himself on being analytic: identify the problem, cut it out."

"Which he couldn't do with Joanne."

"No, he couldn't." She stirred the drink. Eyes down again. Stress lines deeper.

"Bob seems to feel her illness was all emotional depression," I said.

She looked over at a table to the right. Two couples seated a few minutes ago, laughing, drinking. She summoned the waiter over, ordered another gin and tonic.

"Do you agree?" I said.

"With what?"

"That it was all emotional."

"I'm not a doctor, Alex. I couldn't begin to fathom Joanne's motivation." Another glance at the happiness nearby.

"In terms of Eric and Stacy—"

"Eric and Stacy are going to cope and move on, right? That's why I sent Stacy to you."

Her second drink came. We traded courtroom stories and I listened to her go on about municipal politics, the D.A.'s inability to collect child support. That enabled me to steer the conversation back where I wanted it.

"They couldn't get Mate, either."

She stirred gin, nodded.

"I'm not sure Mate was happy about that," I said. "No more prime time."

"Yes, he was a grandstander, wasn't he?"

"The interesting thing is, Judy, he never took credit for Joanne's death. Never even tried, and it's the only case I could find where that was true."

She'd been holding the glass in midair, lowered it slowly. "You've been researching?"

"The police assumed Mate had assisted Joanne, but they never confirmed it."

"I'd say it's a pretty good assumption, Alex. Her body was full of those chemicals Mate used."

Our salads arrived. Big plate of what looked like lawn shavings. A few cashews on mine. My belly was still filled with steak and nothing had transpired to spark my appetite. I pushed leaves around. Judy aimed her fork at a cherry tomato, tried to stab it, but it rolled out from under the tines. For a split second, fury darkened her face. Talking about the Dosses had been an ordeal.

She speared a speck of lettuce. "Even if Richard was stupid enough to give money to that loser, the loser backed out. I'm hoping he didn't try again. After we spoke, I asked around. So far, nothing beyond solicitation. Have you heard anything to the contrary?"

"No," I said.

"Passion, Alex. It makes people do crazy things."

"Richard was passionate about Joanne?"

"I suppose he was." Peeling back her sleeve, she glanced at the Lady Rolex.

"Here comes the egg timer," I said.

She smiled. "I'm sorry, Alex. I'm very tired—not hungry, either. Is there anything else?"

"I'd like to know more about Eric."

"Just what I told you the first time. A genius, perfectionistic. Dominant personality."

"Stacy said he and Ali dated."

Pause. "Yes, they did. Year ago. Ali said he was a bit of a control freak—nothing weird, he just proved too intense for her. She broke it off."

Stacy had said Eric had severed the relationship. Teenage soap opera. Did it matter?

I said, "He sounds a lot like Richard."

"He's Richard's boy all the way. Like a little nuclear weapon with legs."

"And Stacy?"

"You're Stacy's therapist. What do you think?"

"Was she distant from Joanne?"

"Why do you ask that?"

"Because it was Eric who spent time with Joanne during her last days."

She pushed her plate away. "Alex, I think you've gotten the wrong idea about the Dosses and us. We were friends, neighbors, lunched at the Cliffside. But for the most part they kept their problems to themselves and we lived our own life. Richard told Bob that Stacy seemed to be drifting. From the little I saw, she seemed a bit depressed, so I sent her to you. That's all there is. I can't carry any more on my shoulders. I'm sorry I haven't been more helpful, but that's all there is."

She got up, marched to our waiter, who was talking with a colleague, stood there for a few seconds, then said something that caused his head to retract, as if he'd been bitten. He stalked away and she returned, finished her drink while standing. "Snotty little bastard. I'm waiting to tell him we're ready for the check, he's discussing his latest *audition*."

Looking off to one side, the object of her wrath raced over, flung the check at the table and fled. Judy reached for it, but I got there first.

"What?" she said. "Bribing the judge?"

"Thanking the judge for her time," I said.

"That's all I've given you," she said. "Time. Heat, no light."

* * *

Her Lexus had been left at the curb and I waited for her to drive away. As I waited for the Seville, I tried to make sense out of the last half hour.

She'd arrived at the restaurant looking strained— more tense than I'd ever seen her—and each of my questions seemed to yank her psyche's drawstring tighter. Before she left, she warned off further inquiry. So I'd opened some kind of wound but had no idea what it was.

No chance to get to the topic of hospitals, no way to work it into the conversation.

I'd watched her in court, seen her handle the toughest of cases with aplomb, so this was something personal. . . . The closest she'd gotten to autobiography was self-loathing about her teenage obesity.

I was repugnant. . . . But if that related to the Dosses, I was missing the connection.

I can't carry any more on my shoulders.

Burdened by the Dosses, as was her husband? Bob expressing it as anger because he was a man of a certain generation?

Some kind of intimacy gone terribly bad? Bob jealous of Richard and Joanne in the pool—did it all reduce to another sleazy suburban couples' swap?

And had that related, in some way, to Joanne's decline? Something Richard couldn't forgive her for?

Guilt and expiation. Had *Eric* found out?

Eric and Allison breaking up, Becky in therapy, eating disorders, poor grades, Joanne quitting as tutor, Stacy losing focus, Eric dropping out. Bob enraged, Judy on the edge . . . Joanne dead.

Put together a certain way, I could make it sound like a psychopathology stew.

Even so, what did it have to do with Mate's corpse stretched out in the back of a van, geometry on flesh?

Why hadn't Mate taken credit for Joanne?

The Seville screeched to a halt and the attendant held my door with an expression that said I didn't deserve it. Driving away, I went over it again, finally decided I'd wasted my time and Judy's, most certainly damaged my relationship with the presiding judge of family court.

Another day, another triumph. The car was low on gas and I filled up at a station on Wilshire, used the pay phone near the men's room to call my service. Joseph Safer had phoned five minutes earlier from the Dosses' home number.

Richard answered, hoarse, quieter than usual. "Doctor—hold on." A second later, Safer's melodious voice flowed through the receiver.

"Doctor, thanks so much for getting back promptly."

"What's up?"

"Richard and the children are home. Richard arrived four hours ago, but I waited until the hubbub died down before I called you."

"Press hubbub?"

"Press, police, what you'd expect. As far as I can tell, everyone's departed with the exception of a single un-marked police car parked down the block. Occupied by the two gentlemen who accosted Richard at your home, as a matter of fact."

Korn and Demetri on butt-numbing duty. So Milo had regained at least some of the upper hand.

"Not too subtle," I said.

"We-ell." Safer chuckled. "Cossacks aren't generally known for subtlety."

"Did they search the house?"

"They threatened to," said Safer. "We're disputing their contentions, urging the judge to exercise some re-straint. I realize it's an imposition at this hour—however, if you could find time to come over to chat with Richard and the children, that would be marvelous."

"At the house?"

"I could bring them to your office, but with all they've been through . . ."

"No, that's fine," I said. "I'll be right over."

CHAPTER

26

SAFER GAVE ME directions to the house: west on Sunset, past the Pacific Palisades shopping district, a mile beyond the old Will Rogers estate, then a quick turn north.

Twenty minutes or so from the Village, just as close to my home. In all the time I'd spent with the Dosses, I'd never seen them in their natural surroundings. Back when I was an intern at Western Peds, I found time to make house calls, school visits. After I got licensed, I rarely ventured from the comfort of my own furniture. Was I nothing more than a primatologist deluding himself that he understood chimps because he'd observed them scratching and swinging behind the bars of zoo cages?

House calls were impractical.

Practicality could be confining. Now I'd have the chance to stretch.

I found the turnoff easily enough and sped up a very dark street that climbed into the Palisades. No sidewalks, front lawns the size of small parks, walls and gates and talkboxes, night-black shrubbery, towering cascades of old-growth trees.

Close enough to the ocean to feel the breeze and smell the brine. Were ugly September mornings better up here?

I caught glimmers of moon-blanched water between the bulk of big houses. As I continued, the properties got wider, offered broader glimpses of Pacific. Now I was high enough to see all of the moon, gravid and low. The sky was a cloudless indigo comforter.

Very few cars were parked on the street, and the un-marked, fifty yards up, was as inconspicuous as a roach on a fridge. I sped by, vaguely aware of two heads in front, not bothering to notice if Korn or Demetri made me. Assuming they had. Now I was a notation in the murder book.

I cruised, looked for the address Safer had given me, wondered which neighboring structure housed the Mani-tows' dreams and nightmares.

Richard's monument to success turned out to be a two-story Monterey colonial, pale and ambitious above a hillock of ryegrass spacious enough to host several clusters of trees. Coconut palms, Canary Island pines, lemon eucalyptus, pittosporum, all prettified by clean white lighting that created herbal sculpture. Meticulous flower beds kissed the front of the house. Lights from within turned curtained windows amber. The lack of wall and gate implied openness, welcome. So much for architectural cues.

Stacy's Mustang sat in the driveway, in front of a silver Cadillac Fleetwood of a size no longer manufactured. No sign of Richard's black BMW. Perhaps the auto war-rant had gone through and the vehicle was being raked and combed and vacuumed and luminoled in some forensic garage.

I pulled in behind the Caddy. Its plates read SHYSTER.

A Bouquet Canyon rock pathway snaked to a heavy door banded with hand-forged iron. Before I got to the entrance, the door opened and a rabbi gazed out at me. A tall, rangy, black-suited, yarmulked, gray-bearded rabbi in his sixties. The beard was clipped square and blocked the knot of his silver-gray tie. The suit was double-breasted and tailored. He stood with his hands behind his back and rocked. His presence threw me. The Dosses were Greek-Sicilian, not Jewish.

The rabbi said, "Doctor? Joe Safer."

One hand appeared. We shook, and Safer motioned me into a chandeliered entry hall guarded by a pair of blue-and-white vases as high as my shoulder. An iron-railed staircase swept upward to the second story. Safer and I walked under it and continued to another vestibule bottomed by a crimson Persian runner that fed into a wide, bright hallway. To the left was a dining room papered in blue and set up with plum-colored rosewood furniture that looked old. Across the foyer was a high-ceilinged living room. Ivory ceiling, cream silk sofas, cherrywood floors. If the neutral tones had been designed to show off what was on the walls, they worked.

Case after case of brass-framed, mirror-backed, glassed-in étagères, custom-fit to the crown molding. Glass shelves so clear they were rendered nearly invisible. What rested upon them appeared suspended in midair, just as Milo had described.

Hundreds of bowls, chargers, ewers, jars, shapes I couldn't identify, each piece spotlit and gleaming. One side wall of more blue and white, the other filled with simple-looking gray-green pieces, the widest expanse populated by a porcelain bestiary: horses and camels and dogs and fantastic, bat-eared creatures that resembled the spawn of a dragon with a monkey, all dappled in beautifully dripping mixtures of blue, green and chartreuse. Human figurines rode some of the horses. On a seven-foot coffee table sat what looked like a miniature temple glazed with the same multicolored splotch.

"Something, eh?" said Safer. "Richard informs me that those animals are all Tang dynasty. Over a thousand years old. They pull them up out of graves in China, beautifully preserved. Quite remarkable, wouldn't you say?"

"Quite brave keeping them here," I said, "given the seismic risks."

Safer stroked his beard and pushed his yarmulke back on his head. His hair was an iron gray crew cut specked with red. I still couldn't get rid of the rabbinical image. Remembered his comment about the death of his gay son. *His diagnosis sped my learning curve.* His eyes were gray-green, borderline warm. Like many tall men, he stooped.

"Richard's a courageous man," he said. "The children are courageous. Let's go see them."

We continued through the center hallway. Black carpeting muffled our steps as we passed more brass cases. Monochrome bowls of every color, the mirror backs reflecting Chinese inscriptions on white bases, tiny mud-colored figurines, shelves of potters' creations in white and cream and gray, more of that pale, clean green that I decided I liked best. A row of closed doors, two more at the rear. Safer beckoned me through the one that was open.

Cathedral ceiling, black leather sofas and chairs, black grand piano filling a corner. Through a wall of french doors, an aqua pool and green-lit foliage. Beyond the chlorinated water, palm fringes and the hint of ocean. The seating faced rosewood bookshelves filled with hardcovers, a Bang & Olufsen stereo system, a seventy-inch TV, laser-disc machine, other amusements. On an upper shelf, four family photos. Three of Richard and the kids, a single portrait of Joanne as a smiling young woman.

Richard sat upright on the largest of the sofas, unshaven, sleeves rolled to the elbows, kinky hair ragged—pulled-at, as if birds had attacked, seeking nesting material. He wore the usual all-black and blended so thoroughly with the couch that his body contours were obscured. It made him seem very small—like a growth that had sprouted from the upholstery.

"You're here," he said, sounding half asleep. "Thanks."

I took an armchair and Richard gazed up at Joe Safer.

Safer said, "I'll go see how the kids are doing," and left. Richard picked something out of the corner of his mouth. Sweat beads ringed his hairline.

When Safer's footsteps had faded completely, he said, "They say he's the best." Staring past me. "This is our family room."

"Beautiful house," I said.

"So I've been told."

"What happened?" I said. Any way he took that would be fine.

He didn't answer, kept his gaze above me—focused on the blank TV. As if waiting for the set to come on by itself and feed him some form of enlightenment.

"So," he said, finally. "Here we are."

"What can I do for you, Richard?"

"Safer says anything I tell you is confidential, unless you think I'm a direct threat to someone else."

"That's true."

"I'm no threat to anyone."

"Good."

He jammed his fingers in his hair, tugged at the wiry

strands. "Still, let's keep it hypothetical. For the sake of all concerned."

"Keep what hypothetical?" I said.

"The situation. Say a person—a man, by no means a stupid man but not infallible—say he falls prey to an impulse and does something stupid."

"What impulse?"

"The drive to attain closure. Not a smart move, in fact it's the single stupidest, most insane thing he's ever done in his life, but he's not in his right mind because events have . . . changed him. In the past, he's lived a life full of expectations. That's not to say he's wedded to optimism. Of all people, he knows things don't always work out according to plan. He's earned a *living* understanding that. But still, after all these years of building, establishing, he's done very well, gotten sucked in by the trap of rising expectations. Feels he has a right to some degree of comfort. Then he learns differently." He shrugged. "What's done is done."

"His acting on impulse," I said.

He sucked in breath, gave a sick smile. "He's not in his right mind, let's leave it at that."

Crossing his legs, he sat back, as if giving me time to digest. I had a pretty good idea what he was up to. Working on a diminished-capacity defense. Safer's advice or his own idea?

"Temporary insanity," I said.

"If it comes to that. The only problem is, because he's so screwed up, in the process he may have upset his kids. His own peccadilloes, he can deal with. But his kids, he needs help with that."

Murder-for-hire as a peccadillo.

I said, "Do the kids know what he's done?"

"He hasn't told them, but they're smart kids, they may have figured it out."

"May have."

He nodded.

I said, "Does he intend to tell them?"

"He doesn't see the point of that."

"So he wants someone else to tell them."

"No," he said, suddenly raising his voice. A splash of rose seeped from under his shirt collar and climbed to his earlobes, vivid as a port-wine stain. "He definitely does *not* want that, that is *not* the issue. Helping them through the process *is*. I—he needs someone to tide them over until things settle down."

"He expects things to settle down," I said.

He smiled. "Circumstances dictate optimism. So, do we have an understanding of the issues at hand?"

"No knowledge provided to the kids, holding their hands until their father is out of trouble. Sounds like high-priced baby-sitting."

The flush darkened his entire face, his chest heaved and his eyes began to bulge. The surge of color made me draw back defensively. It's the kind of thing you see in people who have a serious problem with anger. I thought of Eric's outburst in the victims' room at the station.

New side of Richard. Before this, he'd been unfailingly contentious, sometimes irritable, but always cool.

He worked at cooling off now, placing one hand on the arm of the sofa, cupping a knee with the other, as if hastening self-restraint. Ticking off the seconds with his index finger. Ten ticks later, he said, "All right," in the tone you'd use with a slow learner. "We'll call it baby-sitting. Well-trained, well-*paid* baby-sitting. The main thing is the kids get what they need."

"Until things settle down."

"Don't worry," he said. "They will. The funny thing is, despite his poor judgment, he didn't actually *do* anything."

"Soliciting murder's not nothing—hypothetically speaking."

His eyelids drooped. He got up, stepped closer to my chair. I smelled mint on his breath, cologne, putrid sweat. "Nothing *happened*."

"Okay," I said.

"*Nothing*. This person learned from his mistake."

"And didn't try again."

He aimed a finger gun down at me. "Bingo." Easy tone, but the flush had lingered. He stood there, finally returned to the sofa. "Okay then, we have a meeting of the minds."

"What exactly do you want me to tell your kids, Richard?"

"That everything's going to be fine." Making no attempt to steer it back to third-person theoretical. "That I may be . . . indisposed for a while. But only temporarily. They need to know that. I'm the only parent they have left. *They* need *me*, and *I* need *you* to facilitate."

"All right," I said. "But we should also be looking for other sources of support. Are there any family members who could—"

"No," he said. "No one. My mother's dead, and my father's ninety-two and living in a home in New Jersey."

"What about Joanne's side—"

"Nothing," he said. "Both of her parents are gone and she was an only child. Besides, I don't need meddling laymen, I need a professional. Not a bad deal for you. I'll start paying you the way I pay Safer—driving time, thinking time, every billable second."

I didn't answer.

He said, "Why do we have this thing, you and I, everything turns into a push-and-pull?"

Lots of answers to that one, none good. I said, "Richard, we have a meeting of the minds on one point: my role is helping Stacy and Eric. But I need to be honest with you: I have no magic to offer them. Information's my armament. I need to be equipped."

"Oh for God's sake," he said, "what do you want from me, confession? Expiation?"

"Expiation," I said. "Eric used that word, too."

His mouth opened. Shut. The flush drained from his face. Now he'd paled. "Eric has a good vocabulary."

"It's not a topic you and he have discussed?"

"Why the hell *would* it be?"

"I was just wondering if Eric had some reason to feel guilty."

"What the hell about?"

"That's what I'm asking," I said, feeling more like a lawyer cross-examining than a therapist easing pain. He was right, this was our script, and I was as much a player as he.

"No," he said, "Eric's fine. Eric's a great kid." He slumped, rubbed his eyes, half disappeared into the couch, and I began to feel sorry for him. Then I thought of him passing cash to Quentin Goad. In the name of closure.

"So there's nothing particular on Eric's mind."

"His mother destroyed herself, his father got hauled in by the gestapo. Now, what could be on his *mind*?"

He resumed staring at the TV screen. "What's the problem here? Do you resent us because we've made it? Did you grow up poor? Do you resent rich kids? Does having to deal with them day in and day out because they're the ones who pay your bills piss you off? Is that the reason you won't help us?"

My sigh was involuntary.

He said, "Okay, okay, sorry, that was out of line, it's been a . . . rough time. All I'm asking for is some help with Eric and Stacy. If I wasn't so close to the situation, I could deal with it myself. At least I have the insight to know my limitations, right? How many parents can you say that of?"

Footsteps sounded from above. Someone walking. Pacing. Stopping. The kids on the second floor . . .

I said, "No stonewall, Richard. I'm here for Eric and Stacy. Are you in any state to answer a few questions about Joanne?"

"What about Joanne?"

"Basic history. At what hospital did she take her medical tests?"

"St. Michael's. Why?"

"I may want to look at her medical records."

"Same question."

"I'm still trying to understand what was wrong with her."

"Her medical records won't tell you a damn thing," he said. "That's the point, the doctors didn't know. And what does Joanne's illness have to do with the current situation?"

"It may have something to do with Eric and Stacy," I said. "As I said, I run on information. May I have a release from you to look at her records?"

"Sure, sure, Safer can give it to you, I signed over power of attorney to him while I was indisposed. Now, how about going up to talk to my kids?"

"Please bear with me," I said. "After Joanne died, you called Mate, but he never called you back—"

"Did I tell you that?"

"No, Judy did when she made the referral."

"Judy." He swiped at his brow with the back of his hand. "Well, Judy's correct. I did try. Not once, several times. The bastard never gave me the courtesy."

"He didn't throw a press conference regarding Joanne, either."

His eyes slitted. "So?"

"Publicity seemed to be a motive for him—"

"You've got that right," he said. "He was a scum-sucking publicity hound. But don't ask me to explain what he did and didn't do. To me he was a name in the papers."

Easy to erase?

I said, "One other discrepancy: by the time Joanne contacted Mate, he'd already shifted from motels to vans. Yet Joanne died in a motel. Would there have been some reason for her to insist upon that? Some reason for her to travel to Lancaster—"

"She was *never* there," he said.

"Never at the motel?"

"Never in Lancaster." He laughed. Sudden, bitter, incongruous laughter. "Not till that night. It was a thing between us. I was out there all the time, did several projects there, building shopping centers, turning shit into gold. Used to copter from the Municipal Bank Building to Palmdale, drive the rest of the way. Spent so many goddamn hours there I used to feel I was *made* of sand. Joanne never saw *any* of it. I used to ask her—*beg* her—to drive out, just once in a while. Join me for lunch, see what we were accomplishing. I told her the desert could be beautiful when you looked at it a certain way, we could find some good, cheap eats, go casual—goddamn Pizza Hut or something, like when we were broke and dating. No way. She always turned me down, said it was too far to drive. Too much traffic, too dry, too hot, too busy, there was always a reason."

He laughed again. "But she ended up there." Turning to stare at me. For once, not a combative glare. Sad, pitiful, seeking an answer.

"Oh Jesus," he said. An abrupt, suppressed sob made him choke. He bounced once in the sofa, as if levitated by pain and slammed back down by fate.

"Goddamn her," he whispered. Then he lost the fight and the tears gushed. He punched air, punched his knees, attacked his own chest, his shoulder, knuckled his eyes. Hid his face from me.

"Fuckin' *Lancaster*! For *that* she goes out there! Oh *Jesus*! Oh Jesus *Christ*!"

He lowered his head between his legs, as if about to vomit, found no comfort in that position and sprang up, running to the wall of french doors, where he turned his back on me and cried silently while facing his swimming pool and his land and the faraway ocean.

"She must've really hated me," he said.

"Why would she hate you, Richard?"

"For not forgiving her."

"What did she do?"

"No," he said. "No more of this, don't strip off my skin, just let me get through this with my *skin* on, okay? I won't try to tell you how to do your job, just let it be. Help my kids. *Please*."

"Sure," I said. "Of course."

CHAPTER

27

THE FOOTSTEPS FROM above resumed. Moments later Joe Safer knocked on the doorjamb. Richard was still staring through the glass. He turned.

Safer said, "Everything all right?"

"Joe, I'm really bushed, think I'll lie down." Trudging to the sofa, Richard removed his shoes, lined them up at the base of the couch, stretched out.

"Why don't you go upstairs to bed?" said Safer.

"Nah, I'll just sack out here. This is my relaxation spot." Richard reached for a remote control, clicked on seventy inches of the Home & Garden channel. Someone wearing a plaid shirt and a massive tool belt building a redwood deck. Making it look as easy as licking an envelope, the way those types always do.

Within seconds, Richard seemed hypnotized.

"Ready for the children?" Safer asked me.

"Ready."

I followed him up a rear staircase, arranging the file cards in my head.

Guilt, expiation. *I didn't forgive her.*

Joanne transgressing—probably exactly what I'd guessed: an affair.

Eric, close to his father, aligned with his father. Had

Joanne's transgression led her son to despise her? Spending time with her as she destroyed herself, loving her but also *hating* her? Could that explain the Polaroids? Documenting her descent—her punishment—then passing the pictures to Richard . . .

That level of filial contempt was hard to imagine, but Eric was explosive and impulsive and he had the genes for it. Now, months later, was he coming to grips with what he'd done? Seeking his own expiation?

Richard had just admitted paying Quentin Goad to murder the death doctor.

Make it look bloody . . . the wrong guy to cheat on. With Richard's need for control, how could Joanne have expected anything but rejection and retribution?

Attempted murder as closure . . . and, if Mate hadn't helped Joanne die, a grand mistake.

If he hadn't, who *had*?

Do-it-yourself job? As a microbiologist, Joanne had access to lethal chemicals, the skills for self-injection. But given her physical condition I couldn't see driving to Lancaster by herself . . .

She hated me. Now I had a reason she'd died in the Happy Trails Motel.

So maybe Mate *had* been there, agreeing to revert back to rented rooms in order to respect Joanne's wishes. Same for the lack of publicity: perhaps Joanne had requested he keep it quiet. For the sake of the kids? No, that made no sense. If she'd wanted to shield Eric, why choose such a conspicuous suicide?

Why kill herself by *any* means?

One thing seemed clear: Mr. and Mrs. Doss had suffered through a troubled relationship. Mrs. had sinned and Mr. had refused to forgive her.

Joanne had bought into Richard's rage. Hating herself enough to self-destruct.

But she hadn't gone out without a parting shot.

Taking control of the last day of her life. Contacting Mate—or someone else—on the sly. Dying on her own terms.

Lancaster. The ultimate screw-you to Richard.

Because she knew Richard well, knew he'd try to direct his anger everywhere else and a corpse in a cheap motel would be something he couldn't escape.

Or so she'd hoped. If funneling Richard toward crushing introspection had been Joanne's goal, she'd failed miserably. As Judy had said, Richard was a blamer.

And Richard liked to crush his adversaries.

A few minutes before, spinning his "hypothetical" tale, he'd brushed off the deal with Quentin Goad as an act of folly, denied he'd made a second attempt.

Yet he'd come prepared with an alibi, was already talking about temporary insanity. Milo would laugh all that off. You didn't have to be a *detective* to laugh it off. Because Richard was a ruthless, self-centered control freak who'd believed himself aggrieved. And as I'd just seen, Richard had a *very* bad temper.

Now here I was in his house, on his terms.

Safer reached the top of the stairs and paused at a small back landing that faced a closed door. "They're both in Eric's room," he said. "Would you like to see them together or separately?"

"Let's see how it goes."

"But together would be okay?"

"Why?"

He frowned. "To be frank, Doctor, neither of them wants to be alone with you."

"They still think I betrayed them?"

Safer righted his yarmulke. "I'm sorry. Richard talked to them and so did I, but you know adolescents. I hope this doesn't turn out to be a complete waste of your time."

Or worse, I thought.

Safer touched the doorknob but didn't turn it. "So how did it go with Richard?"

"Richard seems to feel rosy about the future," I said.

Rosy. The moment I said it I realized it was the same word I'd thought of upon seeing Richard's anger-flush. Poor old Dr. Freud wasn't getting enough respect in the age of Prozac.

"We-ell," said Safer, "a positive attitude is a good thing, wouldn't you say?"

"In Richard's case, is it justified?"

One big, gnarled hand came forward and smoothed the beard. "Let's put it this way, Doctor. I can't promise to bring everything to a close immediately, but I'm feeling positive, as well. Because when you get down to it, what do the police have? The Johnny-come-lately accusations of a habitual felon facing a three-strikes life sentence? Allegedly corroborative eyewitness testimony about some sort of envelope being handed over to someone by someone else in a poorly lit bar for who knows what purpose?"

I smiled. "Richard just happened to be there?"

Safer shrugged. "Richard has no specific memory of that particular meeting, but he says if it did occur, it was to pay Mr. Goad. It's customary for him to pay his workers in cash when they're short of funds—"

"Altruism?" I said. "Or good commerce when you deal with ex-cons?"

Safer smiled. "Richard employs people no one else wants to hire, sometimes helps them out when they're down. I have a long list of other employees who'll testify to his goodwill."

"So the eyewitnesses are a wash," I said.

"Eyewitnesses," he said, as if it were a diagnosis. "I'm sure you're familiar with the psychological research on the unreliability of eyewitness testimony. I wouldn't be surprised if a careful check into the backgrounds of these particular eyewitnesses reveals histories of alcoholism, drug abuse, criminal behavior."

"And poor lighting."

"That, as well."

"Sounds open-and-shut," I said.

"Overconfidence is dangerous, Doctor, but unless I receive an unpleasant surprise . . ." Safer's green eyes narrowed. "Are there any contingencies I should be aware of?"

"None that I know of."

"Good, that's very good. Now, I'll continue to do my job and I'll let you do yours."

The door opened to a long, central hallway that mirrored the corridor downstairs. Bare beige walls, outlet to the front steps at the far end, closets and alcoves to the left, bedrooms to the right, the tinge of dirty laundry in the air. Safer led me past double doors that framed a huge, white-carpeted chamber. Gold-upholstered chairs. Arboreal wallpaper—the paper I'd seen in Eric's snapshots of Joanne . . . I peeked in, saw the sleigh bed, made up with a silk comforter. Had no trouble picturing a disembodied head, bloated body swaddled to the neck . . .

The other bedroom doors were shut. Safer skipped the first and knocked on the second. No answer, he opened the door a crack, then all the way. The dirty-laundry smell intensified.

Faded blue paper—repeating print of tiny athletes in combative poses. A poster on the facing wall said, WELCOME TO THE COMFORT OF CHAOS. Other posters on two other walls, mostly concert mementos: Pearl Jam, Third Eye Blind, Everclear, Barenaked Ladies. A cartoon of Albert Einstein with his pants down and his genitals dangling, looking confused. The caption: WHO THE FUCK SAYS YOU'RE SO SMART?

Academic certificates hung crookedly. National Merit Scholarship, Bank of America Award, General Studies Award, Science Achievement Award, valedictorian. Two curtained windows, doors to a private bathroom and a closet, a chrome-and-glass storage unit stuffed with paperbacks, spiral notebooks, three-ring binders, loose paper, a cheap Tijuana plaster statue of a bull. On a top shelf, a collection of gold plastic men proclaimed the joys of athletic accomplishment.

Double bed, its sheet tangled, wrinkled, half off the mattress. Behind the sleeping platform, stereo equipment, computers, printers. The floor was littered with wadded underwear, shirts, jeans, socks, a pair of dirty sneakers. Empty blue nylon backpack, food wrappers, Snapple bottles, crushed cans of Surge.

Eric sat near the headboard, Stacy was perched at the foot. Their backs to each other. She had on a yellow T-shirt over white capris. He wore black jeans and a black sweatshirt. Like father . . .

Both of them barefoot. Both of them red-eyed.

Eric slid one fingernail under another, flicked something. "Here it comes," he said.

"Son," said Joe Safer.

Eric's upper lip curled. "Yes, *Dad*?"

Stacy shuddered and hugged herself. Raw cuticles on

her fingers. Her hair was unbound, wild and ragged, like her father's.

Safer said, "Dr. Delaware was kind enough to come here at this hour. Your father would like you to talk to him."

"Talk talk talk," said Eric. "Hap-hap-*happy* talk."

Stacy shuddered again. She managed to look at me, aiming but pulling off scared.

"Eric," said Safer, "I'm asking you to be courteous. Your father and I are both asking you."

"How is Dad?" said Stacy. "Where is he? What's he doing?"

"He's downstairs resting, dear."

"Does he want something to eat?"

"No, he's fine, dear," said Safer. "I made him a sandwich a while back."

"Was it *kosher*?" said Eric.

Silence in the stale room.

Safer stroked his beard and smiled sadly.

"Nice kosher pickle," said Eric. "Nize leetle piece of corned *beef*—"

Stacy said, "Stop it, Eric—"

"Nize little matzo ball—"

"*Shut up, Eric!*"

"Stop *what*? What the fuck am I *doing*?"

"You know what you're doing. Stop being *rude*!"

They glared at each other. Stacy turned away first. Gave a small, furious wave, showed Eric her back. Stood up. "Enough of this, I'm out of here—I'm sorry, Dr. Delaware, I just can't talk to you or anyone else right now. If I need you, I'll call you—I really will, Mr. Safer."

"Safer," muttered Eric. "Dad's writing him huge checks, and are any of us any *safer*?"

Stacy shouted, "*You are so . . .*"

"I'm what?"

Another dismissive wave. Stacy moved toward the door. Eric said, "I'm *what*, smart-girl?"

Stacy kept going.

"Go ahead, leave, but don't think you're out of it," Eric called after her. "We're never really out of our misery unless we *put* ourselves out of it."

Stacy stopped. Another shudder took hold of her body. Her face convulsed and white foam bubbled at the corners of her mouth. Turning, she canted forward, tiny hands compressed into hard little fists. For a moment, I thought she'd charge him. Flushed, herself. The Doss flush.

"You!" she said. "You . . . are . . . evil."

She ran out, I followed, caught up with her at the door to the last bedroom.

"No! *Please!* I know you want to help but . . ."

"Stacy—"

She rushed into the bedroom but left the door open. I walked in.

Smaller room than Eric's. Pink and baby-blue paper, ribbons and leaves and flowers. White iron bed with brass accents, pink comforter, stuffed animals piled into an upholstered armchair. Clothes and books strewn about, but not the calculated entropy of Eric's personal space.

She walked to a window, touched shuttered blinds. "This is so humiliating, you seeing us like this."

"These are tough times," I said. *House calls.* How much *didn't* I know about thousands of other patients?

"There's no excuse," she said. "We're just . . ."

She trailed off. Hunched her back like an old woman and tore at a cuticle.

"I'm here to help, Stacy."

No answer. Then: "It's secret, right? Whatever we talk about? Nothing changes that?"

"Nothing," I said. *Unless you're planning to kill someone.*

I waited for her to talk. She didn't.

"What's on your mind, Stacy?"

"*He* is."

"Eric?"

Nod. "He *scares* me."

"How does he scare you, Stacy?"

"By—he—the way he talks—the things he says . . . No, no, forget it, forget I just said that. Please. Just forget it. He's fine, everything's fine."

She slipped a finger between the blades of the blinds and peered out at the night.

I said, "What did Eric say that scared you?"

She spun around. "*Nothing!* I said *forget* it!"

I stood there.

"What?" she said.

"If you're scared, let me help."

"You can't—there's nothing you can—it's—I just—he—Helen—we were sitting there. After we got back from the police station and he started talking about Helen."

"Your dog."

"What's the difference? Please! Please don't make me get into it!"

"I can't make you do anything, Stacy. But if Eric's in some kind of danger—"

"No, no, that's not what I mean—he—you remember what I told you about *Helen* . . ."

"She was sick. Eric took her up to the mountains and you never saw her again. What's he saying about her?"

"Nothing," she said. "Nothing, really . . . Besides,

what's the big deal? It was the right thing to do—she was sick, she was a *dog*, for God's sake, people do that all the time, it's the *humane* thing to do."

"Putting her out of her misery. Eric told you he did it?"

"Yes—never before, not till now. I mean I knew, but he never mentioned before, not once. Then tonight, after we got back. Dad and Mr. Safer were downstairs and we were up here and all of a sudden he starts getting *into* it. *Laughing* about it."

She sat down on the edge of the armchair, crushing stuffed animals. Reaching behind, she took one in her arms—a small, frayed elephant.

"He laughed about Helen," I said. "And now he's talking about people being put out of their misery."

"No—just forget it." Weak voice, lacking conviction.

"You're worried," I went on. "If Eric could do that to Helen, maybe he could do it to a human being. Maybe he had something to do with your mother's death."

"No!" she shouted. "Yes! That's what—he basically told me! I mean, he didn't come out and say it but he kept hinting around at it. Talking about Helen, how her eyes looked—how she was okay with it, peaceful. She looked up at him and licked his face and he hit her over the head with a rock. One time, he said. That's all it took. Then he buried her—it was brave of him, right? I couldn't have done it, it needed to be done, she was so sick."

She rocked in the chair, held the elephant to her breast.

"Then he got a *creepy* smile. Said sometimes you have to take matters into your own hands, how no one knows what's right or wrong unless they're in your shoes. How maybe there really is no right or wrong, just rules that people take on because they're too scared to make their own decisions. He said helping Helen was the noblest thing he'd ever done."

She squeezed the elephant harder and its tiny face compressed to something grotesque. "I'm so *scared*. What if he did another Helen?"

"No reason to believe that," I said, lying because now I had an explanation for why Mate hadn't claimed Joanne. I went on in my best therapist voice: "He's upset, just as you are. Things will settle down, Eric will settle down."

My voice and my brain diverged as I continued to comfort, thinking all the while: mother and son, guilt, expiation. Joanne and Eric planning . . . Eric taking pictures because he knew she'd be leaving soon, wanted to grasp every opportunity for memorial.

Too sickening to contemplate, but I couldn't *stop* contemplating. I hoped the revulsion hadn't found its way into my voice. Must have faked it okay because Stacy stopped crying.

"Everything will be fine?" she said in a little girl's voice.

"Just hang in there."

She smiled. Then the smile turned into something fearful and ugly. "No, it won't. It will never be fine."

"I know it seems like that right now—"

"Hey," she said, "Eric's right. Nothing's complicated. You're born, life sucks, you die." She ripped a cuticle bloody, licked the wound, picked some more.

"Stacy—"

"Words," she said. "They sound nice."

"They're true, Stacy."

"I wish. . . . Things will be better?" More need than challenge.

"Yes," I said. Lord help me.

New kind of smile. "I'm definitely *not* going to Stanford. I have to find my own place. . . . Thank you, Dr. Delaware, this has been—"

Her words were cut off by sounds from below.

From the front of the house, loud enough to filter upstairs and through the door to her bedroom. Screams and percussion, frantic footsteps, more screams—bellows.

The pretty music of shattering glass.

CHAPTER

28

I RAN OUT, rushed down the stairs, followed the noise.

The living room. Figures in black.

Two figures, crouched combatively.

Richard shouted, "What the fuck have you done?" and advanced on his son.

Eric waved a baseball bat.

Behind the boy stood what remained of the display cases. Ravaged, the brass dented, glass doors splintered and ragged. Glass spikes and shards on the carpet, glittery dust like raw diamonds. Broken pottery within the cases and on the floor. Horses and camels and little human figurines turned to rubble.

Richard got closer. His mouth was open. His breath rasped.

Eric panted also. He gripped the bat with both hands. "Don't even think about it."

"Put it down!" Richard commanded.

Eric didn't move.

"Put it the fuck *down*!"

Eric laughed and took another swing at the porcelain. Richard rushed forward, threw himself at the bat, managed to get hold of it as Eric grunted and struggled to wrestle control.

The two of them fell to the floor, entwined black

clothes coating with glass and dust. I dived in, mindful of the bat, aiming for the bat. Reaching it, feeling hardwood, sweaty and gritty, the crunch underneath as fragments bit into my knees. I tugged at the bat. Some give, then resistance. A fist landed on my jaw but I kept my grip.

Eric and Richard kept growling and spitting, flailing at each other, me, anyone, anything.

Another pair of hands entered the fray.

"Stop!"

I extricated myself. Joe Safer stood there, hands pressed to his cheeks, eyes aflame. Eric and Richard were concentrating on ownership of the bat. "Stop, you idiots, or I'm walking out permanently and leaving you all to your misery!"

Richard stopped first. Eric kept growling but his hands loosened, and Safer and I both rushed forward and pulled the bat away from him.

Richard sat down on the floor, letting the ruins of his collection fall through his fingers. He looked stunned—anesthetized. Tiny cuts flecked his face and his hands, one eye was swollen. A few feet away, Eric was down on his knees, looking out at nothing. Other than a split lip, he showed no obvious injury. My jaw was throbbing and I touched it. Hot, starting to swell, but I could move it, nothing broken.

"For God's sake," said Safer. "Look what you've done to the doctor. What's the *matter* with you people? Are you *savages*?"

Eric smiled. "We're the elite. Pathetic, huh?"

Safer pointed a finger at him. "You be quiet, my friend. You keep that mouth of yours shut—don't you dare interrupt me—"

"Why should—"

"Eh-eh, don't test me, young man. One more problem and I'm calling the police and having you hauled into jail. And I can keep you there, you'd better believe I can."

"Who ca—"

"You'll care. Within an hour you'll be anally raped and worse. Now zip the lip!"

Eric's hands began to shake. He glanced at the havoc he'd created. Smiled. Started to cry.

No one talked. Safer took in the ruin and shook his head.

"I'm so sorry," he said to me. "Are you all right?"

"I'll be fine."

"Eric," Richard pleaded. "Why? What have I done to you?"

Eric looked at Safer, requesting permission to talk. Safer said, "Why, indeed, Eric?"

Eric faced Richard. Mumbled something.

"What?" said Richard.

"Sorry."

"Sorry," Richard echoed. "That's *it*?"

Louder mumble.

"Speak up, for God's sake," said Richard. "What the hell led you to . . ." He shook his head, let it drop.

"Sorry, Daddy," said Eric. "Sorry, sorry, sorry."

"*Why*, Eric?"

Eric began to sob. Richard moved to comfort him, thought better of it, plopped back down.

"Why, son?" he said.

"Forgiveness," said Eric. "Forgiveness is all."

Richard had turned pale again. A bad-looking pale, green around the edges. He picked up a pottery fragment. Green and blue and chartreuse. Part of a horse's face.

"Oh my God," said a voice from behind us.

Stacy stood at the entrance to the living room. Hands at her side, eyes so bugged they seemed ready to take off in orbit.

Just moments ago, hearing talk about finding her own way, I'd allowed myself a small hit of self-congratulation. Now, any victory was a joke, demolished as surely as thousand-year-old pottery drawn from the grave.

"No," said Stacy.

"Dear?" said Safer.

When she didn't answer, he said, "No what?"

She didn't seem to hear him, had turned to me.

"No," she said. "I don't want any more of this."

"And you don't have to take any more, dear," said Safer. "You're certain that jaw's okay, Doctor?"

"I'll survive."

"Richard," he said, "is your maid in the house?"

"No," muttered Richard. "Night off."

"Stacy, please get the doctor an ice pack."

Stacy said, "Absolutely," and left.

Safer faced Richard and Eric: "Now the two of *you* will clean up this terrible mess and I'll figure out if you deserve my further involvement in your case, Richard."

"Please," said Richard.

"Just clean it up," ordered Safer. "Do something useful. Do something together."

He shepherded me out of the room, through the dining room and into the kitchen. One of those vast white lacquer and black granite setups—what realtors call catering kitchens. Another L.A. pretense: upscale isolates staking claim to sociability.

Stacy was wrapping ice cubes in a towel. "One second."

"Thank you, dear," said Safer, as she brought it over. I pressed the cloth to my face.

"I'm so sorry," she told me. "So, so sorry."

"No big deal," I said. "It's really nothing."

The three of us stood there. Listening. No sound through the kitchen door.

Safer said, "Please go up to your room, Stacy. I need to confer with the doctor."

She complied.

Safer said, "At least one of them seems normal."

He pushed back his yarmulke, removed his suit jacket and folded it over a chair, sat down at the kitchen table.

"What just happened out there?" he said.

"I wouldn't even guess."

"Not that that's going to change my strategy vis-à-vis Richard. I'll get him past the immediate threat . . . but that *boy*. He's seriously disturbed, isn't he?"

"Very angry," I said. *You'd be angry, too, if you'd helped your mother die, couldn't talk about it to anyone.*

"Do you see him as a danger to himself and others? Because if he is, I'll get a seventy-two-hour hold."

"Possibly, but don't ask me to go there. Get someone else for that."

He massaged the tabletop. "I understand, conflict of interest."

Yet another.

"Speaking of which," he said, "let's discuss Detective Sturgis. I know we've talked about this and please don't be offended, but I believe in an ounce of prevention. What you saw tonight—nothing gets repeated."

"Of course."

"Good," he said. "Taken care of. And again I apologize. Now as far as Stacy's concerned, you do agree she needs to be out of here? At least for tonight."

"Do you have a place for her to go?"

"My house. I live in Hancock Park, have plenty of room, and my wife won't be put out. She's used to entertaining."

"Entertaining clients?"

"Clients, guests, she's a very social person. Tomorrow night's our Sabbath, Stacy can have a multicultural experience. Shall I call Mrs. Safer?"

"If you can get Stacy to agree."

"I think I can," he said. "Stacy impresses me as a very reasonable young woman. Quite possibly the one sane person in this . . . museum of psychopathology."

He went upstairs and I sat in the kitchen nursing my jaw. Thinking about Eric's rage.

Forgiveness is all.

And Richard hadn't forgiven, so now he was paying for it.

He and Eric, two kegs of explosives . . . not my concern. Not unless it affected Stacy, I had to focus on Stacy.

Safer was right, she needed to be out of here. A night or two at his house might work out, but after that . . .

Safer returned. "I convinced her, she's packing a bag. Let me go tell Richard."

I accompanied him into the living room. The mess was partially cleaned—dust and fragments swept into piles, brooms leaning against the shattered cases.

Richard and Eric sat on the floor, their backs to a sofa. Richard's arm around Eric's shoulder, Eric's head against Richard's chest, his eyes closed, his face tear-streaked.

Pietà in the Palisades.

Richard looked different. Not flushed, not pale. Expressionless. Crushed. Dragged to the edge and dropped off.

He didn't seem to notice as Safer and I approached,

but when we got within two feet of the case, he turned slowly and held Eric tighter. Eric's body flopped. The boy's eyes remained shut.

"He's tired," said Richard. "I need to put him to bed. I used to do that when he was little. Tell him stories and put him to bed."

Safer gave a start. Remembering his own son?

"Do that," he said. "Take care of him. I'm bringing Stacy to my house."

Richard's eyebrows arched. "Your house? Why?"

"To keep things simple, Richard. I promise to take good care of her. I'll get her to school on time tomorrow and she'll spend the weekend with us. Or with friends, if she so prefers."

Not the Manitows, I thought.

Richard said, "She wants to go?"

"My idea," said Safer. "She agreed."

Richard licked his lips, turned to me.

I nodded.

"Okay," he said. "I guess. Tell her to come in before she leaves. Let me give her a kiss."

CHAPTER

29

I CLIMBED THE stairs, nursing my jaw. Stacy sat on her bed. Her voice came out small and wounded. "I'm tired, please don't make me talk."

I stayed with her for a while. When I returned to the kitchen, Joe Safer was talking on the phone, elbow resting on the counter near a black-and-chrome coffee machine from Germany. I found a jar of espresso in one of the refrigerators, packed enough for six cups, and sat listening to the drip and thinking about what guilt and expiation really meant to Eric. Safer left the room and kept talking. I drank by myself. A while later, the doorbell rang and Safer came back in the kitchen accompanied by a tall, husky young man with wavy blond hair and a briefcase.

"This is Byron. He'll be staying here tonight."

Byron winked and inspected the appliances. He wore a blue oxford shirt, khakis and penny loafers, had hyphens for eyes and facial muscles that looked paralyzed. When we shook hands, his felt like a bone carving. Safer went upstairs. Byron and I didn't talk.

No sound from the living room. The entire house was too damn quiet. Then I heard footsteps from above and a few seconds later Stacy entered, followed by the lawyer.

Safer was carrying a small floral overnight bag. Stacy looked tiny, shriveled, much too old.

I followed the two of them outside and watched him help her into his Cadillac. Byron remained in the doorway, hands on hips.

"What is he, exactly?" I said.

"Someone who helps me. Richard and Eric seem calm, but just in case."

"Were you an oldest child, Joe?"

"Oldest of seven. Why?"

"You like to take care of things."

His smile was weary. "Don't think I'm paying for that bit of analysis."

He drove away and I watched the Cadillac's taillights disappear. Down the block, the unmarked hadn't moved. The night had turned dank, redolent of fermenting seaweed. My jaw ached and my clothes had sweated through. I trudged to the Seville. Instead of turning around and heading south, I drove farther north till I found it.

Six houses up. Big Tudor thing behind brick walls and iron gates, vines encircling the brick, the tip-off: Judy's white Lexus visible through the rails. Another vanity plate: HCDJ.

Here Come Da Judge. The first time I'd seen it was when I'd accompanied her from her courtroom to her parking space. One of the many times we'd worked together.

All those referrals. This would be the last, wouldn't it?

I stopped in front of her house, looking for . . . what?

Light glowed behind a couple of curtained mullioned windows. Movement flashed on the second story—central window. Just a smudge of a silhouette, shifting, then freezing, then moving again. Human, but that's about all I could say.

Hooking a three-pointer, my headlights aimed through the Manitow gate, I paused, half hoping someone would notice and show themselves. No one did and I headed back toward Sunset, passing the unmarked. Movement there, too, but the drab sedan remained in place.

I drove east, trying not to think about anything. On the way home I stopped at a twenty-four-hour drugstore in Brentwood and bought the strongest Advil I could find.

Friday morning, I woke up before Robin, just as the sun whitened the curtains. My jaw felt tender, but the swelling wasn't too bad. I drew the covers over my face, pretended to sleep, waited till Robin had risen, showered and left. Not wanting to explain. Eventually, I'd have to.

Using the bedroom phone, I called Safer's office.

"Good morning, Doctor. How's your battle wound?"

"Healing. How's Stacy?"

"She slept soundly," he said. "I had to wake her to get her to school on time. Lovely girl. She even tried to make breakfast for my wife and me. I hope she survives her family. Psychologically speaking."

I thought about Stacy's little speech about self-determination, wondered if it would stick.

"What she needs," I said, "is to separate from her family. Achieve her own identity. Richard expects her to go to Stanford because he and Joanne did. She should go anywhere but there."

"And Eric's at Stanford," he said.

"Exactly."

"The boy hasn't separated adequately?"

"Don't know," I said. "Don't know enough about him to pontificate." Don't *want* to know if he sat by a bed in a cheap motel and inserted a needle into his mother's vein. "If you have any influence with Richard, you might guide him toward allowing Stacy some choice."

"Makes sense," he said, but he sounded distracted. "I understand the boy's not your primary patient, but he continues to bother me. That level of anger. Any new thoughts on why he'd explode like that?"

"None. How was he last night?"

"Byron reports that father and son cleaned up, then went to sleep. Eric's still sleeping."

"And Richard?"

"Richard's up. Richard's full of ideas."

"I'll bet he is. Listen, Joe, I need to take a look at Joanne Doss's medical records."

"Why's that?"

"To try to understand her death. If I'm going to help Stacy, I need as much information as possible. The medical tests were conducted at St. Michael's. Richard said you've got power of attorney, so please sign a release and fax it over to their Medical Records office."

"Done. Of course, you'll notify me if you learn something I should know."

"Such as?" I said.

"Such as anything I should know." His voice had hardened. "Agreed?"

I thought of all I hadn't told him. Knew there was plenty he hadn't told me.

"Sure, Joe," I said. "No problem."

Popping more Advil, I iced my jaw, took a short run, cleaned up, walked over to Robin's studio, stuck my head in and got an earful of noise. My beloved, suited and goggled, standing behind the plastic walls of the spray booth as she wielded a lacquer gun. Knowing she couldn't be interrupted and doubting she could see me, I waved and left for St. Michael's Medical Center.

Sunset to Barrington, Barrington to Wilshire. Driving too fast to Santa Monica. No reason to hurry. My reason for checking out the hospital was to look for Michael Ferris Burke, or whatever he was calling himself now. But my fresh suspicions about Eric dimmed any prospects of finding a Michael Burke connection to Joanne's final trip.

Not an evil stranger. Family.

But what else was there for me to do?

And maybe I *would* find something.

That made me laugh out loud. Shrink's denial. I wanted anyone in that motel room other than Eric.

The boy's rage came back to me in a bitter surge, and the facts spat in my face.

Helen, the dog. Guilt and expiation.

That level of anger.

The noblest thing he'd ever done.

Mate's death had stirred up Eric's guilt. Richard's attempt at vengeance had fueled it further.

Eric knowing an innocent man had been targeted, because Mate hadn't brought about Joanne's death.

Wondering what his father would have done to *him*, had he known. Then reversing the anger—turning it on his father. Because Richard had caused it all by not forgiving.

Blaming. Like father . . .

I thought about the way the death plan might've gone down. Weeks, maybe months, of planning between Eric and Joanne. Easy collusion, or had Eric tried to talk his mother out of it? Finally given up and settled for immortalizing her with Polaroids?

How had she convinced him? Telling him it was *noble*?

Or had he needed little convincing—enraged at her, too. One of those terrifying kids who are missing that little, secret shred of brain tissue that inhibits evil?

The scheme, then the night of judgment . . . surreptitious mother-son outing on one of the many nights when Richard was out of town. Eric driving, Joanne riding along.

The long, dark trip to the edge of the desert. Lancaster, because Mom was adamant about that.

Obscene. How could a mother do that to a son? What transgression had she committed that could've been worse than *that*?

I was unlikely to find the answer in her hospital chart. But one did what one could.

One did what was right. And hoped for some final day of judgment.

Transcendence.

Absolution.

The limestone and mirrored mass of St. Michael's filled several square blocks on Wilshire, in Santa Monica, half a mile east of the beach. I'd lectured there a few years earlier, teaching family-practice residents about divorce and child abuse and bed-wetting, but I had no idea how to find Medical Records and the personnel office.

I got directions from a kid with a skimpy blond beard and a badge alleging he was an MD. North side of the complex, adjoining buildings.

I hit personnel first—Human Resources. Most companies call it that now—warm fuzzy twist on the lexicon. Does it ease the pain when they fire you?

The office was small, stark, sterile, occupied by an

imperious-looking black woman in an orange suit who sat entering columns of data into a PC. I was wearing my Western Pediatrics badge, had my I.D. card from the med school crosstown ready as backup. But she smiled when I told her I was in charge of arranging a faculty party and needed some office addresses, and handed over a phone-book-size volume marked Staff Roster. Her openness felt fresh and clean and odd. I'd been hanging around too long with cops, lawyers, psychopaths, other evasive creatures.

She returned to her desk and I thumbed through the book. The professional staff was listed at the front. Pages of doctors. Names, office addresses, photos. No personal data. No one who resembled the various faces of the man Leimert Fusco claimed was the real Dr. Death. The same went for the rear sections listing social workers, physical therapists, occupational therapists, respiratory therapists.

When I brought the book back, the woman in orange said, "Hope it's a good party."

Medical Records was a bit more complicated. The receptionist was one of those pucker-mouthed types weaned on skepticism, and she hadn't seen Joe Safer's faxed authorization. Finally the paperwork materialized and she produced Joanne Doss's inch-thick chart.

"You need to read it here. That fax doesn't authorize photocopying."

"No problem."

"That's what they all say."

"Who?"

"Doctors who work for lawyers."

I took the file across the room. Multicolored pages of lab reports. Numbers in boxes. Motley samples of physician scrawl. Bob Manitow's name appeared only on the referral form. Fifteen other doctors had attempted to discern the cause of Joanne's misery.

Blood work, urinalysis, X rays, CAT scans, PET scans, MRIs, the lumbar punctures Richard had told me about because nothing else had turned up.

The operative word: "negative."

Clear spinal fluid. Normal BUN, creatinine, calcium, phosphorus, iron, T-protein, albumin, globulin . . .

Morbidly obese white female . . .

Complains of joint pain, lethargy, fatigue . . .

Onset of symptoms 23 mo. ago, steady weight gain of nearly 50 kg . . .

Thyroid function normal . . .

All endocrine systems normal, except for glucose of 123. Glucose tolerance borderline, possible prediabetic condition, probably secondary to obesity.

BP: 149/96. Borderline hypertension, probably secondary to obesity.

Repeat of blood work, urinalysis, X rays, CAT scans . . .

No MD's name that matched any of Grant Rushton's incarnations.

The last notation read: *Psychiatric consultation suggested, but patient refused. . . .*

Of course she had.

Too late for confession.

On the way out, I stopped at a pay phone and checked in with my service.

Last guy in L.A. with no cell phone. It had taken me years to buy a VCR, a good deal longer to get cable hookup. I'd stalled at getting a computer even after the libraries at the U. abandoned their card catalogs. Then my electric typewriter broke and I couldn't find replacement parts.

My father had been a machinist. I stayed away from machines. Lived with a woman who loved them. No sense introspecting.

The operator said, "Only one, it just came in. A Detective Connor. That's not the one who usually calls you, is it?"

"No," I said. "What did she want?"

"No message, just to call."

Petra had left her number at Hollywood Division. Another detective answered and said, "She's out, want her mobile?"

I got through. Petra said, "Milo asked me to let you know that we found Eldon Salcido. He thought you might want to take a look at him."

Milo sending a message through her, rather than calling himself. Knowing he and I were firmly planted on opposite sides of the Doss investigation.

Had Safer warned him off, or was he opting for discretion on his own? Either way, it felt weird.

"Did he say why I should take a look?"

"No," she said. "I assumed you'd know. It was a short conversation. Milo sounded pretty hassled, still fighting to get warrants on that fat cat."

"Where'd Salcido show up?"

"On the street. Literally. Messed up—beat up. Looks like he ran into the wrong bunch of butt-kickers. A resident coming out to collect the morning paper found him. Salcido was lying in the gutter. His pockets were empty, but that doesn't mean he was robbed, he might not have carried a wallet. One of our cars got the call, recognized him from a picture I hung up in the squad room. He's at Hollywood Mercy."

"Conscious?" I said.

"Yes, but uncooperative. I left your name with the nurses." She gave me a room number.

"Thanks," I said.

"If you have any problems, call me. If you learn anything interesting from Salcido, you can call me, too."

"Because Milo's busy."

"Seems to be. Isn't everyone?"

"Better than the alternative," I said.

"You said it. By the way, I'm seeing Billy tomorrow. We're going over to see the new science center at Exposition Park. Anything you want to pass along?"

"Best regards and continue doing what he's doing. And keep busy. Not that he needs me to tell him that."

She laughed. "Yes, he's a wonder, isn't he?"

CHAPTER

30

IT TOOK FORTY minutes on the 10 East and surface streets to get to the shabby section of East Hollywood where Beverly meets Temple.

Second hospital of the day.

Hollywood Mercy was five stories of earthquake-stressed, putty-colored stucco teetering atop a scrubby knoll that overlooked downtown. The building had an inadequate parking lot, a cracked tile roof, some nice ornate moldings from the days when labor was cheap, most with chunks missing. City ambulances ringed the entry. The front vestibule was crowded with long lines of sad-looking people waiting for approval from clerks in glass cages. CAT scans, PET scans, MRIs; the same high-tech alphabet I'd seen at St. Michael's, but this place looked like something out of a black-and-white movie and it smelled like an old man's bedroom.

Mate's bedroom.

His son was recuperating on the fourth floor, in something called the Special Care Unit. An unarmed security guard was posted at the swinging doors that led to the ward, and my I.D. badge got me waved through. On the other side was a chunky corridor five doors long with a nurses' station at the end. A black man with a shaved head sat near a stack of charts, writing, and a lantern-jawed, straw-haired woman in her sixties tapped her finger to soft reggae thumping from an unseen radio. I announced myself.

"In there," said the female nurse.

"How's he doing?"

"He'll survive." She pulled out a chart. A lot thinner than Joanne Doss's encyclopedia of confusion. A Hollywood Division police report was stapled to the inside front cover.

Eldon Salcido had been found beaten and semiconscious at 6:12 A.M. in the gutter of a residential block of Poinsettia Place, north of Sunset.

Three blocks from his father's apartment on Vista.

Paramedics had transported him, and an E.R. resident had admitted him for repair and observation. Contusions, abrasions, possible concussion later ruled absent. No broken bones. Extreme mental agitation and confusion, possibly related to preexisting alcoholism, drug abuse, mental illness or some combination of all three. The patient had refused to identify himself, but police at the scene had supplied the vitals. The fact that Salcido was an ex-con with a felony record was duly noted.

Restraints ordered after the patient assaulted staff.

"Who'd he hit?" I said.

"One of our predecessors, last shift," said the male nurse. "Her big crime was offering him orange juice. He knocked it out of her hand, tried to punch her. She managed to lock him in and called security."

"Another day in paradise," said the woman. "Probably a candidate for detox, but our detox unit shut down last month. You here to evaluate him for transfer?"

"Just to see him," I said. "Basic consult."

"Well, you might end up doing it for free. We can't find a Medi-Cal card on him and he isn't talking."

"That's okay."

"Hey, if you don't care, I sure don't. Room 405."

She came out from behind the counter and unlocked the door. The room was cell-size and green, with a lone, grilled window that framed an air shaft, a single bed and an I.V. bottle on a stand, not hooked up. The vital-signs monitor above the headboard was switched off and so was the tiny TV bracketed to the far wall. A low industrial buzz seeped through the window.

Donny Salcido Mate lay on his back, bare-chested, shackled with leather cuffs, staring at the ceiling. A tight, sweat-stained top sheet bound him from the waist down. His trunk was hairless, undernourished, off-white where it wasn't blue-black.

Blue coils squirmed all over him. Skin art, continuing around his back and down both arms. Pictorial arms striped by bandages. Dried blood crusted the edges of the dressings. A swatch of gauze banded his forehead, a smaller square bottomed his chin. Purpling bruises cupped both eyes and his lower lip was a slab of liver. Other dermal images peeked out from within the coils: the leering face of a nightmarishly fanged cobra, a flabby, naked woman with a sad mouth, one wide-open eye emitting a single tear. Gothic lettering spelling out "Donny, Mamacita, Big Boy."

Technically well-done tattoos, but the jumble made me want to rearrange his skin.

"A walking canvas," opined the straw-haired nurse. "Like that book by the *Martian Chronicles* guy. Visitor, Mr. Salcido. Ain't that grand?"

She walked out and the door hissed shut. Donny Salcido Mate didn't budge. His hair was long, stringy, the burnt bronze of old motor oil. An untrimmed beard, two shades darker, blanketed his face from cheekbone to jowl.

No resemblance to the mug shot I'd seen. That made me think of the beard Michael Burke had grown when adopting his Huey Mitchell persona in Ann Arbor. In fact, *Donny*'s hirsute face bore a resemblance to Mitchell's. But not the same man. None of that cold, blank stagnancy in the eyes. These rheumy browns were bouncy, heated, hyperactive. Hundred percent scared prey, not predator.

I stepped closer to the bed. Donny Salcido moaned and twisted away from me. A tattoo tendril climbed up his carotid, disappearing into the beard thatch like a vining rose. Yellowing crust flecked the edges of his mustache. His lips were cracked, his nose had been broken, but not recently, probably more than once; the cartilage between his eyes was sunken, as if scooped by a dull blade, the flesh below a nest of gaping black pores. Orange splotches remained on his skin where he'd been disinfected with Betadine, but whoever had cleaned him up hadn't gotten rid of the street stink.

"Mr. Salcido, I'm Dr. Delaware."

His eyes jammed shut.

"How're you doing?"

"Let me out of here." Clear enunciation, no slur. I waited, got caught up in the skin mural. Subtle shadings, good composition. I got past that, searched for an image that would tie in with his father. Nothing obvious. The tattoos seemed to encroach on one another. This was the junction of talent and chaos.

Bumps in the crook of his arm caught my eye. Fibrosed needle marks.

His eyes opened. "Get these things off," he said, rattling the cuffs.

"The nurses got a little upset when you tried to hit one of them."

"Never happened."

"You didn't try to hit a nurse?"

Headshake. "She aggressed on me. Tried to force juice down my windpipe. Not my esophagus, my windpipe, *get* it? Nasopharynx, epiglottis—know what happens when you do *that*?"

"You choke."

"You aspirate. Fluid straight into the lungs. Even if you don't suffocate, it creates a pleural cesspool, perfect culture for bacteria. She was out to drown me—if she couldn't accomplish that, infect me." A tongue, gray and fuzzed, caressed his lips. He gulped.

"Thirsty?" I said.

"Strangling. Get these things off of me."

"How'd you get hurt?"

"You tell me."

"How would I know?"

"You're the doctor."

"The police say someone hit you."

"Not some*one*. *Ones*. I got jumped."

"Right there on Poinsettia?"

"No, San Francisco. I walked all the way here because this glorious place is where I wanted to be treated." His head rolled toward me. "Better get me outta here or give me my Tegretol. When I'm out of my Tegretol, I get interesting."

"You suffer from seizures?"

"No, stupid. Cognitive dysfunction, affective scrambling, inability to regulate emotional outbursts. I'm prone to a mood disorder, get too unhappy, everything gets scrambled, no telling what I'll do." His wrists shot upward. The cuffs rattled louder.

"Who prescribed the Tegretol for you?"

"I did. Got a hoard at my place, but you supposed healers won't let me get to it."

"Where's your place?"

"Me to know, you to find out."

"What dosage do you take?"

"Depends," he said, grinning. His gums were swollen, inflamed, rotted black at the tooth line. "Three hundred migs on a good day, more if I'm feeling baaad—better be careful, I'm getting that *baaad* feeling right now. The old prodrome: everything turning glassy, circular, convex, pistons pumping, heart jumping. Soon I'm going to be all scrambled, who knows, maybe I could break free of these, eat you *up*—where's your white coat, what kind of doctor are you, anyway?"

"Psychologist."

"Fuck. Useless. Get me someone who can prescribe. Or let me outta here. I'm the victim, once this story gets out you and everyone else associated with it are not going to look good. Assuming the publishers print it. But they won't. They're part of it, too."

"Part of what?"

"The great conspiracy to denude my brain." Smile. "Nah, that's bullshit. I'm not paranoid, I've got a mood disorder."

"Who attacked you?" I said.

"Mexicans. Gangbangers. Punks. Illegal aliens, refuse of society."

"Did they try to rob you?"

"They tried and they succeeded. I'm walking down the

street, minding my own, they drive up to the curb, get out, beat the shit out of me, go through my pockets."

"What did they get?"

"Everything in my pockets." He shook his head. "You're useless, I'm terminating this interview."

"Were you carrying a weapon?" I said.

He began to hum.

"Poinsettia is three blocks from your father's place."

The humming got louder. His eyelids twitched. He started breathing faster.

"Planning a visit to your father's place?" I said, talking over it. "Last time you tried, the lady downstairs interrupted you. How many times have you gotten inside?"

His head snapped toward me. "I *am* going to bite off your nose. Eye for an eye—avenge what that other psychologist did—Lecter. No, he was a psychiatrist, that was a great movie. I watched it and ate fava beans for weeks afterward."

"Did you kill your father?" I said.

"Sure," he said. "Bit off *his* nose, too. Had it with *pinto* beans and . . . some kind of wine . . . why am I thinking Chablis? Get me my fucking Tegretol."

"I'll see what I can do," I said.

"Don't lie to me, degree-boy."

"I'll do what I can."

"No, you won't."

I left him, returned to the station, paged the doctor who'd written the last note—early this morning. A woman named Greenbaum, first-year resident. Meaning she'd only been in training for a few months. She called back, saying she was at County General, wouldn't be rotating back in Hollywood until tomorrow. I told her why I was with Salcido and asked her about the medication.

"Yes," she said, "he claims he needs it to maintain 'internal stability.' He played that tune for me, too. I'm waiting to talk to the attending."

"He's self-medicating for assaultiveness and mood swings. If he's already on Tegretol, he's probably gone through lithium and the neuroleptics. Maybe in prison."

"Maybe, but I can't get anything out of him resembling a clinical history. Tegretol's okay, but there's the issue of side effects. I need blood levels on him."

"Did you have a chance to talk to him?"

"He didn't talk."

"He's a bit more verbal now," I said. "There's some IQ there. He knows how it feels before the assaultiveness comes on, is fighting to maintain control."

"So what're you saying?"

"I'm suggesting that at least in one respect he may know what's best for him."

"Did you see that skin of his?" she said.

"Hard to miss."

"Pretty disorganized for someone who knows what's best for him."

"True, but—"

"I get it," she said. "The police sent you to see him and you want him coherent so he'll talk to you."

"That's part of it. The other part is he's already been assaultive and if something works for him, maybe it should be considered. I'm not trying to tell you how to do your job—"

"No, actually you are." She laughed. "But sure, why not? Everyone else does. Okay, no sense having him freak out and me getting a three A.M. call. I'll try to get hold of the attending again. If she okays it, he gets dosed."

"He says he's been taking three hundred milligrams daily."

"He says? The lunatics run the asylum?"

"Look at Washington, D.C."

She laughed harder. "What do the police want with him?"

"Information."

"On what?"

"A homicide."

"Oh. Great. A murderer. Can't wait to see him again."

"He's not a suspect," I said. "He's a potential witness."

"A witness? Guy like that, what kind of witness could he be?"

"Hard to say. Right now, I'm trying to get some rapport. We're talking about his family."

"His family? What, good old-fashioned psychoanalysis? The stuff you read about in books?"

I returned to Donny's room. He was facing the door. Waiting.

"No promises," I said, "but the resident's calling the supervising doctor."

"How long till I get my Tegretol?"

"If she gets the okay, soon."

"An eternity. What bullshit."

"You're welcome, Mr. Salcido."

He drew back his lips. Half his teeth were missing. The stragglers were cracked and discolored.

I pulled a chair next to the bed and sat down. "Why were you on your way to your father's place?"

"He never came to my place, why should I go to *his* place?"

"But you did."

"I know that, stupid! It's rhetorical—Ciceronian. I'm

questioning my own motives—engaging in introspection. Isn't that good? A sign of progress?" He spat and I had to move away to avoid being the target.

"I don't know *why* I do what I do," he said. "If I did, would I be *here*?"

I said nothing.

"I hope this happens to *you* one day," he said. "Feeling this passive. Weak. You think my skin's so weird? What's weird about it? Every shrink I talked to told me skin wasn't important, the thing was to look within. Get past the surface."

"How many shrinks have you talked to?"

"Too many. All assholes like you." He closed his eyes. "Talking faces, little crushing rooms just like this . . . Get past the skin, the skin, look inside. Man, I *like* the skin. The skin is all. The skin holds it all in."

The eyes opened. "C'mon, man, get these things off, let me touch my skin. When I can't touch it I feel like I'm not there."

"In time, Donny."

He moaned and rolled his head away from me.

"Your skin," I said. "Did you do all that yourself?"

"Idiot. How could I do the back?"

"What about the rest of it?"

"What do you think?"

"I think you did. It's good work. You're talented. I've seen your other artwork."

Silence.

"*The Anatomy Lesson,*" I said. "All those other masterpieces. Zero Tollrance."

His body jerked. I waited for him to speak.

Nothing.

"I think I understand why you chose that name,

Donny. You have zero tolerance for stupidity. You don't suffer fools." Like father . . .

He whispered something.

"What's that?" I said.

"Patience . . . is not a virtue."

"Why not, Donny?"

"You wait, nothing happens. You wait long enough, you choke. Rot. Time dies."

"People die, time goes on."

"You don't get it," he said, a bit louder. "People dying is nothing—worm food. Time dies, everything freezes."

"When you paint," I said, "what happens to time?"

A tiny smile showed itself amid the beard. "Eternity."

"And when you're not painting?"

"I'm too late."

"Too late for what?"

"Responses, being there, everything—my timing's off. I've got a sick brain, maybe the limbic system, maybe the prefrontal lobes, the temporals, the thalamus. Nothing moves at the right pace."

"Do you have a place where you can paint now?"

He stared at me. "Screw you. Get me out of here."

"You offered your art to your father, but he wouldn't accept it," I said. "After he was gone, you tried to give it to the world. To show them what you were capable of."

His lips folded inward and he chewed on them.

"Did you kill him, Donny?"

I bent closer. Close enough for him to bite my nose.

He didn't. Just stayed in place, prone, staring at the ceiling.

"Did you?" I said.

"No," he finally said. "Too late. As usual."

* * *

After that, he shut up tight. Ten minutes into the impasse, the straw-haired nurse came in carrying a metal tray that held a plastic cup of water and two pills, one oblong and pink, the other a white disc.

"Breakfast in bed," she announced. "Two-hundred-milligram morsel with a one-hundred chaser."

Donny was panting. He forgot his restraints, tried to sit up. The cuffs snapped against his wrists and he slammed back down, breathing even faster.

"No water," he said. "I won't be drowned."

The nurse frowned at me as if I was to blame. "Suit yourself, Señor Salcido. But if you can't swallow it dry, I'm not going back to the doctor to authorize an injection."

"Dry is good. Dry is safe."

She handed me the tray. "Here, you give it to him, I'm not getting my fingers bit off."

She watched as I took the pink pill and brought it close to Donny's face. His mouth was already wide open. His molars and most of his bicuspids were missing. Putrid breath streamed up at me. I dropped in the pink lozenge. He caught it on his gray tongue, flipped it backward, gulped, said, "Delicious."

In went the white pill. He grinned. Burped. The nurse snatched the tray and left, looking disgusted.

I sat back down.

"There you go," I said.

"Now you go," he said. "I had enough of you."

I tried awhile longer, asking him if he'd ever actually gotten into the apartment, what did he think of his father's library, had he read *Beowulf*. Mention of the book drew no response from him.

The closest I got to conversation was when I let him know I'd met his mother.

"Yeah? How's she doing?"

"She's concerned about you."

"Go fuck yourself."

I pressed him about novelty shop gags, phony books. Broken stethoscopes.

He said, "What in the ripe rotten fuck are you talking about?"

"You don't know?"

"Hell no, but go ahead, talk all you want, I'm coasting now. Getting smooth."

Then he closed his eyes, curled as fetally as the cuffs allowed, and went to sleep.

Not faking; real slumber, chest rising and falling in a slow, easy beat. The rhythmic snores of one at peace.

I left Hollywood Mercy trying to classify him. Assaultive and deeply disturbed, but bright and manipulative.

Combative and pigheaded, too. Eldon Mate had rejected his son unceasingly, but genetics couldn't be denied.

Zero Tollrance. He'd turned himself into a walking canvas, drifting from squat to squat, numbed his pain with dope and anticonvulsants and anger and art.

Painting his father's portrait, over and over.

Offering his *best* to his father, getting *rejected* over and over.

As good a motive for patricide as any. And Donny had considered it, he'd definitely considered it.

Did you kill him?

Too late. As usual.

Denying he'd followed through. As did Richard. Brilliant, bloody production, and no one was willing to take credit.

Despite Donny's slyness, I found myself believing him.

The mental impairment was real. Tegretol was powerful stuff, end-stage medication for mood disorders when lithium failed. No fun, not an addict's choice. If Donny craved it, he'd suffered.

He'd dissected his father on canvas, but the real-life murder reeked of a mix of calculation and brutality that seemed beyond him. I tried to picture him organizing what had happened up on Mulholland. Stalking, enticing, writing a mocking note, hiding a broken stethoscope in a box. Cleaning up perfectly, sufficiently meticulous not to leave a speck of DNA.

This was a guy who got mugged and left in the gutter. Who got yelled at by an elderly landlady and fled.

My mention of the book and the scope had elicited nothing from him. His clumsy attempt to enter his father's apartment in full view of Mrs. Krohnfeld was miles from that degree of sophistication. His entire life pattern was a series of failed attempts. I doubted he'd ever gotten past Eldon Mate's front door.

No, someone a lot more intact than Donny Salcido Mate had planted that toy. The personality combination I'd suggested at the beginning—the same mixture suggested by Fusco.

Smarts and rage. Outwardly coherent but with a bad temper problem.

Someone like Richard.

And his son. I thought of how the boy had pulverized six figures' worth of treasure.

It kept coming back to Eric.

Dispirited, I headed west on Beverly and considered how Eric might've lured Mate to Mulholland. Wanting to talk about his mother? To talk about what *he'd* done to his mother—*for* his mother. Claiming to Mate that he'd been *inspired* by the death doctor. The appeal to Mate's vanity might have worked.

But if Eric had been the one in that motel room, why butcher Mate? Covering for himself? Thin. So perhaps Mate *had* been involved. And Eric, knowing of his father's hatred for the death doctor, perhaps even knowing about the failed contract with Quentin Goad, had taken it upon himself to act.

Blood orgy to please the old man.

Happy Traveling, You Sick Bastard. The phrasing had an adolescent flavor to it. I could hear the sentence tumbling from Eric's lips.

But if Eric had slaughtered Mate, why was he now striking out against his father? Had he finally come to grips with what he'd done? Turned his anger on Richard—blaming, just as the old man was wont to do?

Father and son rolling, wrestling, snorting on the floor. Tearing at each other, only to embrace. Ambivalence. Apparent reconciliation.

But if what I suspected was true, the boy was unpredictable and dangerous. Joe Safer had sensed that, asked my opinion. I'd avoided an answer, claiming I needed to focus upon Stacy, but also wanting to avoid additional complications. Now I had to wonder if Eric's presence in the house put Stacy—and Richard—in danger.

I'd call Safer as soon as I got home. Hold back my suspicions and keep my comments general—Eric's bad temper, the effects of stress, the need to be careful.

The afternoon traffic had sludged to chrome cholesterol, cars lurching forward in fits and starts, tempers flaring. I allowed myself to be drawn into it, oblivious to petty resentments, thinking about real rage: Eric and Mate on Mulholland. Blunt-force injury to Mate's head. As in baseball bat.

Perhaps the boy had gotten Mate up there with a simple lie: misrepresenting himself as a terminally ill patient pining for the love bite of the Humanitron.

A young, male traveler. Mate, defensive about too many females, those nasty feminist jibes about his sexuality, would have liked that.

The meet, the kill, then weeks later Eric sneaks into Mate's apartment and hides the stethoscope.

Out of business, Doc.

High intelligence, savage anger. The boy had plenty of both.

And sneaking out in the middle of the night was Eric's habit, he'd done it for years.

Helen, the dog . . .

A look at the boy's phone records and credit-card log would be instructive. Had he booked a flight from Palo Alto to L.A. on or around the day of Mate's murder? Made a second trip to pull off the break-in?

Taking all those risks simply to taunt Mate's ghosts.

Or was it the cops he was out to humiliate? Because, after shedding blood, he learned that he *liked* it?

The juxtaposition of blood and pleasure. That's the way it had started for Michael Burke. That's the way it always started.

Someone that young and smart warping so severely. Terrifying.

I wanted to bounce it all off Milo. *Intriguing,* he'd say, *but all theory.*

And theory was where it would freeze because I couldn't—didn't *want* to—probe further.

A horn honked. Someone screeched to a stop. Someone cursed. The air outside looked heavy and milky and poisonous. I sat in my steel box, one among thousands, pretending to navigate.

CHAPTER

31

FOUR P.M. CORNED-BEEF sandwiches and beer in the fridge, a note from Robin pinned to a carton of coleslaw. She and Spike had gone to A&M Studios to sit in on a recording session. The bassist was debuting an eight-string she'd created. Rhythm-and-blues tracks; Spike loved that kind of thing.

The studio was on La Brea near Sunset; I'd been only a few blocks away. Ships passing . . .

Mail was piled up on the dining room table; from the looks of it, mostly bills, and hucksters promising immortality. I phoned Safer. He was in court, unavailable, so I tried the Dosses.

Richard answered. "Doctor. So you got the packet."

"What packet?"

Pause. "Doesn't matter . . . What can I do for you?"

"I was calling to see how you're doing."

"Stacy's fine. Went to school. She's staying away for the weekend." His voice dropped. "I suppose that's best."

"And Eric?"

"On his way back to Stanford. I got him a plane out of Van Nuys."

"You think he's ready for that?"

"Why not?"

"Last night—"

"Last night was an aberration, Doctor. With all he's gone through, he should've blown a long time ago. Tell the truth, I'm glad he finally did. It's just pottery, I'm fully insured. We'll tell the carrier it was an accident— the bolts on the cases came loose."

"Is he going to get some help at Stanford?"

"We discussed that," he said. "He's considering it."

"I think you should be more directive—"

"Look, Doctor, I appreciate all you've done, but frankly Eric doesn't . . . he doesn't feel comfortable with you. Not your fault, everyone relates differently, you're fine for Stacy, not Eric. Probably all for the best, avoiding sibling rivalry. So why don't you concentrate on Stacy and I'll handle Eric."

"I think he needs help, Richard."

"Your opinion has been duly noted."

"What about you, Richard? How are you doing?"

"I'm alone. Guess I'd better get used to that."

"Anything I can do?"

"No, I'm fine—no thanks to your buddy the detective. He keeps trying to search every square inch I own. And hounding Safer, asking for an 'interview.' Talk about euphemism. But that's okay, everyone has to do their job. Safer tells me I'll be free of all this crap soon enough. Gotta go, Doctor, call coming in on the other line. If Stacy needs you, I'll be in touch."

"She doesn't want an appointment?"

"I'll ask her. Thanks. Bye."

I found "the packet" in the middle of the mail stack. Courier-delivered envelope, the return address, RTD Properties. Folded into a sheet of RTD stationery was a check written on RTD business account IV. Fifteen thousand dollars. A typed note:

> Mr. D. *thanks you for your time. He trusts this will cover everything to date.*
>
> Terri, Accounting

I'll be in touch.

Not likely. I knew severance pay when I saw it.

I couldn't talk to Milo, so I called Petra to let her know my impressions of Donny Salcido Mate. She was at her desk, courteous enough, but she sounded busy and I asked her if it was a bad time.

"It's fine," she said. "I just have to run over to Hollywood Pres in a few minutes, start some paper on a new one. Boy meets girl, boy beds girl, boy kills girl, then tries to kill himself. Guy's hooked up to life support, some people can't do anything right. What's up?"

I summarized my bedside chat with Donny.

She said, "Is this guy dangerous?"

"If he doesn't get medicated, maybe. I can't promise you he didn't kill his father, but I wouldn't bet on it."

I explained my reasoning.

She said, "Makes sense. I'll pass it on, see if Milo wants me to hold him on anything. . . . Listen, I know I'm a pest about Billy, but kid care isn't my thing, I'm the youngest in my family. Tomorrow when I see him, I was thinking of bringing him some books. Anything in particular you'd suggest?"

"He's always liked history."

"I've already gotten him plenty of history books. I thought fiction might be a nice switch—maybe the classics? Do you see him as able to handle *Les Misérables*? Or *The Count of Monte Cristo*, something like that?"

"Sure," I said. "Either."

"Good, I wasn't sure. Because of the themes—abandonment, poverty. You don't think it's too close to home?"

"No, he'll be fine with it, Petra. I can see books like that appealing to his moral core."

"He's sure got one of *those*, doesn't he?" she said. "I'm still trying to figure out where it came from."

"If you knew, you could sell it."

"And do something else for a living."

"Such as?" I said.

She laughed. "Such as nothing. I love my job."

Saturday morning I awoke thinking about Eric as a murderer. It stayed on my mind during the breakfast that Robin and I shared out near the pond. Then I looked around, saw how beautiful the world was and wondered if I was just letting my imagination run wild because I couldn't stand nice. After all, not a shred of evidence pointed to the boy—or his mother—even talking to Mate.

Mate's records might shed some light on that. And I was certain that records existed, because Mate had regarded his work as historically significant, would have wanted every detail recorded for posterity.

Milo had guessed Roy Haiselden had them, and he might be right. Now that he had Richard as a suspect, and Haiselden's motive for disappearing had become clear, he was unlikely to pursue the attorney.

No criminal charges had been lodged against Haiselden yet, but domestic violence and child-abuse allegations meant that other detectives would be looking for him, meaning someone might get a warrant. But the Breckenham civil suit had been filed in Baldwin Park, sheriffs jurisdiction. My only sheriffs contact was Ron Banks, a downtown homicide investigator and Petra Connor's boyfriend. I'd met him once, not exactly foundation for a favor.

After we cleaned up, Robin and I went shopping for groceries, then walked in the hills with the pooch. Then she retired for a nap and I went into my office, ignited the computer and gave the Internet another try. Nothing new on Mate except for a couple of cybergossips in a right-to-die chat room exercising their constitutional right to be paranoid.

Am I being too imaginative, wondered whiteknight, *to suggest that following the death of Dr. Mate further attempts are being made to silence those with the courage to face off against The Powers That Be?*

Not at all, responded funnigirl. *I've heard the police from various cities have gotten together to create a task-force on euthanasia. The plan is to kill people then make it look as if the right-to-die folks are behind it. Shades of Grassy Knoll.*

Screenplays were everywhere. I logged off.

Mate's records . . . Time to give the ever-amiable Alice Zoghbie another try? For all I knew, Haiselden had never had the files, they'd been stored at the pretty little vanilla house on Glenmont.

No reason for her to be any more forthcoming.

Unless I pointed out the discrepancies between Joanne's assisted suicide and Mate's other travelers. Suggested Mate *hadn't* helped Joanne, that Richard had killed Zoghbie's mentor for nothing—had turned Mate into the sacrificial lamb she'd claimed.

If she knew that already, hearing about Richard's

arrest would have sent her reeling, she might even be contemplating coming forth. If so, maybe I could tip the scales—turn her grief to my advantage.

Manipulative, but she was someone who believed the infirm should be encouraged not to exist.

At worst, she'd slam the door in my face. Nothing lost; as things stood, I was pretty useless.

I made the drive to Glendale in thirty-five minutes. In the morning light, Alice Zoghbie's house was even cuter, flower beds crayon bright, the copper rooster weather vane vibrating in a breeze I couldn't feel. The same white Audi sat in the cobblestone driveway. Dust on the windshield.

A bit more humanity on the street this time. An old man sweeping his front porch, a young couple pulling out of their carport.

I tapped the goat's-head knocker lightly. No answer. My second attempt, more energetic, was also met with silence.

Making my way back to the driveway, I walked past the Audi to a green wooden gate. Bees buzzed, butterflies fluttered. I called out, "Hello?" then Alice Zoghbie's name, got no reply. Flowers kissed the side of the house. Lights on in the kitchen.

The gate was latched but not locked. I reached around, popped it open, continued along a cobblestone path shaded by the arthritic boughs of an old, scarred sycamore. A small stoop led up to the kitchen door. Four panes of glass gave me something to look through. Lights on, but unoccupied. Dishes in the sink. A carton of milk and half an orange on the counter. The fruit, slightly withered. I knocked. Nothing. Climbing down the stoop, I moved along the side of the house, peeking in windows, listening. Just the bee buzz.

The backyard was small, charmingly landscaped, with hedges of Italian cypress on two sides that blocked the neighbors' views, and a tall wooden fence at the back. Victorian lawn furniture, more flower beds. The kind of flowers that bloom in shade. A dark yard, shrouded by a second sycamore, even larger, stout branches supporting a macramé hammock.

Trunk as thick as two people.

Two people propped against the trunk.

The buzzing, louder—not bees, flies, a storm of flies.

Both of the bodies were tied to the tree with thick rope, fastened tight at chest level and around the waist. The hemp was crusted maroon and brown and black.

Barefoot corpses, insects reconnoitering between fingers and toes. The woman slumped to the right. She had on a blue floral housedress with an elastic neckband. The elastic had allowed the garment to be yanked down without ripping, exposing what had once been her breasts. The killer had hiked it above her waist, too, raised her knees, spread her legs. Wounds everywhere, that same red-black splotching her skin and her clothing, running down her thighs, filthying the grass. Her flesh was green-tinged where the blood hadn't settled.

Triangles sliced into her abdomen, three of them. Her head drooped to her chest, so that I couldn't see her face. A black gaping necklace was visible along her jawline. A helmet of white hair, sparkling where it wasn't fly-crowded, said she'd once been Alice Zoghbie.

The man's khaki shorts had been removed and folded next to his left thigh. His blue polo shirt remained on but had been rolled up to his nipples. Big man, heavy, flabby. Stiff, reddish toupee—a hairpiece I'd seen on TV.

Triangles danced along the swell of Roy Haiselden's abdomen, too, distorted by his paunch. His head lolled to the right. Toward Alice Zoghbie, as if straining to listen to some secret she was imparting.

Not much remained of his face. His genitals had been removed and placed on the grass between his legs. They'd shriveled and shrunk and bugs congregated there with special enthusiasm.

The fingers of his left hand were entwined with Alice Zoghbie's.

The two of them, holding hands.

I'd broken into frosty sweat, wasn't breathing, but my brain was racing. My eyes shifted from the bodies to something else, off to the left, a few feet away. A wicker picnic basket. Propped against it, a tall green bottle, foil-topped. Champagne. Atop the basket, a pair of tiny, gold-lidded jars.

Too far for me to read the labels and I knew better than to disturb the crime scene.

Red jar, black jar. Caviar?

Champagne and caviar, an upscale picnic. Bare feet and her housedress said Alice and the man had no intention of going anywhere.

Posed.

The irony.

A bluebottle fly alighted on Alice Zoghbie's left breast, scuttled, paused, explored some more before taking off in flight—heading toward me.

I backed away. Retreated through the gate, knowing my prints were on the handle, it wouldn't be long before someone would want to talk to me. Leaving it open, I retraced my steps down the driveway, past the Audi, to the curb.

The old man had gone inside. The street had reverted

to torpor. So many perfect lawns. Sparrows skittered. How long before the vultures arrived?

Inside the Seville, I breathed.

Last guy in L.A. without a damn cell phone.

I got out of there, drove to a gas station on Verdugo Road, sweat-drenched, collar tight. I parked near the pay phone, composed myself, got out. Other people pumped gas as I tried to look any way other than how I felt.

The killings were in Glendale PD jurisdiction, but to hell with that, I called Milo.

CHAPTER

32

"ANY IDEA WHEN he'll be back?"

"I think he went downtown to do some paperwork," said the clerk, a woman, one I didn't know. "I can transfer you to Detective Korn. He works with Detective Sturgis. Your name, sir?"

"No thanks," I said.

"You're sure?"

She sounded nice so I gave her the ugly details and hung up before she could respond.

I drove back to L.A., hoping for an empty house. Wanting time to breathe, to sort things out.

Repulsed, still shaken. Sweat came gushing out of my pores as the image of the bodies kept smacking me across the brain.

Milo and I had visited Alice Zoghbie five days ago.

No skin sloughing, no maggots, the beginnings of the green tinge . . . I was no forensic pathologist, but I'd seen enough corpses to guess that not more than a couple of days had passed since the murder. Alice's mail and phone records could clear that up. . . .

Propped, holding hands, a picnic.

Someone canny enough to overpower a big man like Haiselden and a woman who hiked the Himalayas.

Someone they knew. A confederate. Had to be.

The feelings of disgust didn't subside, but a new sensation joined them—strange, juvenile glee.

Not Eric, not Richard. No motive and both their whereabouts were well accounted for during the past two or three days. Same for Donny Salcido.

Propped against a tree. Geometry. Michael Burke's trademarks. Time to give Leimert Fusco's big black book another review.

Time to call Fusco—but Milo deserved to know first.

I was on the 134, driving much too fast, hoping for an empty house, thinking about Haiselden hiding from the civil suit only to encounter something much worse.

He'd probably been hiding out with Alice all along—I recalled the phone call she'd taken when Milo and I had visited. Afterward, she couldn't wait to get rid of us. Probably from her pal, wanting to know if the coast was clear.

The two of them waylaid right there in Alice's house. Someone they knew . . . someone respectable, trusted. A bright young doctor who'd apprenticed to Mate.

No doubt Glendale police had already been dispatched to the scene. Soon my prints on the gate would be lifted and within days they'd be matched to the Medical Board files in Sacramento.

Milo needed to know soon.

If I couldn't reach him, should I go straight to Fusco? The FBI man had said he was flying up to Seattle. Wanting to check on the unsolveds—something specific about the Seattle unsolveds?

The last Seattle victim—Marissa Bonpaine. Plastic hypodermic found on the forest floor. Cataloged and forgotten.

Not a coincidence. Couldn't be a coincidence.

Fusco had left me his beeper number and his local exchange, but both were back home in the Burke file.

I pushed the Seville up to ninety.

I unlocked my front door. Robin's truck was gone—prayers answered. I raced to my office, feeling guilty about being quite so pleased.

I tried Milo again, got no answer, decided sooner was better than later and phoned Fusco's beeper and routing number. No callback from him, either. I was starting to feel like the last man on Earth. After another futile attempt to reach Milo, I punched in FBI headquarters at the Federal Building in Westwood and asked for Special Agent Fusco. The receptionist put me on hold, then transferred me to another woman with the throaty voice of a lounge singer who took my name and number.

"May I tell him what this is about, sir?"

"He'll know."

"He's out of the office. I'll give him the message."

I pulled out the big black accordion file, flung it open, stared at pictures of corpses against trees, geometrical wounds, the parallels inescapable.

All my theories about family breakdown, the Dosses, the Manitows, and it had come down to just another psychopath. I paged through police reports, found the Seattle cases, the data on Marissa Bonpaine, was halfway through the small print when the doorbell rang.

Leaving the file on the desk, I trotted to the front door. The peephole offered a fish-eye view of two people—a man and a woman, white, early thirties, expressionless.

Clean-cut duo. Missionaries? I could use some faith but was in no mood to be preached to.

"Yes?" I said, through the door.

I watched the woman's mouth move. "Dr. Delaware? FBI. May we please speak with you."

Throaty voice of a lounge singer.

Before I could answer, a badge filled the peephole. I opened the door.

The woman's lips were turned upward, but the smile appeared painful. Her badge was still out. "Special Agent Mary Donovan. This is Special Agent Mark Bratz. May we please come in, Dr. Delaware?"

Donovan was five-six or so with short light-brown hair, a strong jaw and a firm, busty, low-waisted body packed into a charcoal gray suit. Rosy complexion, an aura of confidence. Bratz was a half head taller with dark hair starting to thin, sleepy eyes and a round, vulnerable face. The skin around his jowls was raw, and a small Band-Aid was stuck under one ear. He wore a navy blue suit, white shirt, gray-and-navy tie.

I stepped back to let them enter. They stood in the entry hall, checking out the house, until I invited them to sit.

"Thanks for your time, Doctor," said Donovan, still smiling as she took the most comfortable chair. She carried a huge black cloth purse, which she placed on the floor.

Bratz waited until I'd settled, then positioned himself so the two of them flanked me. I tried to look casual, thinking about the open file on the desk, trying *not* to think about what I'd just seen in Glendale.

"Nice house," said Bratz. "Bright."

"Thanks. May I ask what this is about?"

"Very nice," said Donovan. "Care to guess, Doctor?"

"Something to do with Agent Fusco."

"Something to do with *Mr.* Fusco."

"He's not with the FBI?"

"Not any longer," said Bratz. His voice was high, tentative, like that of a bashful kid asking for a date. "Mr. Fusco retired from the Bureau a while back—was asked to retire."

"Because of personal issues," said Donovan. She took a pad and a Sony minirecorder out of her bag, set them on the coffee table. "Mind if I record?"

"Record what?"

"Your impressions of Mr. Fusco, sir."

"You're saying he was mustered out because of personal issues?" I said. "Are we talking criminal issues? Is he dangerous?"

Donovan glanced at Bratz. "May I record, sir?"

"After you tell me what's going on, maybe."

Donovan's fingernails tapped the Sony. Surprisingly long nails. French tips. Her lipstick was subtle. Her expression wasn't. She had no use for civilians who didn't fall in line.

"Sir," she said. "It's in your best interests—"

"I need to know. Is Fusco a criminal suspect?" As in multiple murder.

"At this point, sir, we're simply trying to find him. To help him." Her index finger touched the Sony's REC button.

I shook my head.

"Sir, we could arrange for you to be questioned at Bureau headquarters."

"That would take time, paperwork, and something tells me time's of the essence," I said. "On the other hand, you could tell me what's going on and I could cooperate and we could all try to have something of a weekend."

She looked at Bratz. No signal for him that I saw, but she turned back to me and her expression had softened.

"Here's a summary, Doctor. All you need to know and more: Leimert Fusco was a highly admired member of the Bureau—I assume you've heard of the BSU? The original Behavioral Science Unit at Quantico? Mr. Fusco was a member of the freshman class. Actually, he's Dr. Fusco. Has a PhD in psychology, same as you."

"So he informed me. Why was he asked to leave the Bureau?"

Bratz leaned across and clicked on the recorder, said, "How'd you meet him, sir?"

"Sorry, I'm not comfortable with this," I said, sorry about a lot more. Moments ago, I'd been ready to focus on Michael Burke as the real Dr. Death. If Fusco had lied, what happened to that scenario?

"What's the problem, sir?" said Donovan.

"Talking to you, going on record, without knowing the full picture. I spent time with Fusco. I need to know who I was dealing with."

Another looked passed between them. Donovan's mouth turned up again and she crossed her legs, setting off little scratchy sounds. Short legs, but shapely. Runner's calves in sheer stockings. Bratz snuck a peek at them, as if they were still a novelty. I wondered how long they'd been partnered.

"Fair enough, sir," she said, suddenly sunny. She tossed her hair, but it didn't move much. Leg recross. She inched closer to me. I could imagine some FBI seminar. *Achieve rapport with the subject by any appropriate means.* "But first, let me take a stab at how you met him: he contacted Detective Sturgis and asked to meet with you to discuss a homicide—most likely that of Dr. Mate—because you're the psychological consultant on the case. He told you he knows who the murderer is." Lots of teeth. "How'm I doing so far?"

"Very well," I said.

"Michael Burke," said Bratz. "He wanted you to believe in Dr. Michael Burke."

"Is Burke fiction?"

Bratz shrugged. "Let's just say Dr. Fusco's obsessed."

"With Burke."

"With the *idea* of Burke," said Donovan.

"Are you telling me he made Burke up?"

She glanced at the recorder. Switched it off. "Okay, here's the whole story, but we insist you keep it confidential. Agent Fusco had an honorable career with the Bureau. For several years, he was assigned to the Midtown Manhattan office as director of behavioral sciences. Five years ago, his wife died—breast cancer—and he was left sole parent of his child. A daughter, fourteen years old, named Victoria. What made Mrs. Fusco's death especially traumatic for Agent Fusco was that Victoria had also been diagnosed with cancer. Several years before, as a toddler. A bone tumor, she was treated at Sloan-Kettering, apparently cured. Shortly after his wife passed away, Fusco requested a transfer, said he wanted to raise Victoria in a quieter environment. An administrative position was found for him in the Buffalo office and he purchased a home near Lake Erie."

"Not a career move," I said. "He was devoted to the girl."

Donovan nodded. "Everything seemed fine for a couple of years, then the girl got sick again, at sixteen. Leukemia. Apparently the radiation she'd received for her bone tumor years ago had caused it."

"Secondary tumor," I said. Rare but tragic; I'd seen it at Western Peds.

"Exactly. Agent Fusco began bringing Victoria down to New York to be re-treated at Sloan-Kettering. She went into one remission, relapsed, received more chemo, achieved only a partial remission, started to weaken, tried some experimental drugs and got better but even weaker. Agent Fusco decided to continue her treatment closer to home, at a hospital in Buffalo. The goal was to increase her strength until she was able to tolerate a bone-marrow transplant back in New York. She improved for a while, then came down with pneumonia because chemotherapy had weakened her immune system. Her doctors hospitalized her and, unfortunately, she passed away."

"Was that expected?"

"From what we can gather, it wasn't unexpected but neither was it inevitable."

"One of those fifty-fifty situations," said Bratz.

"A hospital in Buffalo," I said. "Was she cared for by a respiratory tech named Roger Sharveneau?"

Donovan frowned. Looked at Bratz. He shook his head, but she said, "Possibly."

"Possibly?"

"Roger Sharveneau was on duty during Victoria's final hospitalization. Whether he was ever her therapist is unclear."

"Missing records?" I said.

"What's the difference?" said Bratz.

"Was Michael Burke also working there during that period?"

Bratz's eyes narrowed. Donovan said, "There's no record of Burke caring for her."

"But he was circulating through at the time— probably freelancing at the E.R.," I said.

Silence from both of them.

I went on: "When did Fusco become convinced that

someone—Sharveneau or Burke, or both of them—had murdered his daughter?"

"Months later," said Donovan. "After Sharveneau began confessing. Fusco claimed he recognized him from the ward, had seen him in Victoria's room when he had no good reason to be there. He tried to interview Sharveneau in jail, was refused permission by the Buffalo police because the Bureau had no standing in the case and *he* certainly didn't—it was obviously a personal issue. Agent Fusco didn't react well to that. After Sharveneau was released, he persisted, harassing Sharveneau's lawyer. He became increasingly . . . irate. Even after Sharveneau committed suicide, he didn't cease."

"Was Fusco considered a suspect in Sharveneau's supposed suicide?" I said.

Second's hesitation. "No, never. Sharveneau had been in hiding, there's no evidence Fusco ever found him. Meanwhile, Agent Fusco's work product deteriorated and the Bureau sent him back to Quantico for several months. Had him teach seminars to beginning profilers. As a cooling-off measure. It seemed to be working, Fusco looked calm, more content. But that turned out to be a ruse. He was utilizing the bulk of his energies researching Burke, accessing data banks without permission. He was brought back to New York for a meeting with his superiors, during which he was let go on disability pension."

"*Emotional* disability," said Bratz.

"You see him as seriously disturbed?" I said. "Out of touch with reality?"

Bratz exhaled, looked uncomfortable.

"You've met him," said Donovan. "What do you think, Doctor?"

"To me he seemed pretty focused."

"That's the problem, Doctor. Too much focus. He's already committed a score of felonies."

"Violent felonies?"

"Mostly multiple thefts."

"Of what?"

"Data—official police records from various jurisdictions. And he continues to represent himself as a special agent. If all that got out . . . Doctor, the Bureau has sympathy for his misfortune. The Bureau respects him—respects what he once was. No one wants to see him end up in jail."

"Is he off base on Burke?" I said.

"Burke's not the issue," said Bratz.

"Why not?"

"Burke's not the issue for *us*," Donovan clarified. "We handle only internal investigations, not external criminal matters. S.A. Fusco's been identified as an internal issue."

"Is anyone in the Bureau looking into Michael Burke?"

"We wouldn't have access to that information, sir. Our goal is simple: take custody of Leimert Fusco, for his own good."

"What happens to him if you find him?" I said.

"He'll be cared for."

"Committed?"

Donovan frowned. "Cared for. Humanely. Forget all the movies you've seen. Dr. Fusco's a private citizen now, due the same rights as anyone else. He'll be cared for until such a time as he's judged competent—it's for his own good, Doctor. No one wants to see a man of his . . . fortitude and experience end up in jail."

Bratz said, "We've been looking for him for a while, finally traced him to L.A. He covers his tracks pretty well, got himself a cell phone account under another name, but we found it and it led us to an apartment in Culver City. By the time we got there, he was gone. Packed up. Then an hour ago, you called and we just happened to be there."

"Lucky break for you," I said.

"Where is he, Doctor?"

"Don't know."

His hand clenched. "Why were you attempting to call him, sir?"

"To discuss Michael Burke. I'm sure you know I'm a psychological consultant to LAPD. I've been asked to interface with S.A. Fusco." I shrugged. "That's it."

"Come on, Doctor," said Bratz. "You don't want to be putting yourself in an awkward position. We'll be contacting Detective Sturgis soon enough, he'll tell us the truth."

"Be my guests."

Bratz hemmed me closer and I sniffed mentholated cologne. His jaw was set. No more vulnerability. "Why would you care about Dr. Burke? A suspect's already in custody on Mate."

"Being thorough," I said.

"Thorough," Bratz repeated. "Just like Fusco."

"You know, Doctor," said Donovan, "some people say you're kind of obsessive."

I smiled. How long before the prints on Alice Zoghbie's gate got decoded and they found out about it? "Sounds like you've been researching me."

"We can be thorough, too."

"If only everyone was," I said. "Better world. The trains would run on time."

Bratz rubbed a patch of raw skin and looked at the recorder. Nothing of substance had been recorded. "You think this is a joke, my friend? You think we want to sit around with you, bullshitting?"

I turned and looked into his eyes. "I doubt you're enjoying this any more than I am, but that doesn't change the facts. You asked me if I knew where Fusco was, I told you the truth. I don't. He said he'd be out of town, left the cell-phone number. I tried it and he didn't answer, so I phoned the Federal Building. Obviously that's something he didn't instruct me to do, so we're *obviously* not colluding on anything."

"What cell number did he give you?"

"Hold on and I'll get it for you."

"You do that," said Bratz, barely opening his mouth.

I went into my office, stashed the accordion file in a drawer, copied down the number and returned. Bratz was on his feet, studying prints on the wall. Donovan's nylon-glossed knees were pressed together. I handed her the slip.

"Same one we've got, Mark," she said.

Bratz said, "Let's get out of here."

I said, "Even if Fusco had left me a detailed itinerary, why would it be any more credible than anything else he told me?"

"You're saying Fusco just told you about Burke, then dropped out of sight."

"Told Detective Sturgis and myself. We met with him, together, just as you said."

"Where?"

"Mort's Deli. Sturgis didn't buy the Burke theory, basically shunted it to me. As you said, he's got a suspect."

"And your opinion?"

"About what?"

"Burke."

"I need more data. That's exactly why I tried to

reach Fusco. If I'd known it was going to get this complicated . . ."

Bratz turned toward me. "Understand this: if Fusco keeps improvising, it could get real complicated."

"Makes sense," I said. "Rogue agent running wild, psychological expert goes haywire. Public relations nightmare for you guys."

"Something wrong with that? Protecting the Bureau's integrity so it can do its job?"

"Not at all. Nothing wrong with integrity."

"True, Doctor," said Donovan. "Just make sure you're holding on to yours."

I watched them drive away in a dark blue sedan.

They'd labeled Fusco obsessive but hadn't dismissed the core of his investigation. *An internal issue.* Not their problem.

Meaning someone else in the Bureau might very well be looking into Michael Burke. Or they weren't.

When news of the Zoghbie-Haiselden murder broke, Fusco's nose would twitch harder. He'd probably try to contact Milo, even fly back down to L.A. Get snagged by his former comrades, taken into custody. For his own good.

He'd had a tragic life, but right now worrying about his welfare wasn't my job either. I went back inside, gave Milo yet another try. Daring another attempt at the West L.A. station, ready to disguise my voice if the same clerk answered.

This time it was a bored-sounding man who patched me up to the Robbery-Homicide room.

A familiar voice picked up Milo's extension. Del Hardy. A long time ago the veteran detective and Milo had worked together. Del was black, which hadn't mattered much, and married to a second wife who was a devout Baptist, which had—she'd kiboshed the partnership. I knew Del was a year from retirement, planning something down in Florida.

"Working Saturday, Del?"

"Long as it's not Sunday, Doc. How's the guitar-playing?"

"Not doing enough of it. Seen the big guy recently?"

"Happened to see him about an hour ago. He said he was going over to Judge MacIntyre's house, try for some warrants. Pasadena—I can give you the number if it's important. But Judge MacIntyre gets cranky about being bugged on the weekend, so why don't you try Milo's mobile."

"I did. He didn't answer."

"Maybe he shut it off, didn't want to annoy Judge MacIntyre."

"Scary guy, huh?"

"MacIntyre? Yeah, but law and order. If he thinks you're righteous he'll give all sorts of leeway—okay, here it is."

A frosty-voiced woman said, "What's this about?"

"I'm a police consultant, working on a homicide case. It's important that I reach Detective Sturgis. Is he there?"

"One minute."

Four minutes later, she came back on. "He's on his way out, said *he'll* call *you*."

It took another quarter hour for Milo to ring in.

"What's so important, Alex? How the hell did you get MacIntyre's number—you almost messed me up, I was in the middle of getting paper on Doss. Got some, too."

"Sorry, but you were wasting your time." I told him what I'd seen in Alice Zoghbie's backyard. The way I'd reported it to the police clerk, my prints on the gate.

"This is a joke, right?" he said.

"Ha ha ha."

Long silence. "Why'd you go out there in the first place, Alex?"

"Boredom, overachievement—what's the difference? This changes everything."

"Where are you right now?"

"Home. Just finished with some visitors." I began to tell him about Donovan and Bratz.

"Stop," he said. "I'm coming over—no, better if we meet somewhere, just in case they're still watching you. I just got on the 110—let's make it somewhere central . . . Pico-Robertson, the parking lot behind the Miller's Outpost, southeast corner. If I'm late, buy yourself some jeans. And try to figure out if the feebies are tailing you. If they are, I doubt they'll be using more than one car, which will make it damn near impossible for them to pull it off if you're looking out for them. Did you happen to notice what kind of car they were driving?"

"Blue sedan."

"Check for it three, four car lengths behind you. If you see it, drive back home and wait."

"High intrigue."

"Low intrigue," he said. "Bureaucracy's big toes getting stepped on. Zoghbie and Haiselden—did you notice any overt putrefaction?"

"Green tinge, no maggots, lots of flies."

"Probably a day or two at most . . . and you're saying the positioning was similar to the stuff in Fusco's file?"

"Identical. Geometrical wounds, as well."

"Oh my," he said. "Every day brings new thrills."

I wrote a note to Robin and left, drove more slowly than usual, looked out for the blue sedan or anything else that spelled government-issue. No sign of a tail, as far as I could tell. I reached the Miller's Outpost lot before Milo, parked where he'd instructed, got out of the car and stood against the driver's door. Still, no blue car. The lot was half full. Shoppers streamed in and out of the store, business at a nearby newsstand was brisk, cars roared by on Robertson. I waited and thought about putrefaction.

Milo showed up ten minutes later, surprisingly well-put-together in a gray suit, white shirt, maroon tie. Warrant-begging duds. No string tie for Judge MacIntyre.

He motioned me into the unmarked, lit up the cold stub of a Panatela as I eased into the passenger seat.

He scanned the lot, fondled his cell phone, let his eyes drift to the jeans store. "Time to get myself some easy-fit . . . Glendale's at the scene—they've pegged it to an anonymous caller. How does it feel to be an archetype?"

"Glorious. But I won't be anonymous long. The gate."

"Yeah, terrific. I'm waiting to hear back from their detectives. News jackals picked it up, too, it's only a matter of time before they tie Zoghbie and Haiselden to Mate and we're back on page one."

"That's exactly what Burke wants," I said. "But maybe he had another motive for killing Zoghbie and Haiselden: to get hold of any records that incriminated him. He might very well have been planning it for a while, but Richard's arrest might have sped things up: he wouldn't like someone else getting credit for his handiwork. Like Mate, he's after the attention, is eliminating the old guard, telling the world he's the new Dr. Death."

He chewed the cigar's wooden tip, blew out acrid smoke. "You buy the whole Burke thing even though Fusco misrepresented himself?"

"When will you be going over to the Zoghbie crime scene?"

"Soon."

"Wait till you see it. Everything fits. And Donovan and Bratz never dismissed Fusco's findings, they're just worried he'll do something that makes the Bureau look bad. Fusco's convinced Sharveneau and/or Burke murdered his daughter. Personal motivation can get in the way, but sometimes it's potent fuel."

He sucked in smoke, held it in his lungs for a long time, drew a lazy circle on the windshield fog. "So I've been spinning my wheels on Doss . . . who, from what I've been told by business associates, has very complicated financial records—maybe I'll send my files to the Fraud boys."

He faced me. "Alex, you know damn well he solicited Goad to kill Mate, we're not talking Mother Teresa. Just because Goad didn't go all the way doesn't put Doss in the clear."

"I realize that. But it doesn't change what I saw in Glendale."

"Right," he said. "Back to square goddamn one . . . Burke, or whatever the hell he's calling himself . . . you're saying he craves center stage. But he can't go public the way Mate did . . . so what does that mean? More nasties against trees?" His laugh was thick with affliction and anger. "Gee, *that's* a terrific lead. Let's go check out every bit of bark in the goddamn county—where the hell do I *go* with this, Alex?"

"Back to Fusco's files?" I said.

"You've already been through them. Okay, I'll accept the fact that Burke is evil personified. Now, where the hell do I find him?"

"I'll go over them again. You never know—"

"You're right about that," he said. "I never *do* know. Spend half my damn life in blissless ignorance . . . Okay, let's handle some short-term matters. Like keeping you out of jail once those prints cross-reference to the Medical Board. Did you touch anything but the gate?"

"The front door knocker. I also knocked on the side door, but just with my knuckles."

"The old goat's head," he said. "When I first saw it I wondered if Alice was into witchcraft or something. That, combined with all her talk of Mate being a sacrifice. So *she* ends up tied up— All right, look, I'm going to run interference for you with Glendale PD, but at some point you'll have to talk to them. It'll take days for the prints to be analyzed, maybe a good week for the cross-reference, even longer if the med files aren't on Printrak. But I need to work with them, so I'm telling them about you sooner—figure on tomorrow. I'll try to have them interview you on friendly territory."

"Thanks."

"Yeah. Thanks, too." He inhaled, made the cigar tip glow, created another quarter inch of ash.

"For what?"

"Being such a persistent bastard."

"What's next?" I said.

"For you? Keeping out of trouble. For me, anguish."

"Want Fusco's file?"

"Later," he said. "There's still Doss's paper to deal with. I can't let warrants lapse on an attempted murder case. I do that and Judge MacIntyre puts me on his naughty list. I'll sic Korn and Demetri on Doss's office, have them shlep the financial records to the station so I can get moving at Glendale. Maybe the scene will tell me something. Maybe Burke/whatever missed something in

Alice's house and we can get a lead on him." He crushed the cigar in the ashtray. "Fat chance of that, right?"

"Anything's possible."

"Everything's possible," he said. "That's the problem."

By the time I got back, Robin was home. We had a takeout Chinese dinner and I fed slivers of Peking duck to Spike, acting like a regular, domestic guy with nothing heavier on my mind than taxes and prostate problems. This time I went to sleep when Robin did and drifted off easily. At 4:43 A.M., I woke up with a stiff neck and a stubborn brain. Cold air had settled in during the night and my hands felt like freezer-burned steaks. I put on sweats, athletic socks and slippers, shuffled to my office, removed Fusco's file from the drawer where I'd concealed it from Donovan and Bratz.

Starting again, with Marissa Bonpaine, finding nothing out of the ordinary but the plastic hypodermic. An hour in, I got drowsy. The smart decision would have been to crawl back in bed. Instead, I lurched to the kitchen. Spike was curled up on his mattress in the adjacent laundry room, flat little bulldog face compressed against the foam. Movement beneath his eyelids said he was dreaming. His expression said they were sweet dreams—a beautiful woman drives you around in her truck and feeds you kibble, why not?

I headed for the pantry. Generally, that's a stimulus for him to hurry over, assume the squat, wait for food. This time, he raised an eyelid, shot me a "you've got to be kidding" look, and resumed snoring.

I chewed on some dry cereal, made a tall mug of strong instant coffee, drank half trying to dispel the chill. The kitchen windows were blue with night. The suggestion of foliage was a distant black haze. I checked the clock. Forty minutes before daybreak. I carried the mug back to my office.

Time for more tilting, Mr. Quixote.

I returned to my desk. Ten minutes later I saw it, wondered why I hadn't seen it before.

A notation made by the first Seattle officer on the Bonpaine murder scene—a detective named Robert Elias, called in by the forest rangers who'd actually found the body.

Very small print, bottom of the page, cross-referenced to a footnote.

Easy to miss—no excuses, Delaware. Now it screamed at me.

The victim, wrote Elias, *was discovered by a hiker, walking with his dog (see ref, 45).*

That led me to the rear of the Bonpaine file, a listing of over three hundred events enumerated by the meticulous Detective Elias.

Number 45 read: *Hiker: tourist from Michigan. Mr. Ferris Grant.*

Number 46 was an address and phone number in Flint, Michigan.

Number 47: *Dog: black labr. retriev. Mr. F. Grant states "she has great nose, thinks she's a drug dog."*

I'd heard that before, word for word. Paul Ulrich describing Duchess, the golden retriever.

Ferris Grant.

Michael Ferris Burke. *Grant* Rushton.

Flint, Michigan. Huey Grant Mitchell had worked in Michigan—Ann Arbor.

I phoned the number Ferris Grant had left as his home exchange, got a recorded message from the Flint Museum of Art.

No sign Elias had followed up. Why would he bother?

Ferris Grant had been nothing more than a helpful citizen who'd aided a major investigation by "discovering" the body.

Just as Paul Ulrich had discovered Mate.

How Burke must have loved that. Orchestrating. Providing himself with a legitimate reason to show up at the crime scene. Proud of his handiwork, watching the cops stumble.

Psychopath's private joke. Games, always games. His internal laughter must have been deafening.

Hiker with a dog.

Paul Ulrich, Tanya Stratton.

I paged hurriedly to the photo gallery Leimert Fusco had assembled, tried to reconcile any of the more recent portraits of Burke with my memory of Ulrich. But Ulrich's face wouldn't take shape in my head, all I recalled was the handlebar mustache.

Which was exactly the point.

Facial hair changed things. I'd been struck by that when trying to reconcile the various photos of Burke. The beard Burke had grown as Huey Mitchell, hospital security guard, as effective as any mask.

He'd gone on to use another Michigan identity. Ferris Grant . . . the Flint Museum. Another ha ha: *I'm an artist!* Reverting to Michigan—to familiar patterns—because at heart, psychopaths were rigid, there always had to be a script of sorts.

I studied Mitchell's picture, the dead eyes, the flat expression. Luxuriant mask of a beard. Heavy enough to nurture a giant mustache.

When I tried to picture Ulrich's face, all I *saw* was the mustache.

I strained to recall his other physical characteristics.

Medium-size man, late thirties to forty. Perfect match to Burke on both counts.

Shorter, thinner hair than any of Burke's pictures— balding to a fuzzy crew cut. Each picture of Burke revealed a steady, sequential loss, so that fit, too.

The mustache . . . stretching wider than Ulrich's face. As good a mask as any. I'd thought it an unusual flamboyance, contrasting especially with Ulrich's conservative dress.

Financial consultant, Mr. Respectable . . . Something else Ulrich had said—one of the *first* things he'd said— came back to me: *So far our names haven't been in the paper. We're going to be able to keep it that way, aren't we, Detective Sturgis?*

Concerned about publicity. Craving publicity.

Milo had answered that the two of them would probably be safe from media scrutiny, but Ulrich had stuck with the topic, talked about fifteen minutes of fame.

Andy Warhol coined that phrase and look what happened to him . . . checked into a hospital . . . went out in a bag . . . celebrity stinks . . . look at Princess Di, look at Dr. Mate.

Letting Milo know that fame was what he was after. Playing with Milo, the way he'd toyed with the Seattle cops.

Getting as close as he could to criminal celebrity without confessing outright.

It had been no coincidence that he and Tanya Stratton had chosen Mulholland for a morning walk that Monday.

Stratton had come out and said so: *We rarely come up here, except on Sundays.* Resentful about the change in routine. About *Paul's* insistence.

She'd complained to Milo that *everything* had been Paul's idea. Including the decision to talk to Milo up at the site, rather than at home. Ulrich had claimed to be attempting a kind of therapy for Tanya, but his real motive—multiple motives—had been something quite different: keep Milo off Ulrich's home territory, and get another chance at déjà vu.

Ulrich had talked about the horror of discovering Mate, but I realized now that emotion had been lacking.

Not so, Tanya Stratton. She'd been clearly upset, eager to leave. But Ulrich had come across amiable, helpful, relaxed. *Too* relaxed for someone who'd encountered a bloodbath.

An outdoorsy guy—Fusco had said Michael Burke skied, fancied himself an outdoorsman—Ulrich had chatted about staying fit, the beauty of the site.

Once you get past the gate, it's like being in another world.

Oh yeah.

His world.

Amiable guy, but the charm was wearing thin with Stratton. Was she edgy because she'd begun to sense something about her boyfriend? Or just a relationship gone stagnant?

I recalled her pallor, the unsteady gait. Wispy hair. Dark glasses—hiding something?

A fragile girl.

Not a well girl?

Then I understood and my heart beat faster: one of Michael Burke's patterns was to hook up with sick women, befriend them, nurture them.

Then guide them out of this world.

He enjoyed killing on so many levels. The consummate Dr. Death, and one way or the other the world was going to know it. How Eldon Mate's fame—the legitimacy Mate had obtained while dispatching fifty lives—

must have eaten at Burke. All those years in medical school, and Burke still couldn't practice openly the way Mate did, had to serve as Mate's apprentice.

Had to masquerade as a *layman*.

Because since arriving in L.A., he hadn't found a way to bogus his medical credentials, had to represent himself as a financial consultant.

Mostly real-estate work . . . Century City address. Nice and ambiguous.

Home base, Encino. *Just over the hill*. Respectable neighborhood for an upstanding guy.

In L.A. you could live off a smile and a zip code.

The business card Ulrich had given Milo was sitting in a drawer at the West L.A. station. I phoned information and asked for Ulrich's Century City business listing, was only half surprised when I got one. But when I tried the number, a recording told me the line had been disconnected. No Encino exchange for either him or Tanya Stratton, nothing anywhere in the Valley or the city.

Tanya. Not a well girl.

A relationship on the wane with Ulrich could prove lethal.

I looked at the clock. Just after six. Light through the office curtains said the sun had risen. If Milo had been up all night at the Glendale crime scene, he'd be home now, getting some well-deserved rest.

Some things could wait. I phoned him. Rick answered on the first ring. "Up early, Alex."

"Did I wake you?"

"Not hardly. I was just about to leave for the E.R. Milo's already gone."

"Gone where?"

"He didn't say. Probably back to Glendale, that double murder. He was out there until midnight, came

home, slept for four hours, woke in a foul mood, showered without singing and left the house with his hair still
wet."

"The joys of domestic life," I said.

"Oh yeah," he said. "Give me a nice freeway pileup
and I know I'm being useful."

Milo picked up his mobile, barking, "Sturgis."

"It's me. Where are you?"

"Up on Mulholland," he said in an odd, detached
voice. "Staring at dirt. Trying to figure out if I missed
something."

"Son, I'm going to bring some joy into your wretched
life." I told him about Ulrich.

I expected shock, profanity, but his voice remained remote. "Funny you should mention that."

"You figured it out?"

"No, but I was just wondering about Ulrich. Because I
positioned my car where the van was, walked myself
through the scene. When the sun came up it hit the rear
window and gave off glare. Blinding glare, I couldn't see
a thing inside. Ulrich claimed he and the girl discovered
Mate right after sunrise, said he could see Mate's body
through the rear window. Now that was a week ago, and
the van's windows were higher than mine, but I don't
calculate that much of a difference and I don't imagine
the sun's angle has shifted that radically. I was waiting
around to see if the visibility changed over the next
quarter hour or so. By itself it wasn't any big deal,
maybe the guy didn't remember every detail. But now
you're telling me . . . Left the bastard's address back at
the station, I'll run a DMV on him and the Stratton girl.
Time for a drop-in."

"The Stratton girl may be in danger." I told him why.

"Sick?" he said. "Yeah, she didn't look too healthy, did she? All the more reason to visit."

"How're you going to handle Ulrich?"

"I don't exactly have grounds for an arrest, Alex. At the moment, all I can do is scope him out in his natural habitat—my story will be that I'm dropping in for a follow-up, has he thought of anything else? 'Cause we're stumped—he'd like that, right? The cops being stupid, my coming to him for wisdom."

"He'd love it," I said. "If he believed it. But this is a smart man. He'd have to wonder why, after Richard's arrest, you're knocking on his door on a Sunday morning."

Silence. "How about I imply there are complications with the current investigation—stuff I can't talk about. He'll know I mean Zoghbie, but I won't come out and say it. We'll tango around, I can watch his eyes and his feet. Maybe Stratton will give off some kind of vibe. Maybe I'll get her alone, later on in the day."

"Sounds good. Want me there?"

Silence. Static. Finally he said, "Yes."

When I walked into the bedroom, Robin was sitting up and rubbing her eyes.

"Morning." I kissed her forehead and began to get dressed.

"What time is it? How long have you been up?"

"Early. Just a bit. Have to run and meet Milo up on Mulholland."

"Oh," she said sleepily. "Something come up?"

"Maybe," I said.

That opened her eyes wide.

"A possible lead," I said. "Nothing dangerous. Brain work."

She held out her arms. We embraced.

"Take good care of it," she said. "Your brain. I love your brain."

CHAPTER

33

MILO WAS PARKED on the road below the murder site, engine running, fingers tapping the steering wheel. I left the Seville a few yards away and got in the unmarked. He was wearing the same gray suit, but it looked ten years older. Driving east on Mulholland, he reached the Glen, headed north into the Valley.

"Where'd you get the address?" I said.

"DMV. No listings for Ulrich's BMW or any other vehicle in his name, but the Stratton girl owns a two-year-old Saturn, has an address on Milbank. Sherman Oaks, not Encino. Too far east by two blocks."

"Why tell the truth when you can lie?"

"Setting up the scene . . . He just loves this, doesn't he?"

"Every detail," I said. "Remember what you said about the only footprints being his and Stratton's? He cleaned up after himself, but just in case he missed something, he gave himself a legitimate reason to leave behind trace evidence."

"All these years . . . orchestrating . . . goddamn conductor." He took one hand off the wheel, raised it toward the roof. "Lord, grant me the opportunity to shove his baton up his ass. . . . Anything else you think I should know before I approach him?"

"Act friendly but authoritative. Don't go overboard

on either. While you're listening to him, let your eyes roam. Let him try to figure out if it's cop curiosity or you're looking for something. Let's see how he reacts to the uncertainty. Ask him lots of questions, but keep it general. Out-of-sequence questions, like you do so well. Dropping in on him without warning is good. You'll be the one orchestrating. If he gets nervous, he may do something impulsive. Like pack up and leave once he thinks you're gone, or try to hide something—a storage locker. He's likely to have one, can't afford to have Tanya come across his souvenirs."

"You're sure he keeps them?"

"I'll bet on it. Once you leave, can you get surveillance in place pretty quickly?"

"One way or the other, he'll be watched, Alex. If I have to do it myself, he'll be watched. . . . Okay, so you're talking a one-man good-cop/bad-cop show. But keep it subtle. Yeah, I can do subtle. Even without the benefit of alcohol. What'll *you* be concentrating on?"

"Playing impassive shrink. If I can get Tanya alone, I'll take a closer look at her."

"Why, you suspect her, too?"

"No, but she's tiring of him. Maybe she'll say something revealing."

He bared his teeth in what I assumed was a smile. "Fine, we've got our plan. All that accomplished, *then* can I shove it up his ass?"

His gas foot was heavy and the ride took fifteen minutes, whipping us past canyon beauty and the barbered anxiety of hillside suburbia, accelerating into a too-fast left turn across Ventura. The Valley was ten degrees warmer. Encino appeared just past Sepulveda and the low-rise shops of Sherman Oaks gave way to mirrored office buildings and car lots. Very little traffic this early on a sleepy Sunday. The 405 freeway ribboned across the intersection, parallel with the western flank of the white carcass that had once been the Sherman Oaks Galleria. The shopping center was shuttered now, all the more pathetic in death because of its size. Someone had plans for the space. Someone always had plans.

Milo drove a block, turned right on Orion, stayed parallel with the freeway, headed west on Camarillo, circling around to the mouth of Milbank, a shady street with no sidewalks. Single-story houses, well-maintained, dimmed by the luxuriance of untrimmed camphor trees. Off to the east, the freeway thundered.

Tanya Stratton's address matched a white G.I.-bill dream box with blue trim. Carefully tended lawn, but less landscaping than its neighbors. No cars in the driveway, two throwaway papers on the oil spot. Shuttered windows, white-painted iron security grate across the front door, mailbox mounted on the steel mesh. Another white metal door blocked access to the rear yard.

"Someone likes their privacy," I said.

Milo frowned. We got out, walked to the security door. A button was mounted on the front wall of the house, near the jamb of the security door. Milo pushed it and I could hear the buzzer sound inside the house. No answer. No barking.

I remarked on that, said, "Maybe they took Duchess on one of their early-morning walks."

"On Sunday?" he said.

"Hey, he's a fit guy."

He lifted the lid of the mailbox. Inside were four envelopes and two circulars from fast-food restaurants. He inspected the postmarks. "Yesterday's."

He toed the grate. I watched his lips form a silent curse

as he stared at the jewel-bright brass dead bolt. "Who knows what the hell's in there, but Ulrich finding the body ain't exactly grounds for a warrant. Hell, I don't even exercise the warrants I do get."

"You didn't end up serving Richard?"

He shook his head. "So much for any future relationship with MacIntyre. Spent all night with my Glendale colleagues. Who, by the way, will not arrest you for trespassing a crime scene."

"They wouldn't know it was a crime scene unless I trespassed."

"Technicalities, technicalities." He punched the button again. Rubbed his face, loosened his tie, glanced over at the door barring the yard. "Let's go back to the car, try to figure something out. Meanwhile, I'll run searches on Ulrich's aliases. He repeated the hiker M.O., used Michigan twice, so maybe he's recycled an identity."

He tried DMV again, inquiring about Michael Ferris Burke, Grant Rushton, Huey Mitchell, Hank Spreen, with no success. We'd been sitting for a few minutes, alternating between silence and dead-end suggestions, when a small red car drove up and parked across the street.

Nissan Sentra, dark-haired woman at the wheel. She turned off her engine, started to get out when she saw us. Then she flashed a nervous stare and up went the driver's window.

Milo was out in a second, jogging over, flashing the badge. The Nissan's window stayed up. He produced his business card, I saw his lips move, finally the glass lowered. As if in appreciation, Milo backed away, gave the woman space. She exited the red car, looked at me, then at Milo. He had his hands in his pockets, was making himself a bit smaller, the way he does when he's trying to put someone at ease. I joined them.

The woman was in her thirties, slightly heavy, brown hair highlighted with rust, sooty shadows under her bright-blue eyes and a speck of mascara under one of them. She wore a bulky white cowl-neck T-shirt, black leggings, black flats. The rear of the car was filled with fabric samples in binders.

"What's wrong?" she said, eyeing the white house.

"Do you live in the neighborhood, ma'am?"

"My sister does. Across the street."

"Ms. Stratton?"

"Yes." Her voice strained half an octave higher. "What's going on?"

"We came to ask your sister and Mr. Ulrich some questions, ma'am."

"About what happened—about their finding Dr. Mate?"

"Your sister talked to you about that, Ms. . . ."

"Lamplear. Kris Lamplear. Sure, we talked about it. It wasn't exactly an everyday thing. Not in detail, Tanya was grossed out. She called me to tell me they found it— him. Is there some problem? Tanya's already been through a lot."

"How so, ma'am?" said Milo.

"She was sick a year and a half ago. That's why I'm here. She was sick and I'm overprotective. She doesn't like me to be, but I can't help it. I try to give her space, usually we talk only two, three times a week. But I haven't heard from her in a few days, so I called her at work Friday and they said she'd taken some vacation time. I held off yesterday, but today . . ."

She frowned. "She's entitled to her vacation, but she should've told me where she was going."

"Does she usually?" I said.

Sheepish smile. "Honestly? Not always, but I don't let that stop me. What can I say? I decided to stop by this morning early, 'cause my kids have Little League in an hour. Just to make sure everything's okay. So there's no problem, you just want to talk to her?"

"Right, just following up, ma'am," said Milo. He eyed the fabric samples. "Interior-design work?"

"Fabric sales. I work for a jobber downtown." Another glance at the house.

Milo said, "Looks like they've been gone for only a day or so. Do they travel a lot?"

"From time to time." Kris Lamplear's eyes jumped around. "Paul probably took her somewhere on one of his impulsive *romantic* things."

"He's a romantic fellow?"

"He thinks he is." She rolled her eyes. "Mr. Spontaneous. He'll come in and announce they're going to Arrowhead or Santa Barbara for a couple of days, tells Tanya to pack, call in sick. Tanya's ultraresponsible. She takes her job seriously. But she goes along with him, usually. He works for himself, so taking off like that's no big deal. He likes nature stuff, loves to drive."

"Nature stuff," said Milo.

"The great outdoors, he's a member of the Tree People, the Sierra Club, watches birds, actually reads the auto-club magazine. It was *his* idea to be up there on Mulholland at that hour. He's always pushing Tanya to rise and shine, exercise, all that stuff. As if that's going to do the trick."

"Do what trick?"

"Heal her up," she said. "Make sure she stays in remission—she had cancer. Hodgkin's disease. The doctors said it was curable, she's got a good chance of being cured. But the treatment knocked her out. Radiation, chemo, heavy-duty. The whole thing changed her. She *is* fine, I know she'll be okay, but I'm sorry, I'm still the protective older sister, so sue me. She should at least tell me where she's going, don't you think? Our parents are gone, the two of us are it, she knows I worry."

She tugged her shirt down, stared at the house. "I know I'm being neurotic. I'll get home and there'll be a message from her—don't tell her you met me here, okay? She'll get p.o.'d."

"Deal," said Milo. "So you don't keep a house key for her."

"You mean like some people do? That would be nice, wouldn't it. But no, I'd never ask for one. Tanya wouldn't take well to that."

"Wanting to be independent."

Kris Lamplear nodded. "Her having a key to *my* house would be fine. And I'm married, have kids, I wouldn't mind. But she'd be all sensitive. Even when she was going through her treatments she was that way. Telling everyone she could do things for herself, not to treat her like a cripple."

"So Paul's a hands-off guy," I said.

"What do you mean?"

"To get along with Tanya he'd have to respect her independence."

"I guess," she said. "To be honest, I don't know *why* she stays with him. Maybe 'cause he was there for her when she was down."

"When she was sick?" I said.

She nodded. "That's how they met. Tanya was in the hospital for her chemo and he was volunteering there. He ended up spending a lot of time with her. When she couldn't hold food down, he'd be there, feeding her ice chips."

Describing an altruistic act, but she sounded disapproving. I said, "Nice guy."

"I guess—I used to wonder why he was doing all that. To be honest, he doesn't seem like the volunteering type—but what's the difference, she makes her own decisions."

"You don't like him," I said.

"If Tanya likes him . . . No, to be honest I think he's a pompous jerk. I think Tanya may be seeing it, too. Finally." Her smile was reluctant, mischievous. "Maybe it's wishful thinking, but she doesn't defend him as much when I tell her he's a pompous jerk."

I smiled back. "Which hospital did they meet at?"

"Valley Comprehensive over in Reseda. A dump as far as I'm concerned, but that's where her HMO said she had to go. Why all these questions about Paul?"

Milo said, "He and your sister are important witnesses. In a homicide case, we need to be extra thorough. Does Paul still volunteer at the hospital?"

"Nope. Soon as Tanya was discharged and they were dating, he quit. That's what made me wonder."

"About what?"

"About if it was just a technique to hit on women. She's recuperating, and all of a sudden they're dating. Couple of months later, both of them move out of their apartments and they rent this place."

"How long ago was that?"

"Over a year," she said. "I shouldn't put him down if she likes him. He treats her well enough. Does the cooking, the cleaning—*all* the cleaning, now *that's* a good deal. Doesn't leave clothes on the floor—he's real neat, a neat freak, I never saw Tanya live so organized.

He even grooms Duchess—Tanya's dog—can spend a half hour brushing her. Duchess likes him now. At first she didn't, and I'm thinking, Yes, animals have a sense. But then she took to him and I'm thinking, What do *I* know? Or maybe dogs aren't that smart. After all, it was Duchess who got them into this mess by finding—but you know that, don't you."

"What else did Tanya tell you about finding Dr. Mate?"

"Not much. Like I said, she was grossed out—Tanya isn't much of a talker anyway. *Paul* was really into it, though. I'm sure he'll be jazzed that you're back to ask him more questions."

"Why's that?" said Milo.

"He thought it was neat—*fascinating,* he called it. *Learning about police procedure.* After Tanya called me, I came over. To give her support. Paul had the TV on, waiting to see if he and Tanya would be on. So he'll be jazzed at more attention."

"Happy to oblige," said Milo. "Any idea where we can find him?"

"No, like I said, it could be anywhere. He announces to Tanya they're going somewhere and most of the time she agrees. He drives and she sleeps in the car."

"Most of the time?" I said.

"Sometimes she puts her foot down. She doesn't like when her work piles up. When she turns him down, Paul gets all pouty and usually he stays home and keeps pouting. But sometimes he goes off by himself for a day or so . . . I have no idea where they are, but you could try Malibu. That's the one place Tanya likes to go."

"Where in Malibu?" said Milo, keeping his voice casual.

"Not the beach. We've got—Tanya and I own some

land up in the Malibu mountains. Western Malibu, it's more like Agoura, across the Ventura County line and up into the hills. Five, six acres, I don't even know the exact size. Our parents bought it years ago, Dad was going to build a house, but he never got around to it. I never go there because there's really nothing there and it's kind of a mess—dinky little cabin, no phone, gross bathroom, tiny little septic tank. Half the time the electricity lines are down, the road's always washing out. My kids would go crazy from boredom there."

"But Tanya likes it."

"Tanya likes things quiet. When she was recuperating from chemo she went there. Or maybe it was to show she was tough. She can be stubborn. The place is probably worth some money now, I would've sold it a long time ago."

"Does Paul like it?" I said. "Being a Tree Person?"

"Probably. What Paul really likes is to drive, just for the sake of driving—like gas is free and he's got all the time in the world."

"Working for himself in real estate."

"I don't know what he does in real estate—he doesn't seem to work much, but he must be doing okay," she said. "He always has money. Isn't stingy with Tanya, I'll grant him that. Buys her jewelry, clothes, whatever. Plus he cooks and cleans, so what am I complaining about, right?"

Milo copied down directions to the cabin, promised to let her know if her sister was there.

"Great," she said. Then she frowned. "That means she'll know I was here, checking up on her. 'Cause I'm the only one who knows about Malibu."

"Do the people at her job know your number?" he said. "Maybe she listed you as her emergency contact."

Kris Lamplear brightened. "That's true, she did."

"Great. We'll just tell her that's how we reached you."

"Okay, thanks—there's nothing wrong, is there? With Tanya and Paul?"

"What would be wrong, ma'am?"

"I don't know. You just seem awfully eager to talk to them."

"Just what I said, ma'am. Follow-up. It's a high-profile case, we've got to do everything we can to avoid looking stupid."

"That I understand." She smiled. "No one likes looking stupid."

He sped onto the 405. The intersection with the 101 West was nearly immediate, the heavy traffic was flowing east, and soon we were sailing.

"Malibu," he said. "Sounds familiar."

"Oh yeah."

A few years ago, Robin and I had rented a beach house just over the county line. The mouth of the canyon road Kris Lamplear had described was less than a half mile away. I'd gone hiking up there myself, passing campgrounds, the occasional private property, mostly state land walled by mountainside. I remembered long stretches of solitude, silence broken by birdcalls, coyote howls, the occasional roar of a too-fast truck. Brain-feeding silence, but sometimes it had seemed too quiet up there.

"'Paul likes to drive,'" he went on. "Your basic prerequisite for Serial Killer School. A neat freak and the bastard likes to drive. Now, why didn't I think of that? Could've arrested him the first time I met him, saved the city a lot of overtime."

"Tsk, tsk. And don't forget his generosity," I said. "Gives his girlfriend jewelry. I wonder how much of it was previously owned."

He gave a dispirited laugh. "Trophies . . . Lord knows what else he hangs on to."

He exited at Kanan, took it down to PCH and raced north along the beach. The Coast Highway was virtually empty past Trancas Canyon. The ocean was serene, low tide breaking lazily, too blue to be real. We crossed the county line at Mulholland Highway, just past Leo Carrillo Beach, where a handful of beachcombers walked the tide pools.

Back to Mulholland. End of the trail.

No way to travel Mulholland from start to finish. The road was thirty-plus miles of blacktop, girding L.A. from East Hollywood to the Pacific, choked off in several places by wilderness. Nothing important comes easy. . . . Had Michael Burke/Paul Ulrich thought of that when selecting his kill-spot?

A mile into Ventura, Milo hooked right, veering toward the land side. I caught a peek of my rented house on the private beach just ahead, a wedge of weathered wood visible beyond a sharp curve of the highway. Robin and I had liked it out there, watching the pelicans and dolphins, not minding the rust that seemed to settle in daily. We'd stayed there nearly a year while our house in the Glen was being rebuilt. The moment the lease was up, the landlord had handed the place over to his brilliant aspiring-screenwriter son in hopes of spurring Junior to creativity. The only time I'd met Junior he'd been drunk. I'd never seen anything with his name on it at the multiplex. Kids today.

The car climbed into the mountains. Neither of us talked as we searched for the unmarked road that led to the property. Address on the mailbox, Kris Lamplear had said.

The first time, Milo overshot and had to circle back. Finally, we found it, nearly five miles from the ocean, well past its nearest neighbor, preceded by a good mile of state land.

The mailbox was ten feet up the entrance, concealed by a cloud of plumbago vine. Rusty box on a weathered post, its door missing. Most of the gold-foil address numerals gone, too. The three digits that remained were withered and curling.

Nothing in the box. The air was cool, sweet, and the unmarked's idling engine seemed deafening. Milo backed out, parked on the road, turned off the motor, and we returned to the mailbox on foot. Ahead of us, the dirt road—more of a path—swept to the left and flattened in an S that snaked through the greenery. Nothing in the immediate distance but more vines, shrubbery, trees. Lots of trees.

Milo said, "No sense announcing ourselves, giving him a chance to orchestrate. Let's see if we can get a view of the cabin, watch it for a while."

We walked a thousand feet before it came into view, graying clapboard barely discernible through a thickening colonnade of pine and gum trees and sycamores. Old, twisted sycamores, just like the one where Alice Zoghbie and Roy Haiselden had been propped. Had Ulrich/Burke noticed that? I thought he had. He would have liked that, the symmetry, neatness. The irony. Frosting on the old murder cake.

If Milo was thinking that, he wasn't putting it into words. He trudged steadily but very slowly, mouth set, eyes swiveling from side to side, one arm loose, the other at his belt, inches from his service revolver. More tension than readiness for battle. He'd stashed his shotgun in the trunk of the unmarked.

The path finally ended at an egg-shaped parking area

partially edged by large, circular rocks. The border looked
like someone's primitive attempt at hardscape, long dis-
rupted by the elements. Two cars: Ulrich's navy BMW
and Tanya Stratton's copper-colored Saturn.

Ulrich had told us a tale of another dark BMW stationed on Mulholland.

BMW like ours.

I'd agonized over whether the car had been Richard's.
Richard or Eric at the wheel. But it had existed only in
Ulrich's lie.

Orchestrating.

The building was just beyond the cars, at the rear of
the property, and we approached, trying to shield ourselves behind trees, straining for a better look. Finally,
we had a view of the front door. Open, but blocked by a
dirty-looking screen.

Ugly little thing, not much more than a shed, shoved
up against a mountain wall and surrounded by brush.
Tar-paper roof the brown-green of a stagnant pond, the
clapboard, once white, now murky as laundry water.
Nearly hidden by low branches—one bough swooped
within a foot of the door—as if yielding itself to green
strangulation.

Up above, barely visible through the sycamores, was a
mountain ridge crowned by a thick black coiffure of
pines. More state land. No prying neighbors.

We advanced to within twenty yards of the cabin before Milo stopped, ducked off the path and into the
brush, motioning me quickly to do the same.

A second later, the screen door opened and Tanya
Stratton stepped out, letting it slam shut with a snare-
drum rattle.

She wore a long-sleeved tan shirt, blue jeans, white
sneakers, had her hair tucked into a red bandanna. No

dark glasses this time, but she was too far away for us to see her eyes.

She stretched, yawned, went to her car and popped the trunk.

The cabin door opened again, exposing a stretch of arm. Tan arm, male arm. But Ulrich didn't appear. Holding the screen ajar. A good-looking golden retriever bounded out and raced to Tanya Stratton's side.

Duchess. Great nose, thinks she's a drug dog.

"Great," Milo whispered. "So much for surveillance."

Speaking so softly I had to read his lips. But the dog's ears perked and she pivoted toward us, began nosing the ground. Walking. Picking up speed. Tanya Stratton said, "Duchess! Treat!" and the dog froze in her tracks, shook herself off. Turned and ran toward her mistress.

Stratton had pulled a bag out of the trunk. Now she opened it, reached inside, dangled something in front of Duchess's nose.

"Sit. Wait."

The dog settled on her haunches, watched the Milk-Bone that Tanya waved near her nose.

Tanya said, "Good girl," gave her the bone, ruffled the fur around the retriever's neck. Duchess stayed by Tanya's side, waited till Tanya let her back into the cabin.

"Good dog," muttered Milo. He looked at his Timex. "Separate cars. What do you make of that?"

"Maybe Tanya's planning on leaving before him. Work obligations, like her sister said."

He thought about that. Nodded. "Leaving him alone to do his thing. Which could be sticking close to base or taking another drive. Maybe he's got stuff stashed here. Buried here. Meaning I can't afford to mess up any of the search rules. Gonna have to coordinate with Malibu sheriffs to keep it kosher. . . . Maybe the best thing is back off, find somewhere to watch the road. See if Tanya leaves, then what he does—if she's not in immediate danger."

"His pattern with his women friends is to wait until they've gotten ill again, minister to them, then take it all the way. Then again, he may have hastened the process along."

"Poison?"

"He'd know how."

"So what are you saying, forget waiting? Waltz right in?"

"Let me think."

I never got around to it.

The door opened yet again and this time Paul Ulrich showed himself. Fit and well-fed, in a white polo shirt, khaki pants, brown loafers, no socks. Muscular arms, ruddy complexion. Mug of something in one hand.

He drank, placed the cup on the ground, took a few steps forward.

Showed us his face.

Two alert, sparkling eyes, a smudge of rosy skin behind flaring mustaches.

Twin propellers of hair so huge, so flamboyant, that despite my attempt to get past them, to seize upon something—the merest grace note of recognition—that would tie his face into one of the photos in Leimert Fusco's file, my brain processed only *mustache*.

Facial hair could do that.

He retrieved his coffee, strutted around. Flexed a bicep and inspected the bulge of muscle.

Another sip. Big stretch.

So content. Top of the morning.

The mustache made him look like a Keystone Kop. Nothing funny about him.

Milo's hand was square on his gun, fingers white against the walnut grip, scrambling toward the trigger. Then, as if realizing what he was doing, he drew it away. Wiped his hand on his jacket. Rubbed his face. Stared at Ulrich.

Suddenly Ulrich dropped to the ground, as if avoiding gunfire. We watched him peel off fifty lightning push-ups. Perfect form. When he bounced back to his feet, he stretched again, showing no signs of exertion.

He ran a hand over his thinning hair, rotated his neck, flexed his arms, worked on the neck some more. Even killers get stiff . . . all those hours behind the wheel. . . .

Smoothing one mustache, he reached behind and picked at his seat.

Even killers untangle their shorts.

Watching it—the banality—I felt let down. Human. They shouldn't be, but they always are.

Ulrich finished his coffee, placed the mug on the ground once more, walked to his own car. Popped his trunk. Out came something black. Small leather case, the polished surface reflected the filtered sunlight leaking down through the trees.

Doctor's bag. Ulrich stroked it.

I whispered, "There you go."

Milo said, "What the hell does he need *that* for right now?"

The cabin door opened again. As Tanya stepped outside, Ulrich moved quickly, shifting the bag behind his back, inching toward his car. She took only a few steps, was looking away from him, up at the treetops. Ulrich slipped the bag into the trunk, lowered the lid, sauntered over to Tanya.

Not acknowledging him, she started to turn, was about to reenter the cabin when he reached her. Slipping one hand around her waist, he kissed the back of her neck.

She was rigid, unresponsive.

Ulrich remained behind her, maintained his grip around her waist. Kissed her again and she twisted away from his lips. He stroked her cheek, but his face, unseen by her, bore no affection.

Immobile.

Eyes hard and focused. Face slightly flushed.

Tanya said something, broke away from him, disappeared back into the cabin.

Ulrich stroked his mustache. Spit in the dirt.

Walked back to the car. Quickly. Face still expressionless. Flushed scarlet. He popped the trunk and retrieved the black bag.

Milo said, "Not good."

His hand shot back to his gun and now he was stepping out from behind the tree. He'd barely taken a step when the shot rang out, hard and sharp, like hands clapping once.

From behind Ulrich. Above. The growth of pine at the ridge.

Milo ran back to his hiding spot. Gun out, but no one to shoot at.

Ulrich didn't drop. Not right away. He stood there as the red spot formed on his chest, got redder, larger, blossoming like a rose captured in time-lapse. Exit wound. Shot from the back. The leather bag remained in his hand, the mustache blocked out expression.

Another hand-clap sounded, then another, two more roses decorated Ulrich's white shirt. Red shirt, hard to believe it had ever been white . . .

Milo's gun hand was rigid, still, his eyes bounced from Ulrich to the pine ridge.

More applause.

When the fourth shot sheared off the top of Ulrich's head, he let the black bag drop to the ground.

Fell on top of it.

The whole thing had taken less than ten seconds.

Screams from inside the house, but no sign of Tanya.

Duchess was barking. Milo's gun was still out, aimed at the silence, the distance, the trees, that big mustache of trees.

CHAPTER

35

It took a while for the sheriffs to arrive from the Malibu substation, even longer to assemble a squad to travel up to the ridge. A small army of nervous, itchy-fingered men in tan uniforms, each deputy assuming the shooter was still around, wouldn't hesitate to fire.

As we waited for the group to assemble, Milo hung out with the coroner, did his best to let the sheriffs feel they were in charge while managing to inspect everything. He asked me to comfort Tanya Stratton, but I ended up doing nothing of the sort. She shut me out, refused to talk, obtained whatever solace she desired by muttering to her sister over a cell phone and stroking her dog. I watched her from a distance. The deputies had shunted her away from the crime scene and she sat on the ground beneath a silver-dollar tree, knees drawn up, occasionally pummeling herself softly on the jaw. Her sunglasses were back on, so I couldn't read her eyes. The rest of her face said she was shocked, furious, wondering how many other mistakes she'd make over the rest of her life.

While we'd waited for sheriffs, Milo had inspected the cabin. No obvious trophies. Not much of anything in there. A careful search, carried out later in the day, revealed nothing of an evidentiary nature, other than the doctor's bag. Old, burnished leather, gold initials over the clasp: EHM.

Tanya Stratton claimed she'd never seen it. I believed her. Ulrich would have hidden it from her, produced it only when he was ready to use it. A while longer, and she might've lost the opportunity to make any mistakes at all.

Inside the bag were scalpels, scissors, other shiny things; a coil of I.V. tubing, sterile-packed hollow needles in various gauges. Rolls of gauze. Disposable hypodermic injectors, little ampules with small-print labels.

Thiopental. Potassium chloride.

The bag was taken into custody by a sheriff's detective, but he never bothered to ask what the gold initials stood for and Milo didn't volunteer the information. When the search party was ready, he and I rode along, sitting in back of a squad car, listening to nervous-talk from the two deputies in front.

The wounds—the way they'd passed through Ulrich at that distance, the size of the exits—indicated a high-velocity bullet, probably a military rifle, a good-quality scope. Someone who knew what he was doing.

How hard it would be to see the shooter if he'd chosen to barricade himself among the pines.

I knew he hadn't. He'd done his job, no reason to stick around.

Gaining access to the pines wasn't very difficult. The same road that had swept us past the property with the broken mailbox continued its climb for another mile before forking. The right fork reversed direction, descending back down toward the coast, but never completing the journey as it dead-ended at a forest preserve named after a long-dead California settler. A state-printed sign

said scenic views were up ahead, but no path was provided, the curious were proceeding at their own risk.

The party fanned out, weapons ready. An hour later,
it reconvened roadside. No sign of the shooter. One of
the deputies, an experienced backpacker who let us
know he'd walked the John Muir Trail twice and could
navigate without a compass, estimated where the shooter
had stationed himself, thought he probably had the
exact spot.

We followed him to the far end of the forest, where the
outermost trees, granted the best light, grew tallest and
thickest. Nice clear view of the ugly little cabin and adjoining acreage. Nice view of the ocean, too. As the cops
talked, my eyes drifted toward blue. I spotted a steamer
gliding across the horizon, dust specks in the sky that
were probably gulls.

Waiting up here wouldn't have been that bad. How
long had the shooter been waiting?

How had he figured it out? Coming across the same
detail I had? His copy of the file—the original file. The
case of Marissa Bonpaine.

He'd claimed to be flying up to Seattle. Just a few
hours ago, I'd taken him at his word, figured he wanted
to review the details of Marissa's murder, cross-reference
with Michael Burke's med-school schedule, what he
knew about Mate's murder. Discovery by hikers.

Had he flown back to L.A. to trail the "hiker," gotten
here a wee bit faster than Milo and me?

Or had Seattle been a lie and he'd never left. Figuring
it out by doing exactly what I'd done: harnessing the
power of obsession. Then watching, stalking, waiting . . .
He was a patient man, had persisted so many years, another few days wouldn't matter.

Kill-spot with a view.

Had he laid his rifle down lovingly on a rectangle of oilcloth while he ate a sandwich? Drank something from a thermos? Made sure the lens of the scope was clean?

His own little picnic. The irony . . .

The cops kept talking, convincing themselves they needn't search any further, no one else was going to get shot today. I turned away from the ocean, looked down at the cabin, now fronted by coroner's vans and squad cars, tried to see it as Leimert Fusco had seen it.

"Yeah, this has got to be it, the angle's perfect," said the Muir walker. "Look how it gets flat, and there's that rock he could prop his gear against. Maybe he left some trace evidence, let's get the techies up here."

The techies came. Milo told me later they found nothing, not even a tire track.

That didn't surprise me. I knew Fusco couldn't have parked too far from his vantage point and been able to make his escape that quickly. Driving to the left-hand fork and disappearing into hills laced with side roads, most of which ended in box canyons, a few feeding to the Valley, the freeway, alleged civilization.

He'd known which road to take because he was a planner, too.

The main risk had been leaving his car at the side of the road. But even if someone had seen it, recorded the license plate for some reason, no big deal. It would end up traced back to a rented vehicle, hired with false I.D.

So, sure, he'd parked close.

No way he could've hiked far carrying all that gear— the military rifle, the high-grade scope.

Not with that limp.

"Easy shot," said another deputy. "Like picking off quail. Wonder what this guy did that pissed someone off so bad."

"Who says he did anything?" said another cop. "Nowadays, it doesn't take anything to get some nut going."

Milo laughed.

The men in tan stared at him.

He said, "Long day, fellows."

"It ain't over yet," said Muir-man. "We've still got to find the dude."

Milo laughed again.

CHAPTER

36

NOVEMBER IS L.A.'S most beautiful month. Temperatures get considerate, the air acquires the squeaky, scrubbed flavor of a world without hydrocarbons, the light's as sweet and golden as a caramel apple. In November, you can forget that the Chumash Indians called the basin L.A. sits in the Valley of Smoke.

Late in November, I drove out to Lancaster.

A month and a half after the slaughter of Eldon Mate. Weeks after Milo had finished cataloging the contents of four cardboard cartons located in a Panorama City storage locker rented by Paul Ulrich under the name Dr. L. Pasteur.

A key found in Ulrich's bedroom nightstand led to the locker. Nothing very interesting was found in the house itself. Tanya Stratton vacated the premises within days of the shooting in Malibu.

The cartons were beautifully organized.

The first contained newspaper clippings, neatly folded, filed in chronological order, tagged with the names of victims. The details of Roger Sharveneau's suicide had been preserved meticulously. So had the death of a teenage girl named Victoria Leigh Fusco.

Number two held meticulously pressed clothing—

predominantly women's undergarments, but a few dresses, blouses and neckties, as well.

In the third box, Milo found over a hundred pieces of jewelry in plastic sandwich bags, most of it junk, a few vintage costume pieces. Some of the baubles could be traced back to dead people, others couldn't.

The fourth and largest carton held a styrofoam cooler. Layered within were parcels wrapped in butcher paper and preserved by dry ice. The attendant at the storage facility remembered Dr. Pasteur coming by every week or so. Nice man. Big mustache, one of those old-fashioned mustaches you see in silent movies. Pasteur had only spoken to offer pleasantries, talk about athletics, hiking, hunting. It had been a while since his last visit, and most of the dry ice had melted. The largest carton had started to reek. Milo left it up to the coroner to unwrap the packages.

In a corner of the storage locker were several rifles and handguns, each oiled and in perfect working order, boxes of bullets, one set of Japanese surgical tools, another made in the USA.

The papers presented it this way:

Victim in Police Shooting Believed Responsible for Eldon Mate's Murder

MALIBU. County Sheriff and Los Angeles Police sources report that a physician shot in a police-involved shooting in Malibu is the prime suspect in the murder of "death doctor" Eldon Mate.

Paul Nelson Ulrich, 40, was shot several times last week in circumstances that remain under investigation. Evidence recovered at the scene and in other locations, including surgical tools believed to be the murder weapons in the Mate case, indicate Ulrich acted alone.

No motive for the slaying of the man known as "Dr. Death" has been put forth by authorities yet, though the same sources indicate that Ulrich, a licensed physician in New York State under the name of Michael Ferris Burke, may have been mentally ill.

November found me thinking about how wrong I'd been on so many accounts. No doubt Rushton/Burke/Ulrich would've been amused by all my wrong guesses, but teaching me humility would've ranked low on his pleasure list.

I called Tanya Stratton once, got no answer, tried her sister. Kris Lamplear was more forthcoming. She didn't recognize my voice. No reason to, we'd exchanged only a few words when we'd met and she'd assumed I was a detective.

"How'd you know to call me, Doctor?"

"I consult to the police, was trying to follow up with Tanya. She hasn't called back. You're listed as next of kin."

"No, Tanya won't talk to you. Won't talk to anyone. She's pretty freaked out by all those things they're saying about Paul."

"She'd have to be," I said.

"It's—unbelievable. To be honest, I'm freaked, too. Been keeping it from my kids. They met him. . . . I never liked him, but I never thought . . . Anyway, Tanya has a therapist. A social worker who helped her back when she was sick—last year. The main thing is she's still in remission. Just had a great checkup."

"Good to hear that."

"You bet. I just don't want the stress to . . . Anyway, thanks for trying. The police have really been okay through all this. Don't worry about Tanya. She'll go her own way, she always does."

November got busy, lots of new referrals, my service seemed to be ringing in constantly. I booked myself solid, reserved lunchtime for making calls.

Calls that didn't get answered. Messages left for Richard, Stacy, Judy Manitow. A try at Joe Safer's office elicited a written note from the attorney's secretary:

Dear Dr. Delaware:
Mr. Safer deeply appreciates your time. There are no new developments with regard to your common interests. Should Mr. Safer have anything to report, he'll definitely call.

I thought a lot about the trip to Lancaster, composed a mental list of reasons not to go, wrote it all down.

I sometimes prescribe that kind of thing for patients, but it rarely works for me. Putting it down on paper made me antsier, less and less capable of putting it to rest. Maybe it's a brain abnormality—some kind of chemical imbalance, Lord knows everything else gets blamed on that. Or perhaps it's just what my midwestern mother used to call "pigheadedness to the nth."

Whatever the diagnosis, I wasn't sleeping well. Mornings presented me with headaches, and I found myself getting annoyed without good reason, working hard at staying pleasant.

By the twenty-third of November, I'd finished a host of

court-assigned assessments—none referred by Judy Manitow. Placing the rest in the to-do box, I awoke on a particularly glorious morning and set out for the high desert.

Lancaster is sixty-five miles north of L.A. on three freeways: the 405, the 5, then over to the 14, where four lanes compress to three, then two, cutting through the Antelope Valley and feeding into the Mojave.

Just over an hour's ride, if you stick to the speed limit, the first half mostly arid foothills sparsely decorated with gas stations, truck stops, billboards, the red-tile roofs of low-cost housing developments. The rest of it's nothing but dirt and gravel till you hit Palmdale.

Motels in Palmdale, too, but that wouldn't have mattered for Joanne Doss, it had to be Lancaster.

She'd made the trip late at night, when the view from the car window would have been flat-black.

Nothing to look at, lots of time to think.

I pictured her, bloated, aching, a passenger in her own hearse, as someone else—probably Eric, it was Eric I couldn't stop thinking about—burned fuel on the empty road.

Riding.

Staring out at the black, knowing the expanse of nothingness would be among her final images.

Had she allowed herself to suffer doubt? Been mindlessly resolute?

Had the two of them talked?

What do you say to your mother when she's asked you to help her leave you?

Why had she set up her own execution?

I spotted a county sign advertising a regional airport

in Palmdale. The strip where Richard's helicopter had landed on all those trips to oversee his construction projects.

He'd never been able to get Joanne to witness what he'd created. But on her last day on Earth, she'd endured an hour's trip, made sure she'd end up in the very spot she'd avoided.

Prolonging the agony so she could send him a message.

You condemn me. I spit in your face.

The Happy Trails Motel was easy to find. Just a quick turn onto Avenue J, then a half-mile drive past Tenth Street West. Lots of open space out here, but not due to any ecological wisdom. Vacant lots, whiskered by weeds, alternated with the kind of downscale businesses that doom small-town proprietors to anxiety in the age of mergers and acquisitions.

Bob's Battery Repair, Desert Clearance Furniture, Cleanrite Janitorial Supply, Yvonne's Quick 'n' Easy Haircutting.

I passed one new-looking strip mall, the usual beige texture coat and phony tile, some of the storefronts still vacant, a FOR LEASE sign prominent at the front of the commodious parking lot. One of Richard's projects? If I was right about Joanne's motives, just maybe, because the motel was in clear view across the street, sandwiched between a liquor store and a boarded-up bungalow that bore a faded, hand-painted sign: GOOD-FAITH INSURANCE.

The Happy Trails Motel was a single-story, U-shaped collection of a dozen or so rooms with a front office on the left-hand tip of the U and a dead neon sign that pleaded VACANCY. Red doors on each room, only two of them fronted by cars. The building had blue-gray walls and a low white gravel roof. Over the gravel, I saw coils of barbed wire. An alley ran along the west side of the motel and I drove around back to see what the wire was all about.

The coils sat atop a grape-stake fence that separated the motel from its rear neighbor: a trailer park. Old, sagging mobile homes, laundry on lines, TV antennae. As I cruised closer, a dog growled.

Returning to the street, I parked. Nothing crisp about the air here. High eighties, arid, dusty, and heavy as unresolved tension. I entered the office. No reception counter, just a card table in a corner, behind which sat an old man, hairless, corpulent, with very red lips and wet, subjugated eyes. He wore a baggy gray T-shirt and striped pants. In front of him was a stack of paperback spy novels. Off to the side sat a collection of medicine bottles, along with a loose eyedropper and an empty pill counter. The room was small, murky, paneled with pine boards long gone black. The air smelled like every kid's first booster shot. A comb dispenser hung on the rear wall, along with another small vending machine that sold maps and a third that offered condoms and the message *Be Healthy!*

To the old man's right was a glass display case filled with photos. Ten or so pictures of Marilyn Monroe in black-and-white. Scenes from her movies and cheesecake shots. Below the montage and stretched across the center of the case, pinned in place like a butterfly, was a pink satin two-piece bathing suit. A typed paper label, also pinioned, said, CERTIFIED GENUINE M.M.'S SWIMSUIT.

"It's for sale," said the hairless man wearily. His voice was half an octave below bassoon, clogged and wheezy.

"Interesting."

"If you meant that, you'd buy it. I got it from a guy used to work on her pictures. It's all bona fide."

I showed him my police consultant badge. The small print tells them I've got no real authority. When they're going to be helpful, they never bother to check. When they're not, a real badge wouldn't impress them.

The old man barely looked at it. His skin was pallid and dull, compressed in spots, lumped like cooling tallow. Licking his lips, he smiled. "Didn't think you were checking in for a room, not with that sport jacket. What is it, cashmere?"

He stretched a hand toward my sleeve and for a moment I thought he'd touch it. But he drew back.

"Just wool," I said.

"Just wool." He humphed. "Just money. So what can I do for you?"

"Several months ago a woman from L.A. checked in and—"

"Killed herself. So why're you here now? When it happened, the police didn't barely want to talk to me. Not that they should've, I wasn't working that night, my son was. And he didn't know much, either—you read the report, you know."

I didn't deny it. "Where is your son?"

"Florida. He was only visiting, doing me a favor 'cause I was indisposed." His fingers brushed against one of the medicine bottles. "Back in Tallahassee. Drives a truck for Anheuser-Busch. So what's up?"

"Just doing some follow-up," I said. "For the files. Did your son ever talk to you about who checked Ms. Doss in that night?"

"She checked herself in—the coward. Barnett said she

didn't look too good, unsteady on her feet, but she did it all, paid with a credit card—you guys took the receipt." He smiled. "Not our usual clientele."

"How so?"

His laughter began somewhere in his belly. By the time it reached his mouth he was coughing. The paroxysm lasted too long to be trivial.

" 'Scuse me," he said, wiping his mouth with the back of a dimpled hand. "Like you don't know what I'm talking about."

He smiled again. I smiled back.

"Not poor, not horny, not drunk," he said, amused. "Just a rich coward."

"A coward because—"

"Because God grants you your particular share of years, you go and laugh in His face? *She* was like that, too." Pointing to the Monroe case. "Body like that and she wasted it on politicians and other scum. That bikini's worth something, you know. Big money, but no one around here appreciates memorabilia. I think I'm gonna get myself a computer, list it on the Internet."

"Did your son mention anyone with Ms. Doss?"

"Yeah, there was someone out in the car, waiting. Behind the wheel. Barnett never looked to see who it was. We look too hard, we don't get business, right?"

"Right," I said. "Was there anyone else here who might've noticed?"

"Maybe Maribel, the cleaning girl. The one who found it. She came on at eleven at night, was working till seven. Asked for night work because she had a day job over at the Best Western in Palmdale. But you guys already talked to her. She didn't tell you much, huh?"

I shrugged. "Yeah, she was a little . . ."

"She was sick is what she was," he said. "Pregnant,

ready to drop. Already had a miscarriage. After she found . . . what she found, she wouldn't stop crying, I thought we were gonna have one of those real-life video situations right out there in the parking lot—ever deliver a baby?"

I shook my head. "She end up delivering okay?"

"Yup, a boy."

"Healthy?"

"Seems to be."

"Any idea where can I find her?"

He crooked a thumb. "Out back, Unit Six, she's working days now. Someone had a party last night in Six. Longhair types, Nevada plates, paid cash. Should've known better than to give pigs like that a room. Maribel'll be cleaning that one for a while."

I thanked him and headed for the door.

"Here's a little secret," he said.

I stopped, turned my head.

He winked. "Got the Monroe *Playboy*, too. Don't keep it in the case, 'cause it's too valuable. One price gets you all of it. Tell all your friends."

"Will do."

"Sure you will."

Maribel was young, short, frail-looking, in a pink-and-white uniform that seemed incongruously proper for the pitted lot and the splintering red doors. She was gloved to the elbows. Her hair was tied back, but loose strands were sweat-glued to her forehead. A wheeled cart pulled up to Unit Six was piled with cleaning solvents and frayed towels. The trash bag slung from the side overflowed with filthy linens, empty bottles and stink. She gave the badge a bit more attention than her boss had.

"L.A.?" she said, with the faintest accent. "Why're you coming out here?"

"The woman who killed herself. Joanne Doss—"

Her face closed up tight. "No, forget it, I don't wanna talk about that."

"Don't blame you," I said. "And I'm not interested in making you go through it again."

Her gloves slammed onto her hips. "Then *what*?"

"I'd like to know anything you can remember about *before*. Once Ms. Doss went in the room, did she ever come out? Did she ask for food, drinks, do anything that caught your attention?"

"Nope, nothing. They went in after I got here— around midnight, I already told them that. I didn't see them until . . . you know."

"Them," I said. "Two people."

"Yup."

"How long did the other person stay?"

"Don't know," she said. "Probably a while. I was up at the front desk, mostly, 'cause Barnett—Milton's son— wanted to go out and party and not tell his dad."

"But the car wasn't there in the morning."

"Nope."

"Who was the other person?"

"Didn't get a good look."

"Tell me what you did see."

"Not much, I never saw the face." Her eyes filled with tears. "It was disgusting—it's not fair bringing all this up—"

"I'm sorry, Maribel. Just tell me what you saw and we'll be finished."

"I don't wanna get anyone in trouble—I don't wanna be on TV or nothing."

"You won't be."
She pulled at the finger of a glove.
Didn't speak. Then she did.
And suddenly, everything made sense.

CHAPTER

37

JUST WOOL AGAIN.

My best blue suit, a blue-and-white-striped shirt, yellow-print tie, shiny shoes.

Dressed for court.

I pushed open the double doors to Division 12 and walked right in. More often than not, family sessions are closed, witnesses kept out in the corridor, but this morning I got lucky. Judy was hearing motions from a pair of reasonable-sounding attorneys, scheduling hearings, bantering with her bailiff, a man named Leonard Stickney, who knew me.

I sat in the back row, the only spectator. Leonard Stickney noticed me first and gave a small salute.

A second later, Judy saw me and her eyes opened wide. Black-robed and regal behind the bench, she turned away, got businesslike, ordering the lawyers to do something within thirty days' time.

I sat there and waited. Ten minutes later, she dismissed both attorneys, called for recess, and motioned Leonard over. Covering her mike with one hand, she whispered to him behind the other, stepped off the bench and exited through the door that led to her chambers.

Leonard marched up to me. "Doctor, Her Honor requests your presence."

* * *

Soft lighting, carved desk and credenza, overstuffed chairs, certificates and award plaques on the walls, family photos in sterling silver frames.

I concentrated on one particular snapshot. Judy's younger daughter, Becky. The girl who'd gotten too thin, needed therapy, tried to play therapist with Stacy.

Becky, who'd been tutored by Joanne. Whose grades had dropped after the tutoring had stopped.

Becky, who'd gotten too thin as Joanne grew obese. Had severed her relationship with Stacy.

Judy slipped out of her robe and hung it on a mahogany rack. Today's suit was banana yellow, form-fitting, trimmed with sand-colored braiding. Big pearl earrings, small diamond brooch. Every blond hair in place.

Shiny hair.

She reclined in her desk chair. Glittery things occupied a good portion of the leather desktop. The picture frames, a crystal bud vase, an assortment of tiny bronze cats, millefleur paperweights, a walnut gavel with a bronze plate on the handle. Her bony hands found a weight and rubbed it.

"Alex. What a surprise. We don't have any cases pending, do we?"

"No," I said. "Don't imagine we ever will."

She squinted past me. "Now, why would you say that?"

"Because I know," I said.

"Know what?"

I didn't answer, not out of any psychological calculation. I'd thought about being here, rehearsed it mentally, had gotten the first words out.

I know.

But the rest of it choked in my chest.

"What is this, riddle time?" she said, trying to smile but managing only a peevish twist of her lipstick.

"You were there," I said. "At the motel with Joanne. Someone saw you. They don't know who you are, but they described you perfectly."

What Maribel had really seen was hair. Short yellow hair.

A skinny woman, no butt on her. I only saw the back of her, she was getting into the car when I came out to fill the ice machine.

She had this hair—real light, real shiny, a really good color job. That hair was shiny from across the parking lot.

"Mate had nothing to do with it," I said. "It was just you and Joanne."

Judy reclined a bit more. "You're talking nonsense, my dear."

"One way to look at it," I said, "was you were helping a friend. Joanne had made her decision, needed someone to be there with her at the end. You'd always been a good friend to her. The only problem is, that friendship had cooled. For good reason."

I waited. She wasn't moving. Then her right eyelid twitched. She pushed back from the desk another inch. "You're starting to sound like one of those psychic idiots—talking obliquely in the hope someone will take it for wisdom. Have you been under strain, Alex? Working too hard? I always thought you pushed yourself—"

"So friendship would be the charitable interpretation of what brought you out to Lancaster with Joanne, but unfortunately that wasn't it at all. Joanne's motivation for destroying herself was crushing guilt—some sin she couldn't forgive herself for. Richard never forgave her, either. And neither did you. So when she asked you to be there, I don't think you minded one bit about seeing her reach the end."

Her lips folded inward. Her hand reached out among the objects on her desk and found one. Walnut gavel. Brass plaque on the handle. An award. The walls were paneled with tributes.

"Having you there was part of the punishment," I said. "Like when family members of victims are invited to attend the execution."

"This is ridiculous," she said. "I don't know what's gotten into you, but you're talking gibberish—please leave."

"Judy—"

"This *minute*, Alex, or I'll call for Leonard."

"My leaving won't change things. Not for you, not for Becky. Does Bob know? Probably not all of it, I'd guess, because he would've expressed his anger more directly, immediately. Wouldn't have let it sit. But he's mad about something, so he must know something."

She took hold of the gavel, waved it at me. "Alex, I'm giving you one last chance to leave like a gentleman—"

"Joanne and Becky," I said. "When did it happen?"

She shot forward, half standing, and the gavel slammed down on the desk. But instead of making direct contact, the wood twisted, slipping out of her grip, skidding along the leather, pushing a paperweight to the carpet. The glass landed on the carpet with a feeble thump.

Pathetic sound. Maybe that's what did it, or maybe she really wanted to talk.

Her fingers curled into talons that she placed against her breast. As if ready to claw out her own heart. Suddenly they dropped and she sat back down and her hair was no longer in place. Hot eyes, wet eyes, a mouth that shook so badly it took a while for her to speak.

"You bastard," she said. "You goddamn, goddamn bastard. I'm calling Leonard."

But she didn't.

We sat staring at each other. I tried to look as sympathetic as I felt. I'd convinced myself this was all for the best, but now I wondered if it boiled down to feeding my own obsessiveness. A moment more and I might've gotten up and left. But she stood first, crossed the big, beautiful room, locked the door. When she sat back down, her eyes dropped to the gavel.

That's when she reminded me of my oath of confidentiality. Repeated the warning.

I told her of course I'd never talk.

Even then, she kept it theoretical, the way Richard had, could barely stop herself from slapping me, kept drifting into corollary anger.

"What if you were a parent?" she said. "Why *aren't* you, anyway? I always meant to ask you that. Working with other people's kids, but you never had any of your own."

"Maybe one day," I said.

"So it's not a physical problem? Not shooting blanks?"

I smiled.

"Kind of arrogant, Alex. Preaching to other people about how to raise their kids when you don't have any direct experience."

"Maybe so."

"Sure, agree with me—you guys all do that, another one of those little tricks they teach you in shrink school.

Did you know Becky wants to become a psychologist? What do you think of *that*?"

"I don't know Becky, but offhand it sounds fine."

"Why's it fine?" she demanded.

"Because people who've dealt with crisis can develop a special kind of empathy."

"Can?"

"Sometimes it goes the other way. I don't know Becky."

"Becky's beautiful—a beautiful person. If you'd bothered to father any of your own, maybe you'd have a clue."

"You're probably right," I said. "I mean that."

"Think of it," she said, as if talking to herself. "You carry this creature inside you for nine months, rip your body up pushing them out, and that's when the real work starts— Do you have any idea what it takes to nurture a child nowadays in this fucking urbanized, overfeeding, overstimulating world we've created? Do you have a *clue*?"

I kept quiet.

She said, "*Think* about it: you go through all that, feeding them with your body, waking up in the middle of the night, wiping their ass, getting them through all the tantrums and the hurt feelings and the bad habits, getting them past *puberty*, for Christ's sake, and someone comes along—someone you trust—and sabotages all that."

She sprang up, paced the space behind her desk.

"I'm not telling you a damn thing, even if I did you couldn't repeat a word of it—and believe me, if I pick up the merest hint you've let on to anyone—your wife, anyone—I'll make sure you lose that license of yours."

Race-walking the width of the room, back again, another circuit.

"Picture this, *Doctor*: you put all that into another human being, entrust them to someone they've known their whole life. Someone you've done favors for, and what are you asking? Tutoring, stupid *tutoring*, because the kid's smart but numbers have a way—math—just math, not another goddamn thing. And then you walk in and find that person with—with your treasure, this treasure you've wrought, and they've shattered it . . . by the pool, the goddamn pool. And where are the math books? Where's the tutoring? Getting wet on the deck next to the pool while they—wet swimsuits lying all wrinkled—oh that would be just great with you, wouldn't it? You'd let *that* pass, right?"

"Was it the first time?" I said.

"Joanne claimed it was—Becky did, too, but they were both lying. I can't blame Becky for that, she was ashamed—no, it wasn't the first time, I could tell it wasn't. Because it explained all sorts of things. A little girl who used to talk to me, who after she turned sixteen and started getting tutored didn't talk to me anymore. A little girl who'd suddenly cry for no good reason, leave the house, not tell us where she was going—her grades started to drop, even with the tutoring—she was *sixteen*, Alex, and that bitch *raped* her! For all I know it had gone on for years."

"After you found them you never talked to Becky about it?"

"No point. She needed to heal, not be shamed."

More pacing.

"And don't get that accusatory tone. I know the law and no, I didn't report it to the so-called *authorities*," she said. "What would *that* have accomplished? The law's an *ass*, believe me, I sit out there and listen to it bray every goddamn day."

"And Bob?"

"Bob hates Joanne because he thinks she refused to keep on tutoring Becky and that's why Becky flunked math and won't be able to get into a good college. If I'd told Bob, Joanne might've been dead sooner and that's all I'd need—my entire family destroyed."

"You did tell Richard," I said.

"Richard's a man of action."

Translation: Richard would punish her. Shutting her out, forever.

I said, "Joanne was a woman of action. Once sentence had been passed, she carried out the punishment herself."

Killing herself slowly. Richard's contempt had been part of it—excommunicating her, letting her know he had nothing but contempt for her. Threatening to tell the children.

But there'd been more to the deterioration, force-feeding herself like a goose. Getting fat because Becky had gotten skinny.

Joanne had despised herself.

Stacy, the alleged problem child, had been kept out of the loop. Eric, dropping out to tend to his mother, had probably been privy to more. How much had Joanne told him? Not the essence of her sin, just that she'd done something for which Dad couldn't forgive her . . .

Judy said, "She finally did something right, goddamn her."

"She wanted you to see—her last chance at apology."

She shrugged. Drew her finger across her lips. "Leave now, Alex. I mean it."

I got up and headed for the door. "Despite all she did

to your family, you cared about *hers*. That's why you referred Stacy to me."

"Talk about errors in judgment."

"Who else knows?" I said.

"No one."

"Not Becky's therapist?"

"No, Becky and I agreed she could get help without getting into it. And don't tell me I was wrong, because I wasn't. She's fine now. Planning to go to community college. Study psychology. We're back to where we were before, Alex. Becky will take strength from it—develop a higher level of empathy out of this. Be a *great* psychologist."

I turned toward the door.

"You don't know, either, Alex. This conversation never took place."

I reached for the doorknob.

"You're right," she said. "I don't ever want to see or hear from you again."

CHAPTER

38

TWO WEEKS BEFORE Christmas, I called FBI headquarters at the Federal Building and, not expecting any success, asked to speak with Special Agent Mary Donovan.

I was transferred to her immediately.

"Hello, Doctor. What can I do for you?"

"I was just wondering if you've had any success with Dr. Fusco."

"Success," she said. "As measured by?"

"Finding him. Helping him."

"You're serious."

"About what?"

"Helping him. As if we're a clinic or something."

"Well," I said, "there's always the issue of collegiality. And respect for what he once was. No sign of him, at all?"

Long silence.

She said, "Look, I took your call because I thought you might've changed your mind, but this is a waste of time."

"Changed my mind in what way?"

"Being willing to cooperate. Helping us find him."

"Helping you?" I said. "As if I'm a clinic or something."

Another silence.

"I guess my question's been answered," I said.

"Have a nice day, Doctor."

Click.

I sat there holding the phone. Thinking about Alice Zoghbie's claim of being audited by the IRS because she'd rubbed important noses the wrong way. Probably a lie, covering for a call from Roy Haiselden.

But you never knew.

CHAPTER

39

A WEEK BEFORE Christmas, Stacy called.

"I'm so sorry," she said. "It was rude not answering, but things got really busy and . . ."

"Don't worry about it. How's everything going?"

"Actually, much better. Did pretty well on a bunch of A.P. exams, and I just found out I got in early to Cornell. I know it's far away and it gets cold, but they've got a veterinary school and I think I might want to do that."

"Congratulations, Stacy."

"Architecture seemed too . . . impersonal. Anyway, thanks for all your help. That's it."

"How's Eric?"

"He's okay. Dad's fine, too, busy all the time. He doesn't like visiting that probation officer, complains about it constantly, but he's lucky that's all he got, right? Eric changed his major. Psychology. So maybe you had an influence on him—I'm sorry about the way he treated you."

"That's okay."

She laughed. "That's what he says. Taking abuse is part of your job. Guilt's not a big part of Eric's life."

"Ah," I said, knowing how wrong she was.

"Did you hear about the Manitows?" she said.

"What about them?"

"They put their house up for sale and moved out of the Palisades. They're renting a place down in La Jolla. Judge Manitow's quitting and Dr. Manitow's trying to see if he can find work down there."

"No, I hadn't heard."

"They didn't exactly advertise it," she said. "One day I was seeing Dr. Manitow drive off to work, the next day the sign was up and the moving vans were there. Becky's moving with them. Going to some junior college in San Diego. Everyone else can't wait to get out of the house, but she's staying with her parents. Someone told me Becky said that she needs to stay close to home."

"Some people do need that," I said.

"Guess so. Anyway, thanks for all your help. Maybe one day I'll get my DVM and I'll get a chance to work with that cute little bulldog of yours. Pay you back."

"Maybe," I said.

She laughed. "That would be cool."

When a former patient unexpectedly returns to ask for help, Alex Delaware is thrust into the most dangerous and complex case of his career.

Don't miss
FLESH AND BLOOD
a novel from Jonathan Kellerman,
Available in bookstores everywhere.

Read an excerpt from Chapter One ....

Sad truth: Had she been just a patient, I probably wouldn't have remembered her.

All those years listening, so many faces. There was a time when I recalled every one of them. Forgetting comes with experience. It doesn't bother me as much as it used to.

Her mother phoned my office on a Saturday morning soon after New Year.

"A Mrs. Jane Abbot," said the operator. "She says her daughter's an old patient. Lauren Teague."

Jane Abbott's name meant nothing to me but *Lauren Teague* sparked an uneasy nostalia. The number was an 818 exchange; somewhere in the Valley. When I'd known the family, they'd lived in West L.A. I searched my old case files before returning the call.

Teague, Lauren Lee. Intake date, ten years ago, the tale end of my Wilshire Boulevard practice. Shortly after, I cashed in some real estate profits, tried to drop out, met a beautiful woman, became friends with a sad, brilliant detective, learned more than I wanted to know about bad things. Since then I'd avoided the commitment of long-term therapy cases, stuck to court consults and forensic work, the kinds of puzzles that removed me from the confines of my office.

Lauren had been fifteen at referral. Thin file: One history-taking meeting with the parents followed by two sessions with the girl. Then a missed appointment, no explanation. The next day, the father left a message canceling any future treatment. Unpaid balance for the final session; I'd made a half-hearted effort to collect, then written it off.

When old patients get in touch it's usually because they're doing great and want to brag, or exactly the opposite. Either way, they tend to be people with whom I've connected. Lauren

When old patients get in touch it's usually because they're doing great and want to brag, or exactly the opposite. Either way, they tend to be people with whom I've connected. Lauren Teague didn't qualify. Far from it. If anything, I was the last person she'd want to see. Why was her mother contacting me now?

Presenting problems: poor school achiev., noncompliance at home. Clin. impressions: fath. angry, moth. possib. deprssd. tension bet moth and fath -marital strss? Parents agree re: Lauren's behavior as the prim. prob. Uneventful birth hx, only child, no sig. health probs, contact pediatric. MD to verify. School: per Mom: "Lauren's always been smart." "Used to love to read, now hates it." B- aver, till last year, then "change of attitude," new friends—"bums" (fath), some truancy, C's and D's. Basic mood is "sullen" "No communic." Parents try to talk, get no resp. Suspect drug use.

As I leafed through the file, Jane and Lyle Teague's faces came into semi-focus. She, thin, blonde, edgy, a former flight attendant now a "full-time mom." A heavy smoker— forty five minutes without tobacco had been torture.

Lauren's father had been slit-eyed, blank-faced, reluctant to engage. His wife had talked fast . . . nervous hands, moist eyes. When she'd looked to him for support, he'd turned away.

They were both 39, but he looked older. . . . he'd done something in the building trades . . . here it was, *elect. contractr.* A powerful-looking man, fighting the advent of middle age with long hair, sprayed in place, that fringed his shoulders. Black pelt of beard. Muscles made obvious by a too-tight polo shirt and pressed jeans. Crude but well-balanced features . . . gold chain circling a ruddy neck . . . gold I.D. bracelet—how did I remember *that*? Put him in buckskins and he could've been a grizzly hunter.

Lyle Teague had sat with his legs spread wide, consulted his watch every few minutes, fondled his beeper as if hoping it would come through. Unable to maintain eye contact— lapsing into dreamy stares. That had made me wonder about attention deficit, something he might have passed on to Lauren. But when I raised the topic of academic testing, he didn't stir defensively, and his wife said Lauren had been examined two years before by a school psychologist and found to be "normal and extremely bright."

"Bright," he said, putting no praise into the word. "Nothing wrong with her brain that a little discipline won't cure." Accusing glance at his wife. Her mouth twisted, but she said, "That's what we're here to learn."

Lyle Teague smirked.

I said, "Mr. Teague, do you think anything else is going on, besides Lauren's being spoiled?"

"Nah, basic teenage garbage." Another look at his wife, this time, seeking confirmation.

She said, "Lauren's a good girl."

Lyle Teague laughed threateningly. "Then why the hell are we here?"

"Honey—"

"Yeah, yeah, fine."

He tried to tune out, but I stuck with him, finally got him to talk about Lauren, how different she was from the "cute little kid" he'd once taken to job sites in his truck. As he reminisced, his face darkened and his speech got choppy and by the end of the speech he pronounced his daughter, "A real hassle. Hope to hell you can do something with her."

Two days later, Lauren showed up in my waiting room, alone, five minutes late. A tall, slender, copiously busted, brown-haired girl, treated kindly by puberty.

Fifteen, but she could've passed for twenty. She wore a white jersey tank top, skimpy, snug, blue-denim shorts, and ludicrously high-heeled white sandals. Smooth, tan arms and long, tan legs were showcased by the minimal clothing. Pink-polished toes glinted between the straps of the sandals. The strap of a small black patent leather purse striped a bare shoulder. If she'd been studying the hookers on Sunset for fashion tips, she'd learned well.

When young girls flaunt, the result is often a comic loss of equilibrium. Lauren Teague seemed perfectly at ease advertising her body—like father, like daughter?

She favored her father in coloring, her mother in structure, but bore no striking resemblance to either. The brown hair was burnt-umber with rust, thick and straight, hanging halfway down her back, parted dead-center and flipped into extravagant wings at the temples. High cheekbones, wide mouth glossed pink, dominant but perfectly proportioned cleft chin, heavily lined, azure-shadowed blue eyes—mocking eyes. A strong, straight, uptilted nose was dashed by freckles she'd tried to obliterate with makeup. Lots of makeup. It stuccoed her from brow to jaw, creating a too-beige masque.

As I introduced myself, she breezed past me into the office, taking long, easy strides on the impossible heels. None of the usual teenage slump—she held her back straight, thrust out her chest. A strikingly good-looking girl, made less attractive by cosmetics and blatancy.

Selecting the chair closest to mine, she sat down as if she'd been there a hundred times before. "Cool furniture."

"Thank you."

"Like one of those libraries in an old movie." She batted her lashes, crossed and re-crossed her legs, threw out her chest again, yawned, stretched, folded her arms across her torso, dropped them to her sides suddenly, a cartoon of vulnerability.

I asked her why she thought she was there.

"My parents think I'm a loser."

"A loser."

"Yup."

"What do you think of that?"

Derisive laugh, toss of hair. A tongue-tip skated across her lower lip. "May-*be*." Shrug. Yawn. "So . . . time to talk about my head problems, huh?"

Jane and Lyle Teague had denied previous therapy but Lauren's glibness made me wonder. I asked her about it.

"Nope, never. The school counselor tried to talk to me a couple of times."

"About?"

"My grades."

"Did it help?"

She laughed. "Yeah, right—okay, ready for my neurosis?"

"Neurosis," I said.

"We have psych this year. Stupid class. Ready?"

"If you are."

"Sure. I mean—that's the point, right? I'm supposed to spit out all my deep, dark secrets."

"It's not a matter of supposed to—"

"I know, I know," she said. "That's what shrinks always say—no one's gonna force you to do anything."

"You know about shrinks."

"I know enough. Some of my friends have seen 'em. One of them had a shrink give her that shi—that stuff about never forcing her, then the next week he committed her to a mental ward."

"Why?"

"She tried to kill herself."

"Sounds like a good reason."

Shrug.

"How's your friend doing?"

"Fine—like you really care." Her eyes rolled.

I said nothing.

"That, too," she said. "That's the other shrink thing—just sitting there and staring. Saying, 'Ah-ah' and 'Uh-huh.' Answering questions with questions. Right?"

"Uh-huh."

"Very funny," she said. "At what you charge, I'm not coming here forever. And *he's* probably gonna call to make sure I showed up and did a good job, so let's get going."

"Dad's in a hurry?"

"Yeah. So give me a good grade, okay? tell him I was good—I don't need any more hassles."

"I'll tell him you cooperated—"

"Tell him whatever you want."

"—but I'm not going to get into details, because—"

"Confidentiality, yeah, yeah. It doesn't matter. Tell them anything."

"No secrets from mom and dad?"

"What for?" She played with her hair, gave a world-weary smile. "I've got no cool secrets, anyway. Totally boring life. Too bad for you—try not to fall asleep."

"So," I said, "your dad wants you to get this over with quickly."

"Whatever." She picked at her hair.

"What exactly did he tell you to accomplish, Lauren?"

"Get my act together, be straight—be a *good* girl." She laughed, arced one leg over the other, placed a hand on a calf and tickled.

"Be straight," I said. "As in drugs?"

"They're paranoid about that, along with everything else. Even though *they* smoke."

"They smoke dope?"

"Dope, tobacco. Little after-dinner taste. Sometimes it's booze—*cocktails. 'We're mature enough to control it, Lauren.'*" She laughed. "Jane used to be a stewardess, working all these fancy private charters. They've still got this collection of tiny little bottles. I like the green melon stuff— Midori. But I'm not allowed to touch pot till I'm eighteen." She laughed. "Like I'd *ever.*"

"Pot's not for you?"

"Pot's boring—too slow. Like hey, man, let's pretend we're in the sixties, get all wasted and sit around staring at the sky and talking about God." Another gust of laughter, painfully lacking in joy. "Pot sure makes *them* boring. It's the only time she slows *down*. And *he* just sits and vedges on the t.v., munches nachos, whatever. I'm not supposed to be talking about their bad habits. I'm the one who needs to change."

"Change how?"

"Clean my *room*," she sing-songed. "Do my *chores*, get ready in the morning without calling my mom a *bitch*, stop saying 'fuck' and 'shit' and 'cunt.' Go to class and pay attention, build up my *grades*, stop breaking *curfew*, hang out with *decent* friends, not lowlife." She rotated one hand, as if spooling thread.

"And I'm supposed to get you to do that."

"Lyle says no way, you never will."

"Lyle."

Her eyes got merry. "That's something else I'm not supposed to do. Call him by his name, he hates it, it drives him crazy."

"So no way you'll stop."

She played with her hair. "Who knows what I'll do?"